Prai
JadeAnr

MW00576736

The Hydra Effect

Jan M Flynn, award winning author
"JadeAnne heads to Mexico City for a break from her partner and now ex-boyfriend. But her sharp intelligence, curiosity and inability to stay in her own lane land her in a snarl of trouble. In short order she's evading cartel thugs, uncovering a human trafficking network and confronting high-level Mexican politicos with questionable connections, all in a lushly realized setting one can just about smell. And taste—JadeAnne might be in the middle of a gunfight, but she's never immune to the temptation of a good plate of tacos al pastor. She and her loyal dog Pepper are a team you can't but cheer for."

Set Up

Heather Haven, multi-award-winning author of the Alvarez Family Murder Mysteries
"This is a blowout of a story. It starts on the backroads of Mexico in the middle of the night—just a woman, a dog, and Mexican Banditos—and escalates from there. If you are looking for a fast-paced, action-filled thriller about the adventures of a young PI and her lethal but well-trained dog, this will be your cup of tea. Or should I say Margarita? Jack Reacher step aside. You have met your match in JadeAnne Stone.

JC Miller, author of the bestseller, *Vacation*

A routine investigation takes a mysterious, chilling turn when JadeAnne is abducted at gunpoint then deposited in an opulent, albeit creepy manor. Moment-by-moment, her story unfolds in real time as she experiences the sights, sounds and myriad flavors of Mexico, the underworld of political corruption and high-stakes criminal activity roiling beneath the surface. When nothing is as it appears, and no one can be trusted, Jade's adrenaline surges—her mettle is tested. Told with humor and humility, grit and beauty, this page turner delivers.

Judy Penz Sheluk, Amazon international bestselling author
In her debut mystery novel, Author Ana Manwaring offers up more twists and turns than a Mexican rattlesnake. Fast paced, with well-crafted characters and a strong female lead, there's plenty to like about this world of power, politics, and Mexican money laundering. I especially enjoyed the strong sense of place, which Manwaring uses to great effect. Well worth adding to you TBR pile.

NOTHING COMES
AFTER Z
Death and Retribution in Tepoztlán

A JadeAnne Stone
Mexico Adventure

ANA MANWARING

INDIES UNITED PUBLISHING HOUSE, LLC

Nothing Comes After Z, A JadeAnne Stone Mexico Adventure ©
2021 by Ana Manwaring.

All rights reserved. No part of this book may be used or
reproduced in any manner whatsoever, including internet usage,
without written permission from Indies United Publishing House,
except in the case of brief quotations embodied in critical articles
and reviews.

Second Edition August 2022
by Indies United Publishing House, LLC

Cover design by Vila Design
Cover Photo, Ana Manwaring 2010 Tenochtitlán, Mexico D.F.

This is a work of fiction. Names, characters, places, and incidents
are either the product of the author's imagination or are use
fictionally, and any resemblance to actual persons, living or dead,
business establishments, events or locales is entirely coincidental.

ISBN: 978-1-64456-509-4 [Paperback]
ISBN: 978-1-64456-510-0 [Mobi]
ISBN: 978-1-64456-511-7 [ePub]

Library of Congress Control Number: 2022942638

INDIES UNITED PUBLISHING HOUSE, LLC
P.O. BOX 3071
QUINCY, IL 62305-3071
indiesunited.net

To

Marjorie S. Manwaring
January 20, 1924 ~ July 12, 2021

my first editor

"How will you become a writer if you can't spell?"
~Mom

Other Books in the JadeAnne Stone Mexico Adventures

Set Up (2018)
Set Up Audiobook version (2020)

The Hydra Effect (2019)
The Hydra Effect Audiobook version (2022)

Forthcoming from Ana Manwaring
Coyote (2022)

Acknowledgements

I hold deep gratitude for the special folks whose support, consideration, care, and hard work went into developing this series and especially book three, *Nothing Comes After Z*. As always, my deepest love and gratitude go to my husband David Prothero for his steadfast belief in me and my fictional world. Also, without David (and his IT skills) I'd never manage to write or publish anything.

I want to thank my amazing critique groups for helping me shape *Nothing Comes After Z* from start to finish.

To **JAM**, I owe you guys big time: J.C. Miller and Mark Pavlichek. They have worked with me for a decade lifting JadeAnne from idea through her fourth book (2022).

To **Novelistas**: Jan M. Flynn, Heather Chavez, and Crissi Langwell. You each are top notch critique givers and brilliant writers. Your feedback is invaluable to me.

I'm especially thankful to **WordWeavers**: Kerry Granshaw and Malena Eljumaily, who both read every draft and copy edited the final one.

To my beta reading team for your astute comments and direction, Jan M. Flynn (the voice of JadeAnne), Crissi Langwell, Michelle Chouinard, Timothy R. Baldwin, Jeanne Miller, Mark Pavlichek and Lisa Towles, I am forever grateful. Also a shout out to my dear friend Diane Sinawi for the first proofreading, and my editor, Cindy Davis for all the final editing and proofing. You turned *Z* into a book worth reading!

And finally to my **Sisters in Crime Northern California** write-in groups for inspiring me to show up and write.

I cherish you all for your brilliance, generosity, and most of all for your friendship. Without that, I'd never have gotten this far. Thank you.

Chapter 1

A Whorehouse of Her Own

Wednesday, August 22, 2007

Aguirre's town car jerked to the curb and stopped, knocking me into the door handle and sending X-ACTO knives into my healing gunshot wound. What if the Zeta thugs had followed us from the hospital? We had something they'd paid for—me. And from what I'd heard, that group would stop at nothing to get me back. No, Quint—*Dad*—wouldn't let them get near me, would he? How would I know what my long-lost parent would or would not do? I'd only met him eleven days before, but his concern for me while I was in the hospital seemed genuine. I'd go with that. But *Dad* was still hard to say.

"Can I open my eyes now?" I asked.

"Wait a bit, girl. The surprise isn't quite ready," he said as he slid out, slamming the door behind him.

I slumped down in my seat and pain seared my ribs again. Shouldn't they have kept me in the hospital for a few more days? Or at least given me pain killers? Tylenol wasn't cutting it. The Zeta bullet had furrowed a trough deep enough to plant cabbages. They didn't even sew it up. I'd have a scar for sure. Either an interesting conversation hook

1

or the end of bikinis for me.

Where did Quint go? I didn't need to sit in a hot car with my eyes squeezed shut for some absent father's surprise. I needed my dog and the elegant safety of my room at Senator Aguirre's high-rise apartment building in Colonia Polanco. There I'd be safe. I opened one eye.

Quint popped my door open and took my hand. "You're cheating. Slide out."

I squeezed my eyes closed again and clasped my sweaty palm into his calloused paw. All I'd seen in my brief scan was a ubiquitous bougainvillea-covered wall and the shadow of an iron gate. "Where are we, Quint?"

"You'll see."

"Not with my eyes closed."

I lurched against my father's wiry frame as I tripped over an uneven cobble. He snaked his hand around my back to steady me. "Careful," he said to the squeaky whine of the gate opening. "All right then—on the count of three. One... two... "

I heard birds twittering from the trees. The smells of gardenias and freshly mown grass overpowered the stench of smoggy Mexico City.

"Three!"

I opened my eyes. Behind my father rose a three-story pink stucco house roofed in red tile. Rustic-looking wooden shutters and lintels flanked the windows and black wrought iron grillwork. Ivy grew up one side, twining into the balconies, and geraniums trailed from window boxes in brilliant reds, oranges and pinks. Shrubs and flowers crowded around the foundation and the high wall surrounding the property and purple jacaranda petals drifted onto the narrow lawn in the slight breeze. I gasped and inhaled the heady scent.

"This isn't Polanco, is it? Where in the hell are we?"

"Calle Amores in Del Valle. Number 1060. I've rented

it."

A chorus of barks and yips rang above a rhythmic percussion of paws. Pepper beelined toward me from the front door, a golden retriever on his heels and six golden puppies tumbling behind.

"Pepper!" I flung my arms open to my dog and winced at the hot stab in my side as he jumped to his hind legs and I caught him into a hug. Pepper's long tongue slathered my face with doggie kisses while Maya danced around my knees. "You rescued Maya!" I beamed at Quint and let Pepper go, gingerly crouching to hug the dog who saved my life then to tickle her wiggling brood.

"We're home, JadeAnne. Come on, let me show you around," he said as he dragged me back to my feet.

I scooped up one of the squirming pups and tucked it under my arm. "Home? I thought we were going back to the senator's condo. What happened?"

"After you were taken to the hospital, I went back to get the dogs—"

"—the others? In the kennel? What about the ones in the veterinarian hospital?"

"Slow down, Jade. One thing at a time. The vet took over and all the dogs are fine. I grabbed Maya and the pups, and went back to Aguirre's. The puppies pushed him over the top. You know how he is about dogs; he barely tolerates Pepper. The senator has thrown us out," he said as a grin broke across his face. "Lucky for us, his family owns this place and it was empty."

"You mean Lidia. I don't trust that woman. Aguirre's mother has something to do with this mess."

"That's what we're going to find out, ain't it?" Quint said.

"Oh, so you agree."

"I didn't say that, but even the senator knows she owns a working brothel."

"Senator Aguirre's mother is connected to the Zetas cartel somehow, I'm sure of it." As I voiced my suspicion, it sounded ludicrous. She was a society matron. A *Grand Dame* with adult grandchildren.

We entered to the brightly tiled lobby with stairs and an elevator leading to the living area above the street. It reminded me of Anibal's house in Condesa. The polished door to the left must lead into the garage where, I supposed, my combi was housed. "Where's my bus?"

He pointed. "She's got her own barn. Let's go up." He scooped the rest of the puppies into his arms and toed the door open with a *you first* nod of his head.

I headed up behind Pepper and Maya, who looked pretty chummy, wincing with each step as my unused muscles pulled over my ribs under the bullet burn.

"I'm out of shape," I said to the dogs.

At the top of the stairs, the dogs nosed the door open to reveal a smiling Señora Pérez, Anibal Aguirre's housekeeper. My heart stopped. Fear and rage exploded in my gut; I spun to flee, and smacked into my father. He steadied me.

"*Buenos días, señorita. Bienvenidos. ¿Esta bien?*" she asked.

"Thanks, Mrs. Pérez. I'm better," I said over her prattle as she ushered me into the kitchen.

"What's she doing here?" I hissed at Quint.

"She's worked miracles with Lily," he replied.

"Yeah, she was kind to me too, but—"

"But nothing. She came with the house. After the fire, and Anibal's presumed death, she needed a job."

My head swiveled toward Quint. "Presumed? I thought you'd..."

Señora Pérez glanced at me for a beat as she busied herself at the stove preparing tiny *quesedillas* on a *comal*. "I think she speaks English," I mouthed, watching her intently. Coincidence? Or was she Señora Lidia's spy? I hadn't been

4

able to prove it at the house in Condesa. I'd stay on my guard here.

"All right then. Let me show you to your room."

"My things?"

"All upstairs. The vest too. You should have been wearing that."

"Don't nag me, Quint. I was having lunch in the Colonia with a gentleman. It was a date. How was I supposed to know the bastard planned to kidnap me and sell me into the sex trade?" My laugh sounded shrill and my muscles tensed; I wasn't over this. Would I ever be? And why *did* they want me? My Vietnamese build and complexion? Aren't I too old for the trade?

He snorted and his lips flattened into disgust, but he kept quiet.

The stairwell up to the second floor was narrower than that from the ground floor to the kitchen, and it exuded an odor of panting dog and dust. We were quite a parade of feet kicking it up out of the carpet. I sneezed. "Does Señora Pérez vacuum?"

"She just got here today. Give her a break," he replied and set the puppies onto the floor. I put down the two I carried, and they clustered around Maya, peeping and jostling for a teat.

Quint gestured to the end of the hallway. "That's your suite. I'm on the other side. That door is Lily's." He pointed to a door on the left.

"Lily is here?" A wash of guilt engulfed me. "Isn't she under the Embassy's protection?"

"Long story JadeAnne. She's here under the senator's protection."

"A lot of protection that is," I muttered as I surveyed the rose-colored room. "Very, uh, girlie. Whose bedroom was this?"

"A furnished rental, Jade. I thought you liked *Louis XV*."

He laughed. "It's pretty awful, ain't it."

"Maybe Lily would like it. She's only fifteen. Princess rooms might still appeal to her. Where is she, anyway?"

"Nah, she's got her own pink room and bath, and she hides away there most of the time." He frowned before grinning. "You get a sitting room too— Look." He pushed through a silk-draped doorway and opened the door into a den of red velvet accented with gilt trim. Everywhere. Antique oil lamps dotted the black lacquered writing desk and spindly occasional tables.

I aimed my finger down my throat and made gagging noises. "My own bordello."

"That's about the size of it. This was the madam's suite."

"You're kidding me, right?"

"The girls' cribs are smaller, but some have bathrooms. Lily gets one *en suite*." He imitated a bad French accent.

"Doesn't this shout out something revealing about our landlady? Maybe Madam Consuelo did the decorating."

"The senator said he evicted the tenant when he found out what was going on."

"I assume he fumigated?"

I closed Maya and her pups into the "bordello," shutting the door behind me and laying down on the bed. Pepper jumped up, and I wondered if whoever belonged to the frilly dotted Swiss coverlet would mind a shedding dog sprawled across it. I'd have to do something about the decor, but then, would I be here long enough to bother? Maybe now was a good time to go home. Before I got shot again. That idea creeped me out and totally pissed me off. I sat up, disturbing Pepper. He furrowed his brow.

"It's okay boy. I'm not leaving, just thinking."

He woofed softly and nuzzled into my hands. I stroked his head. He sighed and grinned.

I kissed one of his silky ears. "I'm happy to see you too.

I missed you."

Pepper wagged.

"But what are we going to do? Can we turn our backs on Lily? It's my fault her little sister is dead. If I'd just let them go in the helicopter with the rest of the kids..."

I thought back to the day Anibal Aguirre, the senator's half-brother, and I discovered twenty-three filthy children, ranging from six to fifteen, cowering in an airless prison carved from the rock of Mount Ajusco in a southern district of *La Capital*. We sprang them from their jail, and Anibal called his contact for a helicopter. I slammed my fist into a pillow. "How was I so stupid?" I'd believed Anibal was a DEA agent fighting against the drug cartels. At my insistence, he boarded all but the two American girls, Lily and Evie, and the rest lifted off to safety as the traffickers launched an attack on the house. We escaped, but *that* time when I was shot, I'd needed stitches. I ran my hand over my shoulder. Almost time to pull them out. He'd convinced me to stay in Mexico to help him avenge the death of his cousin Lura. Why hadn't I gone home after I found her? That was what I was paid for: find the banker's missing wife in Ixtapa. Take a vacation. Go home. But I stayed.

"I could have lived without *this* vacation, Pepper." He wagged but let out a soft whine. "Oh, you too?" I asked.

Tears welled and streamed down my cheeks. Lura hadn't deserved any of what happened.

A bolt of energy shot though me, and I sprang up from the bed. I hadn't deserved any of this either. "He tricked me, Peppi." Yes, Anibal had meant to sell me into the sex trade from the start, right along with the girls. He was to blame. Anibal might as well have been the man who raped me—he caused it. My skin crawled with the filth I couldn't wash off. My stomach clenched and I felt the burn of bile rising up my throat. I flopped back onto the bed, curled around Pepper and gasped for air. "He was going to give you to Fernando,

Pepper. If he weren't dead, I'd kill him myself."

Anibal was dead, wasn't he? All I'd seen was him trussed like a turkey and tossed into the back of the Zeta's van. "Pepper. What if he isn't dead? What if he comes back?"

Pepper pricked up his ears and turned toward the door. My stomach turned over before I heard the soft knocking and Quint's voice.

"JadeAnne, who are you talking to? You ready to get some lunch and make some plans?"

Pepper answered him by bounding off the bed to the door in two leaps. He woofed and Quint took that as *come in.*

"Aren't you ready?" he asked, scrutinizing my face. "Go wash your face."

What? I wasn't five. This guy was falling into a parental roll too easily.

After we corralled the puppies into a corner of the kitchen, we leashed the other two and headed out on foot where I took in my new neighborhood. Our house, unlike most of our neighbors' was free standing on a double lot. Mature trees shaded our wall and the street, and I now noticed two gates set into the iron fencing, one for people, and the other that would admit a vehicle. That one had an electric sensor. The street itself was narrow, lined with mostly three-story buildings; the compact cars and VW bugs parked in front faced south. A one-way street.

The dogs strained on their leashes, excited to be out for some fun. "Have the dogs been walked today?" I asked. I'd forgotten my dog-poop bag.

"Of course. I've kept dogs before."

"Yeah? When?"

"Growing up, we had dogs."

I looked up at my father and realized I knew nothing

about him. He carried himself like a soldier, but exuded a squirrelly vibe that I mistrusted. Probably exacerbated by the graying red stubble on his chin. He must have been a redhead, or auburn at least. We had that in common. And those startling green eyes—I was staring into my own. "Where'd you grow up?" I asked, cutting off that disconcerting sense of connection I felt looking in his eyes.

"I was born in San Francisco in 1950 and lived in North Beach until I was sixteen and I left home for college. I never went back."

I considered that for a moment as we crossed a street. Would I never go back to my childhood home? My parents weren't anything to crow about, but still, I'd grown up there.

"How could you never go home? Don't you miss your family? Hey, what's my grandmother's name?"

"Take it easy, I can't answer everything at once. I only went to Berkeley. UC Berkeley. Mum came to see me every month. The rest of them? I hated my drunk-ass father, and my three older brothers were just like him. Mean. Greedy. Violent. I was the youngest and learned to defend myself early. My studies were my escape. Mum's dogs were hers. I graduated with degrees in Math and Business Administration in 1970. Got my draft letter the day I graduated." Quint's smile warmed me as he continued, "If I hadn't been drafted, you'd never have been born—whoa Maya, that's a red light!" he said, and reined in the leash, the moment lost.

Pepper sat at the curb patiently as the traffic crawled by. We'd left our quiet neighborhood and emerged into a sunny commercial district. A breeze carried the smell of raw vegetables and I looked around for a market. The light changed and we crossed the street and continued toward the vegetables. "But you said my grandmother lives in Florida. Where? What's her name?"

"Audrey Quint. My father was Morris. He died three years ago, a mean son-of-a-bitch to the end. Mum made me go see him in the hospital before he passed. She hoped we'd reconcile. I hadn't seen him in thirty-eight years. I never understood why she stayed with him."

"So, no sisters?" I asked.

"Yeah, the oldest, but she'd already married and was having babies by the time I came along. Her escape. She was born in Australia—Sydney." He stopped talking and his fist clenched around the leash, jerking Maya.

"Careful, dude," I said, laying my hand on his tense arm.

He blew out a breath and smiled. "Sorry. Thinking about that bastard pisses me off. Dad was a longshoreman. They say he killed a bloke in a tavern brawl and had to pack up the family in a hurry. It was just Mum and my sister then. She died of cancer while I was in 'Nam. I don't know my cousins."

The smells of fruits and vegetables grew stronger and the traffic congested with both vehicles and pedestrians as we came abreast of the municipal market. "Have you been back to Sydney?"

"On assignment. I don't have people there. Mum's people came from Perth and they're all gone. Dad's? They were drunks and thieves." He sounded bitter.

The aroma of cooking meat set my stomach growling. The dogs tugged against their leashes and Quint picked up his pace. My side hurt, but the doctor had insisted I get exercise.

"Here we are." Quint held the door for me. He already knew the area.

I had no idea where we were. I looked at the sign, Don Capitán, as we stepped into a typical Mexican joint with brightly painted wooden tables and chairs. A counter toward the back separated the diners from the grills and *al pastor* rotisseries. My mouth watered. So did the dogs'.

"I can't believe they let dogs in here."

"This is Del Valle. Dogs go everywhere—like the

Condesa. But unlike Condesa, Del Valle is home mainly to families. It's where the young and hip go to raise their kids after they find their mates in the bars and restaurants of Condesa, Roma, or even Polanco. You'll find an organic market here too."

He smiled at me, his look a little too hopeful. Did he think I was going to cook and keep house for him? Oh, no. Señora Pérez would do that. Then again, maybe I should take on the cooking. The señora probably would poison us for killing Anibal. Hadn't he said she was his aunt? Godson?

I must have made a face because Quint's brows furrowed over the top of his menu. "What?" I asked.

He shrugged and went back to the menu.

"Don't you worry about having Señora Pérez in the house? What if she's loyal to Anibal?"

"I thought you were thinking about the organic market." My dad laughed. "Not going to take over the cooking so we can get rid of her?"

Was this guy a mind reader? Could he divine how many fingers I mentally held up?

The waiter appeared to take our orders. I asked for shrimp *al diablo* and a Victoria. Quint went for *pulpo en tinto,* octopus cooked in its ink, and a Coke. Yech.

When the waiter scurried off to get our drinks, I asked, "So, Quint, if this is a family district, how did someone operate a whorehouse on Avenida Amores?

Chapter 2

I'd Recognize His Pointy Head Anywhere

I stuffed a tender shrimp into my mouth and my tongue sparked flames. Shrimp al Diablo, no kidding. The chilies took my breath away. I poured beer down my throat to quench the fire. Quint laughed.

"It's hot!" I spluttered and swilled back another *ampolleta* of Victoria, the lager brewed locally. "The senator's up to his armpits in all this crap, Quint," I said, shaking my fork at him as I considered the possibility of Aguirre's involvement in the human trafficking ring.

"You're not hearing me, Jade. The senator is legit. I've said it all along."

I narrowed my eyes and glared at him. Was he really defending the Aguirre family? Pepper sat up and glared at him too, followed by Maya, although she was more interested in making sure Pepper didn't get the inky rice left on Quint's plate. She glanced at me with a hopeful grin and wagged.

"Sorry girl. All gone." I showed her my empty plate. She wagged harder, casting her eyes toward Quint.

"Get serious, JadeAnne. We have to figure this out. I think you're wrong about Aguirre. He is what he represents himself to be: an honorable guy doing the best he can for his country, his family and his friends." Quint gave me the squint-stare. "He considers you a friend. At the least, an ally."

I opened my mouth to lodge my adamant disagreement, but he tossed up his hands, warding off my attack. "I know he blamed you for Lura's death in Zihuatanejo. He told me he apologized to you. You need to accept it. Look what he's done for you since; isn't it enough?"

I thought for a moment. The chatter of diners rose around us. "Maybe the senator, more or less, sort of meant he was sorry—"

His bearing turned cold. "Christ, girl. He'd just lost his closest relative and still grieves for the deaths of his wife and kids in that car accident. Where's your compassion? Trust me on this. I've known the man far longer than you. He's a good guy."

"Who grows pot for the American market. Who associates with known criminals." I crossed my arms over my chest, wincing at the burn, a smug twist to my lips. When you're right you're right.

"I guarantee in five years states will start legalizing marijuana. No one will care anymore. Now Aguirre funds his campaigns with the profits, and he fights organized crime through his political position. Which criminals are you referring to anyway? His senatorial colleagues? He's not in anyone's pocket, I assure you."

I suppressed a giggle and slowly shook my head side to side. Had he forgotten about Aguirre's family? A bunch of thugs. "Let's start with Lidia, CEO of the Biggest Little Whorehouse in Pedrigal."

"She's his mother. Anibal is his brother. Daniel Worthington was his cousin's husband. Did you expect him to avoid his family? Pretty lonely during the holidays, eh?"

I shrugged my shoulders in exasperation. "Okay, I give up. This bickering isn't going to solve our immediate problem. Are we living in a former brothel owned by Lidia Aguirre? Has she sent Señora Pérez to spy on us? Do her business interests extend beyond running a house of ill repute? I don't really care if she's running brothels if her workers are free hires and compensated fairly. But Quint, what if Lidia is behind the trafficking of kids? Did you ever consider that house Anibal took me to might have been hers?"

"You're referring to the place you found the kids?"

"Yeah. Anibal wasn't clear about how he found it. Maybe he always knew. He was disgruntled over his perceived treatment at the hands of Aguirre and Lidia. She was awful toward him at Lura's funeral and the gathering after. Maybe busting that house was revenge for a lifetime of being treated as a second-class citizen. The poor relative on the doorstep." I glared at him. I was too aware of feeling second best. I'd grown up with it while my father lived another life—not one with me.

"Yeah, your generation studied psychology. Maybe you're right, but I think Anibal was just plain bad. I'll arrange to find out who holds title to the properties in Pedrigal, Del Valle, and Lomas de Pedrigal. You go make nice with the senator and get him to give you a history of our house and his mother's business. Kiss up to him; he'll tell you. Like I said, Aguirre considers you a friend." He grinned what I had come to recognize as his conspiratorial grin. "And the housekeeper? You're being paranoid, girl."

I wrinkled my brow. Could I have been wrong about her? "So, you think Señora Pérez is really just a housekeeper? Not reporting our every move back to Lidia and whatever cartel Lidia's with?"

"What do you mean?"

"Maybe she's connected to the Zetas."

"Mrs. Pérez? Do you know something about her?"

A metal tray clanged to the tiles, making me jump. "Yes.

She told me how she lost her family and rescued Lidia in the big 1980s earthquake." I didn't add how kind she'd been after I'd been shot the first time.

"So Lidia is beholden to her, not the other way around."

Our waiter scurried by, grabbing the empty salsa bowl and replacing it with a full one.

I paused to think. I wasn't so ready to say I might be wrong. "I meant Lidia, but that would be the logical order, yes."

"I rest my case. We'll be glad to have her, unless you want to manage the house." He flashed that charming smile at me. "How about some flan? It's good here."

"Sure. You're buying. Right, Dad?" I smiled and pushed my empty plate aside.

We walked back to the house in silence. I surveyed my surroundings, taking my bearings. This part of the colonia appeared to be laid out in a pretty regular grid of east-west, north-south streets, but I knew from other trips through Del Valle the grid system only went so far. I thought we were walking parallel to one of the City's major thoroughfares, Insurgentes, which bisected Mexico City edge-to-edge on the north-south axis. I'd passed the fancy Del Valle shopping mall and the taqueria Quint and I liked, traveling south on Insurgentes. I'd never ventured into the neighborhood before, and I was sure some oblique boulevard would spear through and trip me up. Or one of myriad dead ends. The city was a perfect metaphor for the Aguirre family and its associations. You had to keep on top of where you were to get anywhere. One wrong turn and you'd be shunted off in the opposite direction with no exits. Was Quint one of those wrong directions?

I pondered the man who claimed to be my natural father while I observed daily life in the colonia. Many of the buildings looked like they'd been constructed during the fifties. Lots of apartments. He probably felt at home here after growing up in a city. Actually, he struck me as someone who felt at home anywhere, or nowhere. A rolling stone or a soldier of fortune. And that's what I mistrusted. That and how he happened to turn up to meet me thirty-two years late in Mexico City. Was I being naïve again? Too trusting? I'd called my dad—my adoptive dad— and gotten confirmation: Quint truly was my progenitor. But something didn't feel right. Why now?

We turned off the main street into our neighborhood. On the side streets, buildings dating from the twenties and thirties loomed over the walls and barred gates between more recent architectural additions. I swiveled my head to admire a lovely facade across the street, and a black SUV caught my eye. I'd noticed one when we first came out of Don Capitán, but in D.F., the Distrito Federal, there're so many black SUVs with smoked windows, it's become a cliché. The thing was, the profile behind the smoky glass had reminded me of Anibal. Maybe I was still weak from my hospital stay, or maybe Quint's motives for reuniting with me had me confused, but was that the same vehicle?

I elbowed my father. "Check out the SUV. I think it's dogging us," I said, tossing my head in the vehicle's direction. Pepper's ears shot up.

We both turned to look; it sped up and passed us. A chill ran up my spine as the driver and I made eye contact. The vehicle turned left at the end of the block before I could get my mouth open.

"Oh. My. God. That driver! We ate dinner with him at Aguirre's. You remember, what was his name? The guy who was helping Lidia with her fundraiser."

"Lobo. Guillermo Lobo," he said, searching my face. "A suspected BLO front man and money launderer. Are you sure?"

"All I know is what I saw, Quint. He recognized me. He

knew me," I said. "That's not all. I saw the vehicle outside the restaurant while the dogs piddled. I swear the silhouette of the passenger in the back seat was Anibal's. I'd recognize that pointy head anywhere."

"Can you I.D. the vehicle? A scratch, dent, something? How do you know this was the same one at the restaurant? It's a pretty big accusation against the senator's friends."

"I told you he hung out with criminals."

He expelled a sharp breath. "I don't think it's the senator who hangs out with that guy."

"Well, he hangs out with one, Aguirre." My head swam and I grabbed Quint's arm as the scene in my mind came into clarity. "He was there when the Zeta tossed Anibal in the back of probably the same SUV."

"What? No, Jade. That can't be right. Lobo isn't a Zeta," he said in a low tone.

I tilted my face up to look into those green eyes. "Oh? Then what is he?"

"Look, I can't discuss an ongoing investigation."

"You had Lobo under investigation? Now he's following me around and you won't tell me what's going on? Wow, Dad. That's really fatherly." My lunch threatened to come back up. I pulled away from him. "Who're you working for —Dad?"

We reached the corner and turned right toward Calle Amores. Maya picked up her pace, dragging Quint along on the leash. She wanted her babies. I wanted safety. Pepper wanted a run, and Quint, what did he want?

I peered up and down the street looking for the SUV. Not in sight. I supposed they knew where we lived. It was just too random they'd find us here on a fluke. Who alerted them? Aguirre? Lidia? Señora Pérez? Or would Anibal have known about this house? Nothing made sense except we'd be moving pretty soon. Or I would. It was not my intention to be sold into sex slavery. I'd grab Lily and we'd fly home.

Maybe I'd adopt her and we'd live with Pepper on my Sausalito houseboat. She could go to Tam High and apprentice as an investigator at Waterstreet Investigations. I shook my head. Where did that idea come from? And if I didn't get home pretty soon, I'd probably lose my partnership. I'd already lost my partner. But I'd think about that another day.

I'd trailed behind Quint and Maya from the corner and caught up to him inspecting the vehicle gate in front of the house. "How'd you open that?" I asked.

"I didn't. It looks like the electric sensor shorted out. Remember how it buzzed? It must have been going out and the gate opened."

Just enough to allow an adult man through and give me a creeping feeling in my bones. "Are you carrying?"

"Of course. Why?" he said.

"I think you better search the premises before I go in."

"You've got an overactive imagination girl. But if it makes you feel better, I'll scout the place out." He pulled a little gun from the small of his back. I'd wondered why he wore a light jacket on such a warm day.

"Pepper, guard Quint. I'll stay here until you tell me the house is clear."

"Do you think you'll be safer on the street?" He snorted. "You've read too many thrillers, Jade. Take the dogs and go inside. I'll check the yard. Unless the lock's been shot out, no one is getting inside."

"What about Señora Pérez? She could open the door."

"She could, but why would she?"

"Force or bribe. They want Lily and me. Where is Lily, anyway?"

"In her room, I expect. Go on up and see. Take your dog if you're afraid."

I cringed. My hands had begun to shake, and tremors crept along my neural pathways. Something was wrong. I was scared. Had they gotten to Lily? Why hadn't I thought to bring my gun?

He activated the gate at the keypad and it rattled open then shut with a clang. "Working now. Let's go."

He unlocked the front door then ushered me and the dogs onto the elevator. I punched 1. The metal cage lurched and groaned up one floor and opened into a wide hall between the kitchen and living room. Maya trotted into the kitchen to see how her babies were doing. Quint followed her.

"Aren't you going to check the house?" I asked.

He turned and leaned into the door frame, grinning. "I'm starting in the kitchen."

I followed and found Señora Pérez cooking one of my favorites, *albóndigas*, meatballs in spicy tomato sauce. I greeted her, and she nodded back at me with a warm smile.

"Has Lily eaten anything?" Quint asked in butchered Spanish and licking his lips.

The señora wiped her hands on her apron and said, "*Comida para mañana, señorita. Sí, la niña comió. Hay una cena lista en el refrigerador cuando quiera.*"

"There you go, Jade. Lily's safe and ate something," he said, giving me an *I-told-you-so* look.

I didn't say anything, but the meatballs smelled so good, my mouth watered, although I was full from lunch. I should get her to teach me some *cocina mexicana* techniques and dishes. I could wow all my friends back home with great Mexican food—and interrogate the housekeeper. If I got on her good side, she'd have pretty boring reports for Lidia or Lobo, or whoever was taking an interest in our occupation of this house.

I settled the goldens, changing the puppy pads then letting Maya into the box, and climbed up the stairs to my suite. I hovered at Lily's door, debating knocking. She'd had a scary and stressful situation and was now plunged into a world of pain, grief, and guilt. Should I let her rest and heal? Pink was a healing color, wasn't it? Better to let her come to me on her own terms rather than barge in and try to cheer her up. I crossed the passageway to my own room.

Coward.

If I couldn't deal with a teen who had lost her sister to cartel gun violence and human trafficking—now didn't that sound way over the top? No one would believe me if I told them the story—if I couldn't deal with Lily, I could call Polo Aguirre instead and make a date to pick his brain. The old-fashioned rotary phone sat on the lacquered desk in the bordello. I dialed. After too many rings, a harried sounding Señora Arias de Barrera answered. "¿Bueno?"

"*Hola señora.* This is JadeAnne. Is the senator in?"

"*Aye, señorita*, we're in a state here. The senator is leaving right now for Guerrero. Some last-minute business. Can I have him call you when he gets back? He'll only be gone overnight."

"I'd like to see him. I need some information. Can you fit me into his calendar?" I heard the rustling of paper and pictured her looking through Aguirre's agenda.

"*Sí*, what about supper on Friday at eight? I know he wants to welcome you back. He was very worried when he learned from Mr. Quint you had been shot."

"Yeah, I'm sure he was. Thank you for the lovely bouquet of flowers, I enjoyed them very much. You arranged them?"

"Of course."

I could hear the smile in the assistant's voice. Señora Arias de Barrera might have missed her calling.

"Tell Senator Aguirre I'll see him Friday at eight."

"*Hasta luego*, Miss Stone."

I hung up. Now what would I do? Hide until Friday? I really should check on Lily. What if she weren't there? What was I thinking? Of course she was. Anyway, Pepper needed some real exercise—so did I after lying around for a week. To hell with the black SUVs. I'd take my dog and my gun for a run. And after exercise and a shower, I'd learn to cook.

Chapter 3

Parque Árboles

After lying around the hospital for a week, the walk and big lunch had tired me out, and .. dropped onto the bed for a little rest before taking Pepper out again. I felt depressed yet restless at the same time. At home, I'd have been kicked out of the hospital in two days; but Aguirre had paid for my stay, so I supposed I should feel grateful.

The smog-filtered sun illuminated my room in a rosy, warm glow as it angled in, making me drowsy. My eyes sank shut and the next thing I knew, Pepper was nudging me awake with a running shoe in his mouth.

"Where did that come from?" I asked him. I hadn't even opened the closet or looked in my bathroom.

Pepper bounded over to a corner by a slipper chair upholstered in wine-colored cabbage roses and did everything he could to pick up the other shoe without letting go of the first. I noticed the leash flopped over the back of the chair.

"So, you want to go out for a run?"

He grinned at me through the mouthful of blue Nike and woofed, muffled by the shoe.

"Okay, let's find the park." I stretched and got to my feet. Two doors with glass knobs and an ornate white and gold dresser with a tilting mirror between them, lined the wall. I chose the narrower door and found my dresses hanging neatly, shoes below. No exercise clothes. Someone had carefully folded the rest of my stuff into the cedar scented dresser. Better than mold, but might have me sneezing anyway.

My workout clothes and bathing suits occupied the last drawer down. Whoever put my things away was not an exercise nut. I used those clothes the most; at home they occupied the top drawer. I wore yoga pants to work most days. Well, not in Mexico City.

The thought of work made me feel guilty. I stretched a pair of blue and white running tights up my legs and tugged a yellow t-shirt over my head. Sure, I'd earned a hefty fee for finding Lura Laylor, but that was way back on the eighth and I hadn't earned my keep since. Waterstreet Investigations could still be considered a startup, and my partner and ex, Dexter Trouette, would be running out of money soon. Especially if he'd been off on another of his salvage dives with buddy Penn. The thought made me frown. This was slippery territory.

I tied a pullover around my waist and rummaged through the narrow top drawer for tennis socks, messing up the neat, color-coordinated rows left by my phantom personal maid.

"God, it wasn't Quint who folded my clothes away, was it, Peppi? That would be creepy." Pepper wasn't saying, too busy standing at attention by the door. I sat down on the rose chair and put on my shoes.

Thinking of my business and my ex-boyfriend had dimmed my enthusiasm for going out. That pink-frosted bed beckoned. It resembled a five-year-old's birthday cake, but it passed the comfort test. I yawned; Pepper whined. My cue. I got up, stuffed my driver's license into my pocket, put the gun and my phone in a fanny pack, grabbed the leash and opened the door. Pepper leaped out and trotted to the elevator; he knew his way around. I followed him, cringing with guilt as I passed Lily's door.

The clock on the stove in the deserted kitchen read five-thirty. I'd slept for two hours. According to the note left on the counter by the coffee maker, Mrs. Pérez had finished cooking our supper and gone home. The house had that dead silence of emptiness, not even the puppies were about. I wondered about Lily again. Maybe she went somewhere with Quint and the goldens. His house keys did not hang on the set of hooks he'd pointed out when we first came in. Mine hung under my initials and I took them. Somebody here was a little Adrian Monk-like. I hoped it wasn't Quint with OCD. I could never measure up to that level of cleanliness or organization.

Outside the shadows angled to the east and the afternoon had cooled slightly. I had no clue where to go and worried the black SUV would turn up. I let Pepper lead. He walked me three blocks south to Pilares and east several short blocks to a big park filled with kids, teens, families playing, strolling, eating ice cream, shooting hoops, biking, and roller skating. We passed plenty of dog walkers and stopped for wags and sniffs often. Pepper knew right where he wanted to go, a turf track circling an area of trees and grass. Most of the dogs on the track were unleashed so I let him loose and he took off at a dead run. I bolted after him and yelped when my wound complained. I panted, holding my side, until the pain subsided.

"Are you all right?" a voice asked. I looked up to see a drop-dead gorgeous man about my age smiling at me. His two dogs, a black and white French Bulldog and a thin-furred black mutt, or *corriente*, wagged at me.

Judging by its ears, the mutt might have Xoloitzcuintli ancestry mixed with a rabbit. I laughed. "I'm fine. Just over-doing it on my first day out of the hospital."

He fell in beside me and we started to walk in the direction Pepper had disappeared. I whistled.

"Why were you in the hospital?"

"Car accident. I'm okay now. Nothing too serious. Bruising on my ribs," I lied. Lying was coming easier since I'd been in Mexico.

"Your daughter didn't say anything about it."

Daughter? I felt my face blanch. Lily had been walking Pepper in the park? I'd have a word about *that* with her.

The man scrutinized my face. "Here, let me help you over to that bench." He took my elbow and guided me to the edge of the track, his dogs trotting alongside, and settled me onto it.

I sat, not because I intended to, but who could resist such a show of kindness after what I'd been through? "Thanks."

"I haven't seen you here before, but I know your dog. He's quite an animal."

"Yeah, my dad has been taking care of him. I'm fine, by the way. Don't let me keep your dogs from their walk." I gave him a sideways glance. He was smiling like he expected it. Minus a point.

"I haven't seen Lily in a couple of days. I thought you'd gone back to California."

"She told you we were from California?"

Pepper thundered up, scaring the little bulldog. He flopped down beside me and the man's dogs moved in for a greeting. Pepper wagged, they wagged, and all touched noses.

"They've met before," I observed.

The man nodded. "You're not from California? I thought —she knew L.A. so well. I lived there while I attended U.C. Medical School."

"You're a doctor? What do you practice?"

"I'm on an ER rotation right now at Hospitál San José," he said and pointed vaguely into the distance, "but I trained as a surgeon. I'm applying at private hospitals for something in surgery." He laughed. "Sewing up kids after skateboarding accidents is great, but I'd rather remove brain tumors. Where are you from then?"

"Sausalito, actually. My girl lived in L.A. with her dad. What brought you back to Mexico? I'd imagine anyone fluent in both languages would have a plum position in the States."

"I had an advantage. My mother is American. Both languages are first languages for me, but I wanted to live in Mexico. I won't make as much in private practice, but I can live like a king. Anyway, the *barbacoa* is better here," he said and shot me a wicked grin.

I licked my lips and murmured, "Yum. I love *barbacoa*."

His eyes twinkled like black diamonds from their fringe of thick lashes. He had full, sensual lips that couldn't stop smiling. And his café latte complexion was smooth as gelato. I couldn't help myself—somebody give me a spoon. I tried not to drool. *Am I crazy? Wake up, Stone.*

"There's a great little taco place out on Insurgentes. Would you like to take the dogs over for a taco or two? I'm hungry. We'll walk slowly."

My stomach knotted. He sounded kind, but so did Fernando Torrens. "No, really, I can't take you away from your dog time. And Pepper needs his run."

"So let him run. He, Noémie and Roger can loop around the track a few times and we'll go."

"Which one is which?" I asked.

"My apologies. I'm Dylan Gael Porras Montero and these are Noémie and Roger."

As he spoke the dogs offered their paws for shaking. Adorable.

"Delighted to meet you all. I'm JadeAnne Stone. This is Pepper—who wants his run." I got up and Pepper watched me expectantly. "Look Dylan, we need to keep moving and

26

get back to the house. The housekeeper has already made dinner. I'd hate to disappoint her after all her hard work. You know how it goes. Maybe I'll see you here another day?" I really did hope I'd see him again. It took all my willpower to let go of this handsome doctor, but a little voice whispered to be careful. I'd learned the hard way. Not everyone was who they seemed.

"I understand. Our Maria sulks if we don't eat her food. So how about tomorrow, JadeAnne? Same time? Walk the dogs then have some tacos?"

His boyish smile disarmed me. "Sure, I'll look forward to it," I said and smiled, too. My traitor eyelashes fluttered. "Come on Peppi, shall we run?"

Pepper took off trailed by Dylan's dogs. Dylan was watching me when I turned and gave him a little wave. I wondered what I was getting myself into. He'd said "we." He was probably married.

No one was going to sneak into my house-of-ill-repute through the elevator. It clanged and groaned and squeaked up to the main floor where it jerked to a stop, announcing our arrival to the neighborhood. Maya greeted us with enthusiasm, sniffing both of us intently for news of our travels.

"That you, Jade?" Quint called from the kitchen.

"Who were you expecting?"

Pepper took his comment as an invitation to head for the kitchen. Maya leaned into me, holding me in place for pets.

"We're about to eat these marvelous meatballs Mrs. P made."

"Yeah, her *albóndigas* are the best. She made them at Anibal's," I said as I walked into the kitchen. "Hey, I thought the meatballs were for tomorrow's *comida*."

Quint shrugged. "She didn't say anything to me about it."

He wore a frilly apron and spooned meatballs and sauce onto a plate. I snorted. He looked ridiculous. Lily sat at the table swiping at her myspace, or whatever, on Quint's phone. Isn't that what all the kids used?

"Hi, Lily. I'm happy to see you. Where'd you go today?"

Lily looked up from her photos and exhaled a long, tortured sigh.

"That good, huh?" I asked, teasing.

"We went to the Embassy. Again. I want to go home."

"To your mother's house?"

"No! If she'd believed me about *him,* Evie and I would never have run away."

"They haven't been able to locate the mother, and the Embassy won't send her to her aunt without a parent's permission. She's only with us through the senator's influence. They were going to put her into child protective services. I called him to intervene," Quint added.

A gloomy shadow played across her face. "They don't believe me about what happened. All that man does is threaten me. Like I'm some sort of criminal, not the people who kidnapped us or, or..." Tears welled from her eyes.

Quint slid a plate of steaming food in front of her and squeezed her shoulder. She hung her head and pushed the plate away.

He met my eyes with a hopeless look. I didn't know what to do either, but I took my plate from his hand.

"She can't get on a plane without a passport or parental permission. Even if the aunt comes for her and she is allowed on the plane, she can't land in the U.S. We could probably grease the wheels at the airport, but not the embassy."

"It's okay, Lily. I believe you; you know I do. I'll go with you next time, but I don't know how to help you without the passport. Have you talked to your mother?" I said.

She shook her head. "She's not answering." Her voice rose into a wail. "It's all her fault. She let him go after Evie. She let him r-rape me. I had to take my little sister away. I had to."

I sucked in a breath as tears sprang into my eyes. These poor traumatized girls. I clasped her hand. "Lily, have you talked to your aunt?"

She gripped me like she would drown if I let go. Maybe she would. I pulled her into a tight hug.

"Yes. I told her everything. She said she'll take custody of me away from Mom and be my guardian until I'm eighteen. And bury Evie." She pulled away, choking on the word, and tears trickled down her cheeks. She swiped at them and continued. "My uncle is a lawyer. He can do it. He even said I can have Eddy arrested and sent to prison. But I have to get home."

I didn't know what to say to her. Hot tears pricked at my eyes. I swiped them with my napkin and took a bite. The meatballs were just as delicious as I remembered. Slightly sweet. Slightly spicy and meaty and moist. I took another bite and pondered the problem. "Quint? Can't we do anything? I could drive her home."

He joined us at the table with his plate. "Same problem getting across the border. It's why the aunt can't come for her."

"But people do it all the time. And Lily is a citizen."

"We're not sending her with a coyote, Jade," he said and chuckled. "This is good. You should learn how to make it."

"Honey, what's your aunt's name?"

Lily looked up from the figure eights she was making in her sauce. "Charlotte and Derrek Medine. They can't find Mom. She left with *him*."

"I'll call my partner tomorrow and get an investigator on her trail. We'll find them."

Lily looked at me, hope lighting her face. "Who's your

partner?"

"I run a private investigation company in Sausalito. I came to Mexico to find a missing woman. My people can find your mom and her monster boyfriend. I promise. You won't have to see her, but we'll get that permission. Quint, where are Evie's remains? When this all comes down, we'll need everything ready from this end."

"Aguirre has Susana on it."

"Susana?"

"Señora Arias de Barrera."

"She never told me her first name."

"Can I be excused?" Lily asked.

Quint and I looked at each other. She hadn't eaten anything, but I suppose in this situation, I wouldn't be able to eat either. We nodded.

Lily scooped the six puppies and the puppy pads into a large basket and trudged out of the room. Maya looked from the meatballs to her children and back to the meatballs. She sighed and with a last longing look, followed Lily. I tucked a meatball into a napkin to slip to her later.

When the stairs door shut behind Lily and the dogs, I turned to Quint. "What's the meaning of letting Lily walk Pepper in the park? I can't believe you've allowed her out of your sight."

"I never let Lily out on her own. Who told you that?"

"Doctor Dylan Gael Porras Montero. I met him in the park today and he asked after my daughter. He was walking his dogs and I realized Pepper knew them."

"Did you speak to him or did he approach you?" he asked.

"Yeah, I thought of that, too. He approached me and was full of questions. But he was so nice and had such cute dogs..."

"So was the bastard who snatched those girls. What are you thinking, talking to strange men? Did you carry your gun?"

"Yes, *Dad*, I had the gun. No, *Dad*, I didn't tell him where I live, or at least not in Mexico."

"Jade, you're too trusting. I suppose you introduced yourself."

"And Pepper. We have a dog walking date tomorrow at five." I popped another meatball in my mouth. "You know, this meal calls for a beer. Get you one?"

Quint frowned. "What about Senator Aguirre. Will you go see him?"

I set two cold ones on the table and sat back down. "Corona or Victoria?"

"Corona. Well?"

"Dinner Friday night

Chapter 4

This is so Abnormal

Thursday, August 23, 2007

Thursday the sun shone brightly and the air smelled unusually fresh. All the trees in this century-old district helped keep the air cleaner. The moment I stirred, Pepper pounced on top of me carrying the leash. As if I'd ever forgotten his walk.

"You wanna take a walk, Peppi? How about a trip to the yard for now?" I asked.

He woofed and leapt across the room to the door. Pepper and Superman, leaping in a single bound. It was a tiny suite. I followed sedately, but with more enthusiasm than I'd felt in almost two weeks. My gunshot wound didn't hurt much today. The doctors were right: yesterday's walking really helped. Dylan said the best medicine was to get up and move. Yeah, so why was I kept in bed for a week? I guessed Aguirre worried I'd instigate an international incident if I didn't get proper care.

I stretched and tossed on a pair of shorts. I could check out my side when I took a shower.

Pepper and I tiptoed down the creaking stairs to the landing. I'd barely explored the house and now would be a good time to do it. The kitchen took up most of the end of the house, if you counted the breakfast room. The many windows let in plenty of light and, I'd noticed the day before, caught the late afternoon sun. Between the kitchen proper and the breakfast room, the back stairs went down to the small garden. I found the key on my ring and opened the door. Pepper pushed ahead of me, thundered down the steep, straight stairs and sat in front of the garden door. He craned his head up to watch me inch my way down.

"What's the matter boy? Impatient?"

He grinned and twitched his tail.

At the bottom, I again tried keys until one fit. I would have to label them. Every door in the house must have a lock, except, of course, my bedroom. I guess the working girls wouldn't dare enter the madam's room uninvited. I wouldn't tangle with Consuelo either unless I had to, but unfortunately, it looked like I might. I was determined to get to the head of the trafficking ring—the kingpin—and put an end to it. I'd make it my mission, and Madam Consuelo knew the players.

The lock turned and we stepped out onto a narrow tiled patio furnished with rusting wrought iron benches and a card table. A couple of stone urns spilled weedy greens and shriveling flowers from their bowls. Pepper scooted around the corner of the house and I hunted a hose. I found a spigot and a bucket. That would have to do. I hauled water to the urns and visibly brightened the flowers' day. The one next to the house grew a trumpet vine that had climbed to the second floor and now was a dried mess. The house came with a housekeeper. Did we also have a gardener? The front looked so tidy and lush, someone must be tending it. Why hadn't the backyard been kept up? I followed Pepper around the corner into a jacaranda shaded tunnel arching over the tiled walkway. Against the outer wall, a little fountain gurgled merrily into a murky well clogged with rotting leaves.

I tried keys until I identified the one to the side door into the garage. My VW pop-top camper, my *combi*, filled about half of the space. I could see a workbench and tools beyond it. Quint had had the bus washed. Thoughtful of him.

I relocked the door and went around to the front. Dappled sun warmed the grass. Pepper rolled on his back in a sunny patch and made happy sounds. The vehicle gate was fully closed and didn't buzz. Quint had finally come through. I was accustomed to a father who did what he said he'd do. My adoptive dad always stressed keeping one's word. *My adoptive dad*—it would take some doing to accept that.

Pepper finished his back rub, trotted around the far corner of the house, and barked. I followed him. A man dangled from the fire escape, holding his feet above Pepper's snapping jaws. I froze, petrified. My gun was in my room. My phone too. Thank God for Pepper.

"Ayúdame, señorita. ¡Porfavor!"

Now shaking, I demanded, "What are you doing here? *¿Quién eres?"*

"Jardinero. Soy el jardinero. Ayúdame."

The gardener. That answered my question. "Pepper. Come," I commanded.

The man dropped to the ground, shaking. *"¿Muerde el perro?"* he asked, watching Pepper with trepidation.

I shot the dog some hand signals. He sat and raised his paw to shake. "No, he's friendly," I replied in Spanish. "What's your name?" I gave him a once-over, assessing he was unarmed.

The man edged away from Pepper, not convinced. *"Tonalli. La señora Aguirre me mandó."*

Lidia sent him. I knew it. "I'm glad to see you, Tonalli. The backyard needs some attention. By the way, how did you get in?"

"La señora gave me the gate code, but it didn't work. I climbed the gate. My truck is on the street."

He pointed toward the street and I could see the tailgate with garden tools peeking above it. What did he think he'd do once in? The gate still required the key code.

"I'm JadeAnne. What did Lidia tell you to do?"

"I am to tell la señora what it needs. She gave me the key to the garden room."

"The garden room? Where's that?"

Tonalli shrugged toward the door next to the fire escape. I saw his keys dangling in it. Did Lidia give him keys to the whole house? "Let's take a look." I turned the key and pushed open the door. Damp and the scent of leaf mold laced the musty air. I breathed in, tasting the earth with a rush of homesickness and wondered if Dex was taking care of my orchids. Tonalli found the switch and bare bulbs washed dim pools of light over the workbench and shelves.

The room reminded me of Mom's garden shed back home. Pots, a potting table, a push lawnmower, clippers, loppers, spades, rakes, shovels and forks lined the walls. A mushroom sprouting pile of dirt filled one corner. Chemicals, fertilizers and toxic sprays stood on a top shelf. I'd discourage Tonalli from using those. Maybe we'd start a compost pile in a corner of the yard. With all the trees, we probably already had one.

"I guess you don't need your truck. Good. I don't know the key code either." I smiled at him. "Let's take a look at the garden."

He nodded and backed out of the room. I locked the door and handed Tonalli his keys. "Do you have keys for any other doors to the house?"

He shook his head. "*No, señorita. La jefa* gave me the code and this key."

"When will you come?" I asked as we surveyed the dry lawn and drooping shrubs.

"Regular maintenance I do every week."

"You'll do the backyard too? Friday?"

"*Sí, señorita*, at eight." He slid his eyes toward Pepper.

"I'll open the gate for you and keep Pepper inside at eight o'clock then."

The gardener nodded and gathered up a hose.

Tonalli had come early. It was barely eight when I set a steaming mug of coffee on the table and opened the paper I'd found just inside the gate. Pepper had eaten, and I'd peeled and cut a bowl of fruit for anyone who wanted it. Lily might like fruit and yoghurt. What did Quint eat? Shrimp on the barbie? I didn't have either.

"Good morning, JadeAnne," Quint boomed from the doorway, making both Pepper and me jump.

"Good morning. How'd you sleep? Out late?"

"Nah, not late. I had a meeting with the senator and some associates. You were sleeping when I came in. You look like you're feeling much better."

How'd he know I was sleeping? "Yeah, I'm just about back to normal. Did you know we have a gardener named Tonalli?"

"No, but Aguirre said something about taking care of the yard. Why?"

"He's outside now, watering. Seems like a nice fellow. Tonalli. What kind of name is that?"

"You're asking me?"

"Lidia sent him. She gave him the gate code and a key to the garden room. I don't know if he has keys to anything else. By the way, the gate was closed fully and the code didn't work. It was cracked open yesterday evening when I came in from my walk. A man could have gotten through, Quint. As if it mattered. Tonalli climbed over."

"So that confirms Lidia owns the house," he said, frowning. "Did you close the gate?"

"I did not."

"We should change the code then, and the locks. I'll work on that today."

"You didn't change it already?"

"No, why?"

I hmmm-ed, eyebrows raised. "He said the code Lidia gave him didn't work."

"I've noticed other inconsistencies," Quint replied.

"Like what?"

He sidestepped my question. "I'm taking care of them."

A man of few words? Or some funny business? I pushed on. "Have you noticed how many keys there are? It's a lot of locks to change."

"We'll just change the locks that give access to the house and property."

The house shook slightly and Pepper cocked his head; he trotted into the hall. I could hear the muffled thumps and giggles of Lily and the goldens in the stairwell. The stairs door slammed open and Pepper crowed. Lily shuffled in wearing an oversized pair of black scuffs and lugged all six puppies, squirming in a comforter. What happened to the basket?

"Good morning," I said, smiling at the girl. "You're feeling chipper today. I'm glad."

"Is Mrs. P here yet?" she asked, checking out the kitchen and pantry.

"Not yet, Lily. She'll be here soon," Quint said.

Lily dropped her gaze and her smile. "I hope she isn't mad. She's gonna have to clean my bathroom, I think." The girl blushed and shrugged. "The puppies.... she trailed off, still contemplating her fuzzy feet.

I nodded. Discussing puppy crap wasn't something she was used to, but having these dogs was a blessing. Lily showed signs of coming out of her depression, but I worried. After her trauma—how could she feel safe?

"Maybe we'll clean up and let Mrs. P get on with other tasks when she comes in," I said. "Quint, when does Señora Pérez come? And you never really told me what she's supposed to do." I cocked my head at him.

"Look at you girls! How did a guy get so lucky to have two beautiful girls discussing dog poop at the breakfast table. Makes an old dad proud." He beamed at us.

The man really meant it. A sure sign of someone who has been lonely too long. I grinned back at him and reached for his hand. Lily giggled and sat down.

"Can I have coffee?"

Quint jumped up. "Of course you can." He went to the counter and poured a cup, setting it in front of her.

I fed Maya and Maya fed her pups, which Lily had deposited on the puppy pads in the boxy enclosure. "Well, those didn't last long. These pups should be getting ready for solid food pretty soon. How old do you think they are? A month? Five weeks? Maybe we should think about weaning them and finding homes. I know someone who might help us."

"No, JadeAnne. Please, let me keep them." Lily's face fell into a frown and her bright mood visibly nosedived.

"I don't mean right now, Lily. It will take a while to wean them and they have to be at least eight weeks before they can be given away. Anyway, where would you keep seven huge golden retrievers?"

"Here with you guys. You love dogs, and Pepper loves Maya."

I couldn't deny that. He'd taken to her like I'd never seen him take to any other dog. "Well for a while, Lily. What happens when you go to your aunt's?"

I sighed. And when would I go home? I missed Sausalito. It would be crystal clear and sunny right now. A breeze would be blowing through the eucalyptus trees, scenting the harbor fresh. I'd be doing exactly this: sitting at the table drinking coffee, but it would be an hour earlier and, instead of worrying about locks, I'd be getting ready then walking the two blocks to my office in the Industrial Center

Building.

"Why so glum, girl?" Quint asked. His green eyes shimmered through the steam coming off the coffee flowing into my cup.

"Thanks. I was just thinking about the Sarasvati."

He made a goofy face. "And that loser Dex, I bet."

"Sarasvati? What's that? Who's Dex?"

I glared at him. "I live on a houseboat at Varda Landing in Sausalito. Dex is my business partner."

"A houseboat! I've never been on one. What's it like?"

"Why don't I tell you all about it while you give me a house tour? I barely know my way around. After, I can show you some photos."

Lily put down her mug and pushed away from the table.

"I meant after breakfast. What do you want? Eggs or fruit and yoghurt, or both?"

"Everything, I'm starving."

"Quint?"

"Eggs and tortillas. Mrs. P left a red salsa in the fridge. Thanks, darlin'."

I searched the packed shelves and found a *salsa fresca* and a flat of eggs. Two kilos of tortillas hid behind milk and orange juice on the top shelf. "Everyone likes tortillas, right?"

"Yeah," Quint and Lily chorused.

"Then *huevos mexicanos* coming up." I grabbed the frying pan from the overhead rack. "I better go to the store and get some decent oil. This processed vegetable oil sucks," I said, eyeing a bottle of corn oil on the counter. I placed a pan of whisked eggs on the burner and lit it and the griddle for the tortillas. Quint grabbed the cut fruit, yoghurt, and plates. In a few minutes, I set the eggs and stack of tortillas wrapped in a towel on the table.

"This is so normal. Like a TV family," Lily commented as she doused her eggs in salsa.

39

"What's normal?" Quint asked.

"She means, sitting down to breakfast like a family. I watched those shows, too. The Brady Bunch."

"The what?" Quint and Lily chorused again.

"Never mind. My family never ate breakfast together."

"Mine either," Lily said.

"Nor mine," Quint added.

"Well, I guess for us, this is so *abnormal*," I said and swigged a mouthful of coffee.

Chapter 5

Chile Rellenos y Tacos al Gusto

"You know the kitchen, JadeAnne, but did you see the breakfast room?" Lily swept her arm in a grand gesture toward the door off the kitchen—Vanna White in frayed shorts and a baggy t-shirt unveiling the prize.

She led me past the door to the backyard and we admired a pretty room with a large table set with French bistro chairs and a matching sideboard on scuffed oak flooring. A white china cabinet with glass doors bulged with dishware and glasses. Four sets of iron-framed windows opened to a narrow iron balcony and rail with pots of geraniums cascading over the rim. Two more sets of windows faced into the jacarandas' canopy along the side of the house. Some kind of vine growing over the stucco framed the back windows, which I hadn't noticed when I went out. I'd only seen the dead vine.

"Pretty isn't it? Maybe we can eat here?" Lily said wistfully.

The elevator clanged into place in the hall and the door scraped open. Señora Pérez trudged out with her shopping bags bulging. "*Buenas días, señoritas.*"

Lily flapped to the older woman, took the bags, and scuffed toward the kitchen, the housekeeper following. "I'll

41

be right back JadeAnne. Mrs. P what's for dinner?" I heard her ask.

It was as if a switch had flipped. Lily acted like a normal teenager. A nice one, at that. She seemed to like Mrs. Pérez. I remembered again how kind the housekeeper had been to me at Anibal's in Condesa. Motherly. Something neither of us had had much of, I thought as I trailed them into the kitchen.

"Mrs. P is planning on making *chile rellenos*, *frijoles barrachos* and pineapple flan. She says I can help. You want to help, too?"

"Yeah, I'd thought of asking her if she'd teach me some Mexican cooking. Let's do it." Cooking lessons from our resident spy. At least something good might come of this disastrous Mexican vacation.

Quint leaned around the doorjamb, Pepper's leash in his hand. "Mind if Pepper takes a walk with me?"

"No. He'll like that. Bring back *pan dulces*. Go with Quint, Peppi."

He clipped the leash on Pepper's collar, wished us happy cooking, and was gone.

"We better finish our tour and you should get dressed before we cook."

"Okay. Here's the dining room," she said, leading me into the next room.

Someone had paneled the room in dark walnut. Empty built-in glass fronted cabinets lined the interior wall and two balconied windows looked into the jacarandas. A worn wool carpet lay under a scarred dining table. The chairs matched the table but their upholstered seats had seen better days. I saw the dirt shadow where framed art had hung over the cabinets, and an oversized dark scene of dead birds and hunting dogs dominated the back wall. Yummm, appetizing.

"Look, you can go straight into the living room through here," Lily said, pointing to a set of pocket doors. She opened them and we entered past a baby grand piano with a veneer of dust coating its casing.

This house needed a good going over. Did Mrs. P clean as well as cook and shop? I sure as hell wasn't taking on housework. The pretty view to the front wall and gate belied living in one of the most populated megacities in the world. Flowers brightened things up in the morning sun, which found its way in through the mature trees. A couple of cityscapes hung on the walls above a grubby L-shaped sectional couch upholstered in white with a matching storage-ottoman-coffee table in front and an Eames chair to the side. On the wall above the chair someone had mounted a 70" flat screen TV. Oh, boy. Three matching threadbare oriental carpets covered the dark planking of the floor, which matched the heavy beams on the ceiling. Not elegant, but that couch looked like it would be perfect for watching *telenovelas* and eating ice cream. For some reason I pictured a Christmas tree trimmed in sequin strawberries and indigenous angels in the corner.

"Maya and Pepper love the couch."

"I guessed. I saw you and Maya curled up asleep when I came in last night. Speaking of sleeping, isn't it time to get dressed? Let's look upstairs."

"The bedrooms are all pink. Even Quint's. Hey, why don't you call him Dad?"

We trudged up the stairs. I noticed the third from the top really squeaked. I'd remember that. "I didn't grow up with him."

"Me either—with mine, I mean. I barely remember my dad. He left after Evie was born."

I heard the break in her voice when she named her sister. Poor Lily. Her life had gone so wrong. "You never see him?"

"No. He doesn't pay child support either. Mom's a hairdresser. A good one. But she doesn't make enough to support us. That's why she always has her loser boyfriends."

We pushed into her room. "Yuck. This really *is* pink."

Lily grinned. "I hate pink. Have you seen the other three rooms? They're pink, too. If we stay, can I paint mine purple and get new curtains?"

I poked into the bathroom. More pink. At least her towels were white.

"Quint bought all the towels," she said, following my eyes.

"Thank God he didn't try to match the bathroom. And sure, if we stay, you can do whatever you want. But we aren't staying. Quint and I have a job to do after we get you safely to your aunt." Or before, I thought. "I don't know how it will play out, but soon we'll go back to our real lives."

A thunder cloud rolled over the girl's face. "Can I visit you on your houseboat?" She asked, her voice sounding anxious.

I hugged her to me. "Of course you can, Lily. I want you to. Bring Maya."

She pulled away excitement in her eyes. "You mean I get to keep Maya?"

"Of course. She's obviously your dog. We'll figure out a way to get her home with you. She doesn't need a passport, permission, or a guardian."

We laughed.

"So I'll see you in the kitchen in a half hour?" I asked.

"We didn't go to the third floor yet."

"What's up there?"

"Your dad's office, a bunch of storage, and the awfulest little rooms you've ever seen. About eight of 'em. I don't really know what they would have been for. Tiny cots, a crummy bureau and hooks on the walls. There's a bathroom, too. Were those servants' rooms?"

"Hasn't anyone told you about this house?"

"No. Quint rented it so me and you would have somewhere to be."

"I bet he got it cheap, too. It used to be a whorehouse.

Those rooms? That's where the working girls lived. The pink rooms? Well, we don't want to think about what happened here," I said, grimacing.

She paled and a tear slipped out of her eye. "This is what would have happened to Evie and me, if-if you hadn't found us and rescued us from those men. I don't want to go up there again."

I nodded. But had she fallen into the hands of the Zetas, it might have been much, much worse.

By three I was ready to go batshit with boredom. Lily, Mrs. P, and I cooked all morning. That was fun. The housekeeper was a patient teacher and had plenty to practice with. It turned out there was a trick to "burning" the *chile poblano* so the waxy skin would lift off without breaking the meat underneath. I wrecked about a dozen before I got the knack of slitting one side open, pulling out the seeds and membranes—without tearing the chile—and stuffing it, again without tearing the chile. Lily was a natural. We made a ton of *rellenos,* filling them with Oaxaca cheese, *queso fresco*, a mixture of tuna, tomatoes, onions, rice, and *pico de gallo*. In another batch we added shredded chicken, Chihuahua cheese and parboiled shredded squash blossoms. Mrs. P planned on freezing several batches. I looked around and wondered where. The freezer in the refrigerator was barely large enough for ice trays and a package of frozen peas.

After we had assembled and packaged the *rellenos*, Mrs. P took us down the stairs into a room I'd missed on my morning yard inspection, a storage room/pantry with two huge chest freezers, another refrigerator, and shelves and shelves of dry goods, kitchenware and appliances. Anything we could want was here—it made me feel a little giddy. I suddenly wanted to cook all kinds of things.

An adjoining room housed the washer and dryer, as well

as a utility sink, drying racks, and an iron left face down on a board. I righted it, hearing my mother's voice, "Never leave the iron face down, JadeAnne. You'll burn the house down."

"What's that big tank over in the corner," I asked.

"Oh my God, that's the coolest thing in the house. It's a built-in vacuum. Mrs. P just has to carry a hose and attachments. There's a plug for the hose in every room and it just starts sucking up the dirt."

"Wow, that sounds pretty fancy," I said. My mother had had one of those systems installed.

Mrs. P herded us back up to the kitchen to learn how to roll the cheese *rellenos* in flour and egg and fry them. Finally, we made a really tasty red salsa with dried *chile guajillos* and *chile de arbol*, packed our dinner into casseroles and stowed it in the fridge for heating and eating later. The thought made me salivate—or was it my next thought?

Pepper saw him first and didn't waste any time herding Dylan, Noémie, and Roger to the bench. I watched Dylan stride toward me. Lanky and fluid in straight-leg jeans and a tightfitting soft grey t-shirt that said "McDreamie." OMG.

"Hey! What did you think—Meredith's *sister?* That was a surprise," I said.

Dylan grinned. "A Grey's fan; I knew I liked you. I have to watch it on the internet, but Mexico gets all the American shows eventually."

"I wouldn't have come during the season," I joked. "I'll get home before the fall premier. What's going to happen between Christina and Burke? You saw her in *Sideways*, no?"

He sat down next to me and unclipped the dogs from their leads. They yipped and twirled into the track for their run. Pepper pricked up his ears in surprise and gurgled. Noémie wiggled her hind end at him. They took off at

Noémie's pace: Roger loped and Pepper pranced. Poor little Noémie ran as hard and fast as she could, but she wasn't a match for the larger dogs. Dylan and I tracked them into the bend.

"So you're here through *el grito*?"

"*El* what?"

"Independence Day. At midnight on the fifteenth of September everyone in Mexico assembles in plazas to shout *'¡Viva México!'*—*el grito*—in honor of Hidalgo and the call to arms against Spanish rule in 1821. We beat 'em, but another ruling class filled the void. Nothing changes," he said, looking a bit crestfallen. "Grey's new season premiers in the last week of September."

"I should be home by then. So what about the Mexican Revolution?"

"Yeah, that was the other ruling class, the *Porfiriato*, after President Porfirio, an absolute asshole who rather fancied himself above the law, or maybe he thought he was the law. He brought a lot of prosperity and generally developed a thriving middle class. But the primarily urban middle class got tired of rigged elections, military force, and provincial landowners dominating policy. They revolted and we got the *ejido* system. Are you familiar with that?"

I nodded. I'd seen those impoverished *ejidos* with their skinny kids and starving animals on my way down the Pan American Highway. *Viva México* my ass. "If it was so great here after winning the revolution, why are millions of Mexicans risking everything to come to my country?"

"I have no answer to that except the rich make sure the poor stay poor."

We sat in silence, pondering the inequities of life until Pepper thundered back to our bench, soon followed by Roger.

"Poor Noémie. You left her behind," I said to Pepper. He panted and drooled down my leg. "Yuck. Thanks, buddy." I wiped off the slobber and swiped my hand across my shorts.

"Don't worry about her. She loves her run. She'll stop and visit people on the way. There's an old lady, Isabela, who brings treats for her. I think it's the highlight of Isabela's day. Her husband died last year and she's alone now. I've suggested she get her own dog, but she waits for Noémie. I check in on her now and then."

"She doesn't have kids or grandkids?"

"Not here. Her sons went to the U.S. and her daughter married a man from Tepoztlán and moved there. The daughter visits every Sunday, but the rest of the week Isabela is on her own."

I was sorry for the woman. People shouldn't be alone when they're old. I said, "Tepoztlán?"

"You haven't visited Tepoz? You must. It's a lovely mountainside town in Morelos about an hour away. Why don't I take you there on Sunday? It's an artist's colony. Artists, writers, actors, professors, all kinds of creative people live there. The ruin in the hills above town is dedicated to *Tepozteco*, the god of drunkenness. They say the area has been inhabited since 1500 BCE. It's a sacred place."

I raised my eyebrows as I cocked my head. "Sacred?"

"Our most important myth and god comes from the area."

"Yeah?"

"*Quetzacoatl*, the feathered serpent in his human form was born in a sacred pool in the river that drains the valley. You know about him, yes?"

"He left Mexico, but before he disappeared, he said he'd return on the back of a bird from the sea to the east, the Gulf. The locals thought Cortez was their god returning," I recited from my sixth grade primer.

"Something like that. No one really knows." Dylan checked his watch. "Noémie is taking too long. We better go look for her. Come on, Roger."

Roger popped up from his nap at Dylan's feet. Dylan had done a nice job training his dogs. Not so well trained as Pepper, who'd taken a second lap around the track, but whose dog was? I got up with them.

"Maybe you should wait for Pepper."

I whistled a piercing note. "He'll find me."

"He's well trained."

"My ex wanted me to have protection. Pepper is my bodyguard," I said as he bounded up the track toward us.

"Mine have had training, but not so much. Roger is naturally protective. Noémie is gregarious and loves people. Especially people with treats. Let's go find her."

"Did you have the dogs trained in the states?" Pepper galloped up to me and heeled, slowing to walk by my side.

"No. Here. There's a great trainer in Tlalnepantla. He breeds and trains guard dogs."

"Tlalnepantla?" An electric shock singed up my spine. I knew that name.

"Yeah, a guy named Fernando Torrens runs a place up there, just past Satelite. He's the best trainer in Mexico. You know the region?"

I tensed. Was Dylan toying with me? I casually hooked my hand over my fanny pack and took a breath. Pepper's ears perked-up. "I haven't been here very long."

Dylan hadn't noticed I'd reacted to the name. Good. My hand relaxed. We walked along the track, joggers passing us. How was I going to get away without alerting Dylan I was catching on?

"It's north on the highway to Querétaro."

"Oh, I hear the best pozole comes from there, or is it San Luis Potosí?"

"I don't know, but we could take a little trip. It's only two hours. Would you like that?"

I shuddered. A few too many trips out of the city. What was going on? When I didn't respond he continued. "I'm

49

partial to green pozole. I go to Cuernavaca for that, but there's a place in Tepoztlán with great red pozole if you like it. My mother cooks it, too. Hey, why don't you come the next time? You'll love it. And my folks would like to meet you."

This was creeping me out. "Your parents live here?"

"Yeah. I grew up in Del Valle. I'm living at home until I can buy something. Mom loves when I bring girls home. She's hot for grandchildren, although I've got her trained to never mention it. They're nice people. All my siblings live in other *colonias.*"

This conversation confused me. Was Dylan for real? Just a good-looking guy attracted to a girl in the park? Or was he hooked into the cartel network? And which one? Was Quint right, I was in danger and way too naive for my safety?

I turned back to him from my contemplation. Dylan had a quizzical look on his face. "JadeAnne is everything okay?"

"Yeah, I was just thinking. Tell me about your family."

He smiled and I saw the love he held for them in his eyes. "Dad is an engineer and teaches at UNAM. He met Mom when they were at University of Texas in Austin. She studied architecture, but took a basic engineering program one summer. We own a small architectural firm and construction company. They're a great team. My older brother is a contractor and runs that side of things. The company has done well. It's how I went to medical school. Guthrie has three kids in high school now. His wife, Conchita, owns a boutique here in the *colónia.* Hey, you should stop by." He looked me up and down. "You'll like her selection."

How did this guy know what I would like? Or was he making a veiled criticism on my wardrobe?

"Baez, our sister, is eight years older than me. She teaches high school literature classes and has twins. My mother is a twin, too. Did you know it runs in families?"

I nodded.

"And Seeger, my baby bro, is turning thirty next month."

"Oh, wow. They sound nice," I said. Lame, but what do you say about people you don't know and will probably never meet, although the family sounded pretty normal. Could Dylan's connection to Fernando be innocent? Maybe he just had his dogs trained there. My recollection of the kennel tour was date-drug hazy, but I thought Fernando had said he organized obedience training classes in that courtyard between the office building and the kennel. For the moment Dylan would be innocent until proven guilty.

Roger shot ahead to the next bench. I presumed that was Isabela with Noémie on her lap. Roger put a paw on the woman's knee and she fed him a treat. Noémie barked.

"Noé, don't be rude," Dylan said as we reached Isabela.

Isabela turned toward his voice and smiled, her wrinkled brown face lighting up. "Good afternoon, Doctor Porras. I knew you must be close by when the little miss came to find me." She gave the dog a hug—something hard to do as Noémie wiggled like the golden pups.

"*Hola Doña Isabela.* Noé looks happy and well fed," he said and winked at the old lady. "*¿Puedo presentarle a* JadeAnne, my friend from California? And this is her *pastor aleman,* Pepper."

The crone held out her arthritic hand and I took it gently. "How do you do, *señora.*" I flicked my other hand and Pepper sat down in front of Isabela and offered her a paw. I thought she would swoon in delight.

Dylan came to her rescue with a steadying hand and her cane. "Can we walk with you a bit, Doña? We're off for tacos at that place out on Insurgentes."

"Thank you, dear. That would be lovely. How's your mother, Dylan?"

"She's recovered from her cold, and back to work. I'm sure she'll stop in. Seeger is having a birthday soon."

They chatted amiably as we slowly made our way to the street and Isabela turned down the block toward home. We clipped our dogs back on the leashes.

"You hungry? Let's walk over to Tacos al Gusto. Come on!" he said taking my hand and gently pulling me toward the street.

My stomach grumbled thinking of the tacos, but I pulled my hand back. Was I safe? Dylan seemed so kind and family oriented. What thug helped old ladies in the park? What thug treated his dogs like cherished children? Even Fernando hadn't treated his dogs so well, and he had worn the King of Dogs crown. But going off with a stranger to a place I didn't know had gotten me into big trouble before. I felt the gun bouncing on my hip. I had to keep my wits about me; the Zetas had paid for me and wanted me back.

The sun gilded a halo around the western edge of the taller buildings as I walked home from *Taqueria Tacos Al Gusto*. It wasn't the same place Quint and I had eaten on our way to Lomas de Pedrigal, but the *tacos al pastor* were to die for. As were the *suadero, papas con chorizo* and *longaniza* tacos. Pepper loved his *carnitas,* too. Dylan and the *dueño*, Humberto, had gone to school together, and he treated us to a royal feast. The men chatted in rapid Spanish. Although I was getting pretty good at keeping up, the dozen tiny tacos I ate engaged most of my attention. But I doubt I'd missed anything. If Dylan was a cartel guy, he wasn't going to advertise it.

I hadn't gotten the impression he and Humberto were still close. Dylan told me he had lost touch with most of his friends while he studied in California. His crowd had finished school, found jobs, married and most moved away from Del Valle. I sensed Dylan felt out of step with his homeland, something I totally understood living here in Mexico City. Something I understood no matter where I was.

Dylan impressed me as a compassionate, kind man. His conversation was smart, interesting, and wide ranging, but he exuded a scent of loneliness. I wanted to fully enjoy his company, yet couldn't shake the notion he might be connected to Fernando Torrens in some nefarious way. He probably thought I was a dullard for my limited contribution to the conversation and when he said "*adios*" at the corner, he made excuses and hurried Noémi and Roger the other way.

Quint was going to have a fit that I met him, let alone walked around the *colonia* with him. That black SUV could have pulled up at any second and the thugs, with Dylan's help, swept me inside in a blink. I might get off a round, but probably not.

The notion sent shivers up my spine. I'd begun to think I was a risk junkie. Thinking about the black SUV knotted my stomach again and it churned through the greasy meat filling it—especially when I found the vehicle gate buzzing and open, again—enough for Pepper and me to squeeze through. Pepper didn't act like anything was amiss, but I wondered why Quint hadn't followed through on his promise. My father would have had the gate fixed two days ago. I left it open; I couldn't push it closed and I'd yet to learn the code.

I unlocked the front door and bolted it behind me. The elevator stood open; Pepper walked in and sat down. I followed and punched 1. We'd made it home safely, but Quint was right and I knew it. I'd risked myself and my dog. They'd wanted the dog, too. At least Fernando wanted him. I wouldn't see Dylan again. Let him think I just wasn't that interested.

Lily, Maya, and the pups dozed on the couch in front of the TV when Pepper and I landed on the main floor. They looked cozy. Dogs did not get on furniture in my home. Stupid rule. I left the sleepers to their dreams and wandered to the kitchen. Maybe I'd find Quint. Instead I encountered a covered clay casserole, a wooden bowl and three place settings at the table. Señora Pérez had left us a supper of the cold chilies in the red salsa we'd prepared, and a salad. I didn't need more food. I fed Pepper and scribbled a note telling everyone to eat, I'd gone to bed.

Chapter 6

So It Was About Me

Friday, August 24, 2007

Quint dropped me off in front of Senator Aguirre's Polanco apartment building and said he'd wait until I was on the elevator to leave the No Parking zone he occupied. As if I were a child—but comforting.

Polo owned the entire floor of the building. To get to his landing, a visitor had to know which elevator to take. I'd learned that when I stayed in his guestroom before Fernando Torrens kidnapped me, but since then security had been tightened up. I presented myself at the counter in the small lobby, passport in hand. Neither of the Shreks were on duty. No one was on duty. Where were the guards? On my past visits, one or another of the ogre-shaped security men had scrutinized me, not letting me in until Polo's team cleared me. Even when the senator took me in after the fire at his step-brother's house where I'd been staying.

I looked around and leaned over the counter to find the phone. For some reason the lobby lighting was dimmer than usual. The monitors and blinking lights on the phones lit the guard station in an eerie glow.

I slid around the counter for a better look and started

punching buttons. My ex, Dex, had worked surveillance on several jobs requiring monitors and operating boards. He'd taught me how to run them, and I now flipped camera to camera, bringing up different areas to view. The emergency exits were closed. The elevators docked. The emergency stairs empty. The monitors showed twelve floors of empty landings, halls, and stairways. That in itself was strange. Where was that guard, anyway? The bathroom? Out for dinner?

I reached for the phone to call up to the senator's, but one of the elevators opened. I dropped to the floor, my heart pounding, and slid as far under the counter as I could. If Shrek I or his clone, Shrek II, caught me here, I'd be in a world of trouble. They wouldn't dare harm me, but I'd have a lot of explaining to do to Senator Polo Aguirre. I curled into the smallest ball I could.

Footsteps came my way. I wasn't sure but I thought it was the third elevator that had come down—Senator Aguirre's. The dust under the counter tickled my nose and I snaked my hand up to cover my face and muffle the building sneeze. Yick. Something sticky transferred from the floor to my hand and now my face. I gagged on the thought of what might be under the Shreks' stool. It smelled like rust. I held my breath. At least three sets of footsteps passed and went out the door. I scrambled to the edge of the counter and peeked toward the entry. All I could see were the men's backs. A cloth bag covered the head of the man being roughly dragged out of the building. Curiouser and curiouser. The thug on the left turned and I saw his face under the entry light for only a second. I gasped. Anibal. My stomach leaped into my mouth and then hell broke loose.

A boom sounded. The front window shattered in a rain of tinkling shards. The man on the left dropped, dragging the captive to the ground, pools of red on his shirt. The *bratatatat* of an automatic weapon returned fire. Another boom. Footsteps clattered away. Car alarms wailed and whooped. People shouted and tires squealed. Stunned, I squatted at the edge of the counter. I shook my head, clearing the ringing in my ears. What was I doing? I needed to scram —hide.

I scuttled crab-like to the other end of the counter where I could see the bank of elevators. Sirens wailed in the distance. I had no time to lose.

Aguirre's elevator door stood open. Anibal hated his half-brother and had promised to get revenge on several occasions. Was it tonight? Or was it a trap for me? No. It couldn't be. That was just arrogance or narcissism speaking. Who would have known of our dinner date? Why would they take the senator before I showed up? I scuttled back to the door view. Two men lay in the doorway. Wait. The hooded man was moving, smearing seeping blood into his dark trousers. Alive. I needed to help him. Oh, why didn't I carry my gun tonight? Because one of the Shreks would have impounded it, that's why.

"Psst. Psst! Can you hear me? Are you hurt?"

The man stopped moving and lay deathly still. I crawled to the wall beside the door. The man's hands were bound underneath him. "Psst. Senator? Is that you? It's me, JadeAnne."

"I'm going to kill that bastard," he said, the muffled reply confirming his identity.

"Okay then, first, help me get you inside. Push with your feet. Yeah, like that."

While Aguirre pushed, I grabbed onto his suit jacket and pulled. Slowly he crossed the threshold and I angled him out of sight of the street. I started picking the knots on the hood.

"Cut my hands free."

The sirens closed in. If I didn't free the senator and get out of here, would I be implicated in something I didn't want any part of? I wasn't so sure Aguirre would vouch for me.

After all, he'd accused me of getting his cousin killed.

"Get the scissors from the desk. Hurry," he ordered.

I jumped up and ran around the counter. Yes, the standard pencil cup with writing utensils, ruler, scissors. I twirled back to Aguirre and snipped the tie wraps and hood strings. He yanked off the hood, threw it on the floor and lumbered to his feet. "Where is the security guard?"

"I don't know. But the floor behind the counter is smeared with blood. Quick. We need to get upstairs." I tugged at Aguirre's arm. "Come on, Senator. Move."

Like an engine suddenly catching, he leapt toward the elevator, pulling me behind him. The police had arrived. The revolving lights turned the lobby into a sick light show.

"Come out with... " over a bullhorn was the last we heard as the elevator closed and began to ascend.

A handwringing Chucho met us at the elevator. "Patrón, are you all right? I called the police. I didn't know wha—"

"Thank you Chucho. You did the right thing. I'm fine. Miss Stone arrived just in time."

"¡Que milagro, señor!"

"I think the *señorita* and I might have a drink in the living room before dinner."

"Sí, Patrón. Please, this way." The houseman ushered me into the elegant living room and I collapsed onto the couch.

Aguirre followed. I saw his hand shake as he accepted the whisky Chucho handed him. He served me a rum and tonic with a twist and a cherry. Good memory. I'd drunk two the last time I was here. Aguirre clinked my glass and shot back the entire drink in one gulp. Chucho reappeared with a second as I sipped my cocktail.

"Senator, what happened? I knew that ass was still alive. It's one of the reasons I asked to meet with you. "

He made a sour face. "My dear little brother bullied his way into my home and the next thing I knew, some thug knocked me down and tied me up. He's done something to my security guard. Horacio was on duty. Anibal must have forced him to activate the elevator."

Shrek I. Well, he was no friend to me, but I was sure it was his blood caking my hands. I looked down. And all over my pale-yellow sundress. I stood up. "Senator, I think this is Horacio's blood." I held out my hands. He blanched. "I'm going to the bathroom to wash up. Try to remember what the other man looked like."

He took a gulp of his whisky and nodded.

Aguirre's cell phone rang as I stepped into the hall. I heard him telling someone he was fine as I slipped into the powder room.

The blood was not coming out of my dress. Drat. I loved this sundress. I took a few more minutes rubbing at the worst stain before I gave up. Better the death of my dress than the senator, I tried to convince myself. But I was still irked he'd ordered me kidnapped off the highway to Zihuatanejo. I really needed to get over it, I thought as I returned to the living room, but kidnapping appeared *de rigueur* in this country.

Aguirre continued speaking into the phone and Chucho met me at the door. "Dinner is served, Miss." He gestured toward the familiar dining room, handing me a smock to cover my dress and in Spanglish asked, "What happened, *abajo*? Señor Anibal barged in here unannounced with *otro hombre*. They both had guns." He held the door open and seated me at Aguirre's gleaming table. "The *señor* will be right here. He's changing out of the bloodied pants."

"Thanks, Chucho. It was a mess. The security guard was gone and one of the kidnappers was shot. I hid," I said.

Chucho stiffened, jaw dropping. He nodded and rushed back through the kitchen door.

Our plates waited at our places. I eyed the several covered serving dishes, my stomach growling. All the excitement had made me hungry, but I waited for Aguirre.

In a moment, the senator joined me wearing clean slacks and a casual sweater. Silently, he poured a deep ruby-colored wine into our glasses, tipping his my way. "Thank you, JadeAnne, you saved my life." He tossed back the wine and poured another.

"I guess we've saved each other, Senator. But I doubt the danger has passed."

"I thought my brother was killed during the incident in Tlalnepantla." He inspected me over the rim of the glass.

"He was thrown into the back of an SUV and taken away. I didn't know if he was dead or a prisoner or what." I helped myself to the nearest dish. Rice with peas and carrots. Aguirre lifted the lid of the dish in front of his place and shoved chicken in a yellowish sauce toward me. I worried for the surface of his beautiful table.

"Quint just told me over the phone you thought you saw Anibal two days ago in Del Valle."

So my father already knew. I stood up and put a serving of rice and chicken on his plate. "That was Quint on the phone? Where the hell is he? He said he'd wait until I got in the elevator. What's in that dish?"

He pushed the third dish to me and I lifted the lid. Grey squash cooked with garlic, onion and tomatoes. I scooped out a generous portion.

"It was he who shot the other man. We'll have the identity soon."

"Yeah. I should have recognized the thunder from that hand cannon of his. Why didn't he come in?" The house phone rang twice. "Vegetable?" I asked, holding out the silver bowl.

He shook his head. "He followed the SUV my brother escaped in."

"Black?"

"They all are."

"So where did it go? This is delicious, by the way. You should try it."

"Oaxacan. Mole Amarillo. The chef is from Oaxaca. The SUV headed north and Quint lost it."

"Why did Anibal come here, Senator?"

"He wants you and the girl, or the money he was paid by the traffickers. He says they will kill him."

The rich flavor of the stew turned sour. So it *was* about me.

Chapter 7

Allies

I over-filled another glass of *vino tinto* and took a swig. Politeness be damned. Mr. high-society, leader-among-men, captain-of-industry, Leopoldo Aguirre could suck it up. It didn't really matter, just look at him, elbows on the table, forehead practically resting in his stew. The guy was a disaster; he wouldn't notice wine rings on his table. And *he* got me into this mess in the first place.

"Damn you, Aguirre. All our lives are in danger because you had me kidnapped off the highway and kicked this whole party into high gear." I glared at my host. He didn't look up.

"I never meant—"

"What didn't you mean? That your cartel activities would impact everyone's lives? That *your* activities would have your precious cousin killed? Look back, man. You caused your wife and children to be murdered."

Aguirre's head swung up. Anger distorted his handsome features and turned his skin the color of black cherries. He lunged toward me, grabbing my arm. "How dare you! I am not affiliated with a filthy drug cartel," he shouted and looked down, realizing he held my arm vise-like. He let me go. More quietly he added, "I am an elected senator of the country of Mexico and I have devoted my life to fighting against organized crime."

"You grow marijuana and sell it somewhere, Senator. That's against the law, last time I checked. You allow your mother to own a whorehouse, also against the law, I'd bet. How do you justify yourself? How do you *live* with yourself?" I shrieked.

He didn't move. The dining room went tomb-silent for a beat before he took a deep breath. "Please, JadeAnne, calm down. I'm in as much danger as you are. We need to have clear heads to assess and plan."

I blew out the breath I didn't know I held and slumped into the back of my chair. "You're right," I answered. "Sort of like you accusing me of Lura's death." I glared at him while I considered his words. Enmity wouldn't get what I needed. I'd play the bigger man here. "I'm sorry. Going off on you is counterproductive." I held out my hand. "Allies?"

With a hint of a smile, he shook my hand and said, "Allies. Friends, I hope JadeAnne. I'm not what you think. Ask your father."

I stiffened. "My father. How long have you known that?"

"Jackman Quint approached me several years ago in regards to the *investigación* he was conducting. It had to do with U.S. government connections in *narcotraficante*. We formed an alliance. I had *información* and *contactos* he could use and he had the same for me. We came to trust, even like, each other. When his *investigación* ended, we arranged to continue working together. He filled me in about his history. A man with his background watching my back, as you Americans say, is very *valuable*. When my family..." he paused, running his hand across his eyes. "When they were killed, he investigated for me. He found out my cousin's husband, Daniel Worthington, was behind the accident. I told you about it when we swam that morning."

I put down my fork. I'd been making like Lily with the

figure eights. "I remember, Senator. Go on."

"I had Jack keep an eye on Worthington. Jack followed him to Sausalito and he discovered the private *investigadora* Worthington hired to get hold of Lura was JadeAnne Stone —Quint's daughter. Jack watched you out there on your houseboat, getting ready to drive through cartel country to find my *prima*. He wasn't going to come back, he told me. He was going to stop you. He feared for you." Aguirre poured his own wine and sipped at it in silence.

I twirled my fork around, a baton. "But where was he the rest of my life?"

"What were you going to say to a father you'd never met? You thought he was dead. What were you going to do when you found out, in his words, 'the father, whose selfish and uncaring behavior resulted in the death of your mother, was not dead and had never sent you a birthday gift'?"

His dark eyes pierced through me. What would I have said? What *did* I say?

Aguirre's voice turned husky. "I've never seen a grown man cry like that. He regrets everything he did. He is a man conflicted. He hates himself. He blames himself for the death of your mother and the loss of his daughter."

I sniffed and wiped my nose on the linen napkin. My mother would have had a heart attack if *she'd* seen that. My adoptive mother. I felt like I'd slipped into another dimension. Ever since Quint turned up, my life had turned upside down.

"He followed you all the way from the Bay Area. He was there in the disco in Culiacán. JadeAnne, what were you thinking? A known *federación* hangout."

"Federation?"

"Shorty Guzman's organization. Who do you think these Zetas are fighting for the Mexico City *plaza*?"

"I don't know anything about any of this. Interesting that you do," I replied with a sneer. "And Senator, if my father was so concerned about my welfare, why the hell'd he let you kidnap me?"

"It wasn't supposed to be a kidnapping. How would we have gotten you to my estate? You had to find Lura. Jack had to meet you. For all he has done for me, I had to give him that. We agreed to let you think it was all coincidence, but I swear to you, *te lo juro*, on the grave of my father, the men were never to use weapons."

"You took me on that jeep ride so Quint could see me. It was all a ruse. My *father* stalked me?" The hair on my arms stood up. "Your story is giving me the willies."

"I'm sorry, the willies? I do not know this expression."

"Oh, just a quaint saying meaning Quint's actions turn my stomach and make me feel like creepy crawlies are walking on my skin. What a coward."

"Yes, your father acted like a coward, but he's kept you safe. On the market stairs in Zihuatanejo, the man you saw was your father."

I thought back to the scruffy guy wearing the captain's cap, gliding down the escalator as I paid for my groceries. "And the man on the stairs to the beach? He wore the same hat, but he stalked me with a gun. Real fatherly."

"I tried to keep you at the Crystal. Jack put two and two together about Esteban Grijalves—Zocer."

"Okay, so I have a creepy, cowardly stalker for a father. Tell me the truth, Senator. Am I safe with him?"

"I trust Jackman Quint with my life."

"Yeah, but if my father is so great, why hasn't he moved us from that whorehouse you gave him? The baddies know where we are, Aguirre. They've been there. Your brother has been there."

"I'm sorry, it's the only house we had available. But what makes you think Anibal and his people know where you are? Why would he come to threaten me if he did?"

"You dummy, that was a classic shakedown. He wasn't

looking for me. Anibal hates you, Senator. You better get all your keys and codes changed. The Shreks need backup. No one in this building is safe anymore."

"The Shreks?"

"Yeah, Horacio and the other one, what's his name? The ogres. Didn't you watch the movies with your children?"

Aguirre's face lit up and he laughed. I laughed too. We hooted and guffawed until our stomachs hurt and tears rolled down our cheeks.

"You have quite a sense of humor, Ms. Stone. Please, apply that to your relationship with your father. He wants to make it up to you, but he doesn't know how. As you say, give a man a break. *Familia* is everything. Family is our anchor, our place. The rest is only what happens while you're away from home. I know this, JadeAnne. Jack needs a family. We all do. Even my *loco* half-brother."

Aguirre was right. We all need a family. We all need somewhere to belong. I'd spent thirty-two years with people who I did not belong to. Look what that got me.

"Okay, Senator—"

"Polo. Please, JadeAnne, call me Polo."

"Polo. I'll cut him some slack for stalking me. I thought he was dead. I never blamed him for not claiming me. He couldn't. Did he tell you he had an agreement with my dad, Charles Stone? Why he honored that when he knew it was my dad who ratted him out for the heroin, I don't understand."

"I'm surprised he's been so forthright. He was risking a lot in telling you of his youthful indiscretions. He's paid his dues and it was a crazy illegal war. I've done some reading on Vietnam. My American neighbors have strange ideas."

"Money, power, control in the name of democracy, Polo." The taste of his name on my tongue was a strange fruit.

The scratching sound of the pocket door sliding open

startled us. *"Lo siento Patrón, ¿les sirvo el postre y una cafecito?"* asked Chucho, bearing a tray with coffee and dessert balanced on it.

"Chucho, shouldn't you be studying? It's late," I asked.

"If the boss will excuse me, after I serve dessert, I'll get to my books, *señorita*."

The houseman winked at me. I turned to Polo. "I could use coffee. If we need something else, I know where the kitchen is. I've stayed here, or have you forgotten?"

"You may leave the dessert and pot of coffee, and retire, Chucho."

"Muchas gracias, Patrón. Buenas noches."

"You too, Chucho. Thanks." I said. "I'm curious why we weren't invited to stay here now, Polo."

Polo snorted and I heard the faint rattle of a doorknob.

"He will not have eight dogs in his house," Quint said, making me jump. He seemed to have the knack of stealth. He slid into the chair across from me and helped himself to a cup of coffee. My cup of coffee. "I told you."

"Did you discover my brother's whereabouts?" Polo demanded.

"I lost the SUV, but I got the license plate. We'll know who Anibal is keeping company with as soon as I can have it run. We'll catch him." He turned to Aguirre. "But you weren't hurt, Senator?"

"No, I'm uninjured. You shot the other man. Do we have any information about him?"

Quint shook his head. "The police have him. I'll find out who he is tomorrow. I want to know who is driving that SUV."

"Quint, I told you," I said, my voice sounding whiny. I took a breath and continued. "It's that Lobo guy. We all ate dinner together with him right here at this table not two weeks ago," I said, glaring at Aguirre.

"Guillermo Lobo? That can't be right. Why would an

entertainment talent promoter be interested in Anibal?" Aguirre asked.

"That's a good question, and one I will look into, Senator. Jade, are you absolutely positive it was Lobo? You were awfully tired and in a bit of shock. Could you be confused? Maybe the driver resembles Lobo."

"He looked right into my eyes and I saw him register recognition. Hey, if the man *registered recognition,* it means they didn't know we would be in the neighborhood, right?"

"Or Anibal didn't mention why he wanted to cruise Del Valle," Quint said.

"It would be like that weasel. He cadges rides most of the time from anyone who will put up with him, and Lobo drives a black SUV. Every vehicle entering our garage is photographed. He parked in one of my visitor spaces." Aguirre pushed away from the table. "I'll call the desk. Jack, have the plate verified."

"Don't bother. No one is there. Why don't I go down to the control room and see what I can find. You two finish your dessert and I'll meet you back here for a drink then take you home Jade." Quint got up and headed for the door. He stopped and whirled around. "Good work down there, JadeAnne. You rescued the Senator."

Chapter 8

How Was I the Last to Know?

I gazed at the expanse of lights filling the Valley of Mexico from Aguirre's swanko-Polanco flat. The city overflowed the original lakebed, and the view from Aguirre's apartment at night took my breath away. Not so much during most days, when the giant living room window overlooked a taupe-colored scene of acres and acres and acres of mismatched buildings swimming in a sea of pollution. At night, the smog cleared a bit and the lights twinkling in the thin mile-high air turned Mexico City into a fairyland. At least from twelve floors up.

"What can I pour for you, JadeAnne?" Aguirre asked from the bar.

"It feels like a port kind of night tonight. Make it a double." I turned back to the scene through the window.

He joined me, approaching soundlessly across the deep wool pile of the carpeting. I'd kicked off my shoes and let my feet sink into its soft warmth. Would I ever live in this kind of elegance and luxury again? Nothing here was more or less rich than both my parents' and grandparents' houses. And this luxurious flat floating in the clouds above one of the world's great capitals felt just as empty as my family seat. Wealth and power wasn't all it was cracked up to be. I'd

69

certainly turned my back on it. Dad, my *adoptive* dad, had expected me to go to Hastings Law School or Stanford Medical School. At the very least, I would attend UC and study for an advanced degree in International Business Administration. Okay, so I did attend Stanford and I did earn an advanced degree. I embarrassed my parents with my degrees in journalism, but at least Dad had paid the bill.

"What are you thinking about?" Polo asked.

"How I've failed my family."

"How so?"

He turned two easy chairs around toward the view and gestured I take one. I sat down, curling my feet under me as he carried a small table from the other side of the room and placed it between our chairs.

"They expected me to step into wealth and power, do something important. Marry someone important. Instead, they have to put up with no son-in-law and a low-class occupation. Poor Mommy and Daddy. They hated that I went into journalism."

"Speaking of that, how is your article on human trafficking coming?"

"Well, I have gained some invaluable knowledge, but haven't had much writing time, what with the excellent drugs your clinic pumped me full of. Thanks, by the way, for taking care of my hospital bill. I would have had to discharge myself the next day with the high cost of care."

"Medical care is affordable in Mexico. The American system is a travesty. I believe the government's job is to provide for the citizens. Mexico has a system whereby all *ciudadanos and* residents can receive medical care. You could have received free care, and I suppose you would have, if I hadn't sent you to my doctors. I didn't want word of your or the American girl's involvement to become public."

"Why not? Isn't hiding the sex trade and trafficking part

of the problem?"

"I imagine your article will reveal your personal experience." Aguirre sighed.

Polo Aguirre struck me as a dichotomy unto himself. His politics leaned into progressive territory yet he was so darned conservative.

"Hey, loosen up, dude," I admonished. "You remind me of my family. Too proper. Life isn't so proper and what I do or don't do does not reflect on you at all."

He exhaled a short burst of air. "And you sound like Lura and my wife. Even my mother calls me a stick-in-the-mud."

"Your mother is another dichotomy. She's so stuck on being proper, yet she's a madam. I don't get it."

His face reddened. "My mother is not a madam. She owns gentlemen's clubs. She's a business woman. She has several restaurants, a hotel or two, a handful of night clubs, many commercial and residential properties, and a car dealership. I don't really keep up with her holdings. There are so many businesses, it's easy to overlook what goes on at some of them." He dropped his head into his hands and mumbled, "My mother mortifies me."

"And this from the guy who grows marijuana."

"Tell me you never smoked it."

"I'd be lying. Everybody smokes at some point in their lives, but it wasn't for me. Neither was cocaine. That was big when I was a teen. What about you? Ever have a stoner phase?"

"Not at all. My grandfather was against using drugs. I idolized him, wanted to be just like him. Mother had other ideas. But Grandfather taught me that marijuana was a crop like any other crop—for selling. I have a private network for selling my crop. I now trade with a Portuguese broker and he arranges transportation. It's legal in Portugal."

"You are more naïve than I, Senator Aguirre. A broker?

Brokers broker deals, and I bet if he isn't hooked into one of the cartels here, he is in Europe. In fact, your Chapo isn't going to let some random broker cut into what he thinks is his *negocio*."

"How did you learn this?"

"Investigative reporter. I talk to people and I read what's being written."

"Is my smarty-pants daughter showing off?" Quint had snuck up on us again, a rocks glass of tawny liquid in his hand.

"Pull up a chair, Jack. What did you find out?"

Quint set his drink on the table and lugged another chair over next to mine. He sank down into it and gazed out the window before speaking. "I found Horacio trussed like a sheep for *barbacoa* in the control center. He'd been bashed in the head and lost a lot of blood. He may have bled out had I not gone down."

My gut clenched. "No! I should have looked for him. This is Horacio's blood on my dress."

"Don't blame yourself, Jade. You had the senator to deal with. I called an ambulance and left him in the hands of the police." He took a long draught of his cocktail and addressed Aguirre. "That badge you gave me came in handy, Senator. The patrolman on guard duty wanted to arrest me. Keystone Cops. It's quite a zoo out there. We'll have to go in and talk to them tomorrow. Call Castillo y Iglesias," Quint directed Aguirre.

The senator replaced his cup into the saucer with a rattle. "It's done."

"Who are they?" I asked

"Not they—him. Attorney," Quint replied.

"Of course. Weird name, Castle and Church. Did you get the license plate? Was it the SUV?.. asked.

"Yes. I'll have my contact run the plate when the offices open tomorrow."

"Tomorrow is Saturday, Dad."

"I'll call him in the morning. I'm sure I can offer him something to get the information."

I laughed. "You mean you'd bribe a public official?"

"Pass me my drink, girl, and quit being so smart. Maybe I employ a hacker."

"Maybe. You keep a hacker on the payroll Polo?"

"Do I keep a what? No don't tell me. I'm going to refresh my drink. May I fix you another one?"

"I'm good."

Aguirre wandered away with his glass. Quint and I sat in companionable silence, sipping our drinks and thinking our thoughts. The view twinkled into the distance and for a moment I relaxed into absolute contentment.

The living room lights had been turned up and the men huddled by the bar, voices low and intense. I must have fallen asleep. I sat up yawning. "Quint? You didn't leave Lily alone, did you?"

"No, Jade. That's what took me so long to get back. I picked up Omar and left him on duty. The house is locked and alarmed. All the locks have been changed and the gate re-coded. I've also had the windows along the fire escape double-locked."

"Can't they be broken and opened?"

"Anything can happen, Jade. But for today, we've done what we can. I have a company coming tomorrow to install a new security system for the house. It will be a fortress. Pepper is patrolling the yard. Lily is asleep; you should go back to sleep. The senator and I have a couple more things to talk about, then I'll take you home."

"Miss Stone, JadeAnne, I will assign a guard detail to the Amores house. Sra. Arias de Barerra will call tomorrow with details. Does that ease your worries?"

"Yes, thanks, Polo, but I think I'll join you for another

drink." I got up and carried my glass to the bar cart. The port looked too thick. I switched to tonic with a splash of lime and another of rum. I tossed two ice cubes into the glass. "So what are we discussing?"

"I'm sorry, JadeAnne, Jack and I have some private *negocio* to clear up. Jack, why don't we go to my office?"

"Don't leave on my account," I snapped. "I'll go watch TV."

"Stay here and watch the view. We'll only be a few more minutes. Enjoy your drink," the senator said.

Soft music floated out of hidden speakers.

"Is *la musica* all right?" Aguirre asked me.

"Yes. Very pretty, thank you. Hey, I forgot to ask something."

"Ask away."

"Polo, did you tell Anibal we were in Del Valle?"

"Absolutely not."

"What about your mother. Would she tell him?"

"My mother will do most anything to avoid talking to the maid's bastard. Does that answer your question?"

"Yeah, I guess. How did Anibal know we were in Del Valle? He's familiar with the house, I'm sure of it."

"How he knows the Del Valle property is a mystery, but since *su casa* burned, I imagine he hoped to move in. Señora Arias de Barerra mentioned he telephoned and wished to discuss his housing situation."

"So I'm the only one who thought he was dead?" I asked.

Quint frowned. "Senator, this is news. We suspected he'd been dispatched by his Zeta friends."

"The message slipped my mind. I apologize. I must make a note to have his house repaired. I can't have him barging in here because he's homeless. Frankly, I'd suggested mother have the house torn down and the lot sold when I made her close down the brothel. I hadn't considered she would appear to comply by moving the operation to El Pedrigal."

"You think tonight's attack is connected to Anibal's house burning?" Quint asked.

"My brother has always been unstable. Lura's death pushed him over the edge. I've tried to bring him into the family, but Mother will have none of him; he hates me for the privileges I have as an Aguirre, which he can never have. I think Anibal Aguirre would do anything to get back at me for being our father's legitimate child and heir. He improved after Beto took him in. California was a good place for Anibal—far from Mother and me." Aguirre shook his head. His face radiated sadness. "There's no reason for any of this in today's world. Mother could have adopted him and it would all have been over. Now he's chosen his path and we will want to stay out of it."

"I'm worried about this," I said. "Anibal is a loose cannon and just as destructive. How can I be sure he won't get to us? Quint, if you're as concerned about our safety as you claim, why have you left us in a house he's familiar with? Why haven't you moved us? *And* our dogs."

Quint's face took on a rosy cast. "Let's figure this out on our own time, daughter. The senator doesn't want to worry about my family."

I stepped into his personal space, looked up into his eyes and said in a hard voice, "Don't you dare 'daughter' me."

He took a quick step back, jaw falling open.

I move closer and punctuated my words with my index finger to his chest. "I will not be patronized or placated." I threw my hands on my hips. "You want to be my dad? You'll need to care about me first. And I come with a teenager and eight dogs. You'll care about them, too."

I felt kind of sorry for the guy. He was trying so hard, but I was tired, scared, and not ready to have my chain jerked.

Aguirre chuckled. "Jack, when you told me you had a daughter, I never imagined she'd be as independent and feisty as you. She's a real, how do you put it—a real flake off the woodblock. You better do what she says."

I shook my head and covered my mouth, trying to stifle the mad giggles bubbling up. I gasped and composed myself enough to say, "I am not a flake, Mister Senator. I'm a chip." I stamped my foot for effect, killing my attempt at seriousness.

Even Quint joined in the mirth. "Yes, ma'am. I'm at your service."

"And don't you forget it," I said, and again punctuated my utterance with a stamp of my foot.

The clock chimed midnight. I yawned and put my half-finished drink on the cart.

"Let's go home—Dad.

Chapter 9

Qadir Finds the Link

Saturday, August 25, 2007

Pepper and I dragged into the kitchen. My head pounded. *Cruda*. I wondered if Mrs. P could make *birria* stew, the best medicine for hangovers.

"Mornin', Lily. Shall I make some coffee?"

Lily flipped a piece of eggy toast and bacon sizzled on the back burner. "Nope, all made," she said, and carried the insulated carafe to the table along with a pitcher of milk. "Can I make you some French toast? Look, there's real maple syrup. Not that fake corn syrup crap my mother used," she said, eyes misting over.

Poor kid, I thought. "Let me have a little coffee first and I'll see if I'm hungry." I poured my cup, took a long draw, and spit it back into the cup. "Ouch! Too hot."

Lily laughed. "Maybe too much to drink at the senator's?"

Sad that a fifteen-year-old knew so much about the effects of alcohol. Pepper nudged me and I got up to feed him.

"I'll feed Pepper. Sit down. You don't look so hot."

I followed Lily's order and crumpled back into my chair.

This time I sipped gingerly at my too hot coffee and dribbled in some more milk. For a moment I contemplated the girl. She was a nice kid. Why had her life been so hard?

"Thanks, kid. You and Pepper look pretty chummy, but where are the goldens?"

"In the yard, I already fed them. You feeling okay?"

I nodded. Lily was right. I'd had way too much port the night before on too empty of a stomach. The dinner had been delicious, as always, but we were too wound up to actually eat. How many drinks had I had? And Aguirre, he must have killed that bottle of scotch. I wondered if he remembered everything he'd told me. He was going to be pretty unhappy he'd admitted he knew what his mother was up to. And I was very happy I'd jotted down everything I could remember before I went to sleep. I felt a tad dull this morning.

"Yeah, fine. The senator's port disagrees with me. Hey, have you talked to him recently?"

"Quint talks to him. I don't have any news." Lily slid her gaze to my cell phone.

My coffee cup was halfway to my mouth but I lowered it back to the table and asked, "You want to call him?"

"No. I, ah, well—do you have news about my mom?"

I tapped the screen and my phone woke up. The time in Mexico City read 8:42 a.m. "It's only 7:42 in Sausalito. The office hasn't opened." Lily's look of expectation crumbled.

"Well, actually, it's Saturday. The office doesn't officially open, but with your pressing case, shall we call and see if we can reach Qadir? Sometimes he comes in really early."

The girl's face lit up again. "Please, JadeAnne. Would you?"

I pressed the office's speed dial button and when my own voice answered, I punched in my computer guy's extension. The line rang once.

"Hello, JadeAnne. I thought you might call. I have some

good news and some bad news. Which first?"

I put the phone on speaker. "Qadir, I've got Lily with me and we're on speaker phone."

"Hi Qadir," she said. "Have you found my mother yet?"

"I'm sorry Lily, that's the bad news. She seems to have vanished for the moment. But don't worry, we'll trace her. She's not going far without using her bank cards or her car, for that matter. It's in the carport at your apartment building."

I squeezed Lily's hand. Tears spilled over her lids and down her cheeks. She swiped them away with the silly apron she wore. "Did anyone look to see if she's home?"

"I sent police two days ago. They said no one at home. Most likely she went somewhere with her boyfriend. Honey, do you remember his name? It could really help. Or his car and license plate?"

Lily spoke right up. "Everyone called him Eddy. But his name was really Edgar, like in Spanish. Edgar Santos. He's Mexican. I stole money out of his wallet all the time and saw his driver's license," she said, turning toward me, her face coloring. "He deserved it for what he did to us when Mom was at work."

"Don't worry Lily, you're not in trouble. You did what you had to," Qadir said, his voice soft.

I knew he was thinking about his own difficult life in his native Pakistan.

"Do you remember where the license was from?"

"Yeah, the State of Mexico. I forget the address but the city was a funny Aztec name. Evie and I always tried to say it. You know, Jade. It's where, it's the place... " Her voice cracked into sobs. I got up and moved around the table.

"Qadir, it's Tlalnepantla." I spelled it for him while I hugged the girl to me and stroked her hair. "That's the city we were taken to. This Santos guy has to be part of the Mexico City trafficking ring. Lily, do you remember his car?"

She nodded and gulped air. I could hear Qadir breathing, and my heart pounding in excitement. We had a lead.

"He drove a cool BMW with smoked windows and little shiny wheels. It was black."

Qadir asked, "A sports car or a sedan? Two doors? Four? Do you think it was new?"

"It was four doors and had that smell cars at the dealership have." She thought for a moment. "We never had a new car, but I went with a friend's family to test drive new cars once."

"Lily, can you tell us anything else about Eddy or his car?"

"I dunno. Would it help if I described him?"

"Absolutely," Qadir prompted.

"He thinks he's Joe Cool and wears sunglasses all the time, even inside." She grimaced. "His hair is modern with it sticking up in front. He uses hairspray," she said, derision coloring her quavering voice. "His eyes are grey or blue, pretty light colored—like his hair." She stopped talking, visibly upset.

I said, "Are you getting this, Qadir?"

"Yes. What else, Lily?"

The girl took a deep breath and continued. "He has these thin lips that you can't see because he has this kind of stringy mustache. And that same kind of beard. He's kind of skinny and ugly." Tears ran down her cheeks and she lowered her head to her hands.

I tensed up. "What does he wear?" I asked, picturing the narco Anibal tried to hide from.

"Cowboy looking clothes, like, all the time but, with all this flashy gold and diamond jewelry. He gave Mom a diamond bracelet once after he beat her up. I was going to sell it. We could've used the money to escape him—" She looked down at her hands, hair swinging over her face.

"It's okay, Lily. Can you remember anything else? Did he work somewhere?" I asked.

"He went places a lot, but he didn't have a job like Mom with regular hours or anything. He slapped me, told me to mind my own business the time I asked, and... he laughed," Lily whispered. "That was the thing, when he laughed it sounded like one of the mean girls at school. High and snotty. After he hurt me, he would laugh like that. I tried to get away, but he worked out and was too strong." Lily paused, gripping the edge of the table and sucking in several more breaths of air. Her voice turned husky. "I hate him."

"As you should, Lily. You've done really well. I've got some good information to go on now. I'll get busy and find Eddy. I'm betting if we find him, we'll find your mother," Qadir said.

"Qadir, thanks so much for everything. Will you be there for a while, say an hour? I need to talk to you about another matter."

"I'll be here, boss. Give me a shout when you're ready." He hung up.

I closed my phone. I knew Eddy Santos. He'd come to Lura's funeral and Lidia's vigil afterward. Anibal called him *The Saint*. This couldn't be a coincidence. I had to talk to Quint.

"Lily, can you take Pepper out? Poor guy has been hopping around needing to go since we got on the phone. I'm going to talk to Quint. I think I may have met your Eddy here in Mexico City back on—I checked my calendar—the eighth. High-pitched laugh, classic Fu Manchu-style mustache and stringy beard? Did you ever hear anyone call him *The Saint*?"

"I never met his friends. I saw them. Tattoos and gangland clothes. I never liked those types. They're mean." She clucked to Pepper, and said, "C'mon boy. Let's go outside."

Pepper grinned and bounded for the door.

I poured coffees for us and climbed up to the second floor. I'd never been in Quint's room, but this couldn't wait. I actually might have a breakthrough in the case. I stopped in front of his door. I could hear a rhythmic grating noise. My dad snored. Well, he'd stop that as soon as I knocked.

Tap tap tap. I rapped softly not wanting to alarm him. No response. I knocked harder and fake whispered, "Quint. Quint, you awake?" I put my ear to the door. Quint sputtered, probably rolled over, and the snoring continued. This time I banged on the door as I called out, "Quint, I've got new information on the case. Might be a breakthrough. Wake up!"

"That you, JadeAnne?" his sleepy voice said.

Definitely hungover. "Yes, it's me. Who else would be pounding on your door? Can I come in?"

"You don't mind seeing your old man in his skivvies?"

"Actually, I do. Put on your pants and open the door. I've got coffee."

"All right. That changes everything."

He opened the door and I stepped into another girlishly pink room. This room, seashell pink with frilly everything. I sat down on a faded red slipper chair facing Quint perched on the edge of the unmade bed.

"Hey, love your suite, Dad. I feel like I'm at a birthday party."

"Yeah, yeah. We'll redecorate later. What do you have for me, girl?"

I recapped the phone conversation.

He listened, his head cocked in my direction, letting me tell the story before speaking. "So, this Santos, you're sure he's the man you saw at the funeral?"

"Quint, I'm not sure of anything, but how many sunglass-wearing Fu Manchu-style mustaches do you meet?

My researcher Qadir, is looking into the car and the driver's license. Don't you think this is a little too much of a coincidence? Tlalnepantla, the place Anibal's contact took me and the girls to sell to the Zetas? This guy could be a Zeta. For sure, he's the guy setting up the meets to lure girls out of L.A. It fits."

"Yes, Jade, it fits, but not the only possibility. You said Anibal tried to avoid him?"

"Yeah. Really weird. In the church Anibal suddenly buried his face in my chest and made like he was sobbing—"

"That ain't so weird. He wanted to get close to you, so to speak." Quint said, eyes twinkling.

"Get serious, old man. As if all that sobbing would be a big turn-on." I grinned and winked. "Later at Lidia's house, her vigil for Lura, or whatever that was supposed to be, Santos showed up and Anibal sank down into his wing chair and hid until Eddy took Lidia into the dining room. I've even talked to Polo about him. Polo hates his mother hanging around with a low-life like that guy. Ask him."

"I know who you're talking about. The senator has complained to me, too. Wants me to investigate the man. If you'll kindly leave my room, I'll get dressed. How about meeting me for breakfast in twenty?"

"Oh. Okay, sure. But, what did you mean? Another possibility?"

"I looked into Lobo when we got back last night. He's got ties to the Beltran-Leyva Organization as the senator said. I can't prove it, yet, but I'd stake my claim the BLO is behind the Mexico City trafficking operation."

"So how do the Zetas fit in?"

"That remains to be seen, girl. Now get out and let me dress."

I backed into the hall, and said, "Let's say thirty minutes. I'm going to shower."

"Slowpoke," Quint said, as he closed the door.

"Qadir, I really appreciate the work you're doing. I couldn't talk in front of Lily."

"I got that, and I've got news."

"You go first then."

"Do you remember that P.I. Conye Jones?"

"Of, course. What about him?" I asked.

"I had the L.A. office send him over to the mother's apartment to check things out. Car still there, missing hubcaps. Had him on speakerphone while he banged on the door. Nothing. Neighbor come out and say no one been there in about three weeks. Not since a big fight. Mother yelling something about giving them back. Neighbor knew it was the boyfriend when he laughed real high and girly-like. Heard doors slamming and nothing since. Complained it smells like the cat died coming through the vent."

"Oh, no. It wasn't the cat, was it?" I said, my heart clenching. Poor Lily. She'd lost her whole family. I teared up.

"Conye busted in. I am sending photos now. Woman is dead and it is not pretty. He did it slow. She was tied up, gagged, and left to bleed. Ugly."

I drew in a settling breath. "I was afraid this would be the end of the story. So we won't be getting any permission slip for Lily to fly home. Senator Aguirre needs to pull some diplomatic strings. I'll call him next," I said, as I quickly swiped my eyes and made notes in my casebook. "Conye called Robinson?"

"Yeah. The lieutenant contacted L.A. What did you want to tell me?" he asked.

"The boyfriend, whose name is Edgar Santos, is a player in my case here. He goes by *The Saint*. He showed up at the funeral for that missing banker's wife. He's friends with the senator's mother, Lidia Sotomayor de Aguirre, and Anibal Aguirre did everything he could to avoid eye contact with him. So far, no one here has had anything to say about him other than Senator Aguirre is chagrined his mother hangs out with a low-life. If you could find him mentioned in the media, maybe I could approach the journalist and get connected here."

"Sure, boss. I'll be happy to pull up what's out there. I probably can get you names of who is writing about cartels in Mexican papers."

"That would be great, Qadir, but I didn't know you also spoke Spanish."

"I don't, but I'm getting hits in English and Spanish. I will send you a couple of names in a few. I guess you don't want Lily to know the man is in Mexico, eh, Boss?"

"Not at all. The kid is traumatized enough. I'm keeping her mother's status under my hat, too."

"You wear a hat in Mexico?"

I chuckled. "An expression, Qadir. It means, to keep quiet about something. I'll look for your text."

Quint's door opened across the hall.

I called out, "Quint, c'mere. New development."

"What's happened?" he asked, as he pushed open my door.

"Lily's mother was killed, left to bleed out in the apartment. The neighbor told my investigator they'd fought about the time the girls disappeared and she heard that high-pitched laugh. Five will get you ten *The Saint* is the killer."

"I didn't know you were a betting woman."

"There's a lot you don't know about me."

"I'm learning. I'll call the senator; it's time we had a chat with Lidia. Also, Jade, I don't think we should tell Lily yet."

"No. My thinking, too. She's had enough trauma. Will you get Aguirre onto a diplomatic solution to getting her home? She's hanging by a thread and needs family."

"Will do, Boss." He grinned wide. "After breakfast."

Mrs. P met us at the stairs door, wringing her dishtowel as she fumed. I could see the smoke. So could Quint. What had we done now?

"*Buenos Días, señora. ¿Qué pasa?* Is there a problem?" Quint asked the housekeeper.

"*Señor*, you must do something for that poor little girl. She's scared, hiding in the corner of the kitchen surrounded by all those beasts."

"What? What are you talking about, Señora Pérez? She was fine thirty minutes ago."

"See for yourself." She led us into the kitchen.

Lily huddled and shook inside the puppy pen with the dogs. Maya lay with her head on Lily's feet, gazing sorrowfully up at her person. Pepper sat at attention, back to Lily, guarding the group. I knew the posture. As Mrs. P approached, he growled softly and Lily shrank away, curling into a tight ball. The puppies jumped and yipped and wagged.

"Pepper, at ease," I commanded him. "Sorry, *señora*. It's his training."

Pepper jumped out of the enclosure and Maya shifted to sit leaning against the girl. Lily didn't look up, but rocked silently.

Quint stepped into the enclosure, squatted down and gathered Lily into his arms. "What happened, Lily?" He patted her tear-stained face with a pocket square.

She nuzzled her head into his chest and mumbled something.

He tilted her chin up. "Tell me again?"

Lily's voice quavered and she spoke barely above a whisper. "I saw him. He was here, at the gate."

"Saw who, Lily?" Quint asked. "Why were you at the gate?"

"I took Pepper out. Some of the puppies had gone into

the front. And... and I looked up and the gate was open and he was there. He was c-coming through the gate." She began to cry again.

Mrs. P put a cup of steaming tea into Lily's hand.

"Could it have been Señora Pérez? She has a key to the gate," Quint said.

"The car gate. It was open. He was there."

"It couldn't have been. I had that gate fixed yesterday. It has a new code."

"Lily, are you sure? Was the man inside?"

"Why don't you believe me? Pepper chased him away then Mrs. P came. She saw it."

I looked at the housekeeper, still wringing her hands. "Did you see this man?"

She shrugged, eyes darting up to the right. Lying? "The gate is open enough for a slender adult to squeeze through. I saw the back of a man rapidly walking away, whistling."

"Lily, look at me," I said. She looked up. "Tell me what man you saw."

She looked down and moved her mouth as though she'd bitten into something rotten then spat out the bad taste. "Eddy. He's here."

That was all we needed. "Quint, contact the senator. Get him and his car. We're going to pay a call on his mother." I twirled toward the housekeeper. "And you will not alert her that we are coming."

Mrs. P colored; a shadow of guilt passed through her eyes. I knew it, Lidia's a spy.

"He spoke to me," Lily said.

I whirled to face the girl. "What did he say?"

Her voice dropped to barely perceptible. "He killed her."

At this admission Mrs. P startled. Proof the bitch speaks English. Perhaps she didn't know what game was afoot. Or maybe she did, but now wasn't the moment to confront her. We needed to get Lidia to call off her bulldog and to tell us where to find Santos. The Saint was going to jail. If not here, in California. But first we would extract every gram of information that bastard possessed. I bet Quint knew something about persuading people to talk. My stomach lurched. I was thinking about—planning—torture of a human being. That wasn't my way. I felt sick.

But was Edgar Santos really a human being?

Chapter 10

Gonna be a Showdown

I paced, Quint tapped his feet, Lily zoned into music videos, waiting for the senator to collect us for the confrontation with his mother. Polo had vowed to have Lidia arrested if she continued her illegal activities. I didn't believe a word of it. But so long as Lily, Pepper, and I made it home, I didn't really care. Well, except the part about putting Anibal out of his misery. I'd crush him for his part in this trafficking ring.

The gate buzzer rang. I slid the drape aside and peered out the living room window "Limo's here, Quint. Someone is with him."

He put his coffee mug on the side table and launched himself out of the easy chair. "Medina," he muttered.

I craned my neck to see through the windshield. "Who?"

He raised his eyebrows in that smug *you'll see* expression of his and stepped into the hall to buzz the gate open. I watched the limo roll in and a stranger slid out of the front seat. He waited while another stranger clambered from the back, pulling a couple of cases off the seat before nudging the door closed with his knee.

"Wait! That's not the senator's limo. What the hell is Aguirre up to?"

Quint snorted and smirked. Obviously *he* knew what

was up. I wrinkled my nose at him and started for the hall. "I'll get the door."

"What?" Lily asked, watching our exchange from the couch.

"We have a change in plans," I called over my shoulder from the elevator. Quint scooted in as the door closed.

"Welcome Señor Attorney General," Quint said, taking the shorter man's proffered hand. "This is my daughter, JadeAnne Stone."

He smiled at me, dropping Quint's paw and reaching for mine. The Attorney General? Of Mexico? Why here? But I automatically switched into my debutante manners, smiled and took his offered hand. "Welcome to our home, señor. Please come in."

He held my hand a beat too long. "Please, not so formal. It's Saturday. I'm Vincente. Vincente Medina." He covered his leer with a smile, perfect teeth shining against his dark complexion, and nodded toward the elevator. "Lead the way." Yuck. And for a casual Saturday, his bespoke linen suit looked well pressed and out of place in the Cathouse.

I gestured and stood aside as the visitors passed into the entry hall, following them to the elevator. Quint held the door while we stepped in. Medina hadn't introduced, or offered to help, the rumpled looking man with the equipment. I took the smaller piece from him and he smiled gratefully and crowded into the elevator after us.

What the hell was going on here? Polo was supposed to pick us up for a little showdown with his mother. I hadn't believed he would have the guts to accuse her formally, and I doubted the Attorney General of Mexico had stopped by to reprimand her, because from what I'd heard, that asshole was as inept—and possibly connected—as they came. But what did I know about Mexican bureaucrats?

Once upstairs, Quint led Medina into the living room

where Lily sprawled on the couch in a heap with Maya and the puppies, eyes glued to a music video. She didn't look up.

Quint waved toward the couch. "Have a seat, Attorney General."

At Medina's look of horror, I directed him to the leather easy chair. "Sir, please. This one is free of dog hair," I shouted doing my best to keep my face neutral. Lily giggled into Maya's ruff. "Lily, turn the TV off and get the dogs out of here, please."

She glared at me, but hit the power button and slinked off the couch with her entourage.

"May I offer you something? Coffee?" I asked.

"*Gracias no,* señorita." He turned to the equipment *burro* standing near the entry and snapped in Spanish, *"Bernal, set up the recorder."* He tipped his head toward the table in the far corner. The agent trudged across the room and found the plug, hooking up a slick looking recorder and mic.

Did the senator know about this? The room suddenly felt stuffy, full of dead air. I wanted to throw a window open. Bernal appeared to be thinking the same. Quint stood, his customary seat taken by señor prig. We waited silently while the man finished testing and adjusting the equipment.

Medina broke the silence with another order. "When Aguirre arrives, we'll seat him there." He waved to a pair of straight-backed chairs on the other side of the room. "You're sure he and Señora Sotomayor are coming?"

Quint dipped his head. "Yes."

"*Bueno, entonces,* señorita, you will sit with him. The girl may join Mr. Quint on the couch. The dogs will be kenneled. I will place Señora Sotomayor in that chair." He pointed at a straight-backed chair next to the recorder and microphone, now dominating the spindly side table.

Quint sat down and checked his watch. Had Polo chickened out? This already wasn't going well.

Fifteen silent minutes and a mug of Lily's coffee later the gate buzzer rang again. Finally. Medina looked at his heavy gold watch and frowned. I nodded to Quint and sprinted for the gate release button then ran down the stairs. Polo and Lidia waited on the front step, bickering. Shrek 2 shot me a quick salute before backing Polo's limo into the street.

"Welcome señora, Polo. Come in." It was déjà vu. Hadn't I already done this today?

I led them across the entry to the elevator. Polo acted nervous, jittery. Lidia frowned at my house—her house—with utter disdain. I kept quiet as we wordlessly clanked and swayed to the next floor where Mrs. P awaited. Where'd she come from? She should have made the coffee—she should have answered the door. I saw the smirk on her face. Vindicated! Lidia's spy. I smiled. She'd be leaving our employ if I had any say.

The housekeeper showed us into the living room where sherry and scotch had magically appeared on the bar cart.

Medina, whisky in hand, lumbered out of the easy chair. "Good afternoon, senator, señora. Miss Stone, please seat our guests," he ordered.

"Vincente, what a surprise," Lidia said, offering her hand as I guided her by. Medina did not take it.

Lidia sniffed as I seated her by the recorder. Polo paced. Mrs. P didn't waste a moment before she was passing sherry to Lidia. Was this a party?

Aguirre spun around, confronted Lidia, his voice apologetic. "Mother we have a problem to discuss with you."

Was Aguirre backing down in front of *Mami* Dearest? I looked across the room to my father lounging on the couch. He kept a pleasant smile plastered to his face, but I could tell by the jiggling fingers at his side, Quint was livid.

Lidia took a moment to arrange her haughtiest expression and asked, "And what do you feel is important enough to discuss in front of these... ?" she said with a dismissive wave of her hand.

Medina interrupted. "Senator, I will conduct the interview." He shifted out of the chair to tower over Lidia.

Lidia's composure cracked and she appeared to shrink, although she hadn't moved.

Medina pulled an envelope from his pocket and unfolded its contents. He cleared his throat, checked the top page and tilted his chin at Bernal. The operator started the tape recorder, identifying the day and time, location, and people present.

Medina bellowed, "Señora Sotomayor, we are aware your house located on Calle San Augustín, in Tlalpan has been used in the illegal trafficking of drugs and humans."

Her head jerked up. Indignation flared in her eyes. "How dare you. Leopoldo— "

"Señora, you can answer my questions here, or be remanded into custody. Which will it be?"

She straightened herself on the uncomfortable chair and glared at Polo. "I don't know what you are talking about."

"Are you acquainted with one Edgar Santos?" Santos asked.

"I demand to know what this is about, Leopoldo. Of course I know him, as do you Leopoldo. He's my godchild, Vincente"

Polo interrupted. "Eddy is involved with human trafficking."

"Oh, come now *hijo*, Edgar is an importer of some sort."

Her tone almost convincing.

"Senator, please," Medina barked. "I am conducting this interview."

Who was this guy kidding? He'd never get between Polo and his mother.

"Your godson rents the premises in Bosques de Pedrigal?" he asked.

Lidia sat stone-like for several moments before speaking. "That house is empty, as I recall."

I knew it was her house!

"Was that house leased by Edgar Santos, agent for service of process of BL Enterprises, S.A. on August tenth of this year?"

"I have a property manager who handles the day-to-day operations of my real estate holdings."

"I have the lease agreement here," he said, producing a paper from the envelope. Is this your signature?" He handed her the contract.

Lidia's hand shook. "This contract has been terminated."

Flying out of my seat, I cut in. "Why? Because your darling Eddie abandoned twenty trafficked children in the sub-basement? Or because he operated a meth lab and money processing room? Don't give us a ration of crap, Lidia," I said, drawing her name out.

"Miss Stone. Miss Stone! Sit down," Medina commanded.

A vehicle backfired around the corner, blowing the raspberry I'm sure Lidia's triumphant expression intended.

I shouted over him, "We don't know what happened to the rest of the children, but two American sisters were in that holding cell, an unlit, unventilated cave deep in the mountain." I paused and glared at the old woman.

On cue, Lily and Maya padded in and jumped onto the couch. Lidia's look of loathing creased her perfectly applied lipstick.

"Yes, Mother, he imports human beings into the sex industry. You know full well Anibal and JadeAnne rescued children from a holding cell in the basement of your property." He watched her intently.

She sat rigid for several moments before speaking. "That house was empty. I don't know anything about—"

Medina held up his hand and shouted *"¡Basta!"*

Enough.

"Señora Sotomayor, the American Embassy has become involved. You will not fare well in prison."

Lidia turned bone pale under her powder. Yep, a shakedown. I glanced at the couch. Curled tightly against my father, Lily watched, loathing and pain creasing her face, tears coursing through. Quint pulled her closer. Rage boiled inside me. I looked back at Polo's mother and saw her wheels turning. She was going to try and spin this.

Medina continued on with his story. "Señora, the American girls were removed from your house by your nephew Anibal Aguirre, and delivered to your employee, Consuelo García, at your gentleman's club located at Calle Lluvia 15, Jardines de Pedrigal. Do you deny this?"

She slid narrowed eyes toward the Attorney General. Her expression wry. "I have no knowledge of this, Vincente. I'm sure you are more familiar with that club than I."

Medina's ears turned pink, but he plunged on. "Who arranged the sale of these girls to members of the organized crime group, *Los Zetas?*"

The room went dead silent. Lidia glared at each of us in turn. I noticed how ugly her face could be, twisted and furrowed in hate. What got me—why would a woman, wealthy in her own right, who appeared to have everything life could offer—and a practicing Catholic— be involved in the ugliest, sleaziest, most devil-infused business on earth? The buying and selling of human beings, especially vulnerable children, youths and women. The sex industry and human slavery were the lowest forms of commerce. There only was one reason for their existence: pure unadulterated greed. Could Lidia be so empty she needed to debase her fellow humans and herself to satiate her empty soul?

"Leopoldo, are you going to allow these outrageous accusations?"

"I'm sorry Mother, these are the facts. You cannot pretend these events have not taken place, and I doubt you are blameless."

Well, yay for Leopoldo Aguirre, I thought, grinning as I beamed to Quint: finally a forty-something man stands up to his mommy. He winked.

Lidia replied, her voice brittle, beaten. "Why are you so cruel to me, *hijo*?"

Aguirre grimaced; his chin quivered. "The Attorney General has a few questions for you. I suggest you answer him. He can destroy your reputation, Mother. Can you hear what your old biddy friends are saying about you? It will be all over the papers. Mother, it's up to you. He's got the power to turn your nightmares into reality."

At least she had the decency to look contrite as she nodded.

We all turned toward Medina who began again. "Who was involved in the kidnapping, transport, and imprisonment pending sale, of the minor American sisters, Evie Flynn, aged ten, and Lily Flynn, fifteen, taken from Los Angeles, California on or about August fifth of this year?"

She avoided looking at the Attorney General. "I have no knowledge of any kidnapping."

"Nor of the illegal operations at your property located in Tlalpan?"

"I have already answered that."

"This document," he said, handing her a yellow highlighted page, "states the property is rented to BL Enterprises—a shell corporation," he added, speaking to Quint before turning back to Polo's mother. "Do you have knowledge of, or information about, BL Enterprises?"

"I do not."

"Our office knows that BL Enterprises is connected to the Beltran Leyva organized crime syndicate, and you are associated with members of this organization. We want information. Señora, your answers will be held in strict confidence unless, of course, you persist in associating with known traffickers. If we are satisfied that your answers are accurate and we are able to stop the trafficking ring operating in Mexico City, we will continue to ignore your gentlemen's clubs and houses. However, I admonish you to begin divesting yourself of these businesses and properties." Medina wanted to placate her. He was letting her of the hook.

"I have no knowledge of this organization or these American girls. I am horrified you would accuse me of hurting children. Consuelo García manages several of my establishments and is in charge of the hiring and firing of employees." She looked at her son, her expression fixed in her haughty sneer.

I jumped to my feet fists clenched and towered over the little crow cowering on her chair. "So you're blaming Consuelo? That fat whore doesn't have what it takes to set up an operation such as the one Anibal and I stumbled into."

Quint coughed. I swung around to face him, and he waved me back to my seat. I exhaled, releasing my hands.

"Mother, for God's sake. This is an international scandal. If the Yanks get wind you're involved with trafficking, we're ruined—my presidential bid... "

Polo was aiming to be Mexico's president? I rolled my eyes and made a face at Quint, who contemplated the wall above my head.

The senator was devolving into emotional pleading to "be good". How was that going to get the information we needed? I'd be strong-arming Lidia all the way. Beating her up might get results. I felt sick again. Mexico was turning me into a liar and a torturer, but that bitch was in the middle of the whole thing. I'd always thought it was Aguirre who was a cartel man.

"Lidia, this is Lily Flynn. Perhaps we should let her tell

you what was done to her in your name," I said in a hard voice I didn't recognize. "Edgar Santos is supplying your sex trade with underage workers."

"Edgar?" The old woman let out a raspy, shrill sound that may have been laughter.

"He isn't alone. He works with your wonderful friend Guillermo Lobo. Lily has provided identification for both."

Her head shot up. "What does this girl know about my godson?"

"He raped me and my sister and killed my mother," Lily replied in a hollow voice.

"How dare you!" she said, her voice hard, and turned to Polo. "She is obviously lying."

Medina replied, "We have witnesses, señora. According to the facts we have, the two American girls were sold to representatives from the Gulf Cartel—a sale allegedly brokered by your stepson Anibal Aguirre. Miss Stone was drugged, detained, and included in the deal."

"I have little to do with my husband's bastard."

I couldn't contain myself. "The ten-year-old is dead, Lidia." I noticed her flinch every time I used her first name.

"We know Consuelo García had possession of the girls, Mother," the senator said.

"Señora Sotomayor, is it possible Anibal and Consuelo are conducting business outside of your authority?" Medina asked.

"It is apparent that Consuelo has become a problem for my business, Vincente. I have suspected for some time that she acts on her own."

Chapter 11

Even If We're Just Dancing in the Park

I couldn't take another minute of that house or the company, and excused myself on some pretext to return to my room. Aguirre and his witchy mother drove me crazy. At least he brought in that Attorney General, or had it been Quint? Whatever—in my mind, the connection was made. BL Enterprises was under the umbrella of the Beltran Leyva Organization. We could have gotten so much more if Medina weren't a scumbag and Aguirre weren't such a mama's boy. They accused her; they placated her. What was up with the waffling? And Quint with his unshakeable belief that Aguirre was a good guy—he—they both—almost had me convinced, but after watching the farce of an interrogation, I wasn't so sure. In a real court it would have gone differently:

"Señora Sotomayor, are you working for organized crime?"

"Please identify which organization you work for."

"Do you buy and sell women for your 'gentlemen's clubs'?"

"Who receives the profits of your businesses?"

"Are your 'gentlemen's clubs' and money laundering organizations for the Sinaloa Cartel?"

Wow, I hadn't given that any thought before. Money

laundering. Those kinds of businesses operated on cash. Another angle. It segued with Lura's husband Daniel Worthington's business, and he'd been having an affair with Consuelo, or so I'd gathered from the talk at Lidia's Celebration of Life after Lura's funeral. I'd have to mention that to Quint, but what on earth would anyone see in that fat, painted cow?

I rummaged through the bureau for a pair of running pants. Pepper and I needed exercise, dangerous as it might be. He'd been cooped up in my room while Aguirre ran his tribunal—not that shit had been decided or adjudicated. Pepper danced around me gurgling and yipping, ecstatic to go out. I don't think he liked this house much. He wasn't allowed to roam and the yard sucked for a dog.

"Peppi boy, you miss home?"

He put his ears up at that.

"Home?" I teased him.

He jumped up resting his paws on my shoulders and licked my face.

"I guess you do," I said, hugging him. "So do I boy, so do I.

I packed Lura's Glock into my fanny pack, and we slipped out the kitchen door to the back yard after tossing a note, *Gone for a run*, onto the table and grabbing my keys. Quint had changed-out my gate key with the new one. I hoped I had a door key too, but I could always ring. Lily wouldn't be allowed out.

I held Pepper on the leash keeping close to the house so no one looking out a window could see us until we broke for the gate. I saw only Polo's limo and driver waiting at the curb. and waved as we jogged by. I scanned for black SUVs or parked cars with watchers inside. All clear. We headed out.

The slow jog to the Parque Árboles warmed us both up,

but I could tell Pepper wanted a hard run. I could use one, too. My bullet wound was almost healed, so I decided to step up my pace. We jogged onto the track and I gave my dog the signal. He shot off like a rocket with me pumping my legs as hard as I could behind him. We rounded the far curve and my traitorous heart gave a little leap—Doctor Dylan and Noémie dead ahead. Roger bounded into our trajectory and paced Pepper. Pepper ran harder, Roger nipping his heels. Who was I kidding? The run had more to do with Dylan than concern for our health.

I still hadn't actually told Quint about him, at least not about the tacos or my desire to see Dylan again. In all this tangle of danger and suspicion, Dylan was an adorable, smart breath of clean air. There, I'd admitted it.

Pepper and Roger thundered past Dylan. Noémie bounced behind the big dogs for a few strides and I caught up to her master. "Hi Dylan. *¿Qué onda?*" I said, hoping I sounded casual.

Dylan's face broke into a grin. "JadeAnne, I hoped I'd see you here. *Mami* wants you to join us for *comida* tomorrow. I would have called, but—"

"You don't have my number. I don't know the house phone and my cell is a US number. Give me yours and I'll call with mine when I get home. What's she making?"

"Her famous red *pozole*. It's my dad's birthday. My family is looking forward to meeting you. Will you come?"

"Is Pepper invited?"

"*Claro que sí.*"

"Then it's a date. What time? What can I bring?"

"Just yourself. Unless you bring my dad a bottle of tequila," he said and guffawed. "It's not like in the States where an invitation requires you to show up with part of the meal. My family is pretty relaxed and we won't be formal. Have you ever had dinner with a Mexican family here?"

We walked side by side with Noémie. The boys romped

101

ahead. Everyone grinned. I sighed as I noticed my shoulders unfold from around my ears. The afternoon glowed in the warm sunshine, and wafts of rose and astringent eucalyptus swirled on the breeze. The bright colors of sports gear popped against the deep greens of the trees and park visitors smiled. A weekend vibe for sure. Dinner with Dylan's family sounded lovely.

"The only family I've dined with is really dysfunctional. You know, I came to town for someone's funeral and have spent time with her people. They're from the *alta sociedad* and not warm and fuzzy at all. I think they hate each other." I took a deep breath and savored the smell of the trees. Some of them looked like bamboo but bloomed with big showy flowers like dahlias. Very pretty. Maybe that was what I smelled.

"I know, the air is sweet. Have you noticed it's clear?"

I looked up. Sure enough, the sky gleamed a silvering blue like a lake reflected on chrome. "The sky framed by those trees is amazing. I've never seen the sky in Mexico City. Only the hazy pollution."

"I appreciated the air in L.A. We have days here where you can't go outside or open your windows. But tomorrow will be like this, too, and we'll celebrate in Mami's garden. We'll eat around two so come by one."

"What kind of tequila should I buy? Does he have a favorite?"

"I was kidding. Mami's got everything we'll need."

"So who will be there? What are their names? What do I call your parents?"

Dylan chatted about his parents and siblings. His dad, Eladio, trained as an engineer. He and Gabriella, his mom, opened the business together early in their marriage. I got about as far as a married sister, Baez and her husband, but started to lose it with the second brother, Guthrie and his wife? Girlfriend? Then he started on the kids. I smiled and mmm-hmmed in the appropriate places, but I regretted I'd accepted the invitation. Holy moly, I was in for a family of about forty. It would be culture shock in more than nationality. I laughed.

Dylan laughed, too. "What are we laughing about?"

"I'm thinking about the continent of distance between your family and mine."

"Yeah, about four thousand miles."

"No, I mean my family consists of my adoptive parents, a dead sister, and a set of grandparents I see maybe once a year. Oh, and the father I met two weeks ago, who I thought was dead."

"What do you mean by that?"

"My birth father, if that's the term, Jackman Quint. I'm staying with him here. He met me through that family I mentioned. My parents told me my real parents were dead, but it was a lie. Quint is telling me about my history. My mother died giving birth to me as the North Vietnamese swept south toward Saigon. My grandmother delivered me as the Viet Cong bombed and burned the village. Charlie, my adoptive father, rescued me and got me on that last Pan Am flight in the Babylift. He and Quint were best friends then, but Charlie double-crossed my dad and took me…" I paused, embarrassed I'd divulged too much of my history. I waved it off with the fly that buzzed around my head. "It's a long story. Boring."

"Boring? Not at all. So you're Vietnamese?"

"Half-Vietnamese co-ed and half American serviceman. Quint has strawberry blond hair. It's where my red hair comes from, he says."

"You all vacationing?"

"You might say that. I met my father at the funeral. But I want to hear about you and the dogs. Tell me about your trainer. I'm so impressed with Noémie's perfect etiquette. Fernando, you called him?" I scrutinized Dylan's face and posture for any hint I'd touch a nerve. I couldn't detect any reaction other than his easy smile.

"Fernando Torrens is amazing. He trains service dogs for various purposes, like guard dogs for businesses. For me, I wanted obedient pets, nothing more, but he trains companion dogs, protection dogs, and rescue dogs. He raises a few labs and goldens for his service dog clients. I think he's the only trainer in the city for that market. That's how I heard about him, of course. As a surgeon, I meet people with need of companion dogs. I called him and went down to tour his operation. Impressive. He's got everything right there including a vet hospital on-site. The vet is a separate operation, but they work together. A woman, I don't remember her name."

"Wow, cool. Where?"

"North about forty minutes in a place called Tlalnepantla. It was a schlep, but worth it."

We'd gone around the track about three times and as we approached the playgrounds Dylan suggested we grab a drink. It was getting on to cocktail hour and sounded like a good idea. I felt more comfortable after hearing his connection to Fernando, but I couldn't be one hundred percent he wasn't BS-ing me. "Where are you thinking? For that drink, I mean."

"Over on the other side of the park by the bandstand a guy sets up with a rolling bar. It's time for the couples dancing. The music will start any minute. Come on, let's check it out."

He let loose with a shrill whistle and in moments Roger and Pepper galloped back to us. It was hard to totally hate Fernando when these dogs were so well trained and happy. Dylan clipped the leash onto Roger's collar then clipped Noémie to him. I hooked Pepper's leash to his harness, and we started across the play area toward the *Blue Danube Waltz* blasting out of over-driven speakers. Dylan grabbed my hand, twirled me toward him, and took a waltzing step.

"Like to dance?" he asked, wiggling his eyebrows.

"Yeah, I love dancing. You, too?"

Dylan hummed a familiar Bruce Springsteen refrain. "Sure, in the park. At the disco, *pues*, not so much. I like ballroom dancing. I took lessons as a kid and actually enjoyed them. I liked the girls, too. I still do." He flashed his perfect white teeth and winked. "*This scalpel's for hire,*" he sang, "Even if we're just dancing in the park."

I grinned, remembering sixth grade dance class. "Mr. Kitchens' dance class every Wednesday after school for the winter I was twelve. The boys were all a foot shorter than me, if you can believe that. I was a scrawny little girl and they didn't want to dance with me because I didn't have boobs yet."

We turned through a break in the trees and emerged at the bandstand. A sort of shell-looking affair with a cement pad filled with couples of every age swaying to the scratchy music. The atmosphere was electric with happiness. Yes, I wanted to dance.

Dylan led me to the outer ring behind where an audience might sit for a concert. A row of carts had been set up selling food and drink—a veritable cornucopia of *comida Mexicana.* I found carts devoted to candies and desserts, *esquites,* corn on the cob slathered in *crema*, *tortas, tacos, quesedillas,* fried fish, *palomitos,* popcorn, soft drinks including my favorite *horchata,* and the bar cart.

We headed toward our margaritas. The dogs headed toward the tacos and needed some convincing to come with us. Several small tables and chairs surrounded our vendor. I sat down at the only free table and parked the dogs around it. No one tried to steal the empty chair. In moments Dylan came back with plastic cups of slushy margaritas. I'd noticed the drinks had been made with actual limes and liquor, not mix. I smiled at my new friend as he handed me a cup and took a taste. Wow!

"This is delicious Dylan," I said. "I'd rate this street margarita as good as my own, and I think mine are the best." I grinned at him. No false modesty here.

"Where'd you learn to make a killer margarita? The ones in bars are too sweet. In America they favor using margarita mix."

"Not mine. Last time I visited Sally in Zihua she had a party in my honor. One of the guys, a British banker, actually, made these incredible drinks and gave me the recipe. It helps to have perfectly ripe Mexican or Key limes and top quality tequila. Then it's the rum, Cointreau and fresh squeezed oranges that sweeten them up. I use sugar, but not so much. I also prefer rocks, but this is like a snow cone with a kick." I slurped up some more of my drink. The dogs settled under our feet to nap.

"Check out that couple," Dylan said, jerking his head toward the swirling mass.

"Which?"

He pointed his index finger surreptitiously toward an old couple dancing on the fringe of the stage. They were shriveled, silver-haired *bailarinos* in dress clothes. He wore a black three-piece suit with a hat. She sported elbow gloves and a satiny gown of deep maroon under her hat trimmed in black feathers and a net veil. They swayed and stepped to the waltz with a stiff grace. It was obvious they had danced together for many years, and she understood all of his cues.

"How adorable. That gives me hope. Life doesn't end just because you get old," I said. "Well, I hope I make it to old. And I hope I find someone to grow old with." I dipped my head and smiled a little too coyly, shooting my eyes obliquely toward Dylan. Christ. What was the matter with me?

"I know what you mean," he said, apparently not noticing my flirtation. "He's ninety. She's eighty-seven. My neighbors. I thought about specializing in geriatric care for a while, but decided having my patients die would be depressing. I wanted to save lives."

"I guess you do that in the ER."

"Yeah, but it's too hectic. I want to get back to surgery. Elective surgery. My plan is to become wealthy," he winked at me, "I need rich ladies who want breast enhancement and tummy tucks." Dylan laughed. "At least in between heart transplants."

"Ah, cosmetic surgery. I've been thinking of getting my eyes done so I look more Vietnamese."

Dylan gave me a shocked look. "You're kidding, right? You're perfect as you are."

I started to giggle. That had always been a joke I told. "No, really. I'm such a round-eye. And the color is all wrong. I tried to order black contacts, but just couldn't see through them." It was a struggle to keep a straight face as I watched horror roll into Dylan's.

He finally caught on. "You're pulling my leg, you kidder. I think you're the prettiest girl I'm going to dance with today."

He held out his hand and I slid mine into it as we stood up. In unison we turned to our dogs and said, "You stay. Guard the drinks." Then Dylan guided me to the dance floor and took me into his arms.

The waltzes had ended and the couples on the dance floor box-stepped and twirled in a fox trot. I loved fox trot. Less energetic than swing, but more interesting than waltz. I'd gotten pretty good at it in dance class. Like twenty years ago.

Dylan caught me around the back and masterfully led me into the beat. His dancing was smooth, firm, and on tempo. I felt like I was floating in air. What a difference from the muddling of the dance class boys. I might like ballroom dancing if I had a partner like this. I sneaked a glance at the oldsters still going strong and Dylan pulled me in a little closer. My heart beat quick-quick in a foxtrot of its own.

Two more foxtrots played and the music shifted to a salsa. The participants roared and came to life. This was one I had not learned at Mr. Kitchens'. Dylan pulled me tight and stepped me toward him then rocked me back. He stepped me back, a step, a rock, and he started me over. In no time, I had the hang of the eight beats. Then he swung me out and hauled me in. Had I ever had so much fun? All I needed was to learn how to swing my hips. Even the old lady could swing her bony butt.

Dylan leaned in to my ear. His warm breath tickled my neck as he suggested we get some food and another drink before he swung me out again, reeling me back and hugging me in a bear hug as the song ended. I melted into his embrace panting, and agreed.

"Sure. Let's try that fish. It smells really good."

Dylan's broad smile said he was down with fish. He grabbed my hand and we strolled through the throng toward our table, getting several dirty looks from drinkers standing just out of reach of Pepper and Roger, who sat on either side of the small bistro table with that 'don't mess around in my territory' look. Noémie slept under the table.

"You don't worry someone might steal Noémie? Roger is too big, people would be afraid of him like they are of Pepper. Well, one person tried to steal him—" I cut myself off. I couldn't exactly tell him the dog trainer he so respected had kidnapped me and tried to steal my dog.

"No, Fernando trained them to go only with me," he said as we joined the queue at the fish stand.

"But anyone could just pick her up."

"Try it. She'll bite you."

"Not me!"

"I dare you to try and pick her up when we get back to the table. Hey, Jade, how about getting several tacos for the dogs while I purchase the fish?" He thrust a wad of pesos into my hand.

"You're on, Porras. Tacos, then I'm picking up your little princess. I'll show you. And if I can do it, can I keep her?" I winked and headed toward the food.

"Only if you keep Roger and her dad, too," Dylan called, his eyes crinkling into that smile.

My heart melted. God, make Dylan one of the good guys, I prayed.

Chapter 12

No, It's All About Money

The sky darkened as sunset turned to twilight. The dancing had ended and the dogs became restless. Noémie nipped me, just as Dylan had predicted. Determined to try again, I'd bring her some treats tomorrow. The taco had helped, but she was a toughie, and I'd need to really pander to her to pick her up. Now I needed to get home. Quint was going to question me. What would I tell him?

"I should be heading home, Dylan. This has been the most fun I've had since I got to Mexico." My S's slurred after four margaritas. Luckily, we'd danced off a lot of the alcohol and filled our bellies with samplings from just about all the carts, or I'd be staggering.

"Yeah, me too. Mami will expect me to eat something with them, but I'm full," he said, slurring, too. "It was so great to run into you today, JadeAnne. I look forward to tomorrow. Shall I come for you?"

"It's okay. I'll find you."

"You're coming, aren't you?"

"Absolutely. If your family is as cute as you, I'll have a great time." I batted my eyelashes in a gross flirtation.

He laughed. "But seriously, JadeAnne, it's almost dark. I should take you home."

"I'm not safe?" The idea made me uneasy. That black SUV was out there somewhere, but Dylan couldn't know that. Or could he?

"Del Valle is as safe as it gets in a city this huge, but, no, you're not. I'll walk you home."

I didn't fight.

We untwisted our leashes and Dylan took my arm as we headed out. The dogs pranced by our sides, happy to get moving again. I wondered if this were a good idea—letting Dylan know where I lived. A good guy. God, please.

My house was only a few blocks, but we took forever to get there. Dylan walked slowly, letting his dogs sniff everything. Maybe he wanted to spend more time with me. That's what I hoped. But the alternative swam around my tequila-soaked brain. He expected the black SUV to show up and planned to push me in. I kept Pepper close and my leash hand rested on my gun-toting purse. I'd forgotten about the gun at the dance pavilion. Had Dylan felt it? Recognized it for a gun? What on earth would he think?

"...friend growing up. I always liked the houses on this block. Look, there's where Victor lived," he said and pointed to an ivy-covered two-story house behind a metal fence. "I wonder what happened to that family. Has that happened to you, too, JadeAnne? Childhood friends moved away and you've lost touch?"

"Most of the kids have moved away. Marin is too expensive. The geeky kids all moved to Silicon Valley and work at Google, or they're in San Francisco and have start-ups. Most of their parents live on the family estates. It's pretty wealthy in Mill Valley. My folks are still there."

"Your dad still working?"

"Yeah, an attorney. Estate planning. The rich working for the richer. My family is pretty well-off. That's my house over there." I pointed to The Cathouse, as we'd dubbed it.

"That was my first girlfriend's house. Rosa Ortiz. She

111

was a sweet little thing. We were ten. We were planning on getting married when we grew up, but her father was transferred to Guadalajara and that put an end to the romance."

Dylan looked down at me with a soft smile. "Maybe I'll be luckier with the current occupant."

Before I realized what I was doing, I was in Dylan's arms and he was kissing me, deeply, softly, exploring my mouth with his tongue. That six-pack I'd felt on the dance floor pressed into me, his heart pounded against my heart. I felt his muscles flexing under his t-shirt and the heat of his bare arms against mine. I slipped away into that blissful land of letting go.

Pepper tugged on the leash and whined. I pulled away from Dylan and looked at the dog as I refocused my eyes. Behind him a black SUV parked at the curb, lights off, engine idling. Pepper yanked free, the hair on his back stood up. He swiveled toward the vehicle and bared his teeth. Roger shifted in next to him and growled. The side door slid open on its track. I let go of Dylan. Pepper leapt toward the van with Roger at his side, snarling. A scream and a string of expletives poured out of a black clad figure. "Fucking Pepper bit me!" a familiar voice said as the door slammed shut and the SUV roared off. I bolted across the street and whistled as I slipped through my gate. Pepper loped across the street, Roger glued to his side, leashes entwining. I opened the gate and caught Roger as Pepper ran in.

"Roger? JadeAnne!" Dylan's voice sounded frantic. He was still on the sidewalk, Noémie in his arms, turning his head back and forth like a spinning top.

"We're here, inside the gate. Call Roger."

He jogged across Amores and grabbed Roger's leash. "What just happened, JadeAnne?" he asked through the opening.

"I guess it's like you said, Del Valle isn't so safe. I'm so grateful you brought me home, and I'm sorry you were worried. Roger is fine. He seems to have attached himself to Pepper. You know Pepper is trained to be my guard dog," I yammered.

"You're shaking. Let's get inside and I'll call the police." He stepped through and took my arm.

I pulled back. "No. Let it go."

"JadeAnne, what are you not telling me? You knew that SUV. He called Pepper by name. Who was he? Your boyfriend?"

"Oh, no, Dylan! I don't have a boyfriend. But this guy is stalking me. His name is Anibal. It's why I'm a little stand-offish. He scares me." I hoped that would be enough to assuage Dylan's imaginings. I couldn't exactly tell him everything. Not at least until I was certain he wasn't hooked up with Fernando, and by association—Anibal. God, please, no! I liked this guy.

He grasped the iron bars and leaned into the gate. "I really like you, JadeAnne. Please don't turn out to be a crazy person. Please be someone I can count on."

My heart caught in my throat. I am that person, Dylan, I wanted to shout. But it would be a lie. I was a girl with too much baggage, and part of the baggage was after me. Anibal Aguirre. What had I been thinking? My voice quavered. "Am I still invited tomorrow?"

He looked at me for a long moment through the gate. Oh no! Changing his mind?

He took my hands and gazed into my eyes. "JadeAnne, it's been a long time since I've been as excited about a woman as I am about you. I want you to come, but you better know, my family will detect if you're not who you say you are." His shoulders sagged and he looked at the pebble he toed with his running shoe. "It's up to you. What are you going to do?"

Well, I was lots of things, but crazy? I wish my

predicament were wild ravings. No, I was sincerely attracted to Dylan. The irony hit me—Dylan questioned the same things about me as I did about him.

I pulled the gate closed and reached through the bars, hooking my hand around his neck, pulling him toward me until I could reach his lips. I kissed him then pulled away. "I'll be there. 1 p.m."

Pepper and I raced up the stairs and skidded along hall into the kitchen to the delight of Maya and the pups, but to the annoyance of Quint and Mrs. P, who frowned. My dog beat me as usual. Race was one of our games, and Pepper loved to play, especially when the "R" was replaced with "CH," which all race games became in about a nanosecond.

"JadeAnne, do I have to tell you not to run in the house?" Quint said.

"Ha ha, Quint. Ya know, the dad role is a little late." I wasn't in the mood.

"Where have you been?"

"Running with Pepper."

"You missed supper and it's dark. We were worried."

I could see Mrs. P nodding at the sink behind Quint. She definitely spoke English. Well, that's a twist on things. I'd keep that quiet for the moment. "Mrs. P worried about me? You mean, she didn't have anything to report."

"Christ, girl. The woman was concerned. This isn't about Lidia Sotomayor; it's about your safety. You didn't have a date with that doctor, did you? Until I've vetted him, he's suspect."

"No, but I couldn't stand another minute in this house with Aguirre and his awful mother. That was a three-ringed circus going round and round and round. Did you feel satisfied you got any answers?" I gave Quint a sharp look. He shook his head. "I thought not."

I crossed the room to retrieve Pepper's bowl. Maya and

the brood crowded around me as I scooped Pepper's kibble from the bag.

"Maya, go lie down." I slid the dog bowl onto the counter, receiving another frown from Mrs. P, and began scooping up puppies. They were getting so big I had trouble hanging onto more than two at a time, but I eventually corralled the litter into their pen. Pepper sat patiently below the bowl. I grabbed it and put it down by a bowl of fresh water. Maya edged in for a sample. "Maya, I see you." She gave me her sad golden look but lay down.

Quint waited at the table for me to finish with the dogs. He wanted to discuss the meeting. I wanted a beer to chase the adrenalin, and some time to unwind. Mrs. P dallied at the sink, probably hoping for some juicy gossip to carry back to Lidia.

Although I'd eaten in the park, I went to the stove and lifted tops off pots, breathing in the tantalizing aromas of some sort of stew, Mexican rice, creamy pinto beans. My stomach growled. "May I fix myself a plate, Señora Pérez?" I asked in Spanish. I didn't see any reason to let on she'd blown her cover.

"Sí señorita, ahorita se la doy."

Great. *Ahorita*, meaning sometime between now and never. I could get my own plate.

"¿No puedo servirme propio?" Can't I get my own? I asked.

"Como le quiere, señorita," the housekeeper replied—the equivalent of *whatever.*

I pulled a plate from the cupboard and dished up a healthy serving, proving I'd been out running and working up an appetite. The question was, why was I trying to prove something? I was thirty-two, for God's sake. I sat down and shoveled a bit of the spicy stew, loaded with tender chunks of beef and chayote in a smoky gravy, which Mrs. P had spiced with a hint of chile, into my mouth. "Señora Pérez, this is *fantastico*. What's it called?" I gave her a big smile.

The housekeeper smiled back and replied, *"Un guisado de res, nada más."*

A slow cooked beef. She might have been Lidia's spy, but the woman could cook.

I shoveled stew into my mouth as though I hadn't seen food in weeks. Not that I was actually hungry—my rumbling stomach more the effect of fear—but I hoped Mrs. P would finish and leave. She continued mopping the clean counters. I dropped my spoon into the bowl and shoved it aside. The housekeeper started toward the table. I held up my hand.

"It's not necessary, *señora*. I'll clean up the rest. Why don't you go home. We've got some cleaning to do tomorrow." I suggested, forcing a bright smile.

She nodded and turned back to her cleaning. I exhaled, exasperated. Okay then, she was asking for it. "So Dad, why are you so worried about Dylan? He's quite nice."

"JadeAnne, the nicest people can betray you. Anibal—"

"Anibal was a hottie. I never said he was nice. Did Lidia say anything about him? What about Polo? Has he told his mother what happened?" I watched Mrs. P's ears perk right up.

"Of course not, Jade. That's between us."

"And Mrs. P and soon Lidia."

"No way. Mrs. P doesn't speak English."

"Oh, yes she does, don't you señora?" I turned to the housekeeper who pretended to attend something in the sink. "Don't you, Mrs. Pérez."

Señora Pérez turned slowly toward the table, her eyes cast down, but defiance shining in her face. *"No entiendo, señorita."*

"Like hell you don't understand. Mrs. Pérez, don't try to bullshit a bullshitter. You're lousy at hiding it. You may not be fluent, but your understanding of English is way beyond rudimentary. Fess up lady, or you're fired." I hoped Quint would back me up. She should be fired regardless. We could get along without a housekeeper, although the meals would suffer. I studied her overly made-up face. Mrs. P was scared.

"Int-quay, ou-tay eak-spay ig-pay atin-lay?"

"Are you kidding me?" he said.

I glared at him.

Quint sighed and said, "Okay, you win. Es-yay aughter-day. So we're going to speak pig Latin now?"

"E-shay eak-spays ing-lay ish-ay."

Mrs. P craned to understand. I laughed, watching her leaning in with a puzzled look on her face. I hunched my shoulder toward the housekeeper and Quint laughed, too.

It was mean, but we needed to have a conversation without Mrs. P. She realized we were pranking her and colored before scurrying out of the room.

I dropped my bowl in the sink and helped myself to a beer from the refrigerator. Quint kept his eyes on me until I sat down again. I couldn't read him. I supposed that was the outcome of not actually knowing your father. The house trembled as the elevator creaked down to the ground floor. I smiled. "She's gone. Let's talk."

"You're making a mistake, JadeAnne. Mrs. P is a good housekeeper and she's breaking through young Lily's wall. We need her for that. She was a nurse, you know."

"Where is Lily?"

"Watching TV in the living room."

"Then why were the goldens here when I came in? Maya follows Lily everywhere."

"Lily and Mrs. P have bonded over the dogs. Our housekeeper is a dog lover. She feeds Maya treats and is anticipating the puppies being weaned. She and Lily are planning puppy meals," Quint said, shaking his head.

"So I'm not to worry that Mrs. P listens to everything we say and reports it back to Lidia?"

"Jade, you heard Lidia today. She thinks Consuelo and

Anibal are conspiring to take business away from her."

"And you're going along with that?"

"We don't have anything else to go on."

"So, where do Consuelo and Anibal think they are going to take the business?"

"We already know where—to the Zetas. Do you know who they are?"

I twisted my ponytail into a knot and took a swig off my Superior. "Not a clue. Some more Mexican thugs trying to get a piece of the pie. You really like this beer? I prefer Victoria."

"The Zetas are the military arm of the Gulf Cartel. Since Calderon took office in December, The Sinaloa Cartel has made a bid for the Juarez plaza. It's a war that the Gulf will not win. Their people are scrambling for smuggling routes and I heard a rumor the Zetas are vying with the Beltran-Leyva Organization, affiliates of the Sinaloans, for the Mexico City plaza. I'm guessing it's not the drugs they're after, but the human trafficking. It's only a theory, but I'm betting El Chapo's group, with the help of the government, is going to shut down the Gulf Cartel and the Zetas are setting themselves up to be a cartel in its own right."

"What are you talking about? Calderon has declared war on the drug cartels. Why would the government help them?"

"Money, JadeAnne. There are billions of dollars at stake. Why do you think the Mexican government, the DEA, and several other agencies have declared war?"

"Uh, because drugs are bad?" I made a *what, are you stupid?* face.

"When did anyone care about good or bad? Everyone is making money. We need to stop the flow of drugs into the U.S. It's a real problem. Congress allocates several million more into the budget for fighting the drug cartels. More agents are hired. Administrators get raises. In Mexico, government officials operate from the deep pockets of the kingpins. Anibal took his salary and the kickbacks from whatever deals he put together. Money to rebuild his house? A fucking joke. He's probably got more money than the senator."

"Do I understand you correctly? This is all about money?"

"And power, but yes."

"So who do you work for?"

"Senator Aguirre."

"No, really. The American agency. DEA? Secret Service? Some black ops?"

"You've watched too many movies, girl. I work for myself. Since prison, I've gone on my own. Pay is better. I'm what you might call a soldier of fortune."

"Then why aren't you selling me and Pepper to the other cartel if all you're after is money?"

"Who says I'm not?" Quint winked and shoved away from the table. "We'll sort this out tomorrow. I'm taking my beer in to the TV. Coming?"

I nodded. "In a minute."

Quint came around the table and bent to kiss the top of my head. "I couldn't have planned for a better daughter."

Yeah. If I was such a great daughter, why did he joke about selling me to the highest bidder. My head was pounding. What if it were true?

Chapter 13

Interrogation

Sunday, August 26, 2007

If I thought the day before was beautiful, the Sunday sun shone down on a crystal-clear Mexico City. Looking into the deep cerulean sky was like looking into a perfect sapphire. I wished I could see the mountains from our house, but the trees and taller buildings to the west blocked the view.

I was first up and put the coffee on. Pepper and I strolled around the house and I checked out the laundry room. I would need to iron a dress for the party later, and wanted to double check the iron worked. As I continued around the house, I was pleased to see our gates locked shut and an armed security guard on duty. I gave him a wave and kept moving. I'd take him a cup of coffee when it was ready.

The guard, Bruno, a captain in the Presidential Guard, gratefully accepted his coffee and we chatted about Pepper's training for a few minutes. He said he was stationed in Tacubaya and I remembered the taco stand with the city's best *tacos suaderos* at the Metro station. Bruno agreed. His favorite, too. He asked if I was the VIP and was.. movie star? I got a good laugh out of that.

This Sunday morning felt normal, well, disregarding an

armed guard at the gate. The clean air and quiet city encouraged me to slow down and smell the proverbial roses. My high stress existence in Mexico was giving me wrinkles and grey hairs, and I needed to get back to my yoga practice. When I'd changed my bandage before bed, I saw the wound was only a pink scratch. I'd test out a few planks and spinal twists today. If they didn't split the wound open, I'd start a class on Monday. I was certain I'd find something close by, if not in Del Valle, I could go to Roma or Condesa. It was time.

I carried my second cup down to the back patio. The sun warmed the stones. Tonalli's ministrations were turning the drab space into a pleasant place to sit. He'd planted petunias and geraniums in all the pots and some new flowering bushes along the patchy back wall. Even some new patio furniture had appeared. This was beginning to feel like the vacation I'd originally thought I would take in Mexico.

I relaxed into my chair and closed my eyes, breathing in to the count of five from the bottom of my solar plexus up through my stomach and into my lungs. I imagined the breath circling around me, calming me, healing me, and exhaled slowly, emptying my solar plexus and back up through my lungs. I felt my body relaxing, my heartbeat slowing, and as I repeated the breaths, a voice whispered: *I am at peace. I am at ease. I am at home*. With each breath, the voice sounded stronger until I recognized it as my own voice and all the sounds of the city, the yard, the house—faded to unimportant.

People and places floated into and out of my vision: the Sarasvati, the fog tumbling over the shoulder of Mt. Tam, Dex, my dad Charley, my sister. Even my pill-popping socialite mother beamed peace and goodwill. It all seemed right, all a part of me. I carried peace with me, and no matter where I landed, peace would remain in my heart.

The scent of jasmine and roses wafted on a breeze. I

pictured Anibal and recognized him for the lonely damaged soul he was. Lura passed through singing a ditty. A lovely dark-haired Asian girl raised her hand in a benediction as little Evie floated in on a beam of light. She smiled and nodded. My heart warmed and I sank further into my meditation. *I am at peace. I am at ease. I am at home.*

A voice floated toward me from a great distance. "JadeAnne? Are you asleep?"

I breathed and acknowledged my world as it streamed past. I am at peace.

"Wake up. JadeAnne, wake up."

Evie and Anibal, hands joined, appeared. I felt a disturbance. What were these two doing together? The disturbance grew, pushing at me, nudging me. *Let me be at peace.*

"JadeAnne!" Lily's voice sounded loud, urgent.

I shook the meditation out of my head and opened my eyes. She was jabbing my arm. "What happened?"

The girl's voice quavered. "That guy, the one who took us to the dog place. He's here. At the gate. He wants to talk to you."

"Anibal?" I asked. Lily nodded, tears forming in her eyes. "Oh, brother!" That's not what I wanted wake up to. For a moment, I'd found some peace, some forgiveness. Anibal, my nemesis, who set me up, who sold the Flynn sisters, and how many other innocents? A jolt of hatred surged through me. He was behind my being shot. And worse, being raped. Suddenly, I felt my face, my body, harden. I wanted to kill him.

Lily sobbed, shaking. "Jade, you're scaring me. Stop!"

I took a deep breath and counted—my old yoga breathing. I needed it now, and exhaled, softening my snarling visage as I climbed out of the chair and encircled the girl in my arms. "Have Quint send him away and let's make those pancakes."

"We already ate the pancakes. Quint said to let you rest so he and I cooked them up."

"You didn't save me any?"

"Yes, Quint left you a stack in the oven. Come on. You have to come." She pulled at my arm with a trembling hand.

The bullet wound flamed across my ribs. I could kill Anibal. Not only for what he did to us, but for ruining my peace right now.

"Where's Pepper? He was here with me."

"Guarding the gate. He won't let that guy in."

"What happened to Bruno, the guard? Isn't he on duty?"

"No. He only comes at night. He left. Come *on*."

I hauled myself up. My brain felt like jellied consommé and my body moved heavily. "I'll go around to the gate. You go back inside."

Lily bolted for the backdoor. I couldn't blame her for that.

"What the hell are you doing here? You are not wanted. Leave. Now," I said as I approached the gate, mindful to stay behind Pepper and out of Anibal's reach. Pepper snarled.

Anibal backed away from the gate. "But Jade—" he said pronouncing my name in Spanish, HA-day.

"Don't try to sweeten things, Anibal Aguirre. We have nothing to discuss. You used me. Go away! Never contact me or my people again." I turned away and headed back to the house.

"Please Jade, just listen to me. Please. I promise you, it isn't what you think!"

I spun on my heel to face him. So much for *I am at peace.* I screeched at him. "You promise? Well, that makes everything all right, now, doesn't it? You fucking asshole. I hope you rot in hell for what you did."

"I told you not to have anything to do with Torrens but you wouldn't listen to me."

"Oh, selling me and the American girls to Tormenta's gang was all his idea? Funny, I heard you and that scumbag Tito discussing it in your office long before I heard from Fernando."

"You spied on me?"

The shock in his voice was hysterical. I laughed; it sounded evil. Good, the devil take him.

"I'd leave Mexico if I were you, Anibal. You'll be in prison before too long if you stay here."

"Jade, let me in. I'll explain everything. I wasn't selling you!"

"And not giving my dog to that horrid rapist?"

"What did he do to you, Jade? He wasn't supposed—"

"Oh! So you admit it. Okay, come on in, but be aware I'm calling the authorities," I said and started toward the gate.

"No, no, Jade! Please. It's not what you think."

The front door slammed and I turned to see Quint and the hand cannon strolling down the walkway. "Look, Dad, we've got a visitor."

"I heard you from the kitchen. The entire neighborhood can hear you, JadeAnne. Keep your voice down. If you and Aguirre want to bicker, let him in."

"Thank you, Mr. Quint. Jade, will you please let me in?"

Quint pursed his lips as though he'd tasted something disgusting. I suppose he had. A car roared down the street farting out clouds of exhaust and making a racket. I missed Quint's reply. It sounded something like he'd rather tear him limb from limb.

Anibal whined. "I came in good faith. To apologize and explain what happened," he said and dropped his voice. "I was undercover. I can't talk about it in the street, Jade. Let me in."

Quint raised the gun. "You don't have the right to make demands here,

Aguirre. JadeAnne, what do you want to do with him?"

"Shoot him in the nuts."

Like a rapper, he cupped his crotch with one hand and waved the other back and forth. "She's crazy! No! I'll leave, I'll leave."

I looked at Quint and we cackled in hilarity. "Do it, Dad,.. said.

Anibal dropped to the ground and curled into a fetal position.

"What a baby," I said to Quint as he stepped next to me.

He lowered his voice. "Let him in. We'll scare some answers out of him. I'll bet he doesn't know you were in that lobby when he kidnapped his brother. You talk. I'll point the gun and we'll both watch for the tells when he lies."

Quint lowered his gun and blasted a shot into the lawn. Anibal shrank and started shaking. Pepper bounded to the gate, jumping against it and snarling, teeth snapping. Good boy.

I caught Pepper. It appeared Anibal was not armed, but I kept just out of reach. I could hear his whimpers. The tough cartel thug was crying.

"Anibal, my father and I have decided to listen to your story. Get up and stop blubbering, you baby."

He slowly unwound and pulled himself up to standing. "Quint, we better take him to the laundry room. He's wet himself," I said, sneering. "I don't want his pissy bottom touching my furniture."

"I agree, daughter," he said as he unlocked the gate and gestured with the gun for Anibal to come in. "Aguirre, any sudden moves and I'll shoot you. Follow JadeAnne."

I whistled Pepper to my side and we walked to the laundry. I opened the door and stood aside. Anibal entered. Pepper growled and nipped his leg as he passed me. Anibal yelped. Quint followed, the gun to his back. This was better than cop shows on TV.

A folding chair had been pulled up to a card table in the corner. I ran for the chair and centered it in the room under the bare lightbulb and facing the windows. Law and Order Special Victims Unit 101.

"Sit there." I positioned myself so he would have to squint into the bright window behind me. "So what do you want to confess, Anibal Aguirre?" I asked.

"I'm sorry, Jade. I never meant to hurt you."

"Just wanted to sell me. Simple transaction, right? No one hurt, everyone goes home richer."

"Believe what you want. It wasn't supposed to happen like it did."

Quint interjected, his voice sounding disgusted. "So how *was it* supposed to go down?"

"I've been undercover for over a year, investigating smuggling routes. I'd been following the money coming back to Mexico and put it together: guns and money travel together south. They go all over the country, but a lion's share comes to D.F, and Cuernavaca. I have connections here, my superiors assigned me to Mexico to find out who's getting the money. It's a no-brainer. The government is here. These cartels can't get away with their activities without help from high places. Who do you think came to mind? My esteemed brother. But the trail dead-ended. I couldn't find any indication he was on the take and started looking into the northbound smuggling. I found the Sinaloans fighting over the border plazas with the Gulf Cartel and taking over from the Arellano-Felix brothers in Tijuana. I decided to stay in the capital and investigate the Mexico City plaza. Who runs it and what they're smuggling. What I found was a web of human trafficking, mostly organized through the Beltran–Levya Organization. BLO is an affiliate of the Sinaloa Cartel, but I predict a split soon. Chapo wants it all."

"So what does this fairy story have to do with me?" I asked.

"Through DEA, yes, I am a DEA agent with a *placa—*"

Quint sprang in front of me, pointing his gun at Anibal. "Hands in the air, asshole!"

Anibal's hands shot up. "No! My badge, I'm getting my badge."

"Slow, *cabrón.*"

Anibal produced a badge. I took it and shrugged. It looked real to me. I tossed it to Quint. Ani continued his story.

"The truth, Jade. Not a story. I became acquainted with Guillermo Lobo, BLO's stateside recruiter and his sidekick, Edgar Santos. You remember The Saint, Jade? It turns out he's my father's wife's godson, the nasty woman I call Aunt Lidia. I thought Lobo ran the show, but I've learned she's the big boss."

Quint straightened out of his slouch. "You're certain of this? Lidia Sotomayor is working for the BLO?"

"You got it, man," Anibal said, his face contorting into something evil. "And I'm going to take her down."

Quint and I exchanged knowing looks. This confirmed it. BL Enterprises—a BLO operation.

"By selling American girls to the Zetas?" I asked.

"That's the thing, Jade, If you get an outfit, you can be a trafficker, too," Anibal retorted.

"Oh, ha-ha, you shit. You think you're some sort of cowboy?"

Quint loomed over Anibal, grinding his fist into his palm. "Aguirre, I'm not sure what you mean by that. I want to know how you knew about the BLO safe-house and who opened fire."

Ani flinched almost imperceptibly. "I'm a buyer of girls for an Arab market, or so they believe. I went to the safe-house to inspect the merchandise and make a deal. Then I organized a raid on the house to clear it of people, and went back with JadeAnne to get the kids. Secret DEA operation. I didn't count on BLO people across the street."

I lurched toward Anibal. Quint blocked my path. "That's a lie! He didn't know there were kids in the house. *I* heard them. *I* figured out how to find them. That house belongs to Lidia. Both the Pedrigal houses do. But you knew that, didn't you?" I said. "The bread truck, the helicopter, the shootout. It was all your Zeta buddies, wasn't it." I wasn't asking a question.

He sneered. "You talking crazy, girl. I don't know who was shooting, but my assets come through your taxes paid to the good ol' U. S. of A."

"Why doesn't the DEA have any record of sending out a helicopter? Moreover, no one has information on the kids you loaded onto that helicopter. I think you, the American girls, and JadeAnne were supposed to be on the helicopter too, and your associates shot up the house to deflect from what really happened. But you and the girls weren't on that helicopter," Quint said.

"I don't know what you're insinuating, Mr. Quint. The copter came from Mexico and the kids were delivered to the appropriate child services agency. The DEA doesn't send helicopters into Mexico because I call. It's arranged through our reciprocal agencies."

"You're full of shit, Anibal," I said.

"Ask Polo. He knows how it's done and he knows I'm with the DEA."

"Senator Aguirre had no knowledge of your operation and cannot find out where the children were taken. But I listened when you agreed to sell me to Cárdenas. He's Z2, isn't he? A founding member of that group. I'm betting that's what's really going on here. You're aiding the Zetas to take over the *Distrito Federal* plaza. To get back at your family. What do you have to say about that?" It was all falling into place. I pursed my lips. Anibal's story smelled of hell.

His jaw tightened as he clamped down on his teeth, then

blew out a breath, jaw, barely perceptible, sawing back and forth. He had a tell. I'd watched his face throughout the interview in the dull shaft of light beaming down from the fixture. I'd heard the truth from him and I'd heard lies. Now I could read the lies. He did it every time. But ask him if he loved Lura? He'd say yes—no jaw. How had I missed that before? Had Quint seen it?

"You're hypothesizing. It's all BS," he said, shaking his jaw. "Polo is lying to protect his mother. He always does."

No shaking when he spoke of Polo. He believed his own words. I was likely to believe that, too.

"You misunderstood the conversation you overheard. What happened to you was your own fault. I had nothing to do with it." Again, near invisible jaw movement.

"How did you happen to find me at the dog kennel if you weren't part of it?"

"I called Torrens. Santos and he were buddies from childhood. They used the kennels for transshipments. He gloated that you'd chosen him, not me. He sounded like a madman. I came as fast as I could."

"You could have called the police."

"I was frantic, out of my mind. After what happened at my house, I knew I had to rescue you. That's all I could think of." Saw, saw, saw.

"Liar. I saw your Zeta pals throw you in the SUV. Window dressing? Or are they pissed at the *pinche* little DEA snitch for a deal gone bad?"

Anibal's mouth dropped open. I'd hit a nerve.

"You didn't know I'd seen that? I saw a lot more too. Your buddy drugged and raped me."

He hung his head and mumbled something.

Quint growled. "What was that, man? I can't quite hear you."

He looked up at me, pain furrowing his brow. "I am so sorry."

129

"Sorry ain't gonna cut it, pal," Quint said, lunging toward Anibal and whacking him across his jaw with the back of his hand.

I jumped in front of him. "Stop! Quint, back off."

"I want to hurt this weasel."

"So do I. So do I. But Dad, let's do it legally. You can take him back to the States and bust him good, can't you? I want him to suffer long and hard." My voice had turned to ice even as pure hot hatred toward this scumbag bubbled up from deep inside.

"Better to keep him in a penitentiary here. He can be with all his buddies, and all of his enemies. What will Lobo and Santos say when they find out Anibal was behind losing that shipment of kids in the safe-house? Eh, Aguirre? You'll be toast."

"Jade he can't do that. Don't let him—"

"Hey, asshole, I'm not going to bust you. I'm calling your bro'. It'll make his day." Quint handed me the revolver and flashed his phone at Anibal before punching some numbers. I trained the gun on Anibal's crotch.

"I've change my mind. I'd rather have the delight of seeing you writhe," I said to my captive. "Dad, if he's in jail, we can't see the pain. I'll just shoot him where it will hurt most. We can have Bruno haul him off somewhere to bleed out. Prison is too good for him."

"We don't need to do anything," Quint said. "I heard Anibal's buddies are coming for him. He got paid for you and the girls—that's the buzz on the street."

Anibal blanched. He squirmed, teeth grinding. "What the fuck are you talking about, old man? Whatever you heard is a bunch of bull. I had nothing to do with what happened at Torrens'. I went to save them. Jade, please, you have to believe me."

"Sheesh! Just listen to him." His jaw belied his words. "Then who took those girls to Torrens? They were in our care—my care—and you took them to a whorehouse? Then what did you do?" I watched his eyes light up. I bet this was going to be good.

"I told you, I needed somewhere safe for them while you got patched up. I was going back to get them," he said, jaw vibrating. "Take them to the Embassy like you said. When I got back, they were gone. It was Consuelo. She did it."

Quint lunged at him growling. "Did what, Aguirre?"

Anibal jumped to his feet, fists swinging. Quint ducked and shoved him back onto the chair.

I asked, "Then why are your Zeta pals coming to you for the money?"

"What are you talking about? I'm investigating those men. Undercover," Anibal said, his voice unsteady from all the jaw scraping.

"And put you up to kidnapping the senator?"

His mouth went hard. Anibal radiated a hint of satisfaction with an evil glint in his eye. What was going on?

"You two are fishing. You don't have anything on me." He laughed a belly laugh that rocked the chair and devolved into a fit of coughing. "Fools. You're going after the wrong Aguirre."

"You deny visiting the senator on Friday and dragging him out of his building with a hood over his head?" I asked. "Was it you or the other thug who clocked the guard? They found him, you know. That will be two witnesses."

"I always thought you were a little melodramatic, JadeAnne. You should have gone home after Lura died," he jeered. "You couldn't keep away from me, could you? Too bad I wasn't that into you. Now you'd do anything to discredit me and burn my cover. No one will believe you."

"I was there. I saw you drag Polo out of the building. I saw the other man get shot, and you run off after firing on someone."

Quint closed in, put the gun to Anibal's forehead. "I was

parked at the corner when you dragged Aguirre out of the building. I shot over your head and you pulled, what, an Uzi? And wasted your pal, you little shit. But you had to leave your prize. Aguirre would never have given you money."

Anibal looked down the barrel of Quint's gun and stopped grinding his jaw. "Okay. They wanted to kidnap Polo to extort a ransom. Consuelo set it up. She lost her commission on the girls. She's the one who took them to Torrens. She and her Zeta contacts think I'm with them, but it's all my investigation. Without your interference, Jade, I'd have made my case. It was coming together. I had them. The BLO. The Zetas, and above all, I had Lidia Sotomayor. You ruined it, bitch," he said, and spit a thick loogie onto my arm. But again the jaw twitched. I wondered what part of this was the lie as I wiped the spit onto my shorts.

"JadeAnne, go get Lily. She can tell us who took her to Torrens."

Now real fear showed on his face. Anibal was going to be accused by his victim. I backed out of the room.

I found Lily playing with the puppies under the watchful eye of Mrs. P. What was she doing here on Sunday? Or at all. Hadn't Quint fired her? Well, no matter. Lily was going to tell her story.

"Is he gone? What did he want?"

She looked at me and must have read my face.

"You won't let him near me will you?"

"Lily, It's time to tell what happened. I want you to come to the laundry room with me and recount how you got to the dog kennel. Señora Pérez, you come too. I want you to hear what the woman you report to does."

Lily jumped off the floor and dashed behind the housekeeper. I was happy she'd bonded and found motherly comfort after her ordeal, but why did it have to be a woman who worked for the enemy? The "she devil," as I was beginning to think of Lidia.

"I'm sorry honey, but Anibal must cooperate with us if we are to catch and prosecute the people behind this trafficking ring. You've done so well giving us valuable information, please come finish the story and we'll take care of getting you your justice."

"No! You can't make me see that man. Mrs. P, don't let JadeAnne take me. Please."

"*Sí... I... eso tiempo...* the *señorita es correcto*. We go together. *Ven*," the housekeeper said, stumbling through her Pidgeon English and pushing Lily toward the back door. *"¿Porque la lavandaría?"* she asked me.

"We aren't letting scum like that into our home, Mrs. P."

She nodded and we started down the stairs, Maya and the pups following.

I stopped Lily at the door. I would have to trust the housekeeper. "Stand here, Lily. Don't come inside. If Anibal gets loose, you and Mrs. P run into the house and lock the doors. Don't stop for the puppies. Just go in."

"He can get loose?"

"Not with Quint's gun held on him. I'm going inside, and when I say, you tell us what happened from the time Anibal took you to Consuelo's."

"Consuelo?"

"The fat redhead with the whorehouse. Just wait one second," I said, and stepped back into the room. "Quint, move aside. Let Lily see Anibal."

He moved and I heard a squeak from the doorway.

"You're okay, Lily. See? Quint has his weapon."

Quint held the gun up then trained it back onto Anibal.

"Quint, give me your phone. It records, right?"

"It's recording now."

"Great. Did you hear that, Lily? Your statement is being recorded. For the record, I am JadeAnne Stone. It is," I looked at my watch, "10:42 in the morning. I, Jackman

Quint, Anibal Aguirre, Lily Flynn, and Pilar Olinda Pérez are in the laundry room at 1060 Amores Del Valle. Lily, please tell us what happened to you on August 10th of this year."

Lily's lip quavered. "I'm afraid, Jade," she said in a small voice.

"It's okay, Lily. Nothing more can hurt you. Mrs. Pérez, please help Lily," I said. I heard the murmuring as she encouraged Lily to talk.

There was a long silence, then Lily began. "I didn't know what day it was. We were in L.A. meeting a man who was going to get me and Evie modeling jobs and maybe into the movies, but he drugged us and took us to a house." She paused, reddening and looking down. Mumbling she added, "A mean woman made us take our clothes off and put on flimsy pajamas, then we were pushed into a van with some other kids and we drove and drove. It was dark and no one spoke English, and we didn't know where we were or why kids had no clothes and then they finally stopped and pushed us out and made us go through a tunnel, and then we were all in a cave and locked in." She shuddered as tears streamed down her cheeks.

Mrs. P held her close and stroked her hair. The basement filled with tension until I broke the silence. "Lily, who was the mean woman? American? What happened next?"

She hiccupped and blew her nose on a tissue the housekeeper handed her. "I dunno, I so tired I really didn't look at her. In the cave, there were around twenty kids and no food or water. It got hotter and hotter and no one could breathe and there was no bathroom and I thought we were going to die."

Her sobs started again. We waited several minutes before she was able to go on.

"Me and another girl about my age took turns banging on a metal pipe with one of the kids' shoes. We banged and banged but no one came. Then after a long time, JadeAnne and *that man*," she pointed at Anibal, her tears a sheet of despair, "came and took us out. She promised me and Evie she'd get us home. But we were so scared and we didn't want to go home because Eddy would rape us. My ten year old sister!"

Again Lily was overcome with sobs, but this time, it was grief.

Unbidden, she continued. "But then the kids flew away on a helicopter and then they started shooting and the house was on fire and we cut our feet and JadeAnne got shot. He," she pointed at Anibal again, "took JadeAnne to a clinic and took me an' Evie to a pretty house and a woman locked us in a tiny room. A girl in a nightgown came with water and food and a lot later *that man* came back and took us in a black van to the dog kennel. It was dark. The man there shoved us into a pen and locked the door. We were there for two more days because it got light in the kennel in the day."

"Which man do you mean?" I asked.

"Him, Ani-b-bal," she whispered, pointing at our prisoner.

Anibal lurched from the chair shouting, "Lies! It's all lies! I—" Quint smacked him across the face and pointed his gun into his chin. Anibal slumped back onto the chair.

I continued. "What happened in the kennel?"

"The dog man brought us tacos and soda. After the food we got sleepy and sick and he took me to another place and I don't remember really. But later, he took Evie and she remembered what he did to her."

By now, Lily was shaking. What would reliving her terror and degradation do to her?

"Then *he* and two other men came and we had to t-take off our nightgowns and they looked at us and t-touched us and even looked at our teeth. He talked about us as if we weren't even there. I knew it was about us even though it was in Spanish. He held my arms away from me so the men could look at me. And he let them touch my sister." Lily stopped speaking and slumped into Mrs. P.

Backlit, I couldn't see Mrs. P's expression but the air seemed to crackle around her, charged. I remembered her kindness when I'd been shot—the first time. In her heart, Mrs. P was a caring woman, a nurse. Maybe we could use her anger.

"JadeAnne, do you believe a lying little whore or me, the man who saved you from being killed on the pier?"

Anibal's voice was quiet, steady, conversational even. He used that soft, rational, vibe I'd been fooled by before. My hands balled. I felt sick and I burned in shame for being taken in by such a smooth operator. The man quivering in front of me had lured me in in order to sell me to the highest bidder. Along with two children. Little Evie was only ten. I felt the tears steam down my cheeks.

"I'm going to crush you, Anibal Aguirre. As God is my witness, I will see you rot in Hell." I worked up a huge wad of saliva and spit it into his face. "Sick. Sick fuck—that's you."

This time I lunged and planted my fist into his face. The room swam awash in black and red.

"For Chrissake Quint, get this woman off of me! I've told you what I know. It's Lidia and Consuelo!" he cried.

I lunged again but Quint caught me and Anibal flew out of the chair. Quint slammed the butt of his gun into the back of his head and he crumpled onto the linoleum floor whimpering, "You're wrong. It's them, not me. It's them."

I caught my breath and stopped fighting against my father. He loosened his grip and I pulled back, darting to Anibal on the floor. A quick glance to the door told me Mrs. P had pulled Lily away. I slammed a sharp kick into his back and fled. Let Quint figure it out from here.

Chapter 14

¡Fiesta, Fiesta! Yo Quiero Más Fiesta

Pepper and I stormed up the stairs; I heard Lily sobbing in her room and Mrs. P trying to soothe her. Now the story was coming out, and the girl couldn't dam the flood. I didn't want to know the rest. The traffickers turned my stomach. Sick abusers of women. These weren't even women. Anibal was involved in trafficking little girls and boys. He and his pals saw these people—me too—as commodities to trade. I felt filthy. I'd slept with that creep. How could I make such poor choices? My ex, Dex? He was a prince compared to the people I'd met as a result of one simple missing persons case. I curled into a ball on my bed, eyes leaking hot tears.

Pepper, not one to tolerate crying, cuddled next to me and licked the salt off my face until I couldn't stand the dog slobber or the taint of rape and trafficking clinging to me like smoke. I had a party to attend and I needed the stink to come off. But was I making another terrible blunder? Fernando had trained Dylan's dogs—and I was lousy at picking men.

"Buck up, Stone," I counseled myself. I didn't want

to adopt a paranoid attitude, but maybe Quint was right. Dylan did pop up every time I went to the park, and he had originally approached me. Could he be part of this ring? A kind doctor, taking care of damaged girls? Kidnapping them and taking them to Torrens' dog training kennels. Didn't he say he'd saved almost enough to buy a house? Did ER doctors make all that much? I didn't know. If he was buddies with Fernando, did he also know Anibal? Was I walking into a trap? I wished I could discuss it with Quint, but he'd forbidden me to go. And what if Dylan was exactly what he claimed to be? When we were together he felt so safe, so kind. What if he really was a sweet, honorable man? Deep down, I wanted to go to his dad's party. How could I find out if it was legit?

Luckily the shower ran hot and strong. I turned it off as the hot water ran out. I was conflicted; the day's interrogation had disgusted and scared me. Maybe I was putting that onto an innocent man. Dylan had said they'd be celebrating in the yard. Maybe I could find a way to see in before I went in? If it was a family, his mom and dad, grandmother, brothers and wives and kids, the crew he'd detailed for me, what harm would it be if Pepper and I went? Maybe I should carry my gun.

"Oh my God, just listen to me, Pepper. A lot of maybes. I'm going to take a gun to a birthday party?"

It was all I could do to go back to the laundry room to iron my sundress. I'd picked the jungle print sundress because it was calf-length and sufficiently modest. With my high-heeled sandals, I'd look smart but not too sexy. I'd noticed many Mexican women loved to show cleavage, but I wouldn't tantalize anyone today. Anyway, I didn't really have a cleavage, I thought as I crept down the stairs to the main floor. My big problem was, how would I get past the kitchen? I guess I could just tell the truth. I wanted to put on a clean, ironed dress because I felt so filthy.

It didn't matter after all. No one was in the kitchen; no one stopped me on the stairs. The laundry room door stood open but the chair had been folded and leaned against the back wall. Anibal was gone. A faint sweaty odor lingered in the basement air and I tensed, reminded of his vitriol and lies. I pulled out the ironing board from its cupboard and arranged my dress over it after plugging in the iron. I found a sprayer bottle next to the sink, filled it, and sprayed the dress. As I performed these familiar tasks, I relaxed. Why was I so worried? Anibal had been a bad choice, but really, "Hasn't all this brought me to my real father? And now I'm going to get to know a lovely, gentle man, maybe someone I could eventually care about. Isn't this normal and good?" I asked Pepper, who lay in the doorway soaking up the sun. He woofed, looking at me with adoring dog eyes.

Once I finished dressing and put on my makeup, I tackled taming my hair. It was a mess since I'd gotten back from the hospital. Maybe braids today? Nothing I tried pleased me. I realized I was stalling, that little ball of fear stuck in my gut like a limpet on a tidal rock. I had to get moving. I was due already and if I didn't leave now, I'd miss the *pozole*. I ran the brush through my hair and realized it had grown about an inch. It would be just fine hanging down my back. Dylan could run his fingers through it while we danced. A shiver ran through me.

I slipped on my running shoes, gathered the rest of my things, including the gun and my heels, into a blue shoulder bag and stuck my head out my door. The coast looked clear, so I sprinted to the stairs, Pepper beating me as usual. We thundered down to the landing where I poked my head into the hall. Again, no one in sight. We raced down to ground floor and pushed outside into the sunlight. I checked my watch. I had fifteen minutes to get across the *colonia* before dinner was served. But first I had to call Lily. Someone needed to know where I was. I left a message.

"Come on Peppi, we need to hoof it."

I keyed open the gate and let it slam behind us. We jogged together south on Amores, crossing street after street until we came to Dylan's and turned right.

We arrived with five minutes to catch our breath and cool down. I sat on the curb to switch out my shoes in front of a sweet pink stucco house with a tiled roof. The lush, well-tended garden overflowed its beds and stretched around the house to a backyard. I followed the music and laughter, definitely a party going on, and I was staking my life on the notion creepy human traffickers didn't engage *mariachi* bands and serve *pozole* in their backyards on Sunday afternoons. I peered along the side of the house to see who might be partying back there. If they looked like tattooed thugs, I'd go home, although, based on looks, I knew I wouldn't be able to tell bad guys. Anibal, case in point. What I saw were several little girls in party dresses as they rushed around the house giggling while two boys chased them, squirting streams of water everywhere but on the girls from their water rifles. The boys looked slicked down and scrubbed, and delighted to chase the girls. I stepped up to the gate.

Dylan smiling, handsome in blue slacks and an open collared shirt, rushed from the midst of the crowd to greet me. Several heads turned my way.

I'd only ever seen him in running shorts. He cleaned up well and I could see from his expression he wasn't worried about my hair.

"¡*Bienvenidos, amiga!* Everybody, JadeAnne is here!" He opened the gate wide and ushered me in.

"You look beautiful, JadeAnne. My family is excited to meet you. Mami can't talk about anything else." He patted Pepper and took my hand to lead me into the festivities. "Poor Papi has almost been forgotten in the anticipation to meet my American girlfriend." He grinned and his face lit up.

That was something I loved about Mexican men. They had a sweetness about them, delighting in their families, their girlfriends, their friends, and didn't seem to have any problem showing their love.

"I'm not too late, am I?"

"Not at all. We've barely gotten started. Papi is happy with his favorite local mariachis serenading him. Everyone is getting drinks and the kids are starting to run wild."

He laughed as the little herd galloped through again, this time the girls squirting the boys. They craned to look at me, but didn't stop.

Dylan watched after the children and said in a wistful voice, "I always loved the parties when I got together with my cousins. We had a ball. The new generation is the same."

We stepped into a deep yard crisscrossed with cut paper streamers and dotted with round tables fitted with colorful umbrellas. Toward the back wall an elaborate barbeque and kitchen set-up steamed and smoked with tantalizing scents. A bartender poured drinks on a ping pong table and two tubs of ice held beer and *refrescos*. Servers wandered the crowd of at least fifty revelers with trays of what looked delicious. My stomach growled.

"Let me introduce you to Papi and Mami, and my sister." He grabbed a dark-haired woman's elbow and began introductions.

"Baez, this is my friend JadeAnne Stone visiting from California. JadeAnne, my oldest sibling, Baez," he said. A slim dark haired woman smiled as Dylan reached out to grab a tall, bearded man talking to one of the children and yanked him into our little circle, "and Pedro, my brother-in-law. Baez and Pedro are responsible for several of the kids." He waved a hand that encompassed most of the guests. Baez and Pedro stepped back in unison when Pepper poked his head around my skirt.

"Hi, how are you? I'm so glad to meet you both," I said and shook hands. "This is Pepper." Pepper, of course sat down and offered a paw to each of them.

"How cute. Pedro isn't that adorable? He doesn't bite or anything, does he?"

"Not at all. He loves kids. Watch this: Pepper, play with the kids," I said in English. "You play."

Pepper grinned up at me and trotted into the thick of

the children's game. The kids scattered back several feet, but Pepper lay down, madly wagged his tail and trumpeted an invitation. The boldest kids approached him, and he rolled onto his back grinning and wagging. In moments, the gaggle of children flocked around to pet him.

Dylan continued to steer me through the party, stopping to introduce aunts and uncles, cousins, cousins, and more cousins. We chatted with several key family members, but mostly just moved through the crowd saying hi. Pepper, in the meantime, jumped into the game of chase. I'd hear a bunch of boys calling him and when he'd run to them, they'd run away. Pepper, no mental slouch, realized he could chase them, but as soon as they turned the corner, he could run the other direction and catch them on the other side of the house. Everyone looked delighted with the game.

The mariachi band had taken a break, and a group of musicians, which Dylan pointed out as his younger brother, Seeger, and his buddies, took over. They tuned up and launched into a set of dance music. I guessed they covered popular tunes and loved oldies. Everyone sang along and the patio crowded with two-stepping couples, the old people down to the kids. One of the little girls got Pepper to get out there and hop around.

"Shall we?" Dylan said.

I grinned up at him." I thought you'd never ask."

The tune was an oldie I vaguely recognized. Something about chocolate. We two-stepped, dipped, and rocked around the circle with the other dancers until a swarthy, white-haired man cut in. Dylan relinquished my hand to his rival, and bowed out, calling over his shoulder, "JadeAnne, meet the birthday boy, Eladio Porras. Papi, this is my friend JadeAnne Stone."

"Happy birthday, señor. What a wonderful day you're having."

"It is truly a perfect day to become another year older," he said, his eyes twinkling down over me.

"So you turned forty today?" I joked.

"Ay, were I to see fifty again! Today is my sixty-seventh birthday."

"I don't believe that. You couldn't be a day over fifty-five." I leaned back and looked at Eladio. He was tall, lean, well-muscled, and although his skin had seen plenty of sun, it appeared firm and plump. Sure, he had plenty of lines and a few grooves, but sixty-seven? No way.

Dylan bumped into us, dancing with an older woman. "Papi, let's trade partners. I can see if I don't reclaim my date, I'll lose her to you, and Mami will get mad."

The woman laughed. Dylan spun her out into Eladio's arms as he drew me into his. "JadeAnne, this is my mother, Gabriella, the crazy woman who loves American folk music and named us after folk icons."

Gabriella, a diminutive woman with short corkscrew curls under a floppy sun hat. smiled at me, her eyes carrying the same twinkle as Eladio's. "Welcome to our home. It's a pleasure to meet my children's friends. I know how Dylan has missed his friends from California. Our home is yours," she said, before Eladio spun her in another direction.

I could see where the Porras kids got their looks. All

of them were tall and handsome with refined features and wavy dark hair. All radiated good humor and kind intentions. I liked this group already. And no one had tattoos or gangbanger pants.

The band played another couple of tunes and took a break. Dylan steered me through the crowd of well-wishers toward a makeshift bar, grabbed a couple of Victorias, and held a chair out for me at a table planted with several people I had yet to meet. I smiled and said "hi" as I plunked into my seat.

Dylan snatched a tray of little quesadillas from a waiter and straddled the chair next to me as he slid the *botanas* onto the table and grabbed his beer. "Everyone, this is the lovely JadeAnne Stone from Sausalito, California, mother to that giant German shepherd. I'm hoping to convince her to stay in Mexico when her work here is done."

I threw up my hands, laughing. "This is news to me."

"JadeAnne, let me present brother number one, Guthrie, and wife Conchita—they're the ones who produced those sub-humans amusing your dog."

Everyone laughed, as one of the sub-humans in question stormed by waving his light saber. Guthrie shook my hand, and Conchita murmured something I didn't catch. Next to Conchita, a tiny, wrinkled apple doll beamed and cackled as she tried to greet me through clacking false teeth. Eladio's sister, *Tía* Eugenia, who everyone proudly said had turned ninety-two on her last birthday. She pointed a twig at a withered cowboy lounging at the bar on his cane, *Tío* Sergio only eighty-eight. Her 'younger man' she called him. Next to Tía Eugenia, another old lady sat straight as a plank, mysterious behind big tortoise shell sunglasses. Great Aunt Judith on Gabriella's side. The third crone looked like the clone of Great Aunt Judith and turned out to be Dylan's grandmother, Gabriella's mother, Frida Montero. In fact, Frida and Judith were twins and greeted me in unison, welcoming me to the party.

We'd gone around the table but for a twenty-something woman who'd just sat down next to me. She was a pretty blue-eyed blonde with long tresses waving over her shoulders. She wore a chic sundress cut from traditionally embroidered Mexican cloth. I reached to shake. "Hi, I'm JadeAnne."

"Dafne," she said, and took my hand. She had a wild, but perfect manicure with what looked like Chinese waterfalls in silver over dragon purple that clashed with her cherry red ruffles. She looked amazing.

"Love the nails," I said, sliding a glance at my toes.

"I've got a girl in Condesa who is masterful at painting the decorations. She's an artist. Asian, tiny slender hands. She can paint the smallest nails." She looked at me. Could she tell I'm Vietnamese? "She doesn't speak much Spanish though. Probably less English."

"I don't need to talk to her, but I could sure use a manicure."

"How do you like Mexico?"

"A fascinating country. I haven't really done much here in the city yet," I said. That is, if you discount being shot at, kidnapped, nearly burned up, drugged, raped, spending time in a hospital, and going to a funeral, not doing much. I tried to keep my face neutral and gripped my hands in my lap to calm the shaking that still wracked me when I thought of the dog kennels.

Dafne's expression said she'd caught my reaction. She was sharp.

"What do you do here? Are you married?" she asked, her English sounding slightly British.

Seeger leaned over her and planted a big kiss on her forehead. "Dafne isn't yet, but if she'd say yes, we'd change that in a hurry."

"Seeger!" she squealed, giggling. "I haven't made up my mind about this crazy family. Watch out, JadeAnne. They're a bunch of lunatics." She dimpled at Seeger and kissed his nose. "Now, go get me another drink while I warn off this unsuspecting innocent."

The *tías* and grandmother twittered behind painted fans. Seeger trotted off.

"*Pues*, a family of *locos*? Should I run now?" I joked.

"Hold off until the party is over. Gabriella's *pozole* is the best this side of anywhere," Dafne said.

"I'm looking forward to the experience. Dylan lured me with tales of delicious food. What do you do?"

"I finished my MBA last year and the family has me training to take over daily operations of our real estate holdings. Property management mostly. We own properties here in the city and its environs and manage leases, sales, maintenance—you know— pretty normal office stuff. The lawyers do all the buying and selling. Our office is in Condesa and I oversee about thirty people, but not the lawyers, of course, as they're too high and mighty for the likes of an MBA." She made a face and giggled. Was that *Lawyers Guns and Money,* she was humming?

Dafne reminded me of Lura, and I felt both sad and oddly lightened. "You remind me of my friend who died. I came for the funeral."

"Here?"

"Yeah, the service was held at the cathedral in Coyoacan."

"That's such a pretty church. I'm sorry you had to come for such a sad reason. What happened. Did she die in Mexico?"

"Yeah, she died in an accident at a pier."

"Boating. I bet some drunk macho was at the wheel. Were the two of you on vacation?"

"Some macho was definitely at the wheel, but it wasn't a boating accident. They said we got in the way of a turf war."

Dafne nodded slowly, thinking. "Unfortunately, that's all too common these days. Did you find out which cartels were at it? Where did it happen?"

"Zihua."

"Beltran-Leyva and Sinaloa? I heard they're splitting. It might be too far west for Zetas, but that crew is the worst, and watch out, they're going to make a big play for power. I predict Sinaloa is going to defeat the Gulf and the Zetas will spin the militia off—"

"Are you airing our laundry to the tourists, Dafne? Don't scare her. She'll go home and tell everyone she knows how violent and drug crazed we are here." Seeger handed Dafne a poisonous looking pink cocktail. He turned to me. "I'm sorry for my obsessed girlfriend. It's all she talks about. Really, we're not all drug kingpins here."

"It's okay, Seeger. I'm not going to give Mexico a bad rap," I said, my face arranged into my most innocent expression. "I'm over the moon with the arts and crafts. The jewelry!"

"Yeah. We've kept many of our traditional crafts and styles alive," Dafne said.

"Unlike in the U.S. where if it's old it's considered bad and discarded much too often."

"I want JadeAnne to tell us why her friend's funeral was here instead of California," Dafne said.

"Isn't that kind of nosey, Daf?" Dylan asked.

"Not at all," I replied. "She's vetting me, just like I'd do with her in the reverse case. "I drove down to find a missing person; I'm an owner of an investigation agency in California. She was a Mexican-American, the wife of a banker. Her trail went cold in Ixtapa. At Christine's, if you know it."

Dylan's eyebrows jumped up. I'd forgotten he had no idea what I did or why I came to Mexico. This Dafne had a way of pulling information out of me. Or was it the margaritas? I grabbed a fresh one off the tray proffered by a circulating waiter.

Dafne's voice took on an edge. "An investigator, how exciting," she said. "We love Christine's. At the Crystal. Seeg, we should take a long weekend and have some fun. You guys come too," she said, her warm smile returning. "Sorry, did you find her?"

"I did. She is the cousin of a senator from Michoacán and she was simply visiting. Unfortunately, he was the target of an attack. The family held her funeral here as they are from the *Distrito*. At least part of the family is. The rest came down from California."

"I knew it, that's Aguirre, the loudest voice against organized crime at Los Pinos. Hypocrite," Dafne pronounced.

"I've looked into him as you can imagine," I said.

Seeger leaned in close to me. "Dafne doesn't need to imagine. She sidelines both as a hostage negotiator and a detective. Property management is dangerous in Mexico City," he said, a frown on his face.

I guessed Seeger opposed Dafne's sideline. "Dafne, is this true?" I whispered.

"Yes, but we don't like to broadcast my business to the family." She shot her eyes toward the old ladies.

"Yeah, I understand. My family thinks I'm the agency's office manager, of course that means they browbeat me for wasting my degree."

Seeger left the table with a big show of kissing Dafne. The band struck up the next set. The crones bobbed and tapped and flittered their fans. Dylan took my hand. We moved onto the dance floor again. I loved twirling in his arms. He was a good dancer. His two-step had rhythm—he could salsa, cumbia and killed the mambo—a ridiculous dance, but fun anyway. I, of course, was only a good follower. I didn't know how to do most of 'em, but we got envious stares from the onlookers.

I was having so much fun, I'd forgotten my poor dog and scanned the yard for him between songs. Poor Pepper, indeed. He and four little girls were in the corner under a low hanging bush having tea with their dolls. Pepper wore a tiny flowered sunhat tied around his big head with a satin ribbon. I laughed. He seemed to be enjoying himself. Perhaps the plate of mini tamales took the sting out of girly dress-up? He'd tell me later.

Another tune ended and the crowd clapped. Dylan escorted me back to the table and he, Baez, and Guthrie joined Seeger on the stage. Several of the cousins hustled a table out in front, and the grandchildren escorted Eladio and Gabriella to it. It was late enough that the sun slanted through the trees casting patchy shadows over the patio and cooling the temperature.

The party hushed expectantly. A couple of men came in with piles of wrapped gifts and set them down in front of the microphones. Seeger opened the ceremony with a welcome and gratitude for having such an old SOB for a dad and the usual remarks kids make to celebrate their parent's milestones. Baez took over and told heartwarming stories of growing up with Eladio. Guthrie turned out to be a true comedian, ripping off one joke after the next until the crowd, especially his parents, held their sides from laughing. Last came Dylan.

"You all know I was the first mistake of the family. I don't think Mami or Papi thought there would be any more kids, but, surprise! Along came the real mistake, Seeger, and blew my whole act!" The crowd hooted. "But I can't really complain. I couldn't have asked for a more loving or wacky family. From a mother who named us after folk singers—because she can't carry a tune even in a tortilla towel—" he said, and paused for the roar of laughter he knew would come. "To a brilliant, loving father who taught me everything and made me the man and the doctor I am today. This day is yours, Papi, and may there be many, many more like it. Now, let's have our dinner!"

The lids came off the three giant *cazuelas* simmering over the *parilla*, and the yard filled with the delectable aroma of pork and *chile*. I hadn't noticed the clay bowls, plates, and plastic spoons being delivered to the long tables set up beside the barbeque, but now the waiters brought stacks of tortillas folded into towels and placed them on the tables behind the plates. Dishes of shredded cabbage and thin-sliced radishes, salsas, diced onions, and dried oregano leaf were marched out from the house and set up with the tortillas. The guests picked up their bowls and lined up to be served by the two chefs in white coats and puffy chef hats. I loved the drama. Seeger and another guitarist played instrumental renditions of popular songs.

Dylan and I stood in the left-hand line, which turned out to be for the traditional pork *pozole*. A whole pig's head had been cooked for hours in water with onion, hominy- type corn, and chile. Later I learned the head had been removed and the meat stripped from the bone and returned to the pot. I didn't know what the chef's secret was, but the *pozole* tasted rich and meaty, yet nutty and perfectly *picante*, not overbearing. I slurped sips of the steaming stew into my mouth as I spooned the condiments over the top. I just couldn't wait to sit down. I caught Dylan doing the same. In fact, pretty much the entire group started eating the moment they were served.

We walked back to our seats next to the *tías* and

abuilita under the umbrella. We had been joined by
Eladio and Gabriella, and Baez fluttered around trying
to be useful while one of her nieces darted to and from
the condiment tables for more of this or that. Baez
demanded a full stack of steaming tortillas. Other than
Baez's directives, conversation at the table was kept to
mumbled appreciation for Gabriella's *pozole*. The chefs
served her recipe, but she'd started the food cooking
early in the morning. After cooking eight hours or so,
she'd created something heavenly. Would Dylan give
me her recipe? Imagine how I could wow my friends
back home with a party like this.

I smiled at Dylan. "This is amazing. Do you know
how to make it?"

"I told you Mami's *pozole* was better than any
you've tasted, and no, I have no idea how she does it—
except for the pig's head," he added before he took
another bite. He tore off a wedge of tortilla and shoved
that into his mouth, too. "Mami, what's your secret for
this *pozole*?"

"My Dylan wants to become a chef now that he's a
doctor," Gabriella said, mostly to the old ladies, who
tittered, shaking their heads, like Dylan cooking
something was totally unheard of.

"*Mi hijo*, you've never cooked anything in your life.
Why start now?" *Abuela* Frida asked.

Tía Judith said, "The boy is trying to impress his
girl. These modern women expect men to cook and
keep house."

They all laughed, a sound somewhere between
crows cawing and rusted cow bells jangling.

"Where did Dafne go? She seems like a nice

person," I said.

"I don't know. She comes and goes. The traditional lifestyle bores her. She's a business woman."

"So I learned." I lowered my voice. "Is she really is a hostage negotiator?"

"*Sí*, but it's usually because she has to run down some tenant or other for the rent. Some of their properties are in rough neighborhoods. I'm surprised the family lets her go out to collect rents and whatever else she does, but she's been at it for years. Her mother is about to retire, and Dafne will be CEO eventually. From what Seeger has told me, Dafne's father is British and went back to Britain when Daf was small. Dortea had to raise the three kids alone."

Cousins Fernanda and Humberto squeezed in around the table with their baby. Frida took little Aimee from her mother and began fussing over her.

Dylan added, "But here we're never really alone in a Mexican family."

That idea was both horrifying and heartwarming. I wondered what it would be like to come from a large family that actually liked each other. What a concept.

After the *pozole*, some more dancing, and a lot more drinking, the party wound down. A huge sheet cake appeared on the serving table as the waiters circulated with glasses of champagne. Seeger called Eladio to the stage. The band played *Las Mananitas* while the guests sang. I was the only one who didn't know the words.

Eladio beamed beneath the blush turning his ruddy complexion redder, but he was a good sport. At the last note, the band launched into *Happy Birthday* and much of the crowd sang along to that, too. Dylan winked at me. Now I blushed.

The music stopped and Seeger raised his champagne glass. "To the best *papi* a man could have. ¡Happy birthday *Papi*!"

Everyone yelled, "¡*Feliz cumpleaños!*" and tossed back the champagne. Cheers and demands for a speech filled the air. Seeger shoved a wireless mic in his father's hands. Eladio looked like a Chioggia, especially with that little tuft of hair at the top of his round head.

"I don't know why you're making such a big deal of me. It's just another birthday. We all have them." He grinned at his family and friends. "*Gracias a Dios* they keep coming, eh *tío*?"

The crowd roared and Eladio patted down the air with his hands. "I couldn't have envisioned a better life for myself. I'm blessed to have family, friends, and enough put aside that I officially retired last week."

For a beat, the assemblage went silent then someone called out, "You did what, you old fart?" and the cheering and catcalls and good wishes rang out.

As the noise died down, Eladio went on. "I'm lucky to have a boy willing to step into my shoes. Everyone, meet the new president of Porras Enterprises." He gestured to welcome Guthrie to the stage. "My oldest boy, Guthrie will take the helm starting tomorrow. Give him a hand."

We clapped and cheered.

"Don't worry, everyone, I'm still Chairman of the Board," Eladio went on. "Now I only have to go in to work when there's a meeting. I thought I'd take up skydiving." Hoots and head shaking. "*En serio*, Gaby and I are going to do a little traveling before we get too old to see the world."

"You're already old, *abuelo*," one of Baez' teen sons shouted.

"Ah, but you're wrong there, Brandon, I'm a youngster in my new life."

I heard scattered applause and some *no mames*—don't shit me—from the younger men.

"I see that no one is listening to an old man anymore, so how about some cake?"

Everyone clapped until Seeger's rendition of Taj Mahal's *Cakewalk Into Town* drowned it out and we all cake-walked over to grab a piece. And. Oh. My. God. it was a giant *tres leches* cake. My favorite!

Pepper turned up at my side about the time I was eating my third piece of cake and downing yet another glass of champagne—fortifying myself for the tongue-lashing I would get from Quint. Lily knew where I'd gone, but my father had called me ten times according to my call log. He would be livid, but why on earth did I care? Hell, I'm an adult. But maybe I'd be safer if I asked Dylan to drive me home. He must have a car, right?

I was collapsed at a table with a couple of the cousins and some old guys after a long set of eighties dance tunes—all sung in Spanish. *Bette Davis Eyes* and *Girls Just Want to Have Fun, I Need a New Drug,* and *Material Girl*. Although I half recognized the tunes, I'd never have known what they were if Seeger hadn't announced in English for me. The group knocked off a

Material Girl in English and the whole party went dance happy. Now they were singing, *Private Eyes* and heads turned to watch *my* every move.

Dylan popped into my vision, and shouted, "They're playing your song."

I grabbed his hand and dragged him back onto the dance floor to do a jerky eighties dance I remembered from the video, clapping at the right time and belting out the lyrics at the top of my lungs. Yes, too much champagne. Dylan grabbed a mic and held it up for me to sing the next chorus. Oh, well. I'd probably never see any of these people again. I jumped up onto the stage riser.

As the song ended, Seeger introduced me to the multitude as a real-life private eye. My fans rushed me as I stepped off the stage. Lucky Dylan was fit and could keep them at bay.

"Dylan, can you drive me home? It's getting dark. I don't think I should walk."

"Sure, let me get Pedro's keys."

"You don't have a car?" I heard a little disdain in my voice.

"Not here, Jade. Is that a problem?"

"Uh, no. It's just, well everybody has a car, don't they?"

"Sure, mine's in Seeger's garage. Taxis, the metro and *peseras* are safer and cheaper to use than parking and tolls and leaving my car on the street."

"You don't worry about being kidnapped and held hostage in a taxi?"

"No. I don't look like I have anything."

We were pushing through the people flocking

around Eladio as he opened his presents. Many folks had gone home. Only the gift-givers still hung out to see how Eladio liked their offerings. I saw the bottle of very expensive tequila I'd brought and handed over to Dyl as I arrived. He caught my eye and heaved himself up to give me a kiss on my cheek.

"*Gracias,* JadeAnne. We are happy you joined us, and I shall enjoy every drop of this ambrosia," he said, nodding to the bottle.

"Happy birthday, Eladio. May your retirement be the happiest time of your life. Thanks so much for sharing your family and friends with me and my Pepper. We both had a wonderful time."

"You're not taking that dog away are you?" His face looked stern, but the crinkles around his eyes deepened.

"No?" I asked.

"What will those little girls do without their tea party pal?"

We laughed and I thanked him and Gabriella again for their hospitality.

"Papi, Mami, I'm taking Jade home," Dylan said as he steered me away from the party.

Chapter 15

You Will Not Dictate My Life

Pedro drove a family-sized Suburban. It was an older model and coughed before Dylan could encourage the engine to turn over, but it beat walking tipsy in the dark. Pepper couldn't protect me from tripping over uneven pavement or falling into one of the ubiquitous holes in Mexico's sidewalks. This was not the land of tort.

"How'd you like my family? They loved you. Baez told me."

"I had a great time. Dylan, thanks so much for inviting me. Your family is so fun-loving and open. So different from the only other family I know here."

"Senator Aguirre's family?"

My heart thumped hard. "How do you know that?"

"I was sitting next to you while you told Dafne your story. Why?"

I blew out my breath. Stupid me. Of course he was, and I blabbed it all. "I was kind of trying to keep my head down."

"Dafne has that effect on everyone. I don't know how she does it, but before you know it, you're spilling your secrets. Makes her a good investigator. And a bad enemy."

"I'd like to meet her again."

"Yeah, she and Seeger want us to come to *comida* on

Tuesday. You free?"

"Really? Wow. I didn't realize I'd made that much of an impression. Her work sounds so important."

"It was your karaoke that did it. *Private Eyes*. Sheesh. I learned all that music on the oldies station my college girlfriend listened to. Seeger was in the U.S. in 2002. He loved it."

"Where?"

"He went to school at University of Denver. Best Hotel and Restaurant Management school around. He's a hot shot administrator over at Vips. Ever eat there?" Dylan asked.

"Yeah, of course. I'd never have guessed Seeger is a corporate drone. He's a wild man."

"It's what makes him good at his job. Out-of-the-box thinking."

We made another turn and Dylan slowed, cruising as though checking addresses.

"Another block. I'll tell you."

"You forgot my first love lived in your house," he reminded me.

"Oh, yeah. Hey," I said, looking at him, "why not come in for coffee, or how about a movie? We've got cable."

Dylan honked at a car backing into the street and maneuvered around it.

"Pull in," I ordered pointing at the driveway and bounced out, Pepper on my heels, as the car stopped in front of the gate. "I'll get it," I shouted.

In a moment, the gate swung open and Dylan drove through. I closed it behind us and we walked to the front door. It swung open; Quint stepped out, steaming.

"Uh-oh," I said and giggled.

Dylan stepped forward and held out his hand. "Hi, I'm Dylan Porras. You must be Quint?"

Quint grasped Dylan's hand. I was relieved he didn't swing him into a hammer lock or something. He grunted a greeting, and asked, "Where have you been? I've left messages."

"I'm sorry, Quint. We've been celebrating Dylan's dad's birthday and retirement. I didn't hear my phone. Come on in, Dylan." I pushed past Quint, dragging Dylan behind me.

We crowded into the elevator for an uncomfortable ride to the main floor.

"Dylan and I are going to get a drink and watch some TV. Want to join us, Dad?

Dylan's eyebrows shot up. "Quint is your father?"

"Yeah, my long-lost dad I never knew growing up. I have another family. Quint and I met, what? About two weeks ago? Is that right, Quint?"

We arrived in the kitchen and Quint opened the fridge. "What'll it be Dylan? Pacifico or Victoria?"

"Victoria, thanks."

"Daughter?" he said, emphasizing our relationship.

"Victoria."

He handed the beers around and grabbed a Pacifico for himself. "What's on TV?"

"I don't know. We can flip channels."

"I'm not interested in TV tonight. Why don't we get to know one another? I'm hoping to see more of Jade," Dylan said.

"Sounds about right," Quint said, his voice a rasping saw.

"Great idea!" I forced a smile... met your family, now you can meet mine. Well sort of. Where're Lily and the goldens?"

"Holed up in her room, I guess. Did she know where you went?"

"Of course. Did you think I'd leave without telling *anyone*? I'm sorry, Dylan. You don't want to listen to my father of two weeks treat me like a teenager. Let's change the topic," I said, annoyance sharp in my voice.

I sat down at the table. The men followed suit, Dylan wrinkling his brow in that cute confused way I'd noticed he had.

"So who are Lily and the *Goldens*?" he asked.

I tipped my head in his direction. "Are you ready for a long story?"

Quint said, "JadeAnne, I don't think this is a good time to tell that story."

"Sure, Quint," I snapped. "But it's not Lily and the *Goldens*, it's Lily and the golden retrievers. We've got a rescued bitch and six pups. Not interested in a puppy, are you, Dyl? They're pedigreed, although the papers have not been delivered to us yet."

"You rescued them? From where?" he asked.

"Well, that's part of the very long story Quint doesn't want to hear tonight." I didn't rein in my sarcasm. Quint had no right to act like my parent.

"Okay, I'm feeling like something is going on here that maybe I'm not meant to be a part of," Dylan said.

"A wise man, your Dylan."

I jumped up and banged my beer onto the table. "Listen, Mr. Jackman Quint, I will not tolerate you butting into my life. You do not get to pick my friends or dictate my activities. Dylan and I are going into the living room. Leave us alone."

As I spun out the door I heard Dylan apologizing for his inconvenient visit.

"Dylan, you coming?"

He hustled after me and we found Lily and the goldens asleep on the couch. Pepper snored on the floor.

"Lily and *The Goldens*," I whispered.

Maya's ears twitched and her head popped up. She beat a tattoo with her tail. I snapped my fingers. She leapt over Pepper and jumped up on me to lick my face. Lily woke up. She peered at us until she recognized Dylan and she too bounced up. Luckily she didn't lick anyone.

"You're Lily? It's great to see you again, kid. How are you doing?"

"I'm a lot better. JadeAnne and Mrs. P are really helping me through it."

I cocked my head up to study Dylan. Did he already know the story?

"I'm glad. It's hard to lose a loved one. I bet the dogs really help, too," he said.

Lily shot him a coy smile. "Yeah. We're all recovering together. Come on, sit down. We can watch something." She tugged him toward the pile of snoring puppies. I stepped over Pepper, scooped several into my arms and nodded to their place. Dylan sat. I rolled the pups into his lap.

"You should get to know them."

Lily cuddled in on one side of Dylan and I on the other. We channel-surfed until we found a rom-com with J Lo. I heard the stairs door slam and Quint stump up the creaking steps. I felt a collective exhale and we relaxed into companionable silence as the movie started.

Chapter 16

Galerías Insurgentes

Monday, August 27, 2007

Quint was not amused after Dylan's visit. He'd stomped off to his room in a huff. What? Was he jealous? But he'd kept his opinions to himself. We had work to do and not much time to fight.

He'd begun to spend most of each day shut into a tiny room on the third floor after converting several of the cramped cribs into an office with phones and computers. Turned out he was savvier with a computer than I'd given him credit for, but he made it clear I was to stay out of his mission control booth.

I took that, and the Dylan détente, as tacit agreement I could go shopping and take Lily with me.

The Del Valle mall was split between a Liverpool on one side of Insurgentes and Gallerias Insurgentes on the other side. We needed sheets, towels, toilet paper in shades not pink. I searched out Señora Pérez in the laundry room. She seemed nervous, glancing toward the back corner of the room where some bins and trunks were stacked. What was up with that? I asked her where we should go. I said I'd buy groceries, too, if she's give me a list. She frowned when I said I was taking Lily.

"Mrs. P, the kid is going *loco*," I said in my imperfect Spanish. "The mall will be safe. What could happen to us there? Anyway, you know Anibal better than I do. After yesterday, will he come back here?"

She glanced again at the corner and raised her voice. "Señor Aguirre is not the *problema, señorita*. These *narcos* will do anything, including shooting up a public place. Read the paper. Everyday there is a headline of some outrage these people perform. You are not safe. I don't understand why you insist on staying here. It would be better if you took the girl and went back to your own country."

Her conviction caught me off guard. But I wanted to say, *Duh, what do you think we're trying to do?* I replied, "Señora, we can't get Lily home without permission from her mother to cross the international border. She must have told you her mother is dead; I assume you and Lily speak English together."

She switched languages. "My *inglés*, not so good. I don't understand *todos*."

"That's your excuse for never speaking English with me?" I asked, baiting the housekeeper. I knew she'd pretended not to understand English to eavesdrop on Anibal and my conversations. A ploy to get the juicy info for Lidia.

She gave me a cold look. "You speak Spanish," she said in perfect English.

"And you, English. Now you can't eavesdrop anymore." I wrinkled my nose into a smirk.

She switched back to Spanish. "*Señorita* JadeAnne, I'm not the enemy you think I am. Nor is Señora Sotomayor."

"We know what Lidia is, Mrs. P. There's no hiding that truth," I responded then in rapid English, I continued, "I believe you have not participated in her illegal activities directly, but finking on us to her makes you an accessory after the fact. If she goes down, you could see the inside of the women's correctional facility, too." I watched her restless hands stretch and clench, and pictured how they'd probably love to wring my neck.

"*No se entiendo, señorita.*" Her words sounded polite, sincere, but the ice in her tone told a different story. Maybe she didn't know the word *finking*, but I'd bet my hand she got the message.

I continued in English, "Of course you don't, but when the time comes, you will." I kept my voice light. It wasn't in my best interest to scare her too much right now. I wished I had a way of listening in on her *celular* and the house phone.

"*Lo siento*, I'm speaking English." I changed languages again. "Make me a grocery list, please, and may I borrow your grocery cart? Also, do you have the number for the taxi?"

"If you insist on this foolish action, *señorita*, I'll have the list in thirty minutes."

"Thanks, Mrs. P. See you in the kitchen."

Lily was ecstatic hearing the news. Shopping at the mall topped her list of engaging activities. I made her promise she would stay with me at all times and pay attention to our surroundings.

"Is it okay with Quint?"

"Ha! We're not telling Quint. I'm sure Mrs. P will as soon as we're out of the house, although she's afraid to interrupt him in his office. Frankly, so am I."

Lily's happy face darkened. "What if those men come after us?"

"I'm carrying my gun."

"In the mall? Don't they have metal detectors here?"

"I have no idea, Lily. I just don't see anyone trying anything in the linens department."

"Can I have purple?"

"You can have anything you want." I looked around her room. Grotesque. "You need some clothes too."

"I can pick?"

"Well, who else would?"

"My mother picked out my clothes, except for the things I bought with babysitting money. I wasn't allowed to wear those clothes around Eddy. He only liked certain kinds of clothes. Kids sometimes laughed at us for our ugly clothes."

"No kids here will laugh at you over your wardrobe. I checked out the mall and it has all the cool stores. We'll both stock up and send the bill to the senator," I said, and giggled.

Lily frowned. "How will you do that?"

"Um, well, good question. But I'm sure I can get him to kick in, especially on the bedroom makeovers. He couldn't want us to live in a brothel. Or, he couldn't want us to look like we live in a brothel."

"What's a brothel?"

"A whorehouse."

"This is a whorehouse?" she squealed.

"It was. You remember the red-headed toad, Consuelo?"

Lily nodded. "I'll never forget her."

"This was her first place. She decorated." I shook my head. "That woman has no taste."

Lily's voice dropped to a croak. "She wanted me to do terrible things." Tears sprang onto her cheeks.

I folded the girl into my arms. "I know, Lily but I've got you now, and what I want you to do is heal. Pick out a few cool outfits and turn your room into the sanctuary it should be."

She hugged me. "I miss Evie so much."

I had no words for that and stroked her silky hair as I held her close.

She pulled away. "I'm okay. Sometimes it just comes over me."

"I understand, Lily. It took me a long time to stop grieving over my sister's death and that was by cancer, not murder."

167

"I'm sorry your sister died, too."

"It's okay. It's been a few years."

"Jade, what should I wear?"

"For the mall? What do you have?"

Lily showed me the clothes Quint had bought her. Jeans and t-shirts. Nothing fancy.

"How about those washed denim jeans and the tank top? I'll loan you a necklace. You could use something with some style."

"I told you."

"How about let's catch that a-hole, Eddy, and make him pay?" I cackled a Cruella Deville laugh.

Lily giggled. "Could you really?"

"It's our plan."

I waited at the gate for the taxi. Lily would stay in the entry until I had the door open and she'd bolt into the car and duck down the few blocks to the big shopping center. A little cloak and dagger, but I couldn't control the street. I'd checked the block before calling and again right before the cab was due. Nothing. Regular traffic. Gas delivery truck, water delivery truck, laundry pick-up truck, moms with small kids and groceries. No men slouched in black vehicles. No SUVs. Unless they'd rented the house across the street, our block lacked Zetas or any other kind of *narco*.

A beep pulled me back to the street. Our taxi. I pushed the gate and pulled open the car door then yelled for Lily. She dashed out of the house and beelined for the car, diving into the backseat. I sat down in front and told the driver where we wanted to go. He looked confused, checking the rearview mirror and furrowing his forehead.

I shrugged. "Teenagers. Who knows what they're thinking?" I said in Spanish.

The driver smiled as he pulled away from the curb. "*Sí*, I've got three at home. The boys are easy—football. But I

168

never know what the girl is thinking."

"I've got the opposite. My ten-year-old is a boy, and he may as well come from outer space. Girls think about boys, mostly."

"That's what I'm afraid of. Her mother works, no one is around to supervise her. The boys play sports after school."

"That's tough. My mother takes care of the kids while we work. Little Johnny is with her at home now." I presented my most sincere face. "I didn't realize how much I'd miss the little bugger. Even if it's only a week." I turned around and glanced at Lily and sighed. "This one doesn't want to do or see anything here. She just looks at that little screen all the time and sends messages to her *amigas*."

"You brought the wrong kid. You here on business?"

"A conference. We stayed to visit my husband's family."

"Here we are." He stopped the meter in a loading zone in front of the mall entry and handed me a card. It gave his name and telephone number. "Call when you're done and I'll pick you up here and take you back."

"Thank you so much, señor, uh…" I read the card, "Gómez. In about two hours?"

"*Claro*. Give me a call."

Lily and I slid out of the taxi and jogged into the center. We'd be taking another cab home with another story and new looks for each of us. There must be a hair salon here.

"Lily, let's get new hairdos and have our nails done. Whaddya think?"

"Purple?"

"You and your purple. Yes, maybe I'll get purple, too."

"Oh Jade, will you?"

I leaned close to the girl and whispered, "Let's have new names today. I'll be Auntie. Who do you want to be?"

"Suzanne."

"Suzanne, where to first?"

The afternoon was cooling by the time we finished at the mall. I'd not only gotten my hair trimmed, but I'd added blond highlights and maroon lowlights. Not exactly purple, but approved by Suzanne. Lily's silky hair was chopped and tipped with blonde. I promised her streaks of hot pink and purple as soon as we were stateside. While her perm cured, she had long, pointed acrylic nails in royal purple affixed to her own nails and then painted with miniature white lilies. I got my nails filed and cuticles trimmed then a swipe of blush polish. It was my toes that enjoyed the grand adornment. Metallic blue with silver stars. And a bliss-filled paraffin treatment. Lily chose a modest plum and nude French pedicure.

I don't think the shop girls had seen the likes of us coming. We went wild. First in linens and housewares. We bought two sets each of towels and bed linens, including blankets and comforters. Quint got navy and grey. Lily found purple and black everything, including a good looking modern shag rug to match. I wanted to feel clean and calm. I couldn't buy new furniture, but I could change the colors. White. Sand. Teal.

And it turned out, they could deliver the next day.

Next, we found a paint store. Well, that changed a lot. "Let's paint our rooms and the furniture, Suzanne."

"Sure auntie, great idea."

I went for white.

I've always been a sucker for girlfriend shopping and Lily proved my match. We tried on every article of clothing in every store leaving dressing rooms looking like a cyclone had hit. I bought a cute pair of sandals and a slinky dress for clubbing. Dylan and I danced so well together, I was sure he'd take me to one of the infamous salsa clubs if I asked. Yeah, a little before the fact, especially after the weird reception by Quint. But if it came up, I was ready.

Lily picked skintight jeans with fancy pocket detail,

cropped leggings and purple low-rise sweat pants. She found a pair of converse tennis shoes that came with pens for customizing. I wondered if she would draw her Mexican experience on her shoes. She bought a ridiculously tiny vest, a pink tube top and two polo shirts with popped collars. Lucky for me she refrained from getting her belly button pierced at the piercing kiosk. Quint would have flipped over that. The sequined midriff top itself would cause a stir. I put my foot down at the thong underwear, sweats that said 'got beer?' across the butt and Ugg boots with fishnet stockings under rolled Soffe shorts. Really? Fur boots and hose in Mexico's summer? But at least she would look like a teenager now, and those choppy streaks across her razor cut tresses made a great disguise.

We crammed our new things into the grocery cart and made for the Superama. I pulled out the list, ripped it in half and we each set out to find Mrs. P's requests. Thirty minutes later we met at check-out stand 11 and took inventory. Lily ran back for guavas and hair ties. Finally we made it through the check-out with two carts of food and household supplies. I asked for two boxes and we re-packed the groceries at the edge of the parking lot. I'd called a taxi to collect us and I kept an eye out. That's when I saw a black SUV trolling toward us. I felt it. It was coming for us.

"Back inside, quick, Suzanne. Now!" I said, my voice a low hiss.

Lily didn't need to be told twice. She sprang for the door and disappeared inside. I put my head down, pretending to be packing groceries for transport, but kept my eyes on the SUV through the curtain of my hair, my hand gripping the gun in my purse. I'd hate to lose my favorite bag, but I'd shoot right through it if I had to.

The SUV inched closer behind the line of cars hunting for parking spaces. Finally the parking attendant whistled and waved the SUV and the line of cars behind it to turn a row before the entrance. I squatted and peeked through my hair as it crept by. I couldn't make out the passenger, but the driver was Eddy, The Saint. I was sure of it. But—why? He was the wrong cartel, wasn't he?

I watched the vehicle move off as our taxi made the turn and pulled into the loading zone. Lily bounded from her hiding place and dove into the back while the driver and I loaded our purchases. If it were really Lidia's crew, they would have come to the house. Was it just a coincidence? I didn't have an answer, but we needed to beat it home and tell Quint the stakes had been raised.

Chapter 17

Two by Land, One by Tree

I dialed Quint from the cab; he answered on the first ring. "Quint, We're on our way. Please be at the gate. We might have a situation."

"This is why I don't want you out attracting attention."

"We can debate that later. Get downstairs. We just turned onto our street." I clicked off, watching the driver for a sign he understood our conversation. If he did, he gave nothing away.

A little voice from the back asked, "What'd he say?"

I craned around to look into the backseat. Lily hunched between the groceries and the bags of clothes. She was almost invisible. A good thing. If the SUV people had only seen me and the stuff, we were safer. Eddy, the unholy Saint, never had me in his sights. But was he really on the other side? Was everyone a Zeta?

"The usual reprimand for going out. One of those 'I told you so' speeches. Let's hope we prove him wrong, eh?"

"I don't want him to be mad at us, but he sure worries a lot."

"Does he? You've spent more time with him than I have, ya' know."

"But he's your dad."

"Like you, I didn't grow up with my dad. Do you know who yours is?"

"Yeah. We lived with him until Evie was five. He couldn't take it and walked out the door one morning," she said, dropping her voice, "and never came back. At least that's what Mom said. They always fought. But Daddy was fun and brought us presents and candy. He never hurt us. Mom said 'good riddance to bad rubbage' but that wasn't true. Daddy worked hard. He just didn't make much money and got laid off." She paused for a moment, a dreamy expression playing across her face. "I wish I'd gone with him. None of this would have happened if I went with my dad."

"Honey, this isn't your fault. Don't think that way. Maybe we can find him."

"Mom made him leave. She was so mean to him because he didn't make any money. She loved money. It's all she wanted. That's why she liked—"

"No names," I said, interrupting.

The taxi slid to the curb, scraping a tire on the cement, and stopped. Quint had the gate open and beckoned us through. I held up a finger as I emerged from paying the driver, opened the back door and dragged our packages out. Lily edged over, grabbing the last bag and made a dash into the yard. Quint helped me move everything inside the gate, although he kept vigilant watch on the street.

As soon as the clothing and groceries passed through the gate, Quint slammed it shut and locked it. "What you really wanted was a *burro* to carry your stuff."

"Well, that too. But I saw Eddy driving a black Escalade into the mall parking lot. I couldn't see the passenger, but someone was in the vehicle with him. I didn't see them park, so it probably wasn't random. Why would he come here to shop? Aren't we kind of out of the flow of things in Del Valle?"

"Not at all," Quint said, handing me another bag.

I was loaded down with three plastic bags slung over each shoulder. "Hey, no more. This is heavy."

"Just one more."

He handed me one of the boxes. I wasn't going to be able to walk.

Quint moved up the walkway and into the house with a load. I staggered behind him and shoved the carton of groceries onto the bench as soon as I was inside. Quint was busy loading bags and boxes into the elevator. I said, "Here, let me in. You lock the door."

He put the last bag into the elevator. "Go on up then. I'll take the stairs."

I pushed the button and the door began to close. I saw Quint reach out to push the front door closed and heard the boom. The elevator door closed and it began to clank and creak up its shaft. What had just happened? I banged on the buttons, but the controls didn't respond and the car continued its slow climb. I was sure the sound had been a gunshot. Had Quint fired his gun? Eddy followed us home? Oh, no! Had Quint been shot?

"Hurry up! Get me out of here," I yelled to the lift, but it inched up at its sedate pace for what felt like a geologic age until the car shuddered and stopped. The door opened.

"What was that noise, JadeAnne? Where's Quint?" Lily asked as I flew out of the elevator and sprinted to the living room window. She followed. "What happened, Jade?"

"I don't know. Lily, stay out of the window." I dropped to my knees and crawled up to the curtain, peering around it. "The gate is open. Lily, hurry. Make sure the doors are locked then hide." Lily jumped up and ran. I heard the stairs door latch. I looked outside again, now holding my gun at the ready, my purse dumped onto the floor. I heard yipping coming from the kitchen.

I couldn't see the front door or the edges of the house

without exposing myself. Nothing moved. Should I call Quint? What if he... ?

Another blast rocked the window glass and a figure jetted into view from around the corner of the house aimed toward the gate. The man with the gun wore a black hooded sweatshirt. Where was Quint? Another cannon blast and the hooded man screamed, dropping to the ground and clutching his leg. He lunged for his gun, which had spun out of his hand and lay in the flowerbed.

Quint stepped into view, gun trained on the hooded trespasser. His voice drifted up through the open side window. "Don't do it, *pendejo*. I'll kill you before you reach the gun. You can't escape."

"*Chíngate guey*," the man growled.

Quint laughed, a cruel bark I hadn't heard before. "Looks like you're the one who's getting fucked 'mano. On your stomach, hands clasped behind you, " he roared, gun thrust into the man's face.

Lily shivered and clutched me, eyes wide. As the man rolled over, Quint ripped the hood down and I got a flash of a face covered in, was that—tattoos?

Quint whipped a couple of zip-ties from somewhere and bound the man's hands while resting his boot on the man's back. The thug let out a groan, but otherwise remained silent. Quint flipped open his phone and tapped a button.

I squeezed Lily close and whispered, "Quint's got him, we're safe. Why don't you take the pups up to your room and watch from your window. I'm going to find out who this cretin is."

"Did you see the tattoos? He was one of the men who brought us to the dog kennel."

Alarm ran through me like electricity. "You're sure?"

"Yeah. I remember him, he's got a wolf's fangs and tears, four of 'em, dripping off the teeth." She shuddered. "So ugly."

"I've got to tell Quint. Go!"

...took the stairs. Faster.

"Quint, Quint! He's one of the thugs who transported Lily and Evie to Tlalnepantla," I shouted from the doorway, aiming the Glock toward the fracas in the petunias.

"Get out here, girl," he demanded. "Hold this guy here. He came from the back," Quint said and stepped aside as I slid into place, gun aimed at the man's back. The thick scent of the trampled flowers filled the air. Poor Tonalli had just planted them.

I watched my father slink around the corner of the house toward the laundry room and backyard. Going where? He disappeared behind the tall sycamore tree growing up from the foundation bed, blocking my view of the rest of the side yard. I heard the laundry room door scrape across the jamb. My captive squirmed and the hood pulled aside revealing his cheek—a fang dripping tears just like Lily had said.

"Don't move." I stomped on the man's bound hands. He let out a groan. I bet that hurt, what with his arms yanked tight behind his back. I could see the strain in his shoulders. He didn't look like the kind of guy who practiced yoga, but from the muscles popping through his jeans, I knew he worked out. If he kicked out at me, he'd knock me over. I took a step back, watching his feet. I could see a dark stain seeping into the dirt below his left leg. This guy was tough. I'd be writhing and crying by now. I hoped the wound didn't fill up with fertilizer and bug spray. Reading my thoughts, tattoo man strained his head up to look at me. Was that a grimace of pain on his lips? Or a sneer. On his neck a tattoo —Z187. My bleeding heart cauterized. A Zeta, coming for Lily and me.

The door scraped closed and Quint's bulky shadow stumped from behind the tree trunk in the twilight, followed by a bounding Pepper. Pepper had been closed into the laundry?

"Hey, what's going on?"

Pepper yodeled a greeting and pranced to the hog-tied Zeta, sniffing and growling. I pulled him away. "Why was my dog shut up in the laundry?" I demanded.

"He was guarding our prisoner, Jade."

I eyed the trussed man on the ground, "I thought this was the prisoner?"

"This pendejo is Z187, a Zeta foot soldier come to either rescue or kill Anibal—"

"Then Anibal... was in the laundry room?" I asked, as a faint dawning of recollection intensified in my mind. Mrs. P nervously looking toward the corner. "Why would he have come back?"

He jerked his ear toward the sycamore. "Yeah. I caught him poking around last night."

I looked up at the tree. It was dark enough I could see lights glowing in the windows of the second floor through the boughs. Lily's and my rooms. "You think Anibal was going to try and kidnap us by climbing the tree?" I puffed out a breath. Ani wasn't exactly Jungle Jim. I jerked my head toward Z187. "So let's give Anibal to him."

The Cretin remained silent—a pro. I'd tied the strip of cloth Quint handed me around his leg to slow the bleeding and pressed a towel against the gunshot wound. We weren't going to be accused of murder. He refused to say anything, but I'd fished his ID out of his pocket, along with several weapons from various locations along his body, and learned this was one Desmondo Vicente Abrigo, age twenty-three of Coatepec, Veracruz.

"He's from Veracruz," I said. "Desmondo. What kind of name is that?"

"Desmond. Like Tutu." Quint laughed the unfamiliar bark, short, mean.

"Gotta love these names, doncha Anibal?" he asked as

he dumped Desmondo in a trussed heap on the floor next to him.

"So what do we do now?"

"You go in and see to moving the girl across the hall next to me until we can install grills on the window. I've got a call in to the senator. Someone will come for this pile of shit," he replied and darted a booted toe into the man's ribs. A soft rush of air escaped his lips.

I had to hand it to the Zeta. He hadn't made a peep during our exchange. Could he know something we didn't?

"JadeAnne, what's going on? I could see you, sort of, but the tree is kinda in the way. Did he come for me?" Lily asked, shaking, fear in her eyes. She was huddled in her bed, the puppies and Maya surrounding her like a soft barrier of warmth and protection.

I pushed into the room. "Quint thinks he came for Anibal. Did you know Anibal was hog-tied in the laundry room? Mrs. P knows."

"Anibal is here?" Her voice rose to a squeak.

"I thought you and Mrs. P were friends now. She hasn't told you anything?"

"You guys think she's a spy for the owner of the house, don't you." A statement, not a question.

"You've been eavesdropping?" I glared at the girl.

Maya thumped her tail and twisted her head up to smile at me. I leaned over the bed and tickled her belly. The puppies squirmed and began to nip and wag at each other.

"Get up, we have to move you across the hall until we clean up this mess. Bring what you need. Oh, and grab some of those towels and sheets. I'll make up your bed." I collected puppies. Lily tossed a shopping bag of linens at me.

While Lily gathered what she needed for the night, I opened the room, dropped the pups in a pile on an easy chair, and made up the couch bed. The room was small and musty, probably a study, but smelled better once I opened the window. It was full dark, now, and I could see a corona of moonlight emerging above the glow of the city. No trees obscured Lily's view, and more importantly, no one could climb in through the window. I noticed the connecting door between this room and Quint's bedroom. He would be on guard duty then. Better him than me. I yawned. It had been a long day already.

Lily, laden with enough clothing and books for a week, came in with Maya and three pups biting at her tail. She dumped the stuff on the bed.

"Do I have to put this away? I like my old room better."

"No, you can pile everything on the table." I gestured toward an antique walnut writing table on the opposite wall. "You can go back to your room as soon as Anibal is gone and we've had the tree trimmed." I'd be looking for an arborist tomorrow.

The dropped books slapped against the wood.

"Lily, what have you heard about what's going on? You didn't tell me." I shoved the puppies over and perched on the edge of the chair. Lily separated books, stuffies, phone, and clothing into piles on the table.

She didn't look at me. "You told me this used to be a whorehouse and it's owned by that mean woman, Senator Aguirre's mother."

"But Mrs. P? What has she said? Or, what has she asked you? What have you told her?"

"She had a bad family life, too. I told her about Mom and Eddie and what happened." Her face scrunched up, holding back her tears. "Her father did—well you know, like Eddy did to me. She told me about the earthquake and saving Senator Aguirre's mother and going to work for her taking care of Anibal's mother."

"Yeah, she told me all that, too. What else? I know how

easy it is to talk to her when she's being nice. Have you said anything about how we don't trust her?"

Lily spun to face me. "I trust her, JadeAnne. She's kind to me and has helped me. Why won't you trust her?"

I was as ready to share my story with Lily as I was to confront the housekeeper, and if Anibal really was tied up in the laundry room and Mrs. P knew about it, she was keeping quiet—wait a minute! How would the Zeta know he was here?

"Lily, by any chance did you hear Mrs. P on the phone this morning before we went out?"

"No. I don't know."

"Think. You were in the kitchen before I came down. What happened?"

"Nothing. I fed the dogs. I—yeah, the phone rang and Mrs. P answered."

"Who was it?"

"I don't know. She said something too quiet for me to hear. Then she said something about *las cinco* and then I guess she was listening because it was quiet again and she said something about Galerías Insurgentes. I recognized the name."

I smashed my fist into my palm and jumped up, disturbing the sleepy pups. I wished Lily were spending her time learning the language, but I could guess our trustworthy Mrs. P had been telling someone we were going to the mall.

Lily stared at me. "What?"

"Isn't five when she goes home?"

"I guess," Lily responded, voiced flattening in boredom.

I ran out of the room, yelling over my shoulder, "I've got to talk to Quint. Why don't you start heating up some food?"

I found him in the communications center he'd set up in the attic. The air was stuffy and the rooms, not more than particle board cubicles that resembled cells, ran in two rows down the length of the house, a narrow hall cutting under the roof peak. Quint's cell, actually two cells joined by a crudely cut opening, sat directly over Lily's second floor suite, the tiny window facing into the tree—something we needed to talk about.

"Quint," I said, knocking on the partially ajar door.

"Yeah? What can I do for you, girl? Come in."

"Dad," I said again as I settled onto a ragged slipper chair covered in flowered chintz, "I'm pretty sure Mrs. P tipped off Eddie Santos, and the Zeta."

"There you go again, Jade, with the accusations. Why?"

"Why what? That I think Señora Pérez is a spy for Lidia, or why do I think she was part of it? And what are you going to do with Ani and the Zeta?"

"You first, daughter. Tell me."

"It's not what I think, Quint. It's what Lily told me. Mrs. Pérez was on the phone with someone and Lily overheard *las cinco* and *Galleria Insurgentes*. She didn't understand any more of the conversation, but Mrs. P leaves at five and that's where we shopped today. What if... what if she was telling someone to be at the gate when she was leaving? She knew Ani was in the laundry room." I gave him an accusing stare.

"You knew he was there?"

"No, but while I ironed my dress, the *señora* kept looking into the corner where all those boxes and furniture are. I thought she heard rats or something. I was going to call an exterminator." I laughed. "I guess I was right."

"How did the housekeeper know?"

"Isn't that the question? But I'm guessing you caught him—when?—and trussed him up for safe keeping. Who were you going to give him to?"

"I can't discuss the details of my investigation, Jade. You know that, but I'll tell you, I caught your ex-boyfriend halfway up the tree."

"Yeah, I'll call an arborist tomorrow. So how'd you get

him down?"

"Shot him," Quint said, grinning.

"Oh. My. God. Quint! Is he alive?"

"Flesh wound. He fell right at my feet." He picked up a tie wrap and twirled it through his fingers. "Always carry a few, girl. They come in handy."

"What about his wound? You aren't leaving him to die are you?"

"Of course not. The senator will take care of him as soon as he's back in town."

"Where is he?"

"On business."

"So how did Mrs. P know Anibal was there, and who was she talking to? If it was Lidia, *she* wouldn't have cared about Anibal. Unless—" I paused.

"Unless Lidia Sotomayor is in league with the Zetas. I doubt this, as does Senator Aguirre."

"What about Lobo? Eddy Santos? Or even Consuelo? It seems like we're going round and round here, chasing our tails. How did Desmondo know Ani was here, anyway?"

"I think we'll have answers tonight, Jade."

"Why tonight?"

"Gonna be dark."

"What? Like all nights aren't dark?"

"Like it's a full lunar eclipse. I need you to get some sleep right after supper. Hey, is anyone getting some food on the table? I'm hungry," he said, his stomach chiming in with soft rumbling. He reached around to his keyboard and clicked a few keys. The computer went into sleep mode.

"I sent Lily to heat up whatever Mrs. P made. We should go down and help. Does she know any of this? "

"No more than she's still in danger. I want her doors locked tonight. Get her to haul all her dog gear in, those dogs need to be well contained. You, too. Don't let Pepper roam around. They'll go for him first." Quint finished shuffling his papers into some sort of order and pushed away from the makeshift desk.

"In the house?"

"Right up that tree, I'm hoping. You'll be waiting for them."

"But they know Ani's in the laundry. I'm not following your plan."

"I'll be waiting for them outside with a couple of Aguirre's men."

Chapter 18

Total Eclipse of the Heart

Tuesday, August 28, 2007

Fourth of July! Fireworks exploding from barges dotting the panorama of Richardson's Bay. Boom! Boom! Boom! I skip to the edge of our deck holding my toddling sister's hand. We look down through the dark. Booming, faster, faster. Hands clutched tightly. All the neighborhood dogs barking; the lights sparkling. It's so pretty Daddy! Bang-bang-bang-bang, like a big canon.

Pepper barked at the door. My eyes flew open. What the hell? I heard Maya and the shrill yaps of the pups across the hall. My room was totally black, the only illumination coming from a thin line under the door. Why was it so dark? Bang, bang, again—the door, someone was banging on the door.

"Get your gun, JadeAnne. It's started. Get up!" he yelled.

"I'm up, Quint," I called back as I rolled out of bed.

I heard his footsteps pound down the thinly carpeted hall and the stairs' door bang closed. The house trembled under his thudding descent.

I'd gone to sleep fully dressed, Lura's Glock in reach. I

strapped it on and leaped for the thin light around the doorjamb, tripping over Pepper, and patting to find the doorknob.

"Stay!" I commanded and rushed out toward Lily's door, standing ajar. "Lily?" I called, poking my head into the room. The moon glowed red like blood against a black sky through her window. "Lily!"

A frightened voice from behind the adjoining room door. "Yeah."

"Let Pepper in. Keep him with you. I'm going down." The lock clicked and the door opened with a soft creak. I whistled. Pepper shot to my side. "Guard Lily," I said and shoved him through the door. "Take my gun and lock that door, Lily. You've got one shot. Aim for the chest." I handed her the Semmerling and gave the door a nudge. "Now!" The lock clicked home.

No sound from outside. Eerily silent. Quint? The Shreks from Polo's building guarding the property? They'd be okay —highly trained and loyal to the senator, but why didn't I hear anything? I pressed my ear to the Cathouse window. Nothing, not even the distant grind of gears or wail of a siren floating in the oppressive blackness. Would they be able to handle an attack of—well, wasn't that the big question? Of Zetas? Or Beltran Leyva people? I tiptoed out to Lily's vacated suite door, put my ear to it. What if someone got up the sycamore and swung onto the fire escape landing at Lily's window? It was a déjà vu from Anibal's Condesa house—that time Tito Tormenta paid a call. I shivered, heart tattooing the inside of my ribs with a bloody Z. But I couldn't just cringe in front of the door. I had to do something to keep out the fear. Now.

I sprinted to the elevator and locked it at our landing. No one would be able to get in that way. Next, I thundered down the stairs and locked the 1st floor door then ran back up and locked the inside of the door at the fourth floor. Panting, I landed back on our floor and locked the stairs from the hall.

Now what? Why weren't sirens roaring down Calle Amores? Didn't the neighbors hear the gunfire? I pressed my ear to Lily's suite and listened again. Was that a clang I heard? Was that rubber on metal? Shivers fanned across my torso, my skin crawling. I held my breath and listened again. But all I heard was the rapid drum of my heartbeat.

I slowly let out the noise in my head with my breath and fished for the keys in my pocket. Their jingle exploded the silence. I grabbed the bunch, muting the jangle and pressed again into the door. There! That scrape. Familiar, like an old wooden sashed window opening. I raised the Glock and stepped to the side of the door.

The scraping turned to a scream of wood on wood. I felt the rattle as the intruder shook the window trying to loosen it in its frame.

I flipped through the keys like performing a magician's card trick. I found the key painted Lily's favorite purple, the color of her nails. Key poised, gun ready, I aimed—

I pushed; the door banged against the wall. I pulled the trigger. Window glass and a scream exploded into a tuneless arpeggio. Blackness weighed heavy in the sycamore outside the shattered glass. Silence fell—a shadow of dread.

But I didn't have time to worry about who I'd hit. Gun blasts. From the back of the house? Or—the laundry room. Was Quint in there? I ran toward the stairs.

I couldn't see anyone from the breakfast room window. The dark settled thick into the shadows. I headed down, avoiding the squeaking steps gun heavy in my hand. I inched the bolts back to open the door and crept out, another shadow edging along the house. The laundry room door was right around the corner, but I didn't have any cover beyond the blackness of the night. I'd have to move fast and silent. The moon, a red-tinged black was emerging from its hazy corona of light. I pulled my own hoodie over my head, flattened myself to the house and peered into the side yard. The shadows had deepened to thick mist under the canopy of the tree. I waited, letting my eyes adjust. The mist shifted into amorphous shadows of deeper black, puddling on the ground and—crouching behind the tree. It was a human, a slight aura of energy the give-away. Ours or theirs? I squatted, eyes on the figure.

A sudden light streaked followed by the dull PFFFFTT! of a silencer. A bullet lodged into the corner of the house where my head had been seconds before. I lurched back, thumping into the stucco.

The laundry door banged against the wall and a blast deafened the night. A scream of pain, another thud, shouting. I beetled to the corner and peeked. This time I could see a shape half sprawling into the side yard through the door. My stomach knotted.

Quint's voice barked, "Horacio, keep this *cabrón* quiet. I'll deal with our visitors."

A sliver of moon peeked from its cover behind me as I eased around the corner toward the laundry door, my stomach still lurching. "Dad, Dad!" I whispered.

He raised an arm, pointing up the tree. I looked. In the smothering blackness, I could barely make out a darker form against the fire escape ladder below the reach of yellow glow from Lily's bedroom. With the barked orders to Horacio, how could he not notice us? I flattened to the wall and edged closer to him, Glock trained on what I thought was the man's torso.

"You got him," Quint said in a low voice. "I heard the shot."

I kept my eyes on the partially tree-obscured intruder and nodded. I saw a slight movement and heard a groan. "I thought I killed him," I whispered. "He didn't make a sound."

"Yeah, okay," Quint murmured and nudged me toward the backyard. I inched toward the corner and he followed. Above, a slice of silver framed the dull ball of moon.

"Is Lily secure?"

I turned to look at him. Goggles. He could see in the dark. "Yes. With Pepper and my Semmerling, but what's going on? I knew you had Anibal. Why?"

Quint herded me around the house toward the front. "We'll let him tell us. First, let's see who else is out there." He scanned the yard. The front wall blocked most of the street.

"You had him tied up in the basement since yesterday and haven't talked to him?"

"Senator's orders," he hissed, reaching behind to hold me back as we approached the front of the house.

I couldn't see anything in the blacked-out yard. "Mrs. Pérez knew he was there," I hissed back.

"She called Aguirre."

I gasped. "Mrs. P?" I was confused. Wasn't she the spy?

Quint snapped me back to the task. "The gate's open and a vehicle is parked blocking the entry. Stay low between the house and the bushes," he growled. "Wait for my signal at the corner. I'll circle along the wall. Signal or shooting, whichever comes first."

"Shouldn't we call the police?"

He snickered. "Yeah, right. Aguirre's deployed a team. AFI."

Zocer's agency, I thought as I crept behind the azaleas and pittosporums. Great. Whose pocket did they live in? Zocer had turned to the Zetas to make a profit off me. I tensed. This was all about getting us back, fulfilling the brokered deal. My head began to pound. I hunkered down behind a juniper at the front edge of the house.

The Zetas had sent a team to grab me and Lily yesterday and, failing, they attacked the house in the dark of the eclipse. We could keep Anibal for all they cared.

Quint reached the gate. I could barely make him out, surveilling the street. I assumed the SUV was empty. I didn't feel any threatening vibes, but the deep darkness was too creepy to really interpret my sixth sense. I craned my head to look up the fire escape. Still too dark to guess who was there, but the amorphous shadow hadn't moved. Maybe he'd bled out into my yard. Tonalli wouldn't like cleaning that up.

Tires squealed, engines gunning, as three cars turned to block Amores, lights off. Headlights pierced the neighborhood as two more vehicles sped toward us against the one-way traffic circulation. The parked SUV roared to life and backed into the street. I heard the transmission race then cough before the van let out a grinding crunch as the driver threw it into drive. The vehicle teetered and shot forward toward the oncoming traffic, honking madly. It swerved between the trees onto the sidewalk, a shriek of metal on metal as it scraped an iron tree guard. Black figures with scary-looking guns poured from the stopped vehicles and sprinted down the street. I watched, mesmerized as I ran from behind my bush.

The lead vehicle screeched to a stop blocking the sidewalk. The SUV swerved again into a sickening crunch as it crumpled into an ancient sycamore. The second vehicle stopped. Only the clatter of boots on pavement rang out. Quint stepped into the street to greet the final vehicle.

Agents swarmed past him into the side yard. Flood lamps illuminated the path. Someone had wrangled the fire escape down, dragged the thug to the ground and cuffed him. Alive. I edged past two balaclava-ed guards; my eye caught a curl of black forelock punctuating a brown mole on the thug's forehead dripping a length of barbed wire toward his nose. I didn't see any Zs.

A groan—or was it a growl? Whatever, it melted into the whoops and shrieks of an ambulance, which pulled in through the gate and disgorged a team of Cruz Roja *paramédicos* and three folded gurneys. Had Ani been hurt? They charged the side yard to shouts of, *"Permiso" "Tuyo." "Permiso." "Tuyo."* and clattered toward the laundry.

A woman clicked open a gurney and a pair of men loaded—Cárdenas. Zetas! Two of the blue, red, and white clad EMTs whisked the gurney back to the ambulance. On the next gurney was my buddy Shrek 2—Omar. My heart sank as I gaped at the carnage around me, the tang of iron filling my nostrils.

"JadeAnne," Quint's voice commanded over the cacophony of boots and medical jargon and misery. "Join us, please."

I picked my way around the medical workers into the basement. Quint trained his gun on Anibal, who perched on a chair under the single bulb rubbing his raw red wrists. Horacio's ham fist rested on Anibal's shoulder. Polo stood to his side—a family portrait. I guess they needed me to complete the tableau.

"Jade! Get me out of here! Did you know—"

Polo's hand darted out and I heard a slap. Anibal struggled to jump up, but Horacio held him down. "I'll kill you, Polo. *Te lo juro.* I swear it!" he threatened his half-brother. He looked up at me and pointed. "This is all your fault! And your *pinche* father!" he shouted.

I stepped forward and bent to look him in the eyes. "What the hell are you talking about, Anibal Aguirre? I trus —"

"Enough, girl." Quint interrupted, silencing me.

"Polo," Anibal whined, glaring at Quint, "he kidnapped me. Are you going to let him get away with that?"

Aguirre made an odd gurgling noise. I realized he was laughing.

"¿Porque no? Little bro'. I'll let him shoot you if he wants to waste a bullet." The laughter had stopped and his

voice turned cold. "Who said turnabout is fair play?"

"He can't shoot me!" Anibal squeaked.

Quint stepped in front of him, grinning. "Yeah, dude. You're right, but I can shoot a trespasser." He laughed. "I did shoot a trespasser—your little hooded buddy—yesterday," he nodded to the trussed Desmondo still in the corner. "No one is going to arrest me for that."

Anibal eyed the gun, body wound tight.

"Hey, old man, give it up. This isn't your game anymore," Anibal said, springing away from Horacio and slamming his fist into Quint's gut.

Quint grasped him in a bearhug and pummeled his back.

I took aim and yelled, "Stop now! Anibal. I can't miss."

His head jerked up and he lost his grip. Quint had him flipped and pinned to the ground in a nanosecond, his gun pressed into Anibal's neck.

Anibal growled and bared his teeth. I was getting tired of him. He seemed hellbent to make my life difficult.

"So, Ani, was your thing with me all about selling me to your Zeta friends?"

He growled again, but Quint toe-tapped him in the kidney. Anibal screamed.

"Show respect for my daughter, *pendejo*."

"You killed my cousin."

"Oh, wow, he sounds just like big bro', doesn't he, Quint? For a guy who claims to hate his brother, he sure tries to act like him." I shook my head and puffed out a derisive sound. "He begged me to help him avenge Lura's death. I guess ruining my life was his idea. Vengeance, not justice. Why'd you shoot Danny then? You could have let him kill me and been done with me."

"You and the dog were worth more to us alive."

"Us? Who are you working with, Ani? I gotta say these creeps have the ugliest tattoos I've ever seen."

"JadeAnne, that's enough. Quit baiting him," Polo said.

"But it's so fun. And for what he's done to me—and you —I think he deserves a little shit pie in his face."

"I'll kill you, Jade. But first I'll make you watch your dog skinned alive. Better be looking ou—"

Quint landed a debilitating kick to Anibal's ribs. Anibal screamed.

"Shut the fuck up, Aguirre," Quint shouted. The tough Zeta boy was crying. Must have hurt.

I laughed. "What a crybaby. Your pal here is the real tough guy and he's barely out of diapers." I pointed at Desmondo trussed and silent, watching.

Okay, so I was exaggerating, but Anibal was a wuss. I began to understand how he'd gotten such a raw deal in his family. He inspired derision and disdain. My stomach flipped. Yeah, and he was the guy I stayed in this God-forsaken country for. What did it say about me?

"Polo!" Anibal whined again. "Let me up. Arrest him," he demanded.

"After your attack on me? I'm sorry, little brother. Mr. Quint has acted on my orders and your agency has been briefed on your activities. These men will see you to the airport and escort you to your employers.

Anibal gasped. "What the fuck, Polo? I didn't attack you. What do you mean?"

"Your lies won't help you now. I'm kicking you out of Mexico."

"But I'm a Mexican!" he yelled.

"What the DEA chooses to do with you is beyond my control. Get up."

Quint reached down and hauled him off the ground as Anibal lashed out with his foot.

"Tsk, tsk, brother. That's no way to act. Thank Mr. Quint for not killing you."

"Yeah, right. Everything was going fine until that asshole showed up, trying to steal my girl."

Aguirre smiled faintly. "You mean his daughter you set up to sell to Tito Cárdenas? Or your side deal to cheat the Beltran-Leyva Organization? Thank your Aunt Lidia for saving your pathetic ass. If I'd left it up to my associate," he gestured toward Quint, "*you* would have been flayed alive."

As they bantered about who would do more damage to the other, the agents, López and Arnaz, I read on their name badges, hauled the Zeta kid to the limo and shoved him into the trunk. He never made a peep.

"Senator, what happens to that kid? Why didn't the ambulance take him?" I asked as we stepped aside to let the agents pass back to the basement for Anibal.

"Don't let your bleeding liberal heart get the better of you, Miss Stone. That boy is a Zeta foot soldier who would rather kill you than look at you. He'll go to an interrogation center and we'll find out what he knows. Probably not much. He's low on the chain. Didn't you see the *Z187* on his neck? Zetas are smart. They aren't going to waste essential manpower on a double agent, but they also aren't going to leave one of theirs behind."

"What does that mean?" The agents perp-walked Anibal past us to the car, tossing him into the back and slamming the door. I heard the locks click, triggering a bad feeling.

"I wish I understood what's going on. For some reason, all this feels off," I said, cocking my head toward Quint. "Dad? Why don't I believe what's going on here?"

"Miss Stone—"

"Hey, what happened to JadeAnne and Polo?"

"JadeAnne, let the man speak," Quint said.

"Okay, but why the formality? It's just us, Polo. Tell me why this whole scene stinks."

"JadeAnne, I will fill you in soon. Now, I must take my leave. Thank you for your service."

With that, he saluted, spun on his heel, and strode to the limo. Arnaz held the door and the senator slid into the back with Anibal. Arnaz closed the door with a thwump and the limo silently glided out of the gate.

Yeah, thanks for my service.

Chapter 19

The Time Is Now

Wednesday, August 29, 2007

The moon reappeared and the traffic drone of pre-dawn Mexico City rose on the cool night air. Our neighborhood slept, quiet and still beyond the locked gates. I needed sleep but something was wrong; I felt it in my bones. I couldn't add it up between the late hour and the strenuous night. I hugged my dog closer to me on the bed. My bullet wound burned again, my head pounded and I felt wasted, aching with worry over Lily. She's safe, I assured myself, but what about tomorrow or the next day? The senator's comment swirled through my head, "... not going to leave one of their own behind."

The clanking lift woke me up after noon. Pepper was gone, hopefully with Lily or Quint. I yawned and stretched. Sunlight filtered through the lacy sheer—I'd forgotten to pull the heavy velvet curtain. I heard birds twittering in the softly rustling tree branches and the gas vendor calling his customers to the street. In the distance the din of traffic was pierced by the ubiquitous emergency wails. Comforting. City life normal under the light of the sun. I rolled off the bed and padded to the bathroom. The stench of the night's horror clung to my skin, my hair. I needed to wash it away.

I stepped out of my bath when the water turned cold and the bubbles had all popped into an oily film. Now the room smelled like a strawberry milkshake. I hoped Dylan liked strawberries. Heck, who didn't like strawberries? I'd wear my white sundress with the red piping and my red espadrilles and do my hair up in a loose chignon. Maybe I'd add those adorable handblown glass and silver strawberry earrings I'd bought. I checked the time—12:45. Dylan would pick me up at 3:00 for *comida* with Dafne and Seeger. Plenty of time to do my hair, nails, and iron my dress. Memories of the night's activities crowded down. I tensed and my head started pounding again. I couldn't go into the laundry—I just couldn't.

And Mrs. P? I'd have to suck it up and apologize. She called the senator, not Lidia, about Anibal breaking in. Because she wanted to bust him? Save him? Why would the spy of cartel-connected Lidia call Polo? I'd had a bitter taste in my mouth last night. Was this it? Something was so wrong about Anibal being tied up in our laundry room, but I just couldn't put my finger on it and I didn't have time to talk to Quint right now. I wondered if he felt the same.

In the kitchen, I found everyone at the table. Pepper wagged and licked my hand. Someone had fed him. Lily blurred around her edges, but Quint looked like hell, sandpaper chin and dark circles under his red eyes. Even Pepper yawned and flopped onto the floor rolling to his side with a thud.

I tossed my dress over the back of a chair. "Morning. Thanks for feeding Pepper, whoever did that."

"You're welcome, *señorita*." Mrs. P said from her station at the stove. "May I pour you some coffee?"

"*Por favor, señora*," I replied, looking at Quint, "No sleep, Dad?"

"No. I followed the senator to the interrogation. Just got back a little bit ago."

Lily thumped her mug to the table, a strange look on her face. "How are you doing, Lil? Where're the goldens?" I asked.

"In the yard. I put them out because Mrs. P was tired of them," she said frowning at the housekeeper who glowered right back at the girl. "But I wonder if they're safe. What if —"

Quint broke in and said, "The dogs are safe, Lily. We're all safe. The senator has left a detail to guard the house. I'll introduce everybody later."

"Did you get any sleep, Lily?" I asked.

"Barely. When can I move back into my room?"

"After the window is fixed," Quint said, reminding me I'd shot it out when I plugged the intruder.

"Has anyone called the glaziers?" I asked.

He leveled a look I didn't like at Mrs. P. "Will you arrange to have Lily's bedroom window repaired today?"

"*Sí, señor* Quint," she murmured, pronouncing his name 'queent.' "*¿Más cafe?*"

I held out my cup for a top-up. I was going to need a gallon of jet fuel today if I were to make it through. Mrs. P's sludge qualified.

"What's on your list today, Jade? I'm going to need a sit-down with you."

I held a fork full of *huevos mexicanos* poised to bite and looked at him. "Yeah, Quint, what was all this about? Why did you send Anibal with Polo? Lidia couldn't have wanted to save him from anything, certainly not himself. She detests him." At the stove behind Quint, Mrs. P scowled.

"I am aware. The only saving, as you put it, was for the senator to have him interrogated."

"Why here? Why us?" I glanced at Lily. She was in this as deeply as the rest, and deserved to know whatever there

198

was.

"That's what we're going to talk about."

Lily's face clouded over. "Can I come, too?"

I reached across the table and she placed her hand in mine. "We'll figure this out, Lily. We'll get you safely to your family. I promise."

"But I should know! This all started because of me. I should know everything." Her tears welled up and spilled over her cheeks. She swiped them away with the back of her hand and leveled a defiant glare on Quint.

He hunched, throwing up his hands and turned toward the housekeeper. "You drive a hard bargain, Lily. Yes, I think we all should meet here at five. You too, *Señora.*"

"I'm having *comida* with Dylan, his brother and girlfriend today. I might not be back in time."

Lily clapped, a grin spreading like the sun through rain. "Cool! Kinda old, but so cute."

I rolled my eyes, but Quint blew out a disgusted sounding breath and slid his head into his hands.

"JadeAnne, I don't think—"

"There's your problem, Dad," I said with my best sarcasm. Who did he *think* he was? Well, he didn't think—he'd said it.

"If I may," he countered in a tone equally as nasty as mine, "I don't think A: going out of the house unprotected is a good idea, and B: meeting people we have not vetted, is smart. What do you know about these people?"

"Dad, I know their family is a whole lot more functional than mine. I know the Porras family love and value each other, their neighbors, and community. I know Dylan likes me."

"You're an adult and I can't stop you, but—"

I cut in. "And you're the father who abandoned me before my birth because packing body bags with heroin to ship back home from Saigon was more profitable than taking care of a pregnant girlfriend. Don't try to pull some parental BS over me, Quint."

Lily's jaw sank, lips forming a perfect O.

Quint's eyes misted. The pain seared across his face, red and radiating. Instantly I felt like a major horse's ass. I shoved out of my chair, stepped around to him and laid my hand on his shoulder.

"I'm sorry, Quint. I'm sorry." I leaned in, threw my arms around his neck, and rested my cheek on his head. "I know you didn't mean to leave us."

He wrapped his arms around mine and muttered, "I will never forgive myself, daughter."

I let him go and looked him in the eye. "It's okay, Dad, I forgive you. But you'd better get that investigation into Dylan's family done by two."

"You look lovely, today," Dylan said as he handed me into his butter yellow Carmen Ghia convertible gleaming in the dappled sun at the curb in front of the house.

I smiled up at him. "Well, thank you, Doctor. You're not half bad yourself. And what a darling car! I see why you keep it off the street." I remembered our conversation about car ownership at Eladio's fiesta.

"My sanity maker during med school, internship and residency. It's a 1967 1500 model. I bought it off an old hippie photographer named Jed." He laughed. "He'd bought it to restore in the seventies, but never got around to it and his wife gave him an ultimatum. Got it cheap."

"You restored it? It's beautiful." But not as beautiful as you, I thought.

Dylan turned the key and the engine roared to life. It sounded like a race car. "I made a few modifications," he said and winked at me. "Top up or down."

I grinned. "Down, of course," I said as a frisson shot through me—we'd be easy targets if the traffickers were looking for us. "Hey, where are we going?"

"Seeger wangled an invite from Dafne's mother. We're going to the big house." Dylan popped a CD into the player. Rihanna and Jay Z belted out something about an umbrella to a perfect low-rider beat as we merged into the slow-moving traffic and cruised out of Del Valle.

"The big house?" I shouted.

He dialed down the volume. "Yeah. It's a mansion. The Olabarrieta family is one of the wealthiest in the capital. They invested in Mexico after *la Independencia*, buying up a shit-ton of Mexico City. Dafne will take over the company from her mother. Dorotea runs it with an iron fist and I don't foresee her letting go of the helm, but Dafne assures us, she'll be keeping the Porras family in high style within a few years." Dylan honked at an idiot cutting us off.

I held my hair with both hands. So much for the loose chignon, I should have worn a scarf. The exhaust wasn't bad for Mexico City, but I should have worn a mask, too. I coughed.

Over the wind, I shouted, "I wouldn't have guessed. How is it her family is letting her marry outside of her social standing? I thought the Mexicans were class conscious."

Dylan snorted as he stopped for a red light. Several cars honked and swung around us into the intersection. He leaned on the horn. "Where'd you hear that? The world is changing, even in Mexico. Anyway, Dafne's mother met a Brit on her big European trip after college and married him, it's kind of family tradition."

"A commoner? Now who's out of touch?" I scoffed.

None of the red light runners crashed, and we continued on into the roundabout at Reforma and jetted west up the grand boulevard.

"I wondered about Dafne's English."

"Yeah, she grew up speaking both, but the marriage didn't work out I guess, and he moved back to London. He's some sort of music promoter or something. Daf went to school in London then on to university at one of those girls' colleges in the East. She took her MBA at Stanford."

"I went to Stanford for my MA. Who else is going to be at dinner?"

Dylan punched the gas pedal and I grabbed the Oh, Jesus! bar as the little car zipped around a slow-moving, diesel-belching *pesera*. We passed the turnoff to Polo's Polanco flat and ahead, I could see the edge of the Museum of Anthropology through the city's scraggly trees. What a shame the pollution was so bad the trees barely survived. I would have liked to see the Valley of Mexico when it was a series of lakes surrounded by forest and topped by smoking volcanoes.

"What did you study?" Dylan shouted over the roar as we began to ascend the mountain.

"Journalism."

"And you own an investigations agency? I guess that makes sense. Do you write? Or are you a TV journalist?"

"Writer. Magazine, internet, or video—you know, in depth long-term investigations—like what I—" I glanced over at him; I felt my cheeks reddening. "Well, I've never actually done anything outside of grad school."

Dylan's hair blew wildly in the wind as traffic sped up the tree-lined straightaway through the ritzy Lomas district. Huge houses towering over ivy and bougainvillea covered walls dominated the neighborhood.

"So you're here in D.F. investigating something?"

"Sort of. You heard I came to find a woman who had gone missing in Ixtapa. Thought I'd get a vacation, but things didn't turn out exactly as I expected."

"Why did you bring your daughter on an investigation?" Dylan shot me a piercing glance.

My heart sank. Obviously he didn't approve. Already I was losing the good one. Something in my gut said to tell the truth. It was time to come clean with Dylan. Or let him go.

"N-no," I stuttered, "Lily isn't my daughter."

We screeched to a stop behind a jagged line of traffic trying to get into the Pemex station at Prado Sur, and Dylan twirled the steering wheel, frowning. He punched the accelerator and shot into the speeding traffic. "What do you mean, not your daughter. You said—"

"I'm sorry Dylan, we couldn't tell you, we—my words blew behind the car in the rush of air as we sped up the mountain. I tried again, shouting. "Dylan! Can we stop somewhere quiet?"

"Yeah. I've got to hear this. But we're late. You can tell us all over *comida*," he said and punched the gas again.

I gripped the door handle. "I can't Dylan. Pull over. Let me explain."

He swerved between two taxis into the left-hand lane and cut across Reforma into a steep, narrow street, dropping into a wooded canyon before slowing. Huge modern homes peaked between the trees, rising up the canyon walls as we descended the curvy, one-lane road. Geometric planes with huge picture windows reflected woodland gardens back at me. Working out what I could tell him, I gazed at the neighborhood.

Dylan down-shifted and gave me a hard look, working his mouth as though he wanted to expel a sour taste. Maybe he did.

"Listen JadeAnne, I don't know you or what's going on, but I won't be lied to. Lily, if that's her name—"

My voice stabbed even me. "Yes, it's her name. She and her little sister were trafficked from L.A." I shut up and grabbled the handle as we spun around a steep curve and started up the north side of the *barranca*. Dylan glared, lips pressed together. I couldn't see his eyes behind his aviator glasses, but I knew he didn't believe me. "Dylan. I rescued Lily, although the younger sister was killed. Quint, his contact and I, are working to reunite her with her family."

He down-shifted into first and the engine growled guttural and menacing as we climbed into the next curve. "What does this have to do with finding a missing person?"

I gave my most convincing smile, "It's a long story, Dylan. Can't we talk about it later? Where are we, anyway?"

"You'll have to. We're almost there. We're in *Lomas Altas* above the third section of the Chapultepec forest."

I studied the scenery. The forest looked greener here than lower in the bowl of the city. It was filled with pines, cedars, and what might have been liquidambars sheltering the estates from each other. I saw the blue of pools in yards below me. We'd crawled almost to the top of the ridge and the air smelled of cedar, flowers and cut grass. On this north side, the air was moist and cool, more like Mill Valley than the dry, dusty Mexico City I knew.

Twisting through the last turn, we popped over the summit into a sunny block of towering eucalyptus, sycamore, poplar, and high adobe walls with the ubiquitous iron gating straddling the ridge. Dylan hit a button stuck onto his dashboard and a tall gate opened, letting us pass into the sandy driveway leading to an impressive two-story ochre colored stucco house.

"We're here," he said as he slid the Ghia to the curb behind a Mercedes and a midnight blue Suburban parked under a lofty porte-cochere.

Chapter 20

Congratulations and Quetzalcoatl

Dafne swung open the heavy carved door and ushered us across the stone tiled foyer into a sunken living room bookended between a large stone fireplace and a white baby grand piano.

"Hi Dylan!" she said, reaching to buss his cheek in the typical greeting. She grinned at me, hand outstretched. I grasped it between mine and she pulled me into a hug. "I'm so glad you could come, JadeAnne. Welcome to the family seat." She drew us toward a bar cart where Seeger rattled a hammered silver cocktail shaker.

"It's about time, Dyl. You were gonna miss the Bailys. Hi JadeAnne, may I pour you a drink?" He winked.

I winked back at him. "What a beautiful home, Dafne. Thanks for including me."

I looked around as Seeger gave the shaker a vigorous shake. Soft creams, sand and shell pink of the walls, carpet, and upholstery created a backdrop to a rainbow of bright blues and greens splashed with the hot pinks and reds of Mexico in an array of modern and indigenous artwork, pillow coverings, and statuary. The effect was casual and energetic, not stuffy or overdone at all. And floor to ceiling French doors leading onto a deep patio overlooking the western mountains let in soft light that would turn golden as the sun set. The architect had oriented the house exactly on the top of the ridge to take advantage of the view.

"Your drink, *señorita*," Seeger said, handing me a martini glass.

I sniffed. It smelled like grapefruit. I raised my eyebrows.

Dafne said, "It's fresh grapefruit and lime with gin, *jarabe*—syrup—and muddled mint."

Dylan handed her a glass, took his own, and we all clinked. *"¡Buen provecho!"*

"What are we drinking to?" Dylan asked, a coy look on his face. "Any news?"

Dafne's cheeks pinked in obvious pleasure under Seeger's adoring gaze. "Wait 'til Mummy arrives. She's on her way from the office. She'll be here in a couple of minutes."

A hen and her chicks, Dorotea took center stage at the meal. "Dafne, sit still and stop playing with your food," she commanded.

Dafne dropped her fork and pushed her barely touched meal to the side, giving her mother an expectant look.

"What is it? Is everything all right?" Doretea asked.

"Mummy, I, uh—we—" she smiled at Seeger— "have some news." They clasped hands and went a bit misty around the edges. Dylan, Dorotea and I fell silent.

"Everybody. Seeger and I have decided to get married," she said and leaned over to give him a kiss.

Dorotea's chair scraped across the tile as she stood up. "Darlings, this is wonderful news!" She plucked her wineglass off the table and raised it. "To my grandchildren!"

Seeger's face reddened. Dylan hooted. I raised my glass, my smile masking my confusion at being invited to this gathering.

"Mum! Not yet. We don't even have a date."

"Congratulations Dafne and Seeger," I said, delighted. "I had no idea this was a special occasion. Thank you so much for inviting me to share it with you." I turned to Dylan. "Did you know?" He grinned and winked. "You rat!" I softly punched him. "You didn't say a word."

Dorotea said, "We've been waiting for the big announcement. These two have mooned over each other for three years now. Dafne, have you thought of a date?"

"No, Mum, not really. We just decided at Eladio's birthday party."

Dylan lit up. "He'll be thrilled to hear that, Seeg. *Felicidades*, bro. You got yourself one of the good ones," he said as he rounded the table and hugged his brother then Dafne. "Welcome to the family, *hermana.*"

Seeger swiped at his eyes and nodded. "I got the best one, Dyl."

Doretea, meanwhile had signaled for champagne and the serving woman came in with a tray bearing a chilled bottle and five glasses. She twisted the cork and poured, passing a glass to each of us.

Dorotea raised hers, excitement and love shining in her eyes. "I've had the wine chilling for the last year, and it's about time to drink it. To Dafne and Seeger!"

We all chimed in. "To us!" "To Dafne and Seeger" "To Dafne!"

I may be a Californian, but I'd never gotten into sparkling wine. My first sip made me a convert. The flavors of Danish pastry hit me first. I took another sip, swirled it around my mouth, and tasted a hint of cocoa, and finished with candied Saville oranges. "This is delicious, Dorotea. What are we drinking?"

"Oh, just a little something Dafne's father sent over from a trip to France." She turned the bottle's label toward me. "It's a 2002 Louis Roederer Cristal. The Roederer family owns three quarters of the vines in the Champagne region. It's an old company. This one, the Cristal, was created in 1876 for the Tsar Alexander II of Russia. They're still making it today. Digby, Dafne's father, knows how much I enjoy it."

"Mummy, quit showing off. Pour me some more."

Dorotea circled around the table and refilled everyone's glasses amid the excited chatter. Everyone talked at once. I'd noticed it at Eladio's birthday party. What a contrast to my cold, formal family. A jolt of envy shot through me.

Dylan clinked his water glass and the conversation quieted. He stood, turned to Seeger and held up his flute. His eyes gleamed softly. "Seeg, I couldn't be happier. You've found the most wonderful girl in *La Capital*—smart, capable, fun. And pretty, too. I'm proud of you, little bro'. To a long and successful marriage!" He swiped at his eyes with his linen napkin.

"Thanks Dyl, I love ya, Dyl. I'm the luckiest man alive right now," Seeger said and blew a kiss across the table to Dafne, "but I know there's a perfect girl for you, too."

Everyone looked at me. Me? My heart skipped a beat and those butterflies from the love songs danced in my heart. I felt the blood rush up through my face and into my ears. I swigged my champagne in an unladylike manner. Dylan leaned over and nuzzled my neck. The butterflies danced faster.

"Maybe I have. Maybe I have."

"Okay, Jade, spill." Dylan's face tightened into a serious frown, his eyes hard. The engine rumbled at the curb outside the gate where we sat in the dappled shade of an ancient poplar.

No more love nuzzles and sweet toasts—I either had to tell Dylan the story or say goodbye. The proverbial "shit or get off the pot". And for sure he was going to think total shit about me after he heard. Or did he already know? Would he turn me over to the Zetas? There probably was a reward. Oh, lord, if only he didn't have that connection to Fernando Torrens. I didn't know what to do—we barely knew each other, but I didn't want to lose him.

I plucked a peso coin from the ashtray. Quetzalcoatl, I came clean.

Impatience loud in his voice. "Jade, what's it going to be?"

I flipped the coin onto the dash. It teetered on its edge, wavering along the slope and circled as it fell with a soft thunk. The plumed serpent returned to lead Mexico—and me —into a new future, come what may.

"Look JadeAnne, either you tell me what's going on, or I'll be seeing you. I like you a lot, but I won't mess around with someone I don't trust. I already experienced that once. What's it going to be?"

"Trust. It's the problem isn't it, Dylan? I don't know you —how can I trust *you*? You seem like a great guy. Strong family values, smart, good job, kind, dog lover, loads of potential, but," I twisted to face him—I'd made my decision, "but you are connected to Fernando Torrens. He did something terrible."

"Fernando? How would you know him? What about that guy Pepper bit the other night?"

"Him, too. They both work for the cartels."

"What? That's *loco*, Jade. What cartel? What the hell are you involved in?"

The tone of his voice sounded like goodbye. Tears overflowed my lower eyelids and tracked down my cheeks. "I drove to Mexico with Pepper in my ex's VW camper to find Lura Laylor who, according to her husband, the former head of CalMex Bank here in the city, had disappeared in Ixtapa. My good friend lives in Zihua. I thought I'd find the wife then take a vacation. I needed to get away, to think. My relationship wasn't going well. I'm the managing partner in the firm, but it isn't what I really want to do. I came to Mexico to sort my life out, and all I found was the huge tangle of my failures." I slapped the dash. "I'm such a loser!"

"No, Jade. I'm sorry. I've made you cry." Dylan reached for me, but I held him away.

"Quetzalcoatl said to tell the story—can I trust you Dylan?"

He wrinkled his forehead. "You flipped the peso to decide whether to tell me what's going on? Okay, tell me."

My chin quivered. What was the matter with me? He hadn't even pretended to answer my question. Why did I want to tell this stranger my secrets? I fished around in my bag for a tissue, sniffed, and dabbed my eyes.

"Well?" he demanded.

A truck rumbled by, its racks filled with glass five-gallon bottles of water, *garrafones*, and turned into one of the driveways. The poplar leaves rustled and a trill of birdsong floated out from the hedging along a neighboring property. I took a deep breath. Dylan wasn't answering me. He wasn't even trying to fool me. I wrenched the door handle and launched myself from the tiny car.

"What the..? Jade what are you doing?"

Startled, the bird darted away. I sprinted for Dafne's gate.

The car door squealed and Dylan lunged toward me, grabbing my arm. I shrugged him off and pushed the buzzer again.

"Jade, what? What did I say?"

"Who are you really, Dylan?"

"I don't know what you mean? I'm me. A doctor building a career, getting to know a woman I'm attracted to. You're the one with the secrets."

"You're connected to Fernando Torrens."

"And so are hundreds of dog owners in *el distrito*. So what?" The crinkled brow and narrowed eyes again. "How do you know him?" A flash of loathing crossed his countenance. "Did you have something to do with him being beaten nearly to death?"

Dafne's gate lock buzzed open. I reached for it to make the run to Dafne's house. Dylan caught my wrist and swung me around to face him.

He glared at me, his lips twisted as though the words were too sharp to spit out. "A colleague of mine set his jaw. Did you—"

Fernando is alive? "No! No, Dylan, Fernando kidnapped and raped me. There! You know my secret," I sputtered, my spit flying. I swiped my mouth and wrenched away, skin burning where he'd grabbed me.

Dylan's hands flew to his head. "Wha—? Jade, oh my God, Jade, I'm so sorry! How? Come here." He folded me into his arms as I sobbed, murmuring, "I'm so sorry. So sorry. How could I have been so blind? Please, please forgive me?"

Chapter 21

Time to Make a Plan

I stumbled out of the Ghia in front of the gate and punched in the new keycode. It rumbled open and Dylan parked in front of the garage. The street remained quiet; no engines starting up, no men rushing the house. I wiped my face with my skirt hem and fished for my house keys. Quint would kill me for talking about the case, but didn't Dylan deserve to know? He was right, it was time. Dylan was already involved, how deeply remained unclear, but weren't we all connected by six degrees? Dylan confirmed Fernando lived. Surely Quint would want to know. My dad and the senator's team could find him, arrest him, or... I cut that thought off. Quint didn't play by the rules. I pushed the door open into the dusty coolness of our entry.

"Come in, Dylan. Let's go up."

"I hope your father can join us."

"And Lily," I added.

The time had come to formulate a plan. Dylan brought a significant piece of information: Fernando was alive. And Fernando might have the key to stopping the trafficking ring.

The elevator made its slow clank up to the first floor and shuddered to a stop, the door sliding open to reveal the anxious face of my dog. He lit up and crooned his pleasure at my homecoming before sniffing at our shoes and clothes, shifting his gaze between us.

I dropped to the floor and hugged him. "It's okay, Peppi. We're home."

He licked my reddened eyes as I tried to push him away.

"That's a tender homecoming, Jade." Dylan stepped around me to offer Pepper a pat on his head.

What did he mean by that? "He's my best boy, for sure." I crooned more to Pepper than Dylan as I clambered to my feet. "Don't yours get excited to see you?"

"Of course, but there's more jumping, and less concern for where I've been. But I probably always smell like the hospital."

"Pepper wasn't with me that horrible day, or the day we found the children in the cave. He worries. Both times I came home injured and he hadn't protected me. It's his job—isn't it, Peppi?" I stroked his head. "Let me get Quint." I opened the stairs door and bellowed for Lily and my father.

We heard a door slam and some thudding. Lily opened the hall door and the goldens thundered into the stairwell. "What?" she yelled over the dogs.

"Get Quint, will you? I want to sit down with all of us."

"Okay. Hi, Dylan! How was lunch?" she called down the stairwell.

"Delicious, Lily. My brother and his fiancée announced their engagement."

"Sweet!" The door slammed and we felt her steps shudder up to the third floor.

I led Dylan and the dogs to the kitchen and gestured to the table. Dylan sat down while I plucked a trio of icy Pacificos from the fridge and plunked them in front of him. "Help yourself." I slid an opener his way. "I've got to let the dogs out. Be right back." I called Pepper and Maya to follow me and the pack thumped down the stairs and out the garden door.

By the time I'd trudged back up to the kitchen, Quint and Dylan were concentrating on swigging from their Pacifico bottles. Lily gazed through the open refrigerator door. I scraped my chair from under the table and lowered myself into it. Rays of late afternoon sun slanted across the counter and illuminated a shaft of dust motes floating toward the floor. Hadn't Mrs. P cleaned recently?

"Where's Señora Pérez?" I asked.

Quint grunted something sounding like "dunno" as Lily, gripping a Coke in one hand and a tub of ice cream in the other, tossed herself into her place. She poured the Coke over the ice cream and slurped.

I frowned. "Fernando Torrens is alive."

Lily blanched.

Quint's jaw tightened.

Dylan gave each of us a quizzical look, settling on Quint. "Mr. Quint, I don't understand." He waited, drumming his fingers softly on the beer bottle.

Quint glared at me. "What have you told Porras about our mission?"

"Not much. Fernando is alive and Dylan has access to him. You'll help us?" I forced a smile at Dylan.

"Look, Jade, I don't know what's going on here."

Lily opened her mouth. I shook my head, and she clamped it shut again. I was certain she'd suggest killing Fernando. I agreed, but it wouldn't solve our problem. Anibal's Zeta friends were out to recover their investment: me, Lily—and Pepper. Polo had Anibal, but what did that really mean?

"Quint, have you heard from the senator? What about Anibal? Will he lead us to the Zetas?"

Dylan looked horrified, but his voice teetered toward anger. "Los Zetas? What are you people into?"

I felt the burn of his eyes boring into mine. The ray advanced from the counter and sliced across the table, flashing a piercing glare off Lily's ice cream spoon.

Quint's chair creaked as he tipped back and cleared his throat. "What do you know about the Zetas, Porras?"

"Only what the news reports. The most vicious, violent gang in my country."

Quint nodded. "What's your connection?"

"Connection? I'm a doctor."

"Cartel members come to you?"

"I sew up knife wounds, remove bullets, set bones, and tend victims of domestic violence as a volunteer on the Sunday nightshift in the free clinic. I took my shift off for *Papi's* birthday Sunday," he said, turning to me.

I got up and pulled more beer out of the fridge. I was confused. "You mean the Zetas are operating here in del Valle?" I clunked the bottles onto the table.

Quint grabbed the Superior, and popped the cap with a hiss, dripping foam across the table as he lifted the bottle to his lips.

"No. Citlali is where the free clinic is run by *Hospital General Iztapalapa*. I've got the drunks, hookers, *sicarios*. Sunday is big day for drinking and fighting. Violence escalates and grudges are settled. We get plenty of bullet-ridden bodies dumped at the door—kids, mostly. Gang activity is a huge problem. Word on the street, it's a turf war between Los Zetas and Beltran-Leyva."

Lily looked up from her Coke float. "Isn't it scary to go there?"

"*Pues, sí,* but I took an oath. Some of my patients are victims. If I don't go to tend them, who will?" he answered, conviction a high note in his voice. "Many of our volunteers are locals. Working to clean up the streets."

I grimaced, picturing deserted parking garages and dark streets. "You drive?"

"No. I grab the metro bus and transfer to the number eight. From my stop it's a five minute walk."

A gut punch vision of Dylan caught in gang-war crossfire, I blurted, "But those five minutes? Dylan you could be killed!"

His eyes crinkled and softened. "I'm careful, JadeAnne." He reached across the corner of the table to take my hand. "Really."

Quint slapped his bottle into the puddle of beer on the table. "What do you know of the gang activity?"

"Not much. Rumors. I overhear gangbangers talking, but they clam up when hospital personnel are around."

"Anything specific?"

Dylan paused. A bird tsked outside the window, drowned out by the sound of an emergency siren.

"We've had an uptick in thefts of penicillin, and the clinic has treated more young women, girls really, and boys, for venereal diseases over the last year."

I jumped at the sudden chorus of barking from the yard below and raised my eyebrow at Lily. She shrugged and slurped the drips from the bottom of her ice cream tub.

"Quint. Another?" I waggled an unopened Dos Eques in his direction. He ignored me, staring pointedly at Dylan. "Dylan?"

"No, thanks, Jade. I've heard our morgue is receiving an increase in female bodies from heroin overdoses, beatings, sexual assault. The wounds are worse than the typical domestic violence cuts, bruising and breaks. Knifings, gun wounds, burns. Blondes, Asian. These aren't local girls."

Quint scratched his stubble. "Where from, then?"

I chimed in. "From Russia, Eastern bloc countries, all over Asia—you remember that little girl at Consuelo's."

"And L.A.," Lily said, casting her eyes toward the table.

I reached over and patted her arm. "We'll stop them, Lily," I said, but the words sounded hollow.

"Mr. Quint—"

"Please, just Quint."

"Quint, then, what exactly do you all have to do with cartels and trafficking?"

The ray finished its creep across the table and pierced the far wall. The sounds of scratching on wood drifted up the stairwell. I would have to replace the door after the dogs shredded it. I jerked my head toward the stairs. Lily hopped up to let them back in.

Quint waited until she'd started down before speaking. "I'm working as a consultant to Senator Aguirre's taskforce against organized crime. We are investigating connections between the cartels, high ranking governmental officials, and money laundering. And you're right, Beltran-Leyva has a stronghold in the *distrito* and Cuernavaca. My work led me to Jade's missing person case. It's a fluke we stumbled across the trafficking ring here in *La Capital*. It was a relative of the missing wife who led us to the trafficked kids, which included Lily."

The pack clambered up the stairs. I put my finger to my lips.

Dylan lowered his voice. "Why hasn't the girl been sent home?"

"Bureaucracy," I said. My shoulders relaxed. I hadn't noticed they'd been tight around my ears, but Quint volunteering information told me Dylan had passed his test. At least nominally. I still worried about the Fernando Torrens connection, and was sure that connection sat foremost in my dad's mind. His paternal concern was sort of touching.

"Dylan, I'm really worried about Fernando Torrens coming after us. Can you find out where he is?" I looked at Quint, who gave a terse nod.

Dylan regarded me stonily. "I don't want to get involved, JadeAnne. It's not my place. I've known Torrens for some years and I can't believe he'd be involved in what you say."

"Porras, will this help you?" Quint pulled out his cell phone and tapped a few buttons. He held it up so we could see the screen. The photo looked grainy, but it clearly showed the entry and signage of Fernando's business. The next showed Tito Tormenta standing next to a black SUV with the signage to the vet clinic in the background. He held a handgun and the photo captured the Z tattooed on his neck. In another, too underexposed, but I could make out myself with my hands in the air above a shadowy form on the kennel floor. A stocky, square-headed silhouette pointed a gun into the frame. Zocer. My heart raced as a scream built in my throat. I fisted my hands and took a deep breath.

"What does that prove, Mr. Quint?"

"How about this one?" Quint thumbed up another photo of me under the warehouse across the street—dirty and blood streaked. "Or this." He sheltered the screen from Lily's view. On it, the next photo showed the crumpled, bullet ridden body of a tiny girl. Evie. I started to silently cry. The photos were date stamped, same day, same three quarters hour.

"Whether or not this proves your dogs' trainer is involved, it ought to convince you these girls are in grave danger. Will you help us?"

Dylan had dropped his head into his hands and gently nodded back and forth. "I can't believe it. I've referred friends to that bastard. A teenager I treated after her dog pulled her over went to Fernando for training. It was tragic. Both she and the dog disappeared although the dog had been well-trained. Her family grieves—could he have done this?" Dylan turned his face up toward mine. Pain seared across his brow.

"Yeah," Lily said, her voice flat. "He bragged to me an' Evie about how he got lots of girls for 'the trade' he called it. And lots of dogs, too. We didn't know what he meant until..."

Dylan regarded Lily's face, gone gray and strained. "I'll find out."

The elevator clanged up its shaft. Eight heads popped up and eight black noses aimed at the doorway as tails drummed a welcome. Mrs. Pérez, I presumed. Lily jumped from her perch at the table and flew at the woman, hugging her then grabbing plaid baskets burgeoning with groceries.

"What's for dinner? I'm starving," she announced as she dumped the bags onto the counter.

"*¡Cuidate niña! Buenos tardes, señorita, señores,*" she said, and nodded toward us as she carefully put the bag from the *panadería* onto the table.

Lily hugged Mrs. P again and gleefully ripped into it and grabbed a *concha*. "*¡Pan dulces!* Look Quint, *orejas.* Your favorite.*"* She pulled a flaky ear-shaped pastry from the bag.

"Lily, don't be a pig. Get a plate and napkins," I scolded.

Her smile faded, but she flounced to the cabinet for a platter.

Mrs. Pérez eyed the empty beer bottles and started making coffee. "Doctor Dylan, you are staying for supper?"

I glanced at the clock. It was already eight. Wasn't it late for a meal? I still felt stuffed with pozole and cake, but—wait a minute. How did she know his name? Dylan raised his eyebrows and cocked his head toward me. I nodded. Another question this man of surprises would have to answer.

"*Con plaser, doña,*" he replied.

"Oh, good. Dylan's staying. Do you want to watch TV? Mrs. P, what's for dinner?" Lily stuffed a raspberry *beso* into her mouth and loaded her napkin with pastries. The dogs watched every move; no guessing who was spoiling them with treats. Maya was looking a little tubby around the middle. Even Pepper drooled, eyes fixed on the plate of *pan dulces*.

"Would you like a *sopa y ensalada de nopal? Fideo?* I have a bag of Rosario's tamales *el señor* likes."

I saw Quint smile. Apparently this little group was fonder of the housekeeper than I thought. But how could

Dylan know her?

Lily interrupted my thoughts. "All of it. I'm starving. Come on, let's watch a DVD while Mrs. P makes dinner."

I got up and pulled mugs from the cabinet, poured the coffee, and handed them to the men. "Lily, grab the *pan dulces* and fresh napkins. I'll help clean up here and be right in."

The herd of humans and dogs shifted from the room in a clatter of shoes, toenails, and puppy yips.

I cleared the empties to the recycling and wiped the crumbs off the table with a fresh cloth. Mrs. P had finished unloading the food and was scraping spines from the nopal paddles while a pot of water came to a boil on the stove. I knew she would have to boil the slime out of the cactus before it would be edible. I asked, "How will you cool down the *nopales*?"

"In an ice bath. Will you slice these into strips for me?" She shoved a cutting board of scraped and peeled cactus to me. I pulled a knife from the holder. "How thick?"

"*Pues,* a little less than two centimeters."

I stacked the paddles and ran the knife edge over the steel then started to slice. A viscous clear sap ran from the cuts. "These are fresh." Mrs. P nodded.

The funkin' beat of Maroon 5's hit *Makes Me Wonder* streamed into the kitchen. Lily had conned Quint and Dylan into watching her favorite L.A. band. I bopped as I chopped, humming along. I wondered if Dylan had lied to me. I *so* didn't want to say goodbye.

"Mrs. Pérez, how do you know Dylan?" I asked, keeping my voice light.

She smiled at me as I handed her the cutting board. "The señora was Anibal's teacher."

"You mean Mrs. Porras? Dylan's mother? I thought she worked in the family business."

The cactus splashed into the boiling pot. "*Sí, señorita.*

220

But after the children came along, she started teaching *la primaria* in La Condesa. You must have walked past the school."

A gut punch. Had Dylan and Anibal gone to school together? They were about the same age. I blew out a breath. "*Claro,* over by the market. I remember. Did Ani and the Porras kids go to school together?"

"No, the Porras children went to school here in Del Valle, but the *preparatoria* served both *colonias*. By then Anibal was in California." She sighed and her shoulders slumped.

I realized Mrs. P was sad. Anibal was the closest she had to a family, and now I'd come in and wrecked that last bit of comfort for her. "Do you hate me, *señora*?"

Her eyes drilled mine, but instead of hatred I saw pain. "Anibal is the builder of his fate. I have shame that he caused you and Lily so much anguish. He has always hated his half-brother and made it his life's purpose to cause Senator Aguirre harm. It is why he was sent to his cousins. He was happier there. He found a family."

The housekeeper had neatly sidestepped my question. I knew she was fond of Lily. Not for the first time I hoped it enough to make her an ally. I rinsed my dishrag under the faucet and watched the spiny bits of cactus scrapings from the counter swirl away. How could Mrs. P be connected to the Aguirre and the Porrras families? I looked at my fingers. Tiny pricks of brown poked into my skin. Could Dylan be part of the trafficking ring with Anibal, Fernando, and Consuelo?

"*Señorita*, soap your hands and wash them in cold water. The *espinas* will come right out."

I followed directions and the cactus spines, hairs really, washed away. Were it so easy to wash away the needling suspicions filling my brain. I needed to talk to Aguirre.

Chapter 22

A Summons

Friday, August 31, 2007

Spicy scented steam twisted from the cup of *cafe de olla* at my elbow. I absently stirred in another chunk of *piloncillo*, the cone-shaped unrefined sugar used in Mexican cooking. I enjoyed the earthy sweetness of molasses and grass, but I wasn't really thinking about coffee. I had more important problems to worry about. Like getting Lily to her family in Denver. Like protecting us from kidnapping and a life of degradation, pain, and fear. Like shutting down the human trafficking ring in Mexico. Like figuring out where I stood with Dylan. I made headings on my pad: 1), 2), 3), but had no idea where to start.

Instead I doodled hearts and roses as my mind drifted off to dancing in the park. Had it all gone south? Would he still see me? I imagined his arms around me, remembering our first kiss on the curb in front of the house. So soft, starting so tender then passionate—Anibal leaping from the SUV, Pepper biting him, Roger prancing around growling. The slice of the door and the screech of the tires as the SUV fled. First, I needed to know exactly what Anibal was into, who he worked for, what his plans were. And more importantly, what Aguirre intended to do with him.

    1) Make an appointment with the senator

Quint had spent the day before conferring with Polo and his colleagues, but our paths

hadn't crossed. I'd spent the day doing everyone's laundry. I cleaned the puppy messes from Lily's bathroom, took a run, and helped make dinner, a cheese-y *Budin Azteca*, which Lily, Mrs. P, and I ate together later. Meanwhile, I'd hovered over the telephone waiting for Dylan to call. What? Was I fourteen?

Lily and the goldens descended onto the kitchen, a tornado of girl and dogs, hungry and ready to go out. The pups tumbled around my legs and I reached down to pet any I could catch.

"Ouch!" I yanked my hand back to the table and inspected a row of tiny punctures. "Sadie just bit me," I said.

Lily bent down to see which pup gnawed on my chair leg. "It's Jack. He's always biting everything. Did Dylan ever call?"

I frowned. "No. How do you tell them apart?"

"Bummer. Jack's the biggest."

"Jack?"

Lily whistled; Maya and Pepper pricked up their ears. She opened the garden stairs door to Maya's yip. "You know, after Quint." She whistled again. The pack funneled downstairs in a clatter of thuds and barks.

Sweet. She'd named her pup after my dad. That probably made him feel good.

    2)Quint needs to brief me on his meetings with Aguirre!!!

    3) Jot down an agenda for the meeting at Aguirre's office

What did we want to talk about exactly? Tap tap tap. I banged my pencil on the

scarred tabletop.

"Don't worry about it, daughter. The senator has it handled. He'll see us after

breakfast."

I jumped, heart dropping into my gut. "Quint, don't sneak up on me like that!"

"You couldn't hear me through the voices in your head and all that pencil tapping. The senator has some answers and his team is making a plan. Is the coffee hot?" He poured a cup from the clay pot I'd used to make it and took a sip. "Tepid sludge."

"Make a new pot then."

"Of real coffee, not this sugary boiled stuff."

"Aren't you from the land down under—Billy tea and all?"

"I'm from the great coffee at Caffe Trieste in North Beach. This—" The sound of grinding coffee beans drowned out the rest of his sentence.

I swigged the grainy swill in the bottom of my cup and pushed it in Quint's direction. "So what are we going to do about Lily?"

He poured the fresh grounds into the filter and punched the Mr. Coffee's on button. At least I'd bought organic beans but, Caffe Trieste or not, I didn't think Quint would notice or care whether he had Organic Sierra Madre Harvest from the Southern Mexican state of Chiapas. He'd drink day-old Folgers. The notes of almonds, honey, and milk chocolate, so rich in my cafe de olla, would be lost on him. "I could do with a refill," I said. "And would you dump the grounds?"

Murky streaks of light washed the kitchen. Another super polluted day. Perfect for meeting Senator Aguirre and his team. I bet myself it wouldn't be Polo and Jade today. Quint set my mug and a painted pitcher of milk in front of me.

"Thanks." I swirled in some milk and swigged at the too-hot brew, burning my tongue. "Hand me a spoon?"

Quint placed his cup on the table across from me and slid a spoon my way. "The senator and his team have confirmed Anibal's mission with his employers. He *is* undercover for HSI—we've contacted his superiors. One will be at the meeting."

"What's HSI? I thought he was a DEA agent."

He inspected his coffee. "Obfuscation. Anibal Aguirre aligns himself wherever it suits him."

"But what exactly is HSI?" I pressed. I'd never heard of anything with that acronym. "Helpful Secret Intelligence? Hellish Shitty Investigations? Are you with this organization?"

Quint coughed a spray of coffee over the table.

"Dad!" I hopped up to get the dishrag and swiped at the droplets.

He grabbed the cloth and blotted his shirt. The spots disappeared into the green and brown jungle print. "Homeland Security Investigations."

"Why didn't I know about this agency? Is it something secret?"

"Not at all. Google it. Your little buddy Anibal was never investigating the drug trade. From what the senator has confirmed, Anibal's legitimate job here was to uncover human smuggling routes and organizations."

"So the helicopter and bread truck were from HSI?" I wanted to believe in Anibal, to find out he'd acted on the side of the good guys. That he tried to save me.

"The bread truck? Possibly. The helicopter, not at all. We already know that cache of kids was stolen from BLO and brokered to Los Zetas." He glowered at me.

I could hear the *What, are you new?* in his thoughts.

I felt a wave of nausea and exhaustion settle over me. "I just don't want to believe Anibal sold me."

"He's going to prison for it. The senator wants to keep him in Mexico. He wouldn't last a week in prison here. Word is out on the street."

My gut twisted. That shit deserved the worst, yet a current of sympathy flowed below my rage. Anibal had led such a dysfunctional life, unwanted. Sort of like me. "What do you mean? He's acting from grief. Lura was everything to him. What's going to happen?"

"Young Aguirre was up to his eyeballs in this business long before Lura's death. It's why I'm here."

"You better fill me in. I don't want to be a complete numbskull in the meeting."

"Speaking of which—" Quint checked his watch and swilled back the last of his cup— "you better get ready. The car is coming in thirty minutes."

It was not yet eight.

Aguirre was nothing if not punctual. The gate buzzer rang exactly on time. I'd put on my only blazer over the same cream-colored dupioni silk skirt and pink crepe de chine blouse I'd worn to the senator's organized crime summit a couple of weeks before. I'd discovered suits were the expected attire at these meetings. I didn't have anything else, anyway. Who packs for business meetings when they're going to the beach?

Zihuatanejo seemed so long ago. Had it only been thirty-four days since Aguirre's thugs kidnapped me off the Pan American Highway? I considered how my life, and I, had changed as I squeezed my feet into a pair of bone pumps. I'd learned life wasn't all tea and debutant balls, and the dark side wasn't a just a device in novels to keep readers reading. I hadn't signed on for this, yet here I was. As I rummaged through my drawers for my dress purse, I considered how greedy, cruel, and violent humans are and felt my coffee churn in my stomach. I'd landed in the sickest world of all. I'd never have conceived of the depth of degradation people can inflict on one another a month ago.

My clutch hid under a pile of dirty clothes on the chair. I grabbed it and banged out of my bordello, Pepper at my heels, and almost ran Lily down.

"Can you take care of Peppi for me, Lil?"

"Sure. You off to the meeting? I heard the gate."

"Yeah. You'll be okay?"

"Mrs. P will be here in a minute, and the dogs will protect me."

I nodded, not trusting myself to keep what I was thinking inside. No sense scaring the girl. "Great. Pepper, you guard Lily," I commanded. He sat down in front of her and wagged.

"Alrighty then, I'm off. Thanks."

Shrek 1, Horacio, held the car door for me. Quint, already riding shotgun, drummed his fingers on a folder of papers he carried.

"Thanks, Horacio. How's Omar doing?"

"As well as could be expected, señorita. He'll recover." He took my elbow and guided me into the backseat.

"What took so long, Jade? We're going to be late."

He sounded agitated. Why the big rush in the land of *mañana*? "Gee, Quint, it's only 8:35."

"8:37 and rush hour."

"What time is the meeting?"

"9:00."

"Shouldn't we align our objectives?" I asked. Good grief, where did that come from?

He swiveled around to look at me. "You will not be required to talk during the meeting. I invited you as a courtesy."

What? "Oh, the boys club doesn't need the input of the *girl?* I'm the only person who's been present at each incident." His mirrored aviators distorted my face.

"We can't have you and Anibal bickering, or a woman crying."

"That's what you think of me?"

"A woman? Yeah. Am I wrong?"

Horacio's shoulders twitched as he held in a laugh. The rearview couldn't disguise the laugh crinkles at the corner of his eyes before he slipped on his shades and set the car in gear.

We took the exit from Insurgentes onto eastbound Viaducto heading toward La Villa and the airport. I didn't remember this as the way toward the area where government buildings were located. I had to renew my visa down there once. A warren of bland buildings housing offices and agencies out in the *Ejes* or someplace. I'd been completely lost. Thank God for the French designed metro system—*it* made sense.

"Where are we going?"

Quint grunted something and turned on the air-conditioning. I guessed we were not going to Aguirre's office. His was in the government building on Plaza Constitución in the Zocalo. I'd wondered how he rated an office in the grand building with the Diego Rivera murals. Was Polo more powerful than I thought? If he wasn't on the take from the BLO, how would he have the pull for luxurious offices in an historic building? Maybe Lidia footed the "power" bill.

I gazed at the graffitied walls of the Viaducto as it dove below street level. How did anyone get in there to spray paint with bumper to bumper traffic zooming along at 60 kpm? Where graffiti didn't mar the surfaces, political emblems, ads for motor oil, and restaurants whizzed by. I imagined figures wearing gas masks hanging upside down from climbing ropes with their spray paint. The exhaust would be enough to kill anyone—forget the vehicles. I closed my eyes.

The car skidded into a fishtail. I grabbed my shoulder harness and rocked with the slowing car. Horacio pulled it to a stop behind a massive pile-up of traffic. Accident? We crept up on the exit for Eje 3 Pte. Maybe we were going to that drab district filled with blocks of government buildings after all. My stomach rumbled. I'd probably find some good street tacos in the area.

"Dad, let's grab some tacos."

"You're hungry again?"

"I only had coffee. And I'm nervous." I checked my watch—it was 8:47—a long time until lunch, but we must be close to our destination.

"Tacos, the Mexican comfort food. You're a true *ciudadena*."

The traffic crawled. Horacio swore under his breath. I could see his lips moving in the mirror. I smiled at him and mouthed, *cálmate.* He nodded and inched the limo onto the *lateral.*

At 9:02 we pulled up in front of a drab five-story block building. Horacio hopped down and came around to open the door; I scooted across the seat and climbed out after Quint. A *pesera* pulled up behind the limo and blasted its horn. Horacio jumped back into the car and pulled away. Quint escorted me into the unnamed building, past a guard and into an elevator. We exited on the fourth floor. 437 had been painted on the opaque glass inset in the wooden door. He rang and the buzzer sounded. Inside, a stout, middle-aged receptionist with vicious red fingernails greeted us, tapped a button on her phone, and announced, "Señor Quint."

A guard stepped through an adjoining door with a metal detector and gave us the once-over. My jewelry obviously wasn't significant; the wand didn't even squeak. Satisfied we didn't carry any weapons, he walked us down a hallway and ushered us into a carpeted room.

"Welcome, Miss Stone, Mr. Quint. Please join us." Aguirre greeted us at the door, hand outstretched. Quint shook it and nodded to a middle-aged man wearing a brown suit and wire rimmed spectacles perched over a Roman nose, fleshy lips, and serious jowls, who sat across the table, a telephone in front of him.

I won the bet with myself—Aguirre was all business. I assessed the surroundings and found the room to be a well-appointed boardroom, bright without glare from recessed lighting. I sat down in the chair Quint held for me at the end of the table facing the hallway. He took his place to my right next to a fair-haired man wearing a western cut jacket over a white pearl-snap shirt. He probably wore cowboy boots, too. This must be the HSI guy—or did Quint say some CIA dude would be here? A young woman wearing a big-shouldered business suit from the late eighties, shiny from wear, poured me a cup of coffee, handed me a napkin, and gestured to the platters of pan dulces on the table. I surveyed the assembly. The man on my left slid the platter my way and smiled. His squarish shaped head reminded me a little of Zocer, but his beautifully cut suit and school tie suggested a captain of government rather than a street agent.

"Thanks," I said, extending my hand. "I'm JadeAnne Stone. Mr.?"

The man half stood and shook my hand. "Farcía Luna, Secretary of Public Security."

Another door opened and Senator Bendicias, whom I'd met at the summit on organized crime, entered, nodding to the group as he pulled off sunglasses.

"Senator, I'm glad you could make it," Aguirre greeted his colleague. "Please sit down." He gestured to the chair across from his. "Help yourself to refreshment. We're waiting for AFI to bring the prisoner." He signaled to the woman who clacked over to Bendicias in flapping sling-backed stilettos. Gotta love the *mexicana* style—even if she could barely walk.

"Bendicias, I believe you know my associate, Jackman

Quint, and his daughter JadeAnne Stone?"

"I remember you, Miss Stone. A journalist?"

I stood to take his outstretched hand. "Yes, and narrowing down my research to the trade in human beings. Apparently *el distrito* and greater Mexico City is a hub for distribution of trafficked people. I'm curious to learn more, senator."

He eased himself into his chair, tightened his lips, and tapped his pen on the polished table. "It's a serious problem, yes."

I backed toward my seat. "And what are you doing about it?"

Aguirre glared at me. The cowboy grinned.

"Jade, let's not get ahead of ourselves. We all know why we're here," Quint said. He held up his cup for another pour.

Actually, I wondered. That, and why didn't the woman put the pots on the table? I jotted names and titles on the notepad conveniently left at each place. Maybe I really would write an article.

The phone buzzed and jowls grunted into it as the door opened to admit a pudgy, dark-skinned man with a briefcase and the aura of attorney about him. He grabbed the first seat, nodded to Aguirre and opened his case, extracting a sheaf of thin files, which he officiously fanned in front of him.

"I see my client has not yet arrived, Senator Aguirre."

I was right. The *abogado,* lawyer for, I guessed, Anibal. My coffee cup rattled in the saucer as I picked it up. I decided not to risk shaking coffee all over the table and my silk blouse and set it down. "Where *is* Anibal?" I didn't want to confront him, the greedy traitor. I never wanted to see him again.

The cowboy interrupted. "Senator Aguirre, let's get this show on the road. I've got a twelve-thirty flight to Phoenix." He tipped back in his chair, exposing a fist-sized turquoise belt buckle.

DEA? HSI? CIA? I mentally shrugged. Who cared? A lot of acronyms, the same bunch of American cowboys. I caught Farcía Luna's expression. He thought so, too.

"We need him here, he's the connection, dammit!" the cowboy twanged.

"*Cálmase, amigo,*" Quint said. "He'll be here in a minute. I'm Jackman Quint, by the way. And you're?"

The cowboy winked and drawled, "An interested party, Mr. Quint."

I smiled my sweetest smile. "The DEA rides to the rescue."

The Mexicans laughed; the cowboy glared; Quint frowned. Well, who was that "interested party" asshole? And why was I here?

The phone buzzer vibrated again and in a moment, a mean-looking scrawny guy with a truncheon prodded Anibal, shuffling, into the room. I could have really made an ass out of myself by saying what I was thinking, *Hey Ani, nice outfit.* He was swaddled in an ill-fitting white jumpsuit accessorized with draconian leg shackles and plastic tie wraps binding his wrists. He looked uncomfortable, but not so much that he couldn't offer me a charming greeting.

"You bitch! You did this to me," he snarled. "I'm not saying anything with Mr. Quint's bastard in the room."

Aguirre and I exchanged a smirk. Apparently Anibal didn't recognize the irony in his statement. The lawyer leaned in and whispered something in his ear. He shut up. You'd need a chainsaw to cut the tension in the room.

Jowls rapped his coffee spoon on the table. "People, let's get on track here. We have a problem and we need to solve it. For those of you I haven't met, I'm Jose Luis Santiago Vasconcelos, head of the Organized Crime Special Investigations Unit. Senators Aguirre and Bendicias, who will be working with me through the SEIDO office, are assessing and cracking down on the human trafficking here in *El Distrito* and Mexico at large. Senator Aguirre is our liaison with consultants from Homeland Security Investigations." He gave a vague wave of his hand in Quint's direction.

I raised my hand.

"Yes, Miss Stone?" Aguirre asked.

"Senator, I don't understand what we're doing here." I looked at the cowboy. "With all these anti-crime agencies and committees present, why aren't you protecting a little girl kidnapped from her home in LA and sold into sex slavery?"

Quint replied, "JadeAnne, it's a much bigger problem—"

I interrupted, "Look, I was a victim here. Anibal Aguirre," I glowered at Ani,

"sold me to the Zetas along with the American teens kidnapped into the sex trade by members of the Beltran Levya Organization. One of the girls was killed. You," I pointed at Aguirre, "won't send the other home to her family."

"The girl is a witness. I understand she has been subpoenaed to testify and is in protective custody awaiting the trial," Farcía Luna said.

"Whose trial? Anibal's?" I asked.

The senator pursed his lips and glanced sideways at the cowboy, who wore a gloating grin plastered to his perfect American teeth. What was up with that? I shot my own look at my father who gave a quick shrug. The power brokers had cut some sort of a deal and Polo wasn't happy about it. No one answered my question.

"I will take your silence to mean either you have not charged Anibal or arrested Zocer Grijalves, Fernando Torrens, Edgar Santos, or Guiellermo Lobo. Or perhaps you're turning a blind eye to their complicity in this activity." I sighed and held up my palm. "No, don't tell me.

I'm not surprised," I said, my mouth twisting into disgust as I gazed in turn at the boys around the table. Anibal's stony expression of hatred chilled me, but he couldn't hurt me now, could he? I turned away. Quint, Aguirre, and Senator Bendicias looked equally disgusted; the cowboy doodled on his pad; the lawyer wrinkled his forehead, confused; Santiago's raised eyebrows said he had no clue what was going on, and Farcía Luna shifted his eyes from mine, a pinkish tinge to his cheeks. Did he know something?

The silence solidified to a chill weight on the room, broken only by the faint whir of the A/C.

"I'm not exactly sure the purpose of this meeting, gentlemen. I want to know why we can't send a traumatized fifteen-year-old, who has lost her sister and mother—" I glared at the cowboy— "murdered by Eddie Santos, the same man who kidnapped her, why can't she join her family in Colorado until she needs to testify?"

"Miss Stone, we cannot protect the girl if she is in Colorado. She is key to our prosecution," Santiago said.

Farcía Luna shifted his weight. "Where is the girl?" he demanded.

"This is about the kidnapping in Los Angeles? You've arrested Santos and Lobo?" I asked. "You, Cowboy, why don't you nab these scumbutts and put them on a plane to stand trial where they'll be convicted?"

"Well, little lady, y'all have a fine idea, but we don't have jurisdiction. Our mission is to recover our asset." He jerked his chin toward Anibal slumping into his chair.

"What's going to happen to him? Shouldn't I make a statement?"

"I'll take your statement after the meeting," he said, dropping the twang.

"Then let's get on with the meeting. I don't know about the rest of you, but I have a vested interest in shutting down the human trafficking rings in Mexico." I looked at my watch. "I'm in a hurry, too."

Quint's eyes twinkled. He was used to these high-powered bureaucratic types and how they spun their agendas and dragged their feet. Senator Aguirre, for one, wanted to protect his mother. I hoped he wanted to protect me and would get the accusations and arrests rolling.

"My daughter is right, we're wasting time. She was also part of the package young Aguirre sold to the Zetas and was instrumental in freeing the American girls."

I watched the men's faces. Farcía Luna scowled.

Quint went on. "JadeAnne. Anibal will be escorted back to the U.S. by Mr. Jones, who's a U.S. Marshal, by the way, to stand trial for trafficking, I'm guessing.

"To answer your question, the senators have called this meeting to brief Mr. Farcía and secure the full cooperation and backing of SSP to stamp out human trafficking in Mexico." Quint's look bored into Farcía Luna.

So I wasn't the only one who thought something was off about this guy. "I'm still confused. If Mexico has not arrested the known perpetrators of the crime, why would Lily be held here to testify? You can't have a trial without defendants, can you? And why haven't I been subpoenaed and put in protection?"

Everyone looked away from the elephant—me—in the room. I was answered by the rustle of clothing, throat clearing, shuffling papers, tapping pencils, cups clacking against saucers, clinking chains as Anibal shifted. A perfect Mexican stand-off.

I tuned out. Something was afoot, as Sherlock would say, and I wouldn't learn the facts here. Santiago questioned Anibal, the lawyer jumped in periodically to council him not to answer. I didn't get the sense he was a very adept attorney, or he didn't care about his client. With a little prodding of the AFI man's truncheon, Anibal pointed fingers at Santos and Lobo, and mentioned Consuelo a couple of times, even as he evaded all the questions about the house on the flanks of Ajusco. He denied connections to Los Zetas.

During the interrogation, Anibal made eyeball communication with Polo, whose expression clearly said, "Leave my mother out of this."

Who was Polo kidding? Santiago and Bendicias, maybe, but Farcía Luna looked like a man who knew the players. I distrusted him and it dawned on me the official had some connection to the trafficking. I'd gotten the impression he was acquainted with Lobo. So this must be it—a government conspiracy in action. Polo and this guy Santiago were after Farcía Luna. It made sense. No way could the cartels get away with their trafficking without the government removing the obstacles. Anibal was just a bit player, and one about to be extradited back to the U.S. Or was that a ruse, too? Was he a shill? Undercover? I'd probably never know.

Quint's voice pulled me back to the table.

"Sorry…what?"

"I asked if you are ready to go, or do you have anything to add?"

I pushed away from the table. The men stood. Farcía Luna reached out to clasp my hand. I brushed him off with a fake smile and started around Quint's side of the table, mostly to avoid Anibal.

"Gentlemen," I said, nodding to the room as I pushed toward Quint. "Let's get some tacos, Dad."

Chapter 23

An Order of Tacos, A Side of Trouble

Back in the limo, Horacio merged onto Circuito Interior Bicentenario.

"I thought Mr. Jones was going to take a statement from me," I said. Was he for real? Right out of the Old West. Was that his real name?"

Quint laughed. "Smart girl. He's a spook."

"But you said—"

"Yeah, I know what I said. He's undercover."

"Doing what? Not taking Anibal back to the U.S. to be prosecuted?"

"Probably not. The senator is livid."

My stomach timpanied, resonating through my limbs, a death march—dum, dum, duh dum-dum. I felt myself tensing as the orchestration of my nervous system altered my rhythm. "That asshole *sold* me into sex slavery and he walks free?"

"Relax, Jade. He's under Aguirre's control. You saw him. The senator ain't giving him up any time soon. Not until we have his Zeta connections and proof of Farcía Luna's involvement. We'll get him, Jade." His expression belied his words.

"So I wasn't making things up, then," I said. "The head

of SEIDO is paving the way for the cartel activity. BLO?"

"Yeah. He's associated with Lobo, we know that, but Lobo associates with most of the power brokers. It's a matter of unraveling the knot and finding out which threads are tied together. The senator has his financial people following the money. Anibal is just a short cut. We'll get the truth. That's Jones's job."

Jones—well, I couldn't go there. I watched the Mexican streetscape flow past my window, a jagged canvas of squat rectangles. Fading pinks and greens and blues and yellows brushed on peeling dun-colored stucco. *Refracciones, panadería, médico, Abrrotes* Sanchez, *Papelería* Lupe, *zona escolar*—the signs of normal life slipping by my window. Kids in school uniforms, women in *batas* with clashing plaid shopping baskets, a beat cop, men with briefcases, a water delivery truck, the ubiquitous odor of gas and cooking tortillas. Miles of city, thousands of *ciudadanos* going about their business. Were they aware of the corruption and evil lurking below their daily routine? Were they secure and satisfied with their lives? Did they feel safe? That was the big question. With people like Anibal and Jones and Farcía in their world, could they be safe?

I exhaled the breath I'd held too long. "What about Lidia?"

Horacio's shoulders stiffened. Of course he knew what was going on.

"Horacio, what do you think about all of this?"

He flicked on the turn signal and wove through a congested district of apartments, shops, traffic.

"Jade, leave him alone. It's not his job. Anyway, it's lunchtime."

"Where are we?" I smelled meat cooking.

"In *el centro.*"

"We're on Calle de Bolivar, *señorita.* Los Cocuyos. The best tacos in town." He guided the limo to a stop in front of a fire plug. "I'll let you off here. There's the line," he said, pointing across the street to an unruly group of people queueing in front of a tiny hole-in-the-wall taco stand.

"What can I bring you?" I asked.

"*Gracias, señorita, que amable.* I'd like three *cabeza*, two *suadero*, and two *tripa* with extra salsa, a Fanta and a side of *escabeche* with *chile manzana.*"

"Water?"

"No, gracias, I've got a bottle." He waggled his Peñafiel at the rearview mirror.

"Okay, then, let's go." I shoved onto the sidewalk.

Quint slammed the door and took my arm, jaywalking me across the street to the end of the line. I leaned against the front of a sporting goods store and checked out the *taqueros* lined up for tacos. Everyone from all walks of life awaited their turns to order: a mom with a school-aged daughter in tow; an ancient, wizened couple, he in a three-piece suit looking like it had come from the 1940s; skinny teens in a gaggle of impatience and laughter; a mail carrier; a pair of short-skirted shop girls; a bespectacled professor type; a tall, skinny man with neck tattoos, drooping pants, and fingerless gloves who half-turned as I gave him the once-over. I froze, the timpani thundered.

"Quint, it's one of the Zetas from the animal hospital," I whispered

"Who?"

"The thug who saw us hiding behind the animal hospital in Tlalnepantla." I kept my eyes on the man. He hadn't seen me. I pressed into Quint. The man turned and I saw his face. No doubt, it was him. "Cárdenas called him Rollo. He wore the same gloves. I'm sure of it."

Rollo and his companion stepped up to the counter and placed their orders. I stared at them from behind the next folks in line. The thugs stepped aside to wait for their food to be served, turning toward us. Even from a distance, I could see it, something tattooed on the second man's chin. I'd pay good money it was a number. "That's the Zeta *sicario* with him—the SUV driver who took us back to Condesa from the clinic after I was sewn up. I think he's the one who threw Anibal into the van in Tlalnepantla. Maybe—I dunno, it all happened so fast."

I felt Quint pull his gun from the holster.

The Zetas' order came and they moved to the end of the counter, selected condiments, then started eating. The line inched closer. What would I do if they saw me? What would *they* do? I slouched behind the man in front of me.

"Should I go back to the car?"

"Yes. Too many people will get hurt if there's shooting."

We shambled another couple of feet closer. I wriggled through the crowd and stepped into the gutter, heading away from the taquería. At the end of the taco line, I craned around to see if they were still eating. The *sicario's* mean eyes bore into mine. As one they tossed their plates onto the counter and shoved off the wall—reaching under their hoodies, heading toward me. I spun, reversing direction back toward Quint, keeping the line between me and the thugs. I was certain they were the same Zetas, and they were after me. The crowd thickened closer to the taquería, and I lost sight of them. My blood hammered through my body; I wouldn't see them if they broke through. I pushed into the middle of the milling diners. Someone pushed me, grabbing at my blazer. I jerked away, frantic, careening into—Quint.

"I've got you. Stay down."

His arm flew up, the gun in his hand. The crowd surged into the street, shoes slapping on cement. Shouts of "¡*Pistola!*" Screams. The people stampeded, stopping traffic. I searched for the men in the fleeing crowd. A car horn blasted next to us. The car door opened and my father was around me, shoving me.

The door slammed behind me. Horacio held his gun

ready and barked, "¡Bájate!"

I ducked between the seats, pressing into the carpet. The din of shouting and outrage muffled. A spray of shots peppered the side of the car. Quint! Then the explosion of a cannon and screams.

"Stay down. Stay down!"

The car was trapped in the flood of people and vehicles trying to flee the scene. I heard the scream of sirens approaching. "Can you see Quint?" I asked Horacio.

"No. What happened?"

"Zetas. The ones who took Lily and her little sister to Consuelo the day we found them. The tall one was there when the younger girl was shot," I replied, my voice quavering and husky.

"They recognized you. Do they know your dad?"

"No. Do you see him, Horacio?" I peeked my head up, scanning for my father. A blast and the window spread with an orbed web. Another crack and the screaming turned shrill as the door opened.

Quint dove into the front. "Get us out of here, Horacio!"

"¡Claro que sí, capitán!" He slammed the car into reverse and lay on the horn. Look-ee-loos backed away and a path opened. He swung the tail end of the limo into a narrow alley between two storefronts and inched around, aiming for the corner, and turned as several police vehicles flooded onto the block.

We were out of the mess, but Polo was going to be pissed about his car.

As my blood pressure dropped and my muscles relaxed, I offered the universe a little prayer of gratitude for bulletproof glass. I wouldn't be safe until I stopped these Zeta maniacs. I glanced at my dad. Sweat still streamed down his forehead and his expression was grim. He'd pulled a cloth from I don't know where to buff the black metal to a dull shine, turning his gun over and over against the cloth.

"Dad, what happened out there?"

"Wha'd you call him? Rollo? He pulled a gun—might've been an Uzi—popular with the urban thugs. He got off a round."

"Into the side of the car. Was that your gun blast I heard?"

"He won't be bothering you again, love."

"And the *sicario*?"

"Scuttled into the crowd like the rat he is. But I'm sure I winged him. He'll turn up in a hospital somewhere. We'll get him."

"Like I ended up in a hospital? Not. They took me to a private clinic."

"Those guys?"

"Sicario. The one that got away; they know where it is. I don't."

"Good to know. He'll head there, then. What were they driving?"

"Dad, I'd been shot, sedated, and woke up inside a van. I don't know."

"Think. Color? Age? Size? Help me, girl. Could it have been the van in Tlalnepantla?"

I closed my eyes and pictured the scene. *My head pounded. My arm ached. I'd been dumped into the back seat of*—of what? I could see smoke-tinted windows. I took a deep breath and slowly let it out, relaxing, clearing my vision. I'd been put there by—*Prison Edition*—floated into my mind. My eyes popped open. "Mr. America. I remember thinking, Mr. America, Prison Edition, but he's dead. You killed him on the way to Polo's after Anibal lit the house on fire." I sank into my recollections again. Mr. America hadn't been driving. He and the shotgun rider went for tacos. The driver was…I pinched my eyes tight. Who, who, who? OMG, yes! "The van was black. Now I remember Sicario drove. Military style buzz-cut. Numbers tattooed on his chin. He spoke English."

"Sicario? The second man. What did he say?"

"Something crude. They all laughed." His mean little laugh—huk-huk-huk rang in my ears. "He knew Anibal was lying about the kids after the helicopter picked them up. I should have remembered. I should have done something." I pounded my fist into my palm.

"Why were you with these people?"

"I don't know. The bread truck must have let us off at—" Anibal's voice sounded loud and clear. "—at Dr. Augustín's consultorio."

Quint started pecking at his cell phone. "I've got one in Colonia Buenos Aires on Calle Bolivar. Horacio, take the Cuauhtémoc exit. It's the next one."

The limo's turn signal clicked as we slid into the right hand lane. We were back on the Viaducto heading home. I wished I were there—home. On the Sarasvati with my orchids and Pepper. And Dex. I wrenched my thoughts back to the limo. I couldn't think about it. Not now.

The car moved up the exit ramp to street level along a *panteón* filled with lawns and acres of stones, crosses, monuments and crypts. Many of the graves I could see were neatly tended and rioting in colorful flowers. Probably plastic. As we circled around the perimeter, I wondered how many of the hundreds of graves held victims and perpetrators of the narco wars. Ever since President Calderon declared war on drugs, news headlines screamed of the thousands dead across the country. Well, I could think of a couple who I'd off in a heartbeat. Okay, that was a little harsh. Life sentences in solitary, maybe.

Quint interrupted my thoughts. "Consultorio Medico Augustín."

We'd threaded through a rundown neighborhood and stopped across from a building marked with a sign to the clinic.

"Look familiar?"

I shrugged, frowning. "I don't know. I came out of the place in an alley."

Horacio shifted into drive and we pulled forward around the block until he came to a narrow *callejon* between buildings and crept back toward the medical office. I studied the buildings, fire escapes, garbage cans, a typical alley. I didn't see anything familiar, except the trash, and how would I identify that? I shook my head. The limo prowled on.

At the end of the block we stopped at a sidewalk lining a broad, traffic-choked boulevard in a dismal looking grey neighborhood I hadn't paid attention to driving in. Something clicked.

"Hey, look at that." I pointed across the street to a blue painted building with iron balconies. The upper balcony had blue Talavera-style pots overflowing with bright flowers in hot colors, which coordinated with the designs on the containers. *That* I remembered.

"What? That apartment building?"

"Yeah. I remember the SUV screeching to the curb, the flowers in the background."

"Horacio, circle and let's find that SUV."

Our driver nodded and edged into the traffic. Find a black SUV? Every other vehicle on the street in this colonia matched the description. I wished I'd paid attention to the license plate.

Horacio zigzagged up and down the streets surrounding the consultorio. I counted five black SUVs, one with tinted windows, a cracked windscreen and no wheels. That wasn't it. *Sicario* might have beaten us to the doctor's clinic, but even the professionals couldn't have stripped the SUV that fast.

"Mr. America told me this is Colonia Buenos Aires, the colonia of car thieves, but we were on a boulevard with metal sculptures in the median strip when he mentioned it."

"Doctores, Calle Doctor Vértiz. That's a fair distance away," Horacio said, brow furrowed in the rearview reflection.

I spent too much time interpreting people from behind. "*Sí.* We'd driven for a while. Near where we had tacos."

Quint chimed in. "I can't find another Augustín in the colonia—"

"That's it!" I shouted and bounced across the seat to peer out the window at the back of an SUV parked in a narrow drive between buildings as we trolled by. Horacio jerked the limo to a stop and backed up.

"Are you sure, Jade?" Quint asked.

"Yep," I affirmed as the word VERACRUZ flashed into memory. "The license plate came from the State of Vera Cruz. I'd forgotten."

"Then all we need to do is wait."

"What are we waiting for, exactly? Call the police."

Horacio pulled.. and squeezed the limo into a spot within shooting distance. Quint dialed Polo and gave our location. "He's sending a team. We'll nab him and the doctor."

"So can we go home?"

I was getting too used to these mysterious vehicles appearing from nowhere and ingesting or disgorging armed black clad figures. I'd looked up and there it idled off our bow—a black box van, this time spitting out a team of men in SWAT gear, or what I associated with SWAT. No insignias, no POLICIA across their chests, just mean-looking guns, black shields, and helmets over balaclavas. "Quint?" My voice quavered.

Quint looked up as the men broke into two lines and streamed around the limo. The last in line tapped on Quint's window and saluted. Horacio started the car and we cast off into the endless stream of traffic in Mexico City.

Chapter 24

You Are Never What You Seem

Lily heard the elevator. She bounded down the stairs with her puppy entourage, shaking the house. Her eyes shone and she giggled in giddy expectation. "Can I go to my aunt now? Did they say yes?"

"Sweetheart, it wasn't that kind of meeting." Quint slung his arm around her shoulders and herded our pack toward the kitchen. "C'mon, let's get some lunch and I'll tell you about it. Is Mrs. Pérez here?"

"Yeah, she's upstairs vacuuming. I don't think she expected anyone for lunch."

"We missed lunch. I don't hear the vacuum. Where is she?" I asked.

"Third floor," Lily said.

Quint dropped Lily's arm and glared at me, anger and—what?—sparking from his expression. "I'll be right back. You girls get some food going." He waded through the bouncing puppies and stormed up the stairs.

"What was that about?" Lily asked.

I opened the fridge and peered in. Three covered containers promised a satisfactory lunch, although I'd bet it was our dinner. "What's this? Did you help make it?" I held up a foil encased baking dish.

"Chili rellenos, Mexican rice, frijoles de olla, and a tomato and cucumber salad. I finally mastered burning and peeling chilies today. We used poblanos. There's salsa, too. But what happened? I thought you were eating out."

I pursed my lips. "Plans changed rather suddenly. So we can't eat this?"

"I don't know, Jade. Tell me what happened."

"The meeting was a farce. In fact, it was a ruse to expose a government guy, someone named Farcía Luna. He heads up some office for Public Safety." I pulled luncheon sized plates painted in bright colors from the cabinet. "You're eating, right?"

"She'll be ticked off. There won't be any dinner."

"We'll order a pizza."

"Pizza! With extra cheese and pepperoni?"

"Anything you want, Lily."

"Then, yeah, I'm eating."

The microwave dinged and I exchanged the beans for the rice and grabbed a third plate. "Lil, finish setting the table while I get the salad and salsa." I tossed down several woven raffia hot pads and set the hot bowl on one.

"They brought Anibal all chained up. A U.S. Marshal was there to take him back for prosecution. Anibal blamed it all on me. Then on Santos and Lobo. They haven't arrested either of them. We are not safe and you're a material witness, although, it doesn't appear that I am." I spat it out—with a hiss. "The whole thing's a pressure drop. Dropped right on us, Lil. Then—"

"Whaddya mean, I can't go? But I want to go home!" Fat tears rolled down her cheeks. "I'm scared. I hate Mexico. Please—"

"Look, kid, if I have to smuggle you across the border, I promise I'll get you home."

Quint stomped in, fuming, with Mrs. P in tow, her head bowed and her expression guilty. "JadeAnne, you're right."

"About what?"

"Our housekeeper is a spy." He pushed her into a chair at the end of the table.

Lily's chin dropped, her eyes wide.

"Mrs. P, we're about to eat. Would you like to join us?" Why did my debutant manners kick in?

Lily put a place setting in front of her. I slammed the now hot rellenos onto the table along with a spatula and several serving spoons. "Serve yourselves. Beer, Quint? Coffee, Mrs. Pérez? Orange, Lily?"

Mrs. P shot me a half smile and a quick nod. I fetched us both steaming mugs and carted the milk, a Fanta, and a beer to the table.

"Mrs. Pérez, what is going on?" I asked.

Silence.

"Aren't you going to eat?" I raised my eyebrows to my companions.

"But Mrs. P can't be a spy. She takes care of me. She's helped me," Lily, breathless, admonished.

The woman looked toward Lily and took on that dreamy smile again. "*Sí.* I take care of you *querida.* But, but I was forced, *señor.* They made me come here and..." Her voice trailed off.

"And what, *señora.* Who sent you here? Lidia Sotomayor?"

"No. Otro."

Quint clambered out of his chair and towered over the housekeeper, who looked frail cowering under his anger.

"Sit down." I ordered. He'd trap more answers with honey. More gently I asked, "Who?"

Quint grunted something and returned to his chili relleno.

Mrs. P mumbled, "Not *la señora.* She's not involved."

"Then who?" He demanded.

"After the fire and... and I need work, I went to the

senator. He hired me to take care of the house and cook, just like before. But *el señor—el joven, me acercarga a conocer que paso aqui."* Her shoulders slumped and she shrank into her chair. "*Me pagó bien, extra.* I needed the money."

"What did she say? She needs money?" Quint's voice thundered through the room. "What young man? How do you report? What do you report?"

"Quint! Lay off. She's scared. Let me."

"I found her going through my desk, reading my papers." His eyes bored into Mrs. Pérez's. "Did you have something to do with the attack on the house?"

Fear rolled up into her eyes. "No. No, *Señor* Quint. I was only asked to watch and to know if you are interested in them."

"WHO ARE THEY?"

We all held our breath. I had my pesos on Anibal.

"*Me llamaran hoy. Pidieron yo les informo—*"

"Speak English, woman!"

Mrs. P shrank again. It's amazing how small a person could get under my dad's scrutiny. I didn't know this side of him. I wanted to tell him to back off, but I was the one who'd insisted she was a spy. Winning the argument didn't make me feel so happy. I'd miss her great meals. I took a bite of my cooling *rellenos*.

"Anyone want their lunch heated back up?" I asked, as I pushed away from the table with my plate.

"Me," Lily said. "Mrs. P, these are the best chili *rellenos* ever!" She smiled at our confirmed spy.

Mrs. Pérez twitched her lips in reply. She had tears in her eyes. I picked up Lily's plate and put it into the microwave.

Quint had shut up and I decided to take up the interrogation. Good cop, bad cop. "Señora, they paid you money to tell them about us? Don't we pay you enough?"

Her half smile morphed to anguish. Or was her high color shame? "*Señorita,* it's not that. Not money. They didn't give me money..."

"But you said—" I stopped and threw up my hands. It didn't matter. "Señora, why would you be disloyal to us? I thought you cared about Lily and the dogs."

Her rosy cheeks flamed across her face and blended into her cropped red hair, a shade rarely seen in nature. Droplets of perspiration dotted her forehead. She patted her face with her napkin. The microwave dinged and I swapped Lily's plate for mine and set the girl's lunch back in front of her. "Why, Mrs. Pérez. Why?"

"They threatened you," Quint said, flatly.

Lily dropped her fork with a clack onto the half-finished plate of food as she leapt to her feet. She leaned over the table toward our housekeeper and shrieked, "Who are they, Mrs. P? I'll kill them. Tell me. Who? That disgusting Eddie Santos?"

Mrs. P barely nodded, rivulets of tears dribbling off her chin. Lily bent down and hugged her. "Quint will fix it. We won't let him hurt you."

"I-it's not me. It's my niece's family in Cuernavaca. My sister's girl. She's my only family since the earthquake. He will kill her family."

My father and I locked eyes. "Cuernavaca you say? Señora Pérez, how would Eddie Santos know you have family in Cuernavaca?"

"Because it wasn't Eddie. It's Anibal—he wants revenge. You heard him today, Quint." Or maybe *he's* been threatened by the Zetas.

"*Sí*, the young Sr. Aguirre. He has visited my niece, too."

Quint sat down. "We'll go get them. Put them somewhere until we've sorted this mess out. Jade, the Zetas —"

"No," I interrupted, "it's the BLO. Quint, the SUV with Luna and Anibal. BLO wants us. Either Anibal was playing both sides or..." I trailed off, pausing a beat before turning to

Mrs. P. "What kind of information do they want from you, Mrs. Pérez?"

She grimaced and pulled her lips into a tight line.

Quint asked again, his voice terse, biting. " What kind of information do they want?"

The housekeeper straightened up, took a sip of her coffee, and thought for a moment.

"No lies, *señora,*" he said.

"No. No *mentiras.* They, Señor Santos and that man Luna, and another, a *jefe* in a suit came to my home. They want to know when I work. How I get in the door. I told them I am buzzed in. They ask about Lily and *Señorita* Stone and her dog, are they here? Can they see them? Are guns in the house? I am to call when the *señoritas* leave the house, where they are going, or when I am here alone with Lily. They want me to open the door for Sr. Santos."

"What were you looking for in my office, *señora*?"

"The *jefe*, he asked for reports. He want to know what you know."

"The boss? What's his name? What did he look like?"

She shrugged and shook her head. "Middle-aged. Heavy face and big lips."

I did my Richard Nixon imitation, shaking my jowls. "Like this?"

Quint snorted. "Farcía Luna."

He excused himself from our tribunal and we listened to the creak of the stairs as he trudged up to his aerie. Nothing had been decided. Lily looked downcast, taking Mrs. P's betrayal hard. I wondered how I could get the truth out of her and what we should do. Lily wouldn't want to let her go, but we couldn't keep a declared traitor in our midst.

"Señora Pérez, how can we trust you now? Look at this girl. She's crushed. Quint is upstairs arranging for your family to be taken to a safe place, but how do we know you'll align with us? How do we know, *señora*?" I banged my cup on the table. "Maybe we should tie you up and toss you in the laundry room until your bosses come to spring you. Lily?"

I laughed at the ridiculousness of the idea. No one would try to rescue her from our makeshift prison, a notion that abruptly ended my laughter.

Both Lily and Mrs. P stared at me as though I'd gone insane. Maybe I had. Maybe this was all too much. Maybe I'd gotten in too deep. An untethered sob rose up from that deep, washing over me. Maybe I was starting to be too much like the traffickers. Should I take Pepper and Dex's camper and go home—leave this phantom father and the troubled, trafficked teen, the duplicitous housekeeper, the well-meaning but ineffectual senators—leave it all behind me in corrupt, greedy, power-mad Mexico?

Mrs. P huddled in her chair, horror painted across her face, her tears cutting *arroyos* through her pancake makeup.

Lily wrapped around her, sobbing, choking out something that sounded like, "Why?"

That overwhelming vision of the Sarasvati settled on me; my orchids blooming beauty and calm into the world, the fog creeping down the canyons of Mt. Tam as the lights of Mill Valley twinkled up the ridges at twilight. I felt the barge softly rocking as the tide lapped against the hull. And Dex— I straightened up, swiped my hand across my face—Dex wasn't waiting for me. But maybe Dylan was. A tiny yellow bird warbled behind its black mask in the tree outside the window. Its sweet notes telling me a secret if I would only listen.

I drew in a ragged breath, willed my tears to stop. "I'm sorry, *señora*. I'm sorry, Lily." I shook my head to dislodge my homesickness. The bird flew away in a flash of yellow and grey. "Listen, we've got to get to the bottom of this. *Señora*, do you want to see Lily sold into sex slavery?"

She shook her head. "*Claro que no, señorita.*"

"Are you willing to help us stop the traffickers?"

She nodded.

"Say it."

"Sí, estoy de acuerdo."

"Lily? Are you in?"

She sniveled, swiping at her runny nose with the napkin.

"Just blow it, Lily. Are you?"

"Yeah," she said. "But I can't go out. Jade, I'm so tired of staying in. I want to do something."

"Well, here's the plan."

Quint loomed in the doorway. No one had heard him coming, not even Pepper, now awake and softly growling under the table. I reached for his head and gave him a scritch behind one ear. He woofed and clambered between the chairs shaking. Maya stood up and stretched a perfect cat and cow then went into downward dog. The pups jumped against the low barrier, yipping. They were getting too big to be contained by cardboard. I stood up and stretched too, but stopped abruptly when I caught his face.

"What is it? What's happened?"

He grimaced and tipped his head toward the housekeeper. She had gotten up and now cuddled the little runt like her life depended on it.

"Mrs. P, will you take the dogs out?"

"I'll help," Lily volunteered. "Come on Maya, let's go out." She pushed from the table and plucked the barrier away. They tumbled out of their nest in a riot of pratfalls, toenails ticking across the tiles and trotted through the stairs door Mrs. P held open, Lily bringing up the rear. "Pepper, come!" she said.

He turned to look at me. I nodded. He tore down the stairs after the goldens. The garden door slammed; a heavy silence crowded the kitchen, broken by the ticking of the clock. I glanced out the window to search for the tiny bright-yellow bird in the leaves, but saw only the hazy dun of

253

pollution on the horizon. "Time for a beer. Want one?"

His voice a low buzz of anger. "Nah. Today calls for something stronger." He reached up to the top cabinet and brought down a bottle of tequila and two shot glasses from the dish cabinet. The clock ticked, again disrupting the silence. Quint poured, the trickle sounding less like the happy gurgle of socializing than despair.

I downed my shot. "What now?"

"They kidnapped Anibal."

Chapter 25

House of Cards

I choked. The burning tequila caught in my throat, triggering a fit of coughing. Booze sprayed across the table. Quint poured me a new shot. I fingered the glass and gulped a breath of air before croaking, "Kidnapped? What happened?"

"The senator called. The van—attacked at the terminal. They were waiting. As soon as the AFI agents unlocked the cargo door, six or eight armed men swarmed in shooting. Both agents killed. Jones shot three of the men before he was wounded, but they grabbed Aguirre, shoved him into a vehicle, and vanished before anyone could stop them."

My heart skipped. I knew that trick. I'd seen the black van, the snatch, and heard the tires squealing into the distance. They'd tried it with me. "In broad daylight? What about bystanders? How does Polo know this?"

"Several witnesses; it was crowded as travelers arrived for the noon flight to L.A."

"Where's the cowboy?"

"Jones and four Japanese tourists were rushed to a hospital. The senator said the police took the bodies. Only one attacker was recovered, dead."

My head felt like it was in a vice. I slid my glass toward

the bottle, as if tequila could wash away the tension gripping me. "Who is he?" I shot back the golden liquid and dropped my head into my hands, my elbows propped in front of me.

"Unknown. Not talking."

I tried to laugh. Quint got up and opened the refrigerator, returning with two limes and a can of Sprite.

I mumbled, "Tattoos?"

"No Zs, if that's what you mean. I doubt this could be Zetas. How would they have gotten the exact time and place? Only one man knew the itinerary."

Light bulbs popped and confetti flew. I straightened up and stared at my father. "Farcía Luna!"

"Smart girl." He poured himself a second shot. "Damn, I forgot the knife," he said and smiled, eyebrows raised.

I sighed and crawled to my feet for the knife and a cutting board. "So it's a Beltran Leyva move," I mused, more to myself than to Quint. "Why would they want Anibal?"

"Think."

I slid a scarred wooden board toward him. He quartered the lime and splashed Sprite over the tequila shots.

"Slammers, Dad?" I asked, my voice sizzling with acid. But I pressed my palm over the glass, banged it twice and swilled the contents. I grabbed my slice of lime, sucked the juice and puckered, savoring the warm fog billowing into my brain. My muscles relaxed. Perfect. "I wouldn't have taken you to be a slammer kind of guy."

"Nor I, but extreme measures are called for," he said, and slammed his own shot.

"Let me get this right. You think that bulldog Farcía Luna tipped off the BLO as to when Jones would be taking Anibal to the airport. It was hardly a secret; he announced he had a twelve-thirty flight."

"He didn't. It was a two-fifty flight to D.C."

"Then why did he say that, and why arrive so early?"

I waved away a second slammer. Quint fixed his and drank it. I'd never seen him have four drinks in a row before. All I'd seen was him sipping a whisky or a beer. Drastic measures indeed.

The moment stretched. Finally he said, "I can't answer that."

"Can't or won't?"

"Can't. The senator probably knows. But what difference does it make now? Jones is in the hospital. I'm waiting for the senator to get back to me," he said.

"But what about the two wounded guys? Didn't you say the cowboy shot three?"

"Yeah, three, according to several witnesses."

I asked, "Hasn't anyone checked the hospitals?"

"In progress. We know one was shot in the leg."

He eyed the tequila bottle. I pushed it away and slid the Sprite toward his glass. The afternoon waned outside the window, fading sun tinting the smoggy sky rosy. I heard the little bird trill in the garden. Had Lily, Mrs. P, and the dogs been gone too long? I stretched around to see the clock. Already past six? I frowned. It was too quiet. I should hear the puppies at least, shouldn't I?

"Dad, how long has Lily been gone?"

He had slumped over the table, his hand engulfing the shot glass and jerked up to eye his watch. "Right. I better go check on them. Why don't you rustle up some food? Didn't I hear something about chicken and poblanos in cream?"

"*Chile rellenos*. We ate them for lunch. But what if they don't go to a hospital?"

"It's a slim chance. We're looking."

"They might go to Dr. Augustín." The sounds of barking floated into the kitchen. A happy bark. I blew out a breath and relaxed. They were back.

"Unlikely. He's the Zeta connection," he said, as he lumbered unsteadily to his feet and stretched, arching like

Pepper after his nap.

"But we're theorizing the tip-off came from Farcía Luna. We don't know they're not Zetas. Couldn't the plan have passed through Anibal and that squirrelly attorney?"

"It's possible, but they ain't going to find Augustín at home, now, are they."

It was a statement. He was right, we'd taken care of that earlier, but still.... watched him cross the room to the stairwell and peer down. The garden door banged open and the pack stampeded up the stairs, Pepper leading the way. I scrambled to fill their food bowls.

The gang safely back in the house, Quint went up to his lair to check in with Aguirre. Lily headed to the refrigerator and stood assessing her options through the open door.

"*Cierralo, niña,* close it,*"* Mrs. Pérez commanded.

"I'm just looking for something to eat." She pried open a Tupperware. "Salad, yuck."

"How hungry is everyone? Shall I order a pizza now?" I asked.

"Dominos! I want extra cheese and pepperoni," Lily responded.

"Mrs. P?"

"*Queso y tomate, por favor.*"

"With basil? Like a margherita?"

"Sí, albahca, pero no margarita, gracias."

"Lily, go find out what Quint wants on his. I'll look up the number." Lily and Maya bounded out and Mrs. P and I listened to the dull pounding on the stairs. Was I ever that energetic and noisy? It felt like another life when I was fifteen. Of course I was discouraged from running or making noise in the house. We wouldn't want to sully the perfection of peace and elegance, now, would we? I wished the suggestion of pizza could lift my mood as much as it was momentarily doing for Lily.

But our elevated mood was short lived. Quint and Lily

joined Mrs. P and me at the table and he was clearly scowling.

"What. You don't want pizza?" I asked.

"I do. Make mine sausage and olive."

I jotted his order onto my list. "Why the scowl?"

"Aguirre says the doctor was released."

"Why?"

"The man, your Sicario, wasn't there."

I snorted, thinking of my experience at that clinic. "Not locked in the storage closet?"

"No. The senator said AFI and police made a thorough search of the *consultorio* and his records for the past several months. They didn't have enough to hold him."

"What did they expect to find in the records? Anibal paying for me to be sewn up? He's taking cash from Zetas and not reporting bullet wounds."

"He's not cleared, but that kind of investigation takes time, Jade."

"Yeah, okay. And the hospitals?"

"Look, we can only do what we can do here," he said, his tone defensive.

"'Never mind, I'm ordering the pizza. Quint, you know where the Dominos is?"

"I'll find it."

I went out to the hall to the phone and dialed. Quint followed me. After I read over the order, I handed him the list to check at pick-up and gave him the address.

"I didn't want to get into it in front of the others, come downstairs with me," he said as he opened the elevator door and pulled me in."

I shouted, "Lily, I'm seeing Quint out. Be right back." The door clanked into place and the elevator slowly descended.

He remained silent for the slow drop to the *planta baja,* and his frown deepened. We juddered to a stop and he wrenched the door open. "Listen, Jones is in intensive care. They don't think he'll make it. The U.S. is making noise, putting pressure on Mexico to return Anibal."

"Where is he? Who has him?" I asked, as we stepped from the elevator. Outside the window I could see the guard's back in the dim porch light.

"No one has come forward. He's probably dead." He flipped on the entry lights and gestured to the settee. I sank onto it in tempo with my sinking heart.

Anibal had betrayed me, but I'd never wanted him brutally murdered. If the Zetas got him, he'd dissolve in acid. The BLO? I didn't know their tactics, but it would be terrible. No! I couldn't accept it. Anibal's kidnapping was something else. A rescue?

"No, Quint, don't say that. He's a bargaining chip. Two cartels want us. One of them is going to try and make a deal, although, I can't believe either group thinks Polo would trade us for a brother he detests."

"Unless his mother pressures him," he observed.

"She hates Anibal more than Polo does."

"Jade, you were always right about her. She's part of the BLO people trafficking ring."

"You have confirmation?"

"Bendicias reported SEIDO shut down the Pedrigal house today. They've got Consuelo. She's singing like a lark."

I huffed. "And they believe what she says? She's a liar and delusional; you told *me* that."

"Aguirre says they nabbed a couple of important government officials in the house raid. Even if it goes no further, that operation is completed, and Lidia Sotomayor has been implicated. It's a start."

"Polo isn't going to give her up," I said, my voice flat. We were circling.

Headlights sliced across the hallway as the limo nosed

into the driveway, and the guard rapped on the glass.

"Dad, you made Horacio drive across town to take you to get the pizzas? Really? Why didn't you get a cab? Or take my bus. Or I could have asked for delivery. Now we won't have enough pizza for everybody."

"Four large pizzas? No worries. Go on up, girl. I'll be back soon."

The old fashioned house phone jangled as I stepped out of the elevator. I sprinted across the room to answer. "*¿Bueno?*"

"Good, you answered. I've got a guy here I think you'll be interested in—"

My heart started to clog-dance, "Dylan?"

"I only have a moment, Jade. I've got a man prepped for surgery at the clinic. You and Quint will want to know. "

"You're in Iztapalapa? I thought you worked Sundays."

"I swapped with another surgeon." His voice dropped to a whisper, "I overheard his friends in the hall saying he was shot at a taquería in *el centro* today. They're planning revenge on your dad."

"Oh no! What did they say? How do you know?" I could hear the PA calling for someone in the background, but the name garbled.

"Hold on, I think they're calling me." The phone muffled.

I waited. Dylan had Sicario on his table? What were the chances of that? Static and muffled PA announcements streamed through the line. Polo needed to know. I paced to the end of the telephone cord, impatient. If we could get him we could find out who's behind the trafficking... we could... the line went dead. Blood surged through my limbs. We had a lead. I dialed the senator.

"*Bueno?*" It was Señora Arias de Barrera—Susana.

"Señora, it's JadeAnne. I need to talk to the senator right

now."

"He's not here, Miss Stone."

"Please call me JadeAnne. Where is he? How do I get in touch?"

"He's been in meetings all day at his senate office. May I leave him a message, JadeAnne? I'm about to leave for the day. He'll be home after his dinner meeting." Her voice sounded tentative, as though she needed to feel the sounds in her mouth. "Please call me Susana, too. Mr. Quint does."

"Thanks, Susana. But where's he having dinner?" I paused for a beat and rushed on, "Listen, this is really important. Dylan, the surgeon I'm dating? He's on duty at the clinic in Iztapalapa and has a man in his operating room we think is one of the Zeta shooters from the taquería today. Polo needs to have him arrested!" I sucked in a breath and slowed my pounding heart. We might be close to stopping this mess. Sicario would know where Cárdenas was.

"But you don't know?"

I shivered, picturing the man. "I will when I get there. I can ID him. So can Lily."

Susana's voice squeaked. "You can't go to Iztapalapa at night! Nobody does."

"Why not? As soon as Dylan calls back and we eat. Horacio can take us."

"He's with the senator."

"No, Horacio drove my dad to pick up pizzas."

"Who's with the senator?" Now she sounded worried. "I don't know where he's having dinner, JadeAnne."

"Well, who's he dining with?"

"Let me check."

The sappy hold music started. I paced toward the elevator to the length of the receiver wire, stretching the wire straight, and back to the spindly telephone table. I studied the cord as it sagged and curled into a U, which twisted upon itself into a tangle. I couldn't have expressed it better. My stomach clenched, heart racing.

"It's not in his book—there's nothing."

"Doesn't he carry a cellular phone?"

"You can try the car. Horacio will know where Senator Aguirre is. Do you need the number?"

"Quint has it. They'll be back soon. Okay, Susana, thanks." My anxiety notched higher. "I'd better leave the line open for Dylan to get back to me."

Susana's voice quavered. "Sorry I couldn't do more. I'll see if I can track him down."

Chapter 26

Pepperoni and Plans

The smells of cheese, garlicky tomato sauce, and sausage preceded Quint from the elevator. My stomach rumbled. Lily and I had set the table while Mrs. P fluttered about in anxiety. I tossed down a stack of paper napkins on my way to the fridge for the pitcher of *agua de jamaica* and the salad Lily had identified earlier.

"Hi, Horacio!" Lily said.

I turned toward the door. Quint carried a stack of five steaming pizza boxes. Horacio swung a Domino's bag onto the table. He appeared at ease. He must know where Polo was.

"Coke and Fanta," he said.

Lily rushed to empty the bag while Mrs. P bustled to set Horacio's place. I pulled another chair from the dining room and placed it at the table. "Quint," I said, "I have news."

He held up his hand, stopping me. "Let's have some pizza first." He looked at Shrek I and said, "*Siéntate, mano. Cerveza?*" and waggled a Superior in Horacio's direction.

Horacio nodded and sat down at the new place, smiling broadly. "*Gracias señoritas, señora, que amable.*"

I couldn't believe I was sitting down to eat with Shrek I. It had turned out he was as lovable as the real Shrek, although it hadn't hurt that I'd saved his life when Anibal and his pals tried to kidnap the senator. I realized how lost in the mists of time and events that seemed now. It had been only days ago.

"The boxes are marked. Help yourselves," I said, and grabbed a piece of my favorite: sausage, black olive, bell pepper, onions, and extra cheese.

For a period of time the only sounds were the smacking of lips, the rustle of pizza boxes, the clack of salad servers against the bowl, and the gurgle of dressing pouring from the cruet. I darted in for a third piece, this time the margherita. "May I, Mrs. P?"

She smiled and said, *"Claro, señorita."*

"This is better than Dominos at home. Can I have that last pepperoni?" Lily asked, pointing to the meaty wedge.

I shoved the box across the table. "Since we're all here, maybe we should come up with a plan. Have you discussed the situation with Horacio? Where's the senator, by the way?" I asked the driver.

Horacio pushed his plate aside and wiped the drip of sauce off his chin. "I left him at the offices. He said he would call when he needed me to take him to his dinner meeting. Why?"

I dropped my fork onto the dregs of dressing-soggy salad on my plate and reached for Horacio's empty plate, placing it on mine and got up. "I called Susana and she doesn't know where he is."

"Senator Aguirre doesn't always have her schedule his evening appointments," he said.

Then why had Susanna sounded so alarmed? "That must be it. By the way, Dylan called and may have something for us. I'm waiting for his call back. He thinks Sicario is on his operating table. Maybe Horacio can take us to the clinic after dinner?"

Quint's brow wrinkled. "Not one of the kidnappers?

Here in Del Valle?"

"No, Iztapalapa. Anyone else done?" I asked.

"You'll need to verify it's him before we can have him arrested," Quint said.

I nodded, balancing the dishes on my forearm, and raised my eyebrows at Lily. She looked scared. Mrs. P held up her plate, sliding it on top of the stack. I carried them to the counter and turned back to the table. Horacio's expression alarmed me.

"Horacio, ¿que pasa?

"*Señora Arias de Barrera no sabe adonde es Senator Aguirre?*" He looked at his watch. "I should have picked him up by now."

"Horacio, it's barely suppertime here—not even seven. Wouldn't his dinner start later? Eight, nine or even ten?" I asked, slipping into Spanish.

Lily gulped down the last bite of pizza. "What's going on, Jade?"

She couldn't follow our rapid Spanish. "Hey, don't bolt down your food, you'll choke," I said. "Horacio is worried. He thinks he should have heard from the senator by now. I thought it seemed really early. Dinner in the capital is late. Anyone need anything while I'm up?"

Lily shook her head again and poured another glass of Fanta from the bottle on the table. "Where's he going? Maybe someone else picked him up," she said.

"Maybe," Quint said. In terrible Spanish he asked the driver if it could be possible.

Horacio shrugged. "*No sé.* He doesn't usually go out without one of us protecting him, and Señora Arias de Barrera generally knows where he is. This doesn't feel right."

"Who's filling in for Omar?" I asked.

"*Nadie,* no one. I've been working double shifts."

My trouble meter ticked up a couple of notches. What if

— what if *what*? He was in a high security government building for crissakes. "Horacio, you know they kidnapped Anibal—"

"What?" His face colored.

"You didn't tell him, Quint? At the airport. Could they have gotten to Senator Aguirre?"

"*Ching*—" Horacio began, stopping with a glance toward Mrs. P, who frowned, but got up and started filling the sink to wash up.

As if she'd never heard a swear word before. "Yeah— holy shit!" I finished his interjection.

Quint was already punching numbers into his cell phone as he excused himself from the table. "I'll be back. Jade, get your phone and see if you can track down Dylan. Confirm who he operated on. Then check in with Susana. Maybe she has news." He turned at the door. "Mrs. P, here's your chance to prove yourself." He gave the housekeeper a piercing glare. She paled, shrinking against the counter. "Call Lidia Sotomayor and find out anything you can about Anibal's kidnapping."

She nodded, brushed past my father to the hall, the goldens following, probably angling for treats. I held Lily back.

"Listen, we're going to have to go out. I don't want to risk leaving you here alone. Let's go up and put on warmer clothes, dark, long pants, and running shoes."

"Okay, but do I hafta see him?"

"The Zeta? No, I'll make the ID. C'mon. Let's go up. Pepper!"

Mrs. P was definitely talking to someone on the hall phone as I passed by. I couldn't be sure if it was Lidia or whomever her contact was. All I heard before the stairs door slammed behind us was, ...alive? Yes, Tepoztlán..."

Tepoztlán? Wasn't that the place Dylan said he wanted to take me? I wondered as Lily and I trudged up the stairs,

Pepper crowding our heels.

At our floor, we split off to our own rooms to change. Twilight filled the shadows between the buildings and trees outside my window and the city had quieted from the evening commute. Eerie. I flipped on the light, shocked as ever to find myself in the over-plush red Madam's quarters. Consuelo wasn't much of a decorator, I mused for the nth time. But where she was going, she wouldn't need to worry about it. Pepper nosed around the closet and found my running shoes, laying one then the other at my feet while I rummaged in the dresser for black running tights and a charcoal long sleeved tee.

"Good boy, Peppie," I said and bent to give him a hug. The feel of his fur and the ripple of his muscles instantly calmed me. I hadn't realized just how much tension I was holding. Christ, my shoulders had crept up to my temples. I sank to my knees and took several deep breaths, taking in his familiar doggie smell as Pepper leaned into me with a sigh. "Peppie, do you miss home, too?" He woofed and wagged, wiggling around to lick my face. "But you have to stay here and guard the house."

My door cracked open as Quint called in, "I don't know if anyone is safe here. I didn't reach Aguirre, but I contacted his colleague, Bendicias. He's arranging a couple of men to guard the house and calling around to find Aguirre. He said the senator was to meet with him, Jose Luis Santiago, and a couple other blokes over dinner at Fonda el Refugio at seven and never showed."

"If he didn't have Horacio and the limo, how was he getting there?" I asked.

"Yeah. That was my question. Bendicias said he was catching a ride with one of his aides."

"Are his people vetted?"

"We'd hope so. Bendicias is sending people to the offices to check on his movements. There's nothing we can do beyond find out what Mrs. Pérez learned from Lidia."

Pepper whined and tapped my thigh with a shoe. "I think you better let me get ready, Quint—someone is anxious to go out." I kissed Pepper's head and Quint laughed. At least we could still find some humor amid all this.

"Yeah, I'll go down. We need a plan. What did Susana say?"

"I haven't called anyone yet. I'm *trying* to get dressed," I said as I shoved my dad out the door.

"I'll call, then. You get Lily sorted."

He closed my door and I pulled on my "eveningwear," topped by a lightweight black quarter zip, which was baggy enough to hide my gun, and grabbed my phone and purse. "Let's get Lily," I said to my dog.

Lily had taken the dark clothes to another level: black Doc Martins, raggedy faded black cut-off s over black fishnets—my black fishnets, I bet—and a midriff-baring muscle tee. She'd topped her outfit with a black knit cap and added a couple of black tattoos to her neck, cheeks, and hands—a flower, a lightning bolt, vines. "Good grief, Lil. Belly piercing? Tattoos?"

"To blend in. Don't roll your eyes; everyone has tattoos."

"Do they come off?"

"Duh, Jade. They're just transfers."

Nothing like a teen to make you feel totally stupid. "Okay, then let's go hear what Mrs. P found out. She was talking to someone."

"Can I have some ice cream?"

"It's not a party, Lily."

"It's so boring just sitting there while you all talk, talk, talk," she said. "Pepper, race you down." She opened the stairs door and took off. Pepper bounded after her.

In the kitchen, Mrs. P sat at the table with a cup of what smelled like chamomile tea. Quint looked like he needed one, pacing angrily back and forth in front of the sink. Maya sat up and wagged, her pups sleeping in a heap at her feet.

"What happened?" I asked.

"Ask Mrs. Pérez."

We all turned to look at her, even the dogs.

The housekeeper clutched her mug, her face taking on a defensive expression. The overhead light cast a sharp glare across the room. Funny, I hadn't noticed that before. "So? I heard you talking to someone. Who?"

She looked down. "*La señora Lidia no estaba en casa.*"

"Speak English," Lily demanded.

"She-she wasn't home."

"Where is she?" Quint demanded.

"I heard her mention Tepoztlán," I said, nodding toward Mrs. P. "Is that where Lidia went?"

Our housekeeper turned her head slowly side to side and slumped further down on her chair. I studied her. She wasn't trying to be evasive she was—

"Well, *señora*, spit it out. No lies." He towered over the older woman, his stance menacing. Even I cringed.

"She's not lying, Quint. Look at her. She's afraid." I reached across the table for her hand. She slid it into mine. "What is it, Mrs. P?" I asked gently.

"It's something to do with Senator Aguirre."

Quint roared, "Where is the senator?"

Lily closed the freezer door and went to Mrs. P. "Stop shouting at her," she demanded. "Mrs. P, tell us what's happened."

She rested her head against Lily as a tear slid down her cheek. I squeezed her hand and said, "Lidia went to Tepoztlán?"

"*Sí, señorita.*"

"Why!?" Quint shouted, banging his fist on the table.

"Sit down, Dad. Mrs. P, did they tell you?"

"*Sí,* to meet her godson. She said he boasted that he's

made a deal with Los Zetas."

I considered this for a moment. It didn't answer why she seemed to be so afraid, and it didn't tell us any more about Anibal's or Polo's whereabouts. "Let's go to Iztapalapa. Maybe we can get some answers there."

The phone rang. I pushed away from the table and returned to the hall, Pepper on my heels.

"*¿Bueno?* Oh Dylan, I was just about to call. Have you identified the man?"

"Our team is removing the bullets now. Your sicario's name is Javier Solis Carrillo, Z53. It's on his chin. Have you notified the authorities?"

"No. We can't connect with Senator Aguirre. Should I come identify him? He's one of the shooters at the kennels, maybe the one who killed Lily's sister."

"I'll send a photo. What's the email address?"

I told him then held the receiver away and yelled, "Quint, Dylan is sending a photo of the guy to your email. Thanks Dyl. We have another problem—the senator is missing. Can't you plant a spy to listen to his *cuates* or something?"

Dylan's baritone chuckle swelled through the wire. "Jade, I can do better than that. He's sedated. It's like truth serum. I'll question him before he fully comes to."

"Quint will want to hear this. We're coming, and bringing the authorities—" *I hope.* "How long do you think before you'll start?"

"I don't know, Jade. It's dangerous here at night and if these knuckleheads see you—"

Giggling, I interrupted, "Knuckleheads! Where did you get that?"

Dylan warmed my ear again with his laugh. "Three Stooges. Loved 'em as a kid. But to continue after your rude interruption, it's dangerous and I won't have time to visit. If his friends see you, you could be in big trouble."

"Dylan, I'm already in big trouble. So is Lily. But we'll be with Quint and Horacio—armed."

"I've a premonition of how life will be with you, Jade," he said.

A bolt of electricity zinged through me. *How life will be with you.* I felt my face heating up—good thing Dylan couldn't see me. "You got it, pal. Send the photo. I wish we could see his friends. I want to know who's heading up this trafficking."

"JadeAnne, I wish you'd leave things to the authorities."

I exhaled, disgusted. "Ha! Don't trust the authorities. We sat in a meeting today with the head of one of the big government agencies. The director is one of the traffickers, or at least he's paving the way for the trafficking. We're going to get the bottom of this. And I promise you, some corrupt officials are going down," I said with more bravado than I actually felt. The situation seemed like a giant tentacled, hydra-headed monster. The more we uncovered, the more we were choked off.

"...break at twelve-thirty, if you want to meet me for coffee," Dylan was saying.

"Coffee at midnight? Maybe. Anyway, I'll either see you or I won't. First Quint has to make some calls to arrange for Solis's arrest."

Dad swept past me, motioning the universal "hurry up" signal.

"I gotta run Dyl. Thank you so much," I said and hung up. I scurried after Quint into the stairwell. "Wait!" I called at his retreating back.

He slowed down and I caught up. Pepper had beaten us both to the second floor and waited, impatiently wagging, his paw on the closed door to Quint's third floor staircase. Dust floated on the doggy hall air.

"We need to open some windows and the stairs doors. It stinks up here."

He opened the stairs door and ushered me through. "I think the air is the least of our concerns. What did Dylan say?"

"He's digging bullets out of Carlos 'Carlito' Solis Carillo, Z53 from his tattoo." I said over my shoulder. Our feet kicked more dust into the close atmosphere.

"Why does he think it's your *sicario*?" he asked, huffing from the climb.

"His knucklehead *cuates*—friends—were talking about the taco incident outside the exam room. Dyl is sending pictures of Solis and I suggested photographing the friends, too. I wonder if one is Cárdenas? If we got him, we'd topple this ring."

"Solis won't be with the top dog, Jade; he's not a boss. Don't get your hopes up. If we can't get hold of anyone to authorize the arrest, these knuckleheads, as you put it—"

"As Dylan put it," I said between pants. The altitude still got to me.

"Yeah, okay, but these men are walking free."

I'd reached the third floor landing and stepped through the open door to the hall. "You should close the doors. We've seen how fires move in these old houses."

"You just instructed me to close them." He winked as he passed by me to unlock his den.

Chapter 27

Mrs. P Comes Clean

I shoved a stack of papers off a chair and plopped down facing the back of Quint's computer screen. I couldn't see it, but I heard his keys clacking. "Who are you contacting?"

"Bendicias. He's working on this and can authorize his team to make the arrest."

"Why don't you call him?"

"His team will locate him." He held up his hand then resumed a flurry of clacking. "They're finding him. Hold on."

I sat silently. Would Bendicias know anything about Polo? Why would the senator disappear? Unless he were forced. I was sure it had something to do with Anibal's kidnapping, but really, Polo wasn't in love with his little bastard bro'; he'd never go after him. Or would he?

Quint's phone line rang. "Bendicias, what you got?" He paused. "Yeah, but we've got another situation... uh-huh, yeah. Iztapalapa, my girl's surgeon friend is pulling my slugs out of one of the men from the taquería incident today... No, I don't believe in coincidences. The encounter at the taquería was random, but the hit at the airport was not—although we don't know that it was Los Zetas ... Yeah. Anibal's kidnapping and Aguirre's disappearance are connected we think... Aguirre's mother has taken off suddenly." He listened for a moment. "Tepoztlán. Yeah, that's the place."

I jumped up and waved, getting Quint's attention.

"Hold on a sec," he said, into the receiver. "What?" he asked me.

"I overheard Mrs. P on the phone. She said Lidia's gone to that place."

He held up his finger and spoke into the phone again. "Senator, that's the connection." He listened for a moment. "Lidia Sotomayor has gone there. I think that's where they've taken young Aguirre... No... No, I haven't heard anything more. But I'm guessing the senator went after his mother—" He held the phone away from his ear. "Jade, get Señora Pérez. Bring her here. Now."

"Tell him Mrs. P said Lidia went to meet her godson. That's Eddie Santos," I said as I leaped toward the door, clearing the pile of papers I'd stacked on the floor and aiming for the elevator.

I heard Quint's last words before the elevator door shut. "A BLO safe-house—" It was all coming clear. We were up against two cartels, both tied to Anibal, but only one with government sanction. BLO, Beltran Leyva Organization. Did they hit the transport at the airport?

Downstairs, Mrs. P was putting the dishes away as Lily dried and handed them to her. The pizza boxes had been cleared and the drinks returned to the refrigerator. Only the lingering scent of pizza remained. Horacio was eating a bowl of ice cream slathered in chocolate syrup and *crema*.

"Mrs. P! Quint wants you right now. C'mon." I turned back toward the door and nearly broke my neck tripping over a puppy. Horacio flung out his arm and caught me before I crashed into the table. "I guess we're even,.. said. His brow wrinkled, puzzled. I smiled. "*Gracias*."

We rode the elevator to the third floor in silence. I wondered what Mrs. P had been looking for in his office earlier—it was her chance to explain it. Or not. What could it have been and who was she giving it to?

Pepper met us at the landing and escorted us to Quint, who gestured to the chair I'd already cleared. Our housekeeper sat down, her hands trembling slightly. I laid my hand on her shoulder. "It's okay, Señora Pérez. Just tell us what we want to know and we'll take care of you."

He glared at me. *What?* I glared back. The stale air and crowded quarters felt heavy, stifling in the silence.

Quint cleared his throat. "Señora Pérez, what do you know about this place, Tepoztlán? Where is it? Why would Lidia go there? Tell us everything you know."

She exhaled and let her shoulders slump. "*Señor*, Tepoztlán is a town about an hour to the south of the city. It is not unusual for her to go there; it is where Señora Lidia has a weekend home, and she sits on the arts commission. They have an art festival coming up this fall."

"You said she was meeting her godson. Isn't that Eddie Santos?" I asked.

"*Señor* Eddie and his *jefe, el Señor* Lobo, are helping with the festival."

"She told us Lobo was producing a fundraiser for her next year. Why would they go to Tepoztlán to meet? And why did you sound upset on the phone?"

Mrs. P shook her head and looked at the floor.

"What upset you, *señora*?" he demanded.

She shook her head but remained silent.

I spoke rapidly in English. "I think Lidia has something over her. It's time to fire her."

Her head swung up. "No! They've taken Anibal there. That's what I know. Señora Lidia wants to stop them."

"From doing what?" Quint bellowed.

Mrs. P's tremors turned to visible shaking. "*Señor* Eddie made a deal..." she exhaled heavily. "Los Zetas. It is with them."

A deal between BLO and Los Zetas for Anibal. That explained everything. "The airport hit—BLO. It's why no one ended up at Dr. Augustín's clinic. Quin—"

The computer emitted a tone. Quint opened the file. "It's the photo from Dylan. Jade, is this the man?"

I leaned around the screen. The face of *Sicario* filled it, his tattoo clearly visible. "It's him. He was in the vehicle the day we found the trafficked children and he was there at the vet hospital."

Quint scrolled through a couple more images. Poor quality shots of three gangbanger types lounging around in what I figured was the hospital waiting room. Cárdenas was not among them. "I don't recognize these others. Can Senator Bendicias have them picked up?"

"He's on his way," he said then rounded on Mrs. P. "Have you been to this house in Tepoztlán?"

She nodded. "Yes, I know it. I have helped at parties and meetings many times."

He clicked at his keyboard for a few moments before shutting down the computer. "I let Dylan know the team would be there soon." He picked up his cell phone and hit a button. In a moment he said, "It's him. Send a team... yeah, four men... The doctor is expecting you." He listened for a moment, and replied, "I'll keep you posted. We'll probably need a team in Tepoztlán. We're getting the address and directions now."

I assessed my father at work. He looked tough, like that soldier of fortune playing dominos in the shack on Polo's plantation. Like that scruffy man eavesdropping on Lura, Anibal, and me at Las Velas bar at the Cristal Hotel in Ixtapa. A lifetime ago. And not a lifetime I'd want to revisit.

"Girl, you'll need your gun."

"I'm wearing it, and the Semmerling is in my pocket. What about Lily? And her." I jerked my head toward our turncoat housekeeper. "Are they safe to stay here?"

"I don't want either of them to stay here," he said as he locked his office door and strode to the elevator, ushering us along. I punched the button and the door opened. Quint guided Mrs. P inside and stepped out, saying, "We'll deal with you later. For now you and the girl will go into protective custody. " His tone was brisk, authoritative.

Mrs. P looked horrified as the door closed.

We made for the stairs and raced down, Pepper leading. Lily met us at the first floor landing, holding out the phone receiver. "Dylan."

"Thanks, Lil." I took the receiver as our housekeeper stepped out of the elevator. "Take Mrs. P to the kitchen. Quint and I have a couple more things to discuss, and then we'll get going."

Lily linked arms with Mrs. P and they returned to the kitchen, trailed by Quint and Maya. Pepper knew something was up and stuck to me like a burr. I stroked his ear as I asked into the phone, "What's happening?"

"He's in recovery, still out cold. His friends are getting restless. I saw one of them on a cell phone. As I passed by the waiting room, I overheard Aguirre's name."

"Which Aguirre?" I shifted my weight foot to foot.

"That's all I heard. They look like they're getting ready to go."

"You can see them?" I heard the blare of the clinic PA system in the background

"Yeah, I'm at the desk. It's a straight shot down the hall."

"Dylan, stall them. Can't you say someone has to wait to take him home when he wakes up?"

"I'll try. You and Quint are coming?"

"Someone is on the way."

"Has something happened?"

"Yes. We need somewhere safe for Lily."

"Take her to Seeger and Dafne."

"At the big house?"

"No, Seeger has a townhouse on Calle Oklahoma over in Napoles. Not far. I'm calling now." The line went dead. I joined the crew in the kitchen, Quint paced while Lily drummed her fingers on the table. Mrs. P stood at the sink, a statue.

I felt more optimistic and said, "Lily, we're taking you to Dylan's brother, Seeger. You'll be safe there and if anything happens, Dylan will get you to Colorado."

She frowned. "What about my dogs? And Mrs. P. She's not safe here, either."

I grabbed Quint's arm as he paced by. "What will we do with her?" And Pepper. I wouldn't risk taking him to a potential gunfight.

He stopped next to the housekeeper and gently turned her around. "*Señora*, go somewhere safe. We'll deal with you later. Don't go home."

She nodded and started for the door, collecting her handbag from the shelf. She gave Lily a last look, tears spilling over the reddened rims of her eyes.

"You can't send her away like this!" Lily yelped and ran to her, throwing her arms around the woman.

"We're sorry, Lily. When this is over we'll figure things out. For now, we need to get out of this house—all of us."

"But what about the dogs?"

I looked at my father. He shrugged. "I don't know. The house will be guarded, they're probably safe here. Bendicias' guards should be here. We need to leave as soon as they're briefed."

I eyed Lily up and down. "You might want to get a sweater and your toothbrush. We could be gone all night."

Quint nodded and escorted Mrs. P to the elevator. Lily hugged her one last time and disappeared into the stairwell.

"Thanks, señora," I said, and closed the elevator door as the phone rang again.

"¿*Bueno?* JadeAnne speaking. "

"Hi, it's Seeger. Dylan said to call."

"Oh, good, Seeger. May we drop Lily off with you? I have no time to explain, but we'll fill you in as soon as we can."

"We're looking forward to meeting her. Is she bringing the dogs?'

"May she?"

"Dafne can't wait to meet them. She's a big dog lover."

"Great! I'll pack up some dog food. Maybe Daf would like a puppy or two? They'll be ready for homes in a few weeks..."

"Jade, hurry it up," Quint yelled from the stairwell. "Security has arrived."

"Sorry, Seeger. Your address?"

He rattled off his address and directions I wasn't very clear on. I hoped Horacio knew where Calle Oklahoma was. "Thanks, see you soon." I hung up.

"Lily, get the dogs!" I yelled and turned to Quint. "You get the bowls and some food; I'm grabbing Pepper and my jacket."

"The senator isn't going to like having all those dogs in his car," I heard him mutter.

He was giving instructions to the four security men when I arrived at the ground floor. Lily herded the puppies toward the limo where Horacio waited with Pepper and Maya. I picked up two of the pups and dropped them on the backseat. Maya hopped in with them, grinning as always. Lily carried two more to the car, and we hunted down the last two. The little trouble makers, Roli and Poli. Roli squealed like a little pig when I grabbed him. "Oh shush, *tzcuintle*."

I got into the car with Lily and our menagerie and handed the address and my sketchy directions to Horacio. He read the paper and nodded.

"You know where that is?"

"*Claro que sí, señorita,*" he said as Quint slid into the shotgun seat. With a shotgun.

"Where'd the gun come from?" I asked, as we pulled through the gate. I swiveled around but didn't see what happened to the security team.

"Bendicias sent weapons with the team. You've got yours?"

"Yes, Dad, of course."

"Where's mine?" Lily laughed. I wasn't sure if it was better she was joking or if she should be afraid. Maybe she *was* scared. I certainly had a case of tremors going. I hoped I wouldn't have to shoot my gun, because unless the person were directly in front of me, I'd never hold that monster Glock still enough to hit him—or her. I might be shooting Lidia. No, what was I thinking?

About eight minutes later, I was introducing Lily, Quint, and Horacio to Dafne and Seeger. Pepper and Lily shared that forlorn, hang-dog expression as we climbed back into the car, but Maya was happily introducing herself to Dafne, who already held three of the squirming fur balls. I waved as we pulled away, my heart breaking. What if I never saw Pepper again?

Chapter 28

Down to Tepoztlán

Horacio turned on a cool jazz program and adjusted the volume down. "Miss Jade, it's going to be almost an hour's drive. Why don't you relax? Is the music loud enough?"

"Thanks, Horacio, it's fine. Quint, what's our plan?"

"Horacio and I are talking about it now. Take a nap. We'll fill you in when we get close."

"You got the address?"

"*Sí*, I've driven the senator there many times. *No te preocupes*."

We'd entered the *periférico,* the peripheral ring circling the city. It inched along with traffic. I slumped against the door and, as I watched the exits crawl by, something niggled. Something was off. The *laterals* were typically choked with vehicles, but most of the vehicles seemed to be getting off, and as we got closer to the exit to the toll plaza in Tlalpan, the traffic thinned. I'd driven south out of *la capital* before and 1 remembered we had to pass through a couple of toll booths.

I called over the seat, interrupting the men's conversation. "Horacio, if you didn't drive the senator tonight, how would he get down to Tepoztlán?"

Quint's expression said he'd been wondering the same

thing.

Horacio shrugged and started the climb up the mountain, *"No sé."*

I sat up and slid over to the left side of the car. As we ascended, the lights of Mexico City filled the Valley of Mexico, creeping up the mountainsides and twinkling through the layer of smog we climbed above.

The cityscape glittered vast and magnificent. I couldn't look away until we'd reached the summit and the city vanished. The blackness at the top consumed everything. It must be before moonrise. It couldn't be so dark—hadn't we just had a full moon? Time was bending in that weird way it does when too much goes on. I felt like I hadn't had a moment to catch my breath since the attack during the moon eclipse. Yet that seemed to have happened in another dimension. Had it only been three days ago?

Up front, Horacio wagged his head in time to *Take 5* as he navigated the steep descent into Cuernavaca. The highway was broad, smooth, and fast. I peeked over his shoulder—120 km. I wondered what the speed limit was as we flashed by a cluster of roadside restaurants. We were around the next bend and enfolded in pine shrouded darkness before the tantalizing smell of tacos reached me. My stomach growled. Pizza had been hours ago. I checked my watch, 10:14, okay not *that* long ago, but the tacos smelled good.

"Hey, can we stop for tacos next time?"

Horacio grunted something I took for, "We're not on a Sunday outing."

Quint stirred then resumed his soft snore. The blinker clicked on just as the lights of Cuernavaca flashed in front of us, but we were already exiting under the *carretera* overpass, and shooting out along the shoulder of the range as we angled toward the east and the now visible moon.

"How much farther?" I asked.

"Half hour or so. We'll be hitting surface streets in about fifteen minutes."

Car lights were coming up pretty fast behind us. Horacio had slowed down to about 110 km, and that driver was taking a risk. The drop-offs disappeared into blackness far below and the switchbacks angled steeply. "Horacio, that car is going too fast."

"I'm watching it. It picked us up in Coajomulco. Someone knew we were coming."

"What? You said not to worry," I screeched, flying up from my slump against the window.

"Uh! Hey, hold it down, Jade," Quint muttered, covering his ears. "Where are we? Did I fall asleep?"

I turned to watch through the back window. The headlights raced toward us; my pulse raced in my veins. "They're after us. Horacio says they knew we were coming. Why'd you let Mrs. P leave? I know she finked our plans. I know it!"

"It wasn't the housekeeper—"

I interrupted, "What do you mean. You sent her out. Lily and I watched—"

"Yeah, she left, right into custody. I wasn't about to have her picked up in front of the girl. We had a man waiting on the street. She's being questioned. She'll talk."

"What about her family? She said—"

"I know what she said, and we're moving them now. What do you think I've been doing, girl?"

He sounded annoyed. Maybe just cranky without his coffee. I'd learned over these couple of weeks that my father needed his java before he was fit company. Something I took after.

"—who is the mole in the senator's operation, Horacio?" Quint was asking.

"Possibly the senator himself. His phone could be tapped. La Señora Arias de Barrera reported clicking sounds on both house and office lines yesterday."

"Clicking means eavesdropping?" I asked.

"Amateur job if that's the case," Quint said.

He had his side mirror aimed to see behind us. The dash lights lit him up enough that I could make out his tension and hear the thumb drumming on his leg. He had his gun ready.

"Getting close, Horacio. Can we outrun them? Jade, have your gun handy."

"*Claro, jefe,* but they'll catch us at the toll both."

"Can we blow through?" I asked.

"Then we'll have the federal police on our tail," Horacio said.

"Can't they arrest these guys?"

Horacio barked a laugh. "*Estos gueyes* son *los federales.*"

A gut punch—the car following us was protecting the kidnappers of an American citizen and a Mexican senator? I choked out, "The feds? How do you know, Horacio?"

"*Placa. No se acercan sigilosamente a nosotros.* They plan to attack at the toll booth."

My brain scrambled to translate—it was the license plate. They weren't trying to sneak up on us. I saw his mouth flatten into a line as the vehicle closed in and paced us. I clutched my gun. Ahead the lights of the toll booth flashed into view and disappeared as we rounded another bend. Cuernavaca spread far below us. The low barrier marking the edge of the cliff wouldn't stop the limo if it started over. Nausea roiled in my belly and threatened to send up the pizza. I looked away. Horacio slid the car toward the double line and hugged it. He'd had the same thought. An oncoming semi flashed its lights and blared its horn as it passed, grinding into low to start the climb up to the tollway.

The lights of the toll booth and a settlement beyond appeared. Speed limit signs said to slow down, prepare to stop. I felt the limo slow in time with the gripping of my gut.

"We're not—" My breath caught in my throat. I inhaled deeply and held it for several beats of my racing heart— "stopping, are we?"

My dad reached back and held out his hand. I took it. "Keep breathing, Jade. Get on the floor. Keep your gun ready. This tank is armored."

Why didn't his words calm me?

I could clearly see the black SUV with a D.F. government plate and two men in the front. Yep, dark blue uniforms, balaclavas, assault rifles. Shotgun pointed at my head while the driver punched a burst on the siren. The noise pierced through me. I clapped my hands over my ears. The toll-taker ducked.

"*Detenerse*. Pull over." Scratched through a loudspeaker.

Horacio dropped the toll out of his window, punched the gas, and the limo bolted forward, a quarter horse off and running as the toll plaza lit up with flashing lights and sirens. We shot through the booth before the gate dropped. I swiveled on the seat to watch as the SUV crashed through it and was suddenly surrounded by local police cars and highway patrol. That was fast. My heart hammered in my chest.

We roared ahead, clearing the toll plaza and careening around a corner into the outskirts of a town. "Tepoztlán?" I gasped, trying to catch my breath.

Horacio nodded. "Hang on."

The highway dropped over the shoulder of the mountain, shrinking into a steep, narrow street twisting into a wooded canyon dotted with lit houses and dark roadside businesses. The lights hadn't appeared behind us. Horacio tapped the gas, swerving across the road in front of a delivery truck lumbering up the canyon. We were swallowed into a black alleyway between buildings and bumped along the cobbles a short distance before turning down another steep incline. He flicked on the brights. The light disappeared into the inky distance as the high walls on either side of the street closed in.

"You know where you're going?" Quint asked, his voice low.

"Short cut," our driver replied, and skidded around a corner into an alley running horizontally along the mountainside.

Mist was appearing in the trees, and on tops of walls. I felt the tires slip on the cobbles.

I scooted up, folding my arms over the seats. "Will they come after us?" We'd sure see any headlights. This neighborhood was like the dark side of the moon.

He turned toward me. "They know where we're going, Jade, but this gives us time to make a plan."

"You guys mean you haven't come up with anything yet? What were you talking about?"

"Horacio briefed me on what he's found out."

"Which was?" I demanded.

I clung to the grab handle as the car turned downhill again and jounced through a deep pothole, banging the undercarriage, then slewed through a deep rut. Horacio braked as he fought the steering wheel.

"Are we lost?"

"*Lo siento*. No, not lost, *señorita*. We'll come up behind the house. We can assess the situation before moving in."

"That's the plan?" I asked.

"For the moment."

I exhaled my exasperation. The limo crept through what I guessed to be a washed-out road, jogging back and forth, up and down. What if we got stuck? What if the bottom of the car fell off—we'd scraped and banged it enough. Could that even happen? I tried to relax my tense muscles, roll with the jounces. The limo made another left turn and the roadbed smoothed out some. We passed several parked vehicles and gates lit by electric lights mounted on their posts. Had we arrived in the real town? We accelerated slightly until we came to a barrier marking.. intersection. In front of us, a mountain rose in the misty moonlight, faced by sheer cliffs and strangely sculpted outcroppings.

"We're not going there, are we?"

"Nah. Below it," Quint said.

Horacio turned left uphill. Through the rear window I saw the grid of the town marked by street lamps and house lights.

"What do you mean? Where are we, Horacio?" Was he randomly testing the maze of Tepoztlán's streets? My heart skipped. All the streets looked alike in the dark.

"We're just above *el centro*. We need to cross the main street at the foot of the cliffs. There won't be any traffic or pedestrians. We'll circle behind the old part of town and that outcropping over there," he said, and gestured toward one of the odd shadows, "then down along the base of the range until we get to the *inmuebles, hacienda*. There's a *callejon* that runs along the north wall between estates. We'll be able to assess the situation from there."

Quint asked, "What about the car?"

"We'll leave it in a stand of oak and scrub. In the dark, it will be invisible," Horacio rattled off in Spanish.

"Jade?"

"He said we'll leave the car in some trees. So what exactly are we going to *assess*?" I asked, emphasizing the word. "And why are we going uphill if we're supposed to go down the valley?"

Horacio spun the steering wheel and we rolled over a paved bridge. "We needed the *puente* to cross the *barranca*. We'll turn down in a couple of blocks. When we get to the *inmuebles*, we'll watch."

For? I wondered. The back tires skidded on the damp cobble. This seemed like the long way around. I'd forgotten why we were on this mission. "Quint, I don't get it. We're going to watch? Watch what? It's an estate—isn't that what *inmuebles* means?— how will we see anything?"

He shrugged. "I dunno. From what H says, the living room opens to the patio and pool. Most of that side of the house is windows. He thinks we'll see the senator and his mother. He expects we'll see who else is there with them."

I tried to picture it. "What about Anibal and guards? A place like this will have guards."

"We have binoculars and infrared goggles. We'll keep our distance until we determine where Aguirre is and if he's being held. We hope to identify the kingpins of the trafficking ring."

"So it's a rescue attempt?"

"What did you think, Jade?"

"Oh Christ, Quint. I don't know." Could my voice sound more disgusted? I thought we were meeting the authorities to arrest Anibal and maybe his BLO pals. It's what I *wanted*.

The car banged through another ditch and rolled to a stop at the curb in front of a stop sign. We'd reached the paved road. Horacio turned off the lights and we sat in silence but for the ticking of the cooling engine. Nothing moved and, other than the street lamps, the buildings, mostly businesses, stood dark. I saw a curve to the left where the road disappeared into the trees.

"If they know this route, they'll be waiting ahead," Horacio said, voice low. He'd turned off the jazz back at the top of the ridge.

Tick... tick... In the stillness the sound of crickets swelled.

Ranchero music floated from someone's apartment. Through my cracked-open window I smelled Mexico, a combination of gas leak, old tortilla oil, chilies burning and garbage. But here, something else, too. Forest. Dylan wanted to bring me here. He'd called it a *Pueblo Mágico*. I smiled.

We'd need his magic tonight.

The vibration of the engine turning over brought me back. We were rolling. I guessed if the men thought there was danger, we'd still be at the curb. We motored into the bend and were suddenly out of town and on a wooded road.

Horacio pointed up the road as we turned right onto another cobbled track. "The way to the ruin. You should hike up to it next time you come. And eat at Axitla after you hike down. It's on the road near the entrance to the park. I bring my family during *Carnaval*. *Tepoztlán es un pueblo mágico.*"

"Dylan said he wants to invite me here. Are we close to the house yet?"

"Maybe fifteen or twenty more minutes depending on how bad the roads are," he said.

"Isn't it too late to see people sitting around the pool?"

"Not here. They won't have gotten back from dinner before eleven."

I checked my watch. 11:25. "You're kidding. Some assholes have kidnapped Anibal Aguirre and possibly a senator and then they went out to eat?"

"Yes. Lidia Sotomayor doesn't keep a chef at the house. He comes in during the day when people are in residence and prepares the meals, but since this will have been an unplanned visit, she will treat her guests to dinner at the Posada del Tepozteco. We passed it on our way to the bridge over the canyon."

"Where a limo was parked?" I pictured the limo and a flash of some well-to-do types coming out of a door in the center of a non-descript stucco building.

"It's famous now because they filmed the birthday party scene there in *Clear and Present Danger*. You saw that film, *¿no?*" Horacio asked.

"Yeah, I loved that movie." I replied.

"I was always a Tom Clancy fan." Quint said, adding,

"The author. You say it was filmed here?"

"Some of it. In '93 or '94. I'd brought the kids that weekend. It was a mess, traffic, streets blocked off, film crews jamming the restaurants. The kids loved it. "

Had I stepped into the twilight zone? My newly acquainted father, a security guard-slash-driver and I were on our way to kidnap a kidnapped senator, sneaking the back alleys of a "magic village" and discussing movies and books like we were old friends at a coffee klatch.

We'd arrived in the valley. Without the headlights, the limo glided along the hard-packed, sandy lane. The lane skirted walled compounds to the east and dense scrub toward the mountains. I made out scrubby oak and nopal cactus as well as plenty of brush I couldn't identify in the soft moonlight. As we crossed.. intersection a black SUV pulled through tall iron gates. A dark clad figure closed the gates behind it, the shape of a rifle slung across his shoulder. I shivered.

"Hey, did you see that?" I asked.

"No. What?" Quint replied.

"Armed guard at the gate of that property."

"Tonalli. He mans the gate for Señora Sotomayor when she comes down," Horacio said.

"Say what?" I asked. "Tonalli the gardener?"

"You know him?" Horacio said, surprise in his voice.

"He's supposed to come tend the garden for us. Quint, it's Friday. Did he come?"

He shrugged. "Maybe Lily knows."

I had a bad feeling. Maybe Lily had told him what was going on. She'd been out with the dogs for an awfully long time. "Quint—"

"Jade—"

We spoke at the same time. I said, "You go..."

"Mrs. P couldn't have known we were coming here in time to have communicated with anyone."

"My thoughts, Dad. Unless Lily told her earlier. But Lily didn't know. We were talking about going to the clinic. Somehow, I doubt this is about Mrs. P. She looked shocked when we talked about Anibal being kidnapped. I don't know what Lidia's part in it is, but I'll give you two to one that fat creep Farcía Luna has something to do with the kidnapping."

"Why would Farcía be interested in young Aguirre? He's got no political capital," Horacio asked.

The car slowly crunched along the sand. The road seemed to have all but disappeared. I hoped we didn't get stuck and have to go to the house for help. Now that would be irony. I thought about Horacio's question for a moment. Duh! Pieces of the puzzle fit. "Farcía is high in the trafficking ring. It's payback for Anibal turning on them."

"*Tal vez sí.* But I think they're coming after you, *señorita*, and Miss Lily."

"It's not like they don't know where we are."

Quint's eyes flared and his skin glowed ghost like. "It's a trap."

"What is?" I asked.

Horacio nodded. "I got it. The whole thing—young Aguirre, Señora Sotomayor, the senator missing—even the housekeeper prowling your office, Mr. Quint. You were meant to come here tonight."

My voice rose. "You mean Polo is in on it too?"

Horacio turned at the end of the west wall to follow the north wall. "I wouldn't have thought it before," he said.

This was a track, overgrown and barely passable. A hundred yards in, the block wall ended and was replaced by a lower rock wall topped with barbed wire fencing. It looked like volcanic rock. Horacio steered into a narrow break in the underbrush and stopped the car in a small clearing surrounded by oaks and more brush. He was right, unless you were looking, you'd never see the car.

"We'll stay here until the car cools and we're certain we

haven't been followed. Stay in the car. I will collect the equipment." He opened the door silently after popping the trunk. I had to hand it to Mercedes, it didn't make a sound. In a few moments, he returned with two black duffels and slung them onto the front seat.

Quint unpacked, handing me items I'd need: my bulletproof vest, infrared goggles, a wide-billed black cap, binoculars, a radio commlink, or I guessed it was. "A commlink?" I held it over the seat.

"Put your vest on and sweater over it."

"I have my knit cap," I said as I shrugged into the vest and did it up.

"Not good enough. The cap is wired to the mics."

I put it on at a rakish angle. The bill was a little big.

As if reading my mind, Quint said, "You'll be glad if a floodlight is turned on you. Here let me tighten up your goggles."

I handed them over the seat.

He tossed them back to me. "How's that?"

I put them on. Not too snug fit, but weren't going to slip. "Good. Now show me how to use this thing."

Horacio slid back into the car wearing combat blacks. He spoke slowly in English. "It is clear. We go."

The men tested their radios and I heard everything clearly. Quint showed me the button to activate the mic and demonstrated how to push once for no and twice for yes. Couldn't be easier. We got out, careful not to slam the doors. Quint clipped my mic into position and Horacio tossed him a scary looking weapon. I felt a little sick. My heart raced and perspiration moistened my hairline and scalp. What the hell was I doing?

"I don't get one?" I quipped, trying to lighten up.

"Not a chance, girl. Your job is lookout. We'll plant you where you can see what's going on and you'll tell us who is where and what they're doing. Keep your Glock ready."

Alone? I stiffened. "What about dogs? I should have Pepper with me."

"Only the *señora's* pets. Follow me. Miss Jade, you behind your father."

Chapter 29

My Leopoldo Is Not Part Of The Deal

Saturday, September 1, 2007

We crouch-walked along the wall in single file until we were directly opposite the patio off the living room. The way the house had been sited on the lot, we were so close we could hear voices, although not the words. A bank of bushy roses protected us, a sweet vanilla scent wafting in the air. Lidia's guests couldn't possibly see us. Horacio waved me ahead and pointed out a narrow stile leading into a path through the bushes. I could see the dim outline of a small structure.

Quint tugged on my sweater's hem, flicked his hand toward the structure, and tapped his goggles. I put mine on. The scene brightened. I clearly saw the structure, although everything took on the hue of green slime. I realized it was a child's playhouse. Quint wanted me inside it to watch and report. I stepped over the stile, edging through the roses. A half-pint door leaned ajar, jammed open by a rose sucker coming up between it and the building's frame. I crawled in.

The playhouse hadn't seen a little girl in many moons. Possibly since Lura and her sister, Alex, were children. Instead of tiny tea sets, it was filled with dead leaves, creepy crawlies, and a chandelier caked in spider webs. Were there poisonous spiders in Tepoztlán? Horacio had told me about the millions of scorpions. Even the lamp posts we passed had iron scorpions decorating them. I was glad of the hat and the gloves Quint had handed me at the last moment.

I stood up, almost hitting my head on the ceiling, but got a better look at the playhouse as I stepped in front of the two windows. One was shuttered and overgrown by a trumpet vine, but the window directly facing the patio was open. My breath caught in my throat. Could I be seen? I jerked back. A little wooden table sat under the window with two child-sized chairs, which I could tell from old scabs of paint, had once been bright hot-pink and turquoise. I silently brushed the debris off the table and arranged myself in a half-lotus behind a sagging shutter. The other shutter gaped wide letting me see clearly.

And there he was in a padded pigskin chair with a fat cigar stuffed in his mouth—Farcía Luna. Lidia sat primly across from him on a matching settee, a wineglass perched on the low table in front of her. Eddy Santos leaned on the back of the settee on folded arms, drink in hand.

I took a few deep breaths and settled in, clicking the, "I'm in place," signal over the commlink.

As I relaxed my mind and body with my yoga breathing, my eyes adjusted to the ambient light, which, through the goggles took on almost daylight intensity. Well, if you were on Mars. The night sounds amplified: the grating whir of cicadas, the alarmed warble of a night thrush, the sharp clink of ice on glass and Lidia's voice, "You will keep my son out of this."

I tuned in, cocking my head to point an ear in their direction. The house, almost entirely glass facing the patio and pool, was built in a wide V with the tiled patio slightly sloping to the lawn, which dropped gently to the wall. I realized it acted as an amphitheater. Horacio must have known.

Farcía Luna growled something, his vocal range below my hearing.

Lidia again, angry. "You've been well paid, Genero. My Leopoldo is not part of the deal. We've got my husband's bastard, and he'll be turned over to Cárdenas to close this deal. And good riddance."

Farcía slammed his drink onto the table and shouted, "Your stepson cheated us and is going to pay."

Lobo came in carrying a tray laden with a brightly colored gourd-shaped bottles and small glasses. "Your liquor cabinet is impressive Lidia. Farcía, ever taste an Asombroso Reserva? Two thousand dollars a bottle. Best sipping tequila in the world. Let's enjoy a glass and stop bickering. Lidia has a—" His voice muffled as he turned his back to me and set the tray on the table.

Lobo, the jackass, was helping himself to her expensive booze, and Lidia, already fuming, steamed. "It was a gift from a client," she said, her voice sharp.

Eddy giggled and came around to take a glass. as Luna handed them out. Each held their glass up and said, *"¡Salud!"*

"*Madrina*, what do you want me to do with Polo?" Eddy asked.

She flew off the settee, a tiny yellowjacket in her yellow dinner suit, angrily buzzing the giant blundering into her nest. "What do you mean, Eduardo? What do you have to do with Leopoldo? Where is he? I've called and he did not answer."

Luna busied himself pouring another round. Farcía had the good sense to look contrite as the fury rounded on him. She waved the glass away.

"What have you done to my son?"

"Nothing, Lidia, nothing." He drew out her name slowly, coyly. "He's fine."

I felt the winter in her look from the bottom of the

garden. Lidia was no slouch. She knew something was afoot. "How would you know, Genero? Your meeting ended before lunch." She plucked her wineglass off the low table.

Eddy's creepy, high-pitched giggle bounced off the building, echoing around the yard. Lobo glared at him. "*Cállete, mano.* You're not helping anything here." He extended his hand toward Lidia as she paced past him, her glass held like a knife in her hand. This was too good! Was Lidia about to smash her glass and stab Farcía? If only...

I whispered into the mic, "Lidia doesn't know where Polo is. I can hear her clearly. She's pissed off. Farcía has done something. Where are you guys?" The commlink clicked, but neither man spoke.

Eddy followed Lidia as she stormed into the living room. His tinny voice bounced off the windows. "*Madrina,* let me pour your wine. We—"

I could no longer hear them, but I watched Eddy take her glass from her fingers and fill it, a little too full, from the bottle he carried, giving her a one-arm hug as he handed it back. Placating. I recalled *madrina* meant godmother. I wished I could hear what Farcía and Lobo were saying and considered trying to get closer. Where were the guards? I remembered Tonalli. He had struck me as a wuss, afraid of my dog, not a tough cartel guard. Quint wasn't going to hurt him, was he?

The men hunched over their cigars, leaning toward each other as they held a hushed, but animated discussion. Lidia vanished into the interior of the house; Lobo checked his watch; Eddy stepped back onto the patio, and said, "Yo, *hermano*, shouldn't they be here by now? She's checking on him, although there's no way he could have gotten loose."

This is what I needed to hear. I whispered, "I'm certain they have Anibal here. Cárdenas is coming for him."

Quint's voice filled my ear. "Do you know where they have him? What about the senator?"

"Lidia is in the house somewhere. She said Polo isn't answering. She's worried. Farcía knows where he is, but he's not saying, at least not loud enough for me to hear. Anibal is in that house. You have to find him."

"I'm in. H, you done?"

"Three neutralized. Kid still on the gate. Fourth patrolling in direction of the *señorita*."

I froze. What would I do if he caught me? Could I shoot a human being at close range? Adrenalin surged through me. I'd have to, or I'd be sold into slavery, the sex toy of some Arab oligarch. My shaking morphed into a full-body shudder. No way Jose! I'd shoot.

"Jade, get out of there and get ready. And for God's sake be quiet."

As if I'd make a racket, I thought as I unwound my limbs and slithered off the little table into the deep shadows on the back wall. I crept to the mini door, a hatch more like, and crawled out. The bushes were too thick for a guard to push behind the playhouse. I reckoned I'd be safe.

Chapter 30

The Sting of the Scorpion

The sounds of the night stilled. I no longer heard the people, but I saw a green shadow through the rose hedge moving toward me, bright flashlight beam bobbing along its path. I was glad now for that wide bill. The light was blinding through my glasses. The guard closed in. The crickets fell silent. I held my breath.

He stepped into the crack of visibility along the edge of the structure. I pulled back before daring another look. The squeal of rusty hinges screed into the night—he was pulling on the closed shutter. He'd moved in front of the playhouse.

A shout from the patio. "Hey, you there! Everything quiet? The package secure?" It was Farcía.

"*Sí, jefe*. Making my rounds. *Buenas noches*." The structure rocked when he shoved closed the shutter.

I heard him push open the second shutter and felt him lean in to shine his flashlight around. Light spilled from the hatch but didn't reach me. I didn't dare breathe.

The guard's radio squawked, rending the night's calm. My heart hammered. Was I having a heart attack? It squawked again and a voice scratched, *"¡Ouxilio! ¡ Mayday!"*

"Go ahead. Over," the guard responded.

300

"José is down. I repeat, José is down. We have guests. Over."

"Roger. Over."

I looked around the corner. The man already loping across the lawn, shouted, "Get inside. Intruders."

But Lobo and Farcía were up and moving to the patio door. Lobo had the bottle of tequila in his hand.

"Watch out. They found one of the guards," I said into my mic. He's going toward the front." A surge of excitement zipped through my body. I was on top of it. I had important information.

Two clicks—affirmative.

"Where are you?" I said.

"Inside," Quint answered.

"Horacio?"

"Gate secured, sentry neutralized. Joining you *ahora, jefe. Momentito,*" he said and clicked "out."

"What do I do now?" I asked.

"Move to the road and stay hidden. Three clicks when Cárdenas shows." He paused. "Jade, don't try anything. Stay hidden."

"Okay, *jefe.*" I clicked out and slinked toward the stile as low to the ground as I could get. It made me appreciate the mountain climbers my personal trainer made me do. I felt like a jaguar and wanted to roar.

I slouched along the low wall, barbed wire, and thorny hedges until the wall shot up to its full height. It was topped with glass and razor wire. From the pallets of cinderblocks and sacks of cement piled up, it looked like the project wasn't finished. That must be why the compound wasn't fully enclosed. Lidia didn't strike me as one to let an important detail slide, but what did I know. I stopped before reaching the corner bordering the road. Lights on the top of the wall. I wondered if they were motion sensors and if I'd missed Tito Tormenta's arrival. I waited, listening. I was well hidden by the cover of brush and what looked like a stand of willow trees against the wall to the neighboring property. One without glass or razor wire.

Sure enough, in a couple of minutes, the lights flipped off. How did Quint and Horacio get around the corner? The good news: I couldn't hear any vehicles, voices, or clanging wrought iron gates. Maybe Cárdenas hadn't arrived. But maybe I just couldn't hear anything. I backtracked to the beginning of the high wall where I could still see the road, and into the compound to double check. I'd come around the house. It looked like a kitchen garden and sheds filling up this corner. I got out my binoculars and surveyed what I could through the hedging. Yep, I could see the gate and part of the entry. A squarish shape merging into the dark just beyond my focus was probably an SUV. No Zetas. How many would come? Quint and Horacio were going to need me. And I had a little vendetta to collect. I gritted my teeth and climbed over the wall into the cover of a patch of corn.

I made my way toward the sheds. Lidia said Polo wasn't "part of the deal" and that told me he had to be here. But where? I kept to the shadows until I reached the closest structure. The door was open. I listened. Nothing but the sounds of crickets and dogs barking in the distance. I flashed my light. Garden tools. I crept on to the next structure. It was larger and smelled like a garage when I put my face to the crack of the sliding doors. Pitch black. I'd have to go in. I cocked my ear to the opening. Silence, no groans or breathing or anything. God! He wasn't dead, was he? I pushed the door a couple of inches and shot a beam into the garage, staying low in case there were windows I hadn't seen. A tractor, chainsaw, ladders, shelving of paint cans, a pallet of adobe blocks. I didn't see windows or doors—or bodies.

I had one more building to investigate. Getting to it meant crossing a swath of the driveway with no cover. I crouched at the edge of the equipment barn and assessed the risk. The house had windows, although most were dark. I could clearly see the gate and gatehouse, which meant Tonalli could see me, except, hadn't Horacio taken care of him? My gut wrenched. What exactly did that mean? Tonalli was a gardener, liked the goldens and had been kind to Lily. He wasn't one of *them*, was he? Anyway, it was obvious he wasn't there. In fact, looking again, the gate stood open.

I considered my route. I could zig back toward the garden and mingle with the tomatoes to reach the water tank, circle around it, and sprint the short distance across open ground to the third structure. I could sprint directly from here, but it was much farther. The tank was close to the wall and motion sensor lights. Would there be sensors aimed into the compound? I closed my eyes trying to put myself in Lidia's mind. How would she design her security? Silly! She didn't have the place walled in. She wouldn't have the sensors pointed into her yard. I zigged.

The sandy ground softly crunched under my shoes and the lights did not blaze to give me away. My only problem was the lock on the door. I'd read in a book once that good sleuths always wear a couple of hair pins to pick locks. I pulled one from my hair and fiddled with the lock until it popped open. Ha! You would think someone as wealthy as Lidia Sotomayor could afford decent padlocks. But I was in. I closed the door and turned the beam onto my surroundings. Storage. Boxes, furniture and—pay dirt.

"Polo!" I whispered.

He lay on the floor, gagged, arms and feet tie-wrapped, eyes wide in fear. I pulled off my cap and goggles. "It's me, JadeAnne. We've come for you. Are you okay?" I pulled the dripping rag from his mouth. Yech.

He coughed and sputtered then croaked out what might have been "yes." I guessed a disgusting rag caused severe dry mouth. I pulled the knife Quint had given me out of its ankle sheath and sliced through the tie wraps around his wrists and ankles. He rolled to a sitting position.

"JadeAnne. Thank you," he said, rubbed his wrists. He kicked his feet together to get circulation going. His skin looked pasty.

I put my finger to my lips and tapped the mic once.

Quint's voice responded, "Yeah."

"I found the senator. He's okay."

"I told you to keep an eye on the road."

"Sensor lights. I came through the garden."

"Give him your gun and get to your post."

"On my wa—" I stopped talking. I clearly heard a vehicle door slam. Then three more. "They're here," I said as I inched toward the door.

"How many?"

I scooted out the door and peered around toward the driveway. They'd pulled in front of the house. I counted three, no four, armed black-clad figures filing toward the door. A movement behind them caught my eye. Another man guarded the vehicle. "Five. Coming in, fully armed."

"Can you get him back to the car?"

"I dunno. One's in the driveway—unless there's a back door, we're pretty stuck."

"I'm coming. H has the package."

"But, the—" The man looked right at me. Was I talking too loud? He couldn't possibly see me. I scrambled away from the door, hissing, "Hide!" and darted behind a row of boxes. Polo let out a low groan as he moved around a stack of chairs.

Neither of us made a sound as the door swung open and the man stepped inside, his combat boots clacking on the cement floor. Through a sliver of space between cartons, I watched him swing his light around the room, stopping on the pile of furniture shielding Polo. I prayed he didn't see the senator. The weapon he carried could shoot through any of this junk. But my Glock could take him out. I guessed the gods were going to answer my existential question. The man turned the light away from Polo's hiding spot and advanced into the storage room—in my direction. My stomach churned. I had to kill him.

He started down the aisle leading to my row. I shifted my weight, stabilizing my body, and aimed. The moment he came around the boxes, I'd pull the trigger. My gut roiled. But I wasn't going to die and neither was the senator. The corona from the Zeta's flashlight beam edged the tower of boxes. I squinted to ward off the light about to blind me and slowly depressed the trigger.

The blasts had my ears ringing, but the piercing scream and a stack of toppling boxes said I'd hit him. I scrambled for Polo.

"We've got to get out of here right now." I yanked on his arms to help him up.

He lumbered into a standing position. "No, the gun. I've got to—"

I interrupted in a hoarse whisper, "Get out, *now*!" He ignored me, shoving boxes out of the way to reach the gun. "They had to have heard the shots. Hurry!"

He stood up, cleared the gun's chamber, checking the magazine, and reloaded before pumping the man's ugly, lethal weapon. Polo knew how to shoot it? I sure didn't. I grabbed his sleeve and hauled him toward the door. Shouts and gunfire erupted inside the house. I held Polo back and scanned the entry and drive. The moon was fully up, giving the compound a ghostly glow.

"RUN!" I commanded and bolted out the door toward the water tank. Polo was slow, lagging. I dove behind the tomatoes and sprinted around the tank to safety, edging to where I could keep watch on the front door. It banged open. I heard shots and three men poured out, taking up positions to shoot anyone following them. I recognized Tito Cárdenas, and one of his gunmen from Tlalnepantla. Cárdenas moved toward the storage unit.

Polo was not behind me. I scrambled around the tank to find him. Not there. Had he stayed in the storage building? Shots peppered the yard. I heard bullets thunking into the side of the storage tank through a rain of vegetable matter. Christ, the assholes were shooting up the garden? Water streamed out of the tank, drenching me. If they didn't shoot me, I was going to drown. I took one more look at the yard and fixed each man's position in my mind. Then I saw him. Polo was down, belly crawling through the destroyed tomatoes. His leg dragged behind him. What should I do? I tapped the mic three times, hoping Quint or Horacio would come, but the shooting in the house continued. I heard one click. Someone responded.

I croaked, "Behind the water tank. Senator down in the tomatoes."

Horacio answered. "*Vengo*. Coming."

I ran around the tank again. I couldn't get to Polo, but I had to cover him. That was all I could do. Horacio was coming. He would stop them. Back in position behind the shrubs masking the tank from the front of the house, I checked the Zeta positions again. Cárdenas was missing, either in the shed or behind it. One of the men had the SUV running and turned around ready to split. The back doors were open. For Anibal, I realized.

The other man still covered the door. That meant the fourth man was inside. Why the show of force? Why didn't Cárdenas waltz into the house, take possession of Anibal, and shake hands with Farcía? I heard Quint's voice saying, *think, JadeAnne.* Because they went in blasting. They wanted to take out their rivals. How stupid. If they worked together, they'd have an invincible trafficking ring.

A shout from the entry and Cárdenas appeared from behind the shed, walking toward the house. He said something. The last Zeta pushed Lidia through the front door and sent her sprawling. Eddy Santos landed next to her, arms tied behind him. Where were the others? Dead? And Quint?

One click sounded through the commlink. I tapped twice.

"Quint has the house controlled. I'm coming around the sheds now," said Horacio. "We'll take them out."

"They have Lidia."

"Senator Aguirre?"

"I can't see him." I took a quick look at the scene in the entry. Lidia was climbing to her feet. Eddy curled in a ball on the ground pleading, a big gun aimed at him. I could see him shaking, hear his whiny voice. The tough Saint, quaking —like Lidia ought to be, but she had regained her feet and stood like a statue.

Cárdenas stepped into her face and shouted, "You work for me now, bitch!" then backhanded her across her face, knocking her to the ground. She screamed. Jesus H. Christ, Lidia was an old lady! I needed Polo's gun. I started to ease out of my cover to circle around to Polo as a volley of shots rang out from the other side of the tank. I swiveled toward the scene. Eddy Santos on the ground, a guard crumpled half on top of him, skull turned to pulp; Cárdenas running behind the SUV; the driver turning his weapon toward the garden and firing an interminable round. The fire returned and sparks flew off the armored SUV. I saw the driver slump, and the gun silenced. Horacio. I ran for the tomatoes and Polo's gun, but it no longer lay in the vegetation. Lidia dragged herself off the ground.

"Mother, stay down!" Polo rose from the corn, the Zeta's weapon aimed at Cárdenas. He stalked forward, Frankenstein's monster with an AR-15. "I'll kill you if you dare to touch her again. I'll wipe you and your dirty organization off this earth." His voice was calm, cold.

Cárdenas laughed.

Horacio stepped into view, aiming toward the SUV. "*Jefe*, get down. Get down!" he shouted to Aguirre.

"Leopoldo! Do as he says." Lidia sprang toward Polo, arms outstretched, a mother protecting her child.

Cárdenas popped over the hood and strafed the yard, shots lodging above my head in the wooden cistern. Polo crumpled. Lidia screamed.

"Leopoldo! *¡Mi amor, mi hijo!* Nooooooo!" Her words, an anguished sound, speared my heart. But it was cut off by more shots inside the house and a short burst of Cárdenas' weapon. Lidia toppled and lay still, red petals blooming across her back.

I saw Polo twisted into the peppers, and, beyond him, Horacio crouched behind the equipment barn. Cárdenas laughed again and called into the house. "Escopetito, bring the package."

Suddenly Quint was in the doorway, aiming his handgun at the Zeta. "Not so fast Cárdenas." Tito Tormenta had nowhere to cover.

Horacio stepped from the shadows of the barn. I bolted from behind the tank and ran to Polo, sprawled on his back. I searched for a pulse and felt weak throbbing at his neck. "He's alive!"

Quint stepped out, gun on Cárdenas. Cárdenas raised his own weapon and aimed at my father. I heard sirens in the distance. Cárdenas looked toward the sound. I rushed forward, dropping behind a planting by the shed.

"Drop your weapon," Quint ordered.

Cárdenas looked at the door. I sprang up and sprinted to the front of the SUV. I could lean around the grill and shoot the bastard. I *wanted* to shoot the bastard.

He let loose his insane laugh again. Quint twirled to the door, blasting his gun. Escopetito fell across the threshold. Cárdenas raised his weapon, pointing at my dad. I leaned around the fender and shot, grazing his leg.

Quint and Horacio converged on the SUV, but not fast enough. Tito Tormenta had shoved over the dead driver and thrown the vehicle into gear before they could stop him. He peeled out of the gate, turned toward the back road away from the sirens converging on the hacienda like a swarm of hungry mosquitoes and roared away, a rooster tail of dust billowing behind him.

"Come on, we've got to go," Quint shouted. "I'm getting Anibal. You two head for the car. Leave the Zetas." He disappeared into the house.

Horacio grabbed my arm, tugging me straight through to the patio. The sirens whooped over the screech of brakes and the shouting of men. My survival instinct cleared my head, and I ran for my life toward the stile. I wasn't spending the best years of my life in a Mexican jail.

Chapter 31

Can a Scorpion Sting Twice?

I settled into the backseat, wrapped in a blanket Horacio produced from the trunk. The engine turned over and caught. We'd be ready to blast out of here as soon as Quint...

I tensed, had he been caught? My mouth felt like the Sonoran Desert and my thoughts churned. Had one of the BLO men shot him? Or had Anibal over powered him? What happened to Anibal, anyway?

"Horacio, where's my dad?" I croaked.

"Cálmate. He's getting Anibal. We're meeting at the pick-up point in," he checked his watch, "three minutes."

"I don't like these commando missions."

No, they raised too many questions and made me think of death way too much. But who was to blame for my involvement? Yet something felt right about that shooting. He'd killed Lidia, injured Polo, and Cárdenas would do worse to me. I let my eyes close in an attempt to blot out the existential questions like, would my father and the senator make it? Would I be able to live with myself now that I'd killed that man in the shed?

Horacio's disembodied voice filled the dark cabin, a rich bass, sonorous. But I couldn't understand his words. "Again, Horacio? Tell me again why we left him. Polo was still alive."

"*Señorita* Jade, I called the ambulance. The medics were picking him up before we crossed the wall. If God wills, he'll live."

"It's my fault." I felt the burn of tears filling my shuttered eye sockets.

"How so, *señorita*? You are a soldier. You fought valiantly."

The tears spilled down my face, burning my cheeks. "I'm not a soldier. I'm the managing partner of an investigations office. I do billing and personnel scheduling."

A breeze had come up. Shadows cast by the moon through the copse jittered and shifted across the interior of the limo. "What's taking Quint so long?"

"Young Aguirre wasn't fully cooperative."

"You mean belligerent."

"*Sí*, fighting us every moment."

"Didn't he know he was on his way to a barrel of acid? I've been reading about what the Zetas do to people."

"*Negación.* Denial," Horacio said, and we lapsed into silence.

The night sounds swelled in the absence of human sounds. Had the police and ambulance already gone? The windows slid closed. I felt the shift in air as Horacio reached for his gun. A deeper shadow fell across the trunk, reaching toward my seat. My heart hammered. Fright Night.

"Get on the floor under the blanket."

I slid down and made myself as small as I could.

The limo roared to life and shot backward, rocking me against the front seats. I felt the thud and heard the howl of pain. He shifted gears and we shot forward, clipping an accomplice, whose diatribe took swearing to new lows. We spun around the corner onto the track and raced for the back road.

"Quint! We can't leave him." I said, climbing onto the

seat and buckling myself in.

"He'll be there with young Aguirre. Hold on."

"He better be!" I muttered under my breath. And it hit me. A lifetime of wondering, of being different, of not belonging—Quint was my dad and accepted me. He loved me! No longer did I stand outside an invisible divide. I belonged. He *had* to be okay.

I held my breath as we slewed around the westside facing wall for about a hundred yards—and there he was, in the road, waving us down. The brakes squeaked and the back end skidded, but Horacio righted our course and stopped. He popped the trunk and dashed out to help Quint load the gear. The rear of the car sagged; I felt the drag. Quint opened the back door and dumped the duffle of equipment onto the floor behind his seat. In another second Horacio was behind the wheel, Quint riding shotgun, rolling fast along the sandy lane.

"Ani?" I asked after a few minutes of random-seeming turns through the colonia of walled estates.

"In the trunk. He wasn't pleased to be coming with us."

I was shocked. "Really? Why?"

"Why in the trunk? Did you want to sit with him in the backseat? Maybe share a beer?"

I ignored Quint's sarcasm. Horacio navigated us to a paved road and we turned left, down valley, not up. "Where are we going? Not home?"

"Scenic route, Jade," he said, sounding cheerful.

The road dipped along a tree-lined creek and up a little hill before we came to a stop sign at an intersection marked Yautepec to the right, Amatlán straight ahead. We turned right and weaved our way out of the mountains. As we descended, the air grew heavy and warm. Periodically I caught a glimpse of the valley below us with several settlements laid out in grids.

The road finally straightened and we passed shadowy

ruins Horacio said were former sugarcane plantations from before the revolution. I was too tired to listen to the entire history lesson, but figured he was only telling us about it to keep himself awake. My watch said it was 3:26.

The *pueblo* sprouted up around us. We twisted through several narrow streets before stopping at a red light. Pounding and muffled shouting sounded from the trunk. Ani was awake.

I sat up. "Is he going to do that the whole way?"

Horacio punched a CD into the player. Jazzy salsa muted the thumps. Quint snored.

I woke up to the scrape of our gate opening. I stretched, rubbing my eyes. The limo jounced in and the gate clanged closed. Horacio opened the trunk as Quint hustled out of the limo. I heard his voice speaking to someone and opened my door to listen. Quint and a man with a snappy haircut in a black or navy uniform, weapon slung over his shoulder stood just to the side of the open trunk, looking in.

"Have your men move Mr. Aguirre into the house and post a guard. I don't want him wandering off before his escort shows up. Do I need to remind you this is top secret? No one communicates outside this property until the prisoner is secured into U.S. custody, Captain," he ordered.

The *marinero* snapped to and replied, "Yes, sir. Will you be needing the full detail?"

"Yes. On high alert. One of the kidnappers got away. We may see trouble."

I groaned inwardly. All I wanted was to go to sleep— with my dog. But Pepper was at Seeger's. I'd have to wait for a reasonable hour, and, I supposed, Anibal's removal, before I could retrieve him. And the goldens. And Lily. I shoved the blanket off, and started to climb out of the limo. How would I face Lily with the news she was still in danger? And with Polo gone— my chest heaved in an involuntary sob. A black wave of sorrow smothered me. I slumped into the side of the car; tears streamed from my eyes.

Horacio surrounded me, pulled me into a hug. "Shush now, *señorita*. Shhh. It'll all look better in the daylight."

I gulped air and sputtered, "But Polo is probably dead and we didn't stop them. We have Anibal, but what about Lily and all the others sold into slavery?" I pulled away and looked at him. Tears moistened his eyes too. He looked more like Shrek than ever.

"I've been with the senator for many years. He has been a compassionate and generous employer. I am praying he will pull through. But we must complete his mission and take out the Beltran Leyva Organization's trafficking ring. Remember, *señorita* Jade, we're soldiers."

I took his hand and squeezed it then turned and trudged into the house and up to my room.

I dragged down to the kitchen to find Señora Pérez bustling about over a large pan of sizzling something. *Déjà vu.* But the coffee pot was full and smelled fresh. I poured a cup and loaded it with cream and sugar—not my usual fare, but I need a huge dose of energy. "Good morning, Mrs. P," I said.

"*Buenas tardes, señorita,*" she replied, emphasizing the "afternoon" part.

I looked at the clock. Twelve-thirty. Okay, I'd had about six hours of sleep plagued by frightening nightmares of explosions and tattooed monsters. Oh! That was my evening last night. Silly me.

"How is it you are here?" I asked.

"The *señor* requested I be brought back. He is in his office, but when he is finished, he will talk with me," she said, adding, "He saved my family." She smiled and punctuated her relief with a flourish of her spatula.

I saw rolled, stuffed tortillas dripping in hot oil nestled in a bed of paper towels, and inhaled. Beef *taquitos*, refried beans, something smoky. My stomach growled and I looked around. A blender steaming with a thick red salsa. Yummm. I was starving!

"May I have some of those?"

"Mr. Quint authorized *el almuerzo*. The men will come in a few minutes and you can eat then. *Ahora*, set the dining room table for eight. I'm almost done with these taquitos. There's a salad in the refrigerator."

I got up. Mrs. P had gotten pretty bossy since yesterday. "Sure. What plates?"

She nodded to the *barro* we'd been using in the kitchen. I pulled mats from the cupboard and counted out eight plates. The low-fired clay clacked together. I'd have chosen the others. *Barro* glazes were lead based. I deposited the load on the dining table and returned to the kitchen for a soapy rag. The table was veneered in dust. Wow! I'd dusted only two days ago.

After washing and drying the table, I set the places, adding silverware, mugs, and glasses then rounded up more chairs. Dad had "authorized" lunch, Mrs. P had said. Odd. Usually overcautious, it wasn't like him to leave the house and our prisoner unguarded. Unless, of course, the U.S. Marshal's office had sent a team to collect him, or the men ate in shifts. I guess I'd find out.

The room gave a tiny shake and I heard the hall door open. Quint had descended from his lair. I met him in the kitchen.

"Hungry? Mrs. P has lunch made and I've set the table. You're not leaving a guard?"

He shook his head. "The relief team is coming on. Carrillo is briefing them now," he said and took the platter of taquitos Mrs. P handed him. I grabbed the bowl of beans and we went through to the table. The housekeeper followed with a tray of salsa, *agua de tamarindo* and the pot of coffee.

"Carrillo is that captain you were talking to last night?"

"Yeah. Why?"

"No reason. I just thought Anibal would be gone by now and we'd be able to get back to normal. I want Pepper back, and Lily and the puppies." I looked at him, eyes narrowed. "We need to get Lily home and move on with our lives. I have to go home."

A clatter of voices and shoes echoed up the stairwell and Horacio and four tired-looking men tromped into the kitchen. Quint ushered them into the dining room, inviting them to help themselves. A lot of *Gracias*-es and clacking of forks on clay. I sat down to fill my plate before the locusts picked the platters clean.

The men did not chat over the meal. Mrs. P brought another platter of taquitos and a bowl of cut fruit dusted with *piquin* chili. It wasn't long before that disappeared, too. I was dying to find out what was happening, but Quint cut me off before I got started.

"JadeAnne, fix a plate for Aguirre. Carrillo will take it down."

"What's happening with him?"

"Report to me in my office after lunch. You too, Horacio."

Poor Horacio looked like he'd been up all night. I supposed he had. "Horacio, did you have a chance to get some sleep?"

He nodded.

The security team clomped to the kitchen and I heard a chorus of, "*Muy rico señora.*" "*Que amable.*" "*Muchas gracias.*"

Then the thuds of boots on the back stairs. I turned back to my father and Horacio.

"That's some decor in there, *jefe*," Horacio commented.

"Which room were you in?" I asked.

"Red flocked walls, gilt furniture. At the end of the hall."

I laughed. "Yeah, they all look like that. Welcome to the Cathouse. Rumor has it Consuelo decorated. This is Lidia's house, you know."

"Actually, Jade, it may be young Aguirre's house now," Quint said as he rose from his chair."

"What?" I shrieked.

He gazed down at me. "Lidia is dead. Her heir was the senator."

"Are you sure?" Of course he was sure. I saw her cut down trying to protect Polo. A jolt buzzed through my heart. Could I love anyone that much? I sucked in a sharp breath. "But how would it get to Anibal?"

Quint stacked plates from the table to carry back to Mrs. P in the kitchen. "Just conjecture. Aguirre said he'd left his estate to Lura, and we know Lura's went to Anibal."

"Polo is dead?"

Horacio looked up from about his tenth taquito and said, "I haven't gotten through to the hospital yet." He frowned then grinned and held up a dripping taquito, and said, "Best taquito in town."

I saw the sorrow in his eyes. "Well, Anibal will be in a U.S. penitentiary soon. Too bad for him. Good for us, though."

"Which hospital was he taken to?" Quint asked as he started for the kitchen. "Don't hurry, Horacio. If you want more, Mrs. P has hot ones," he called over his shoulder.

"I could eat another," I yelled after him.

Gunfire erupted outside. Bursts of automatic fire. Shouts. A scream. Quint yelled something. Horacio flew from his chair, knocking it over, and ran toward the hall.

Stunned, I sat paralyzed. Fear cemented me to the chair. The men leapt down the stairs and the garden door banged against the house. The noise broke the spell. Someone was after Anibal. No! I ran to the duffle still lying in the hall, and grabbed a gun and my vest and flew down the front stairs.

I'd sneak up on them through the garage.

I heard more shots as I picked my way through the dark garage, fastening my vest as I went. I was going to crawl through the trapdoor Tonalli had shown me. I patted around the far wall until I found the door. A shaft of light filtered through its filthy window. Three black shadows staggered past it toward the gate. I opened the hidden door and emerged into the laundry behind the washer and dryer platform. The outside door stood partially open and I could see Anibal was no longer hog tied on the floor.

I rushed to the outside door. The squeal of tires and the roar of an engine told me I was too late. I tried to push the door wider, but something blocked it. The tang of iron told me it was a body. I squeezed past, my heart in my mouth. Please! Not Quint! Not Horacio! I begged any deity paying attention.

It was one of the men I'd eaten lunch with. My taquitos lurched up my gullet.

"Jade, get back."

Quint. Thank you, God.

I pulled back into the opening and flipped on the light. The handsome captain slumped in the corner, his neck sliced open. The refried beans came up. Not the Zetas, I thought. Wouldn't they'd have raided the house for me, Pepper, and Lily? Who then?

Horacio came in. "You okay, Miss Jade? *Dios*, what's that smell?"

"Mrs. P's regurgitated beans," I replied in English. "Who did this?"

Quint strode in. "How did you get into the laundry?"

"Secret door. Quint, they took Anibal! Why? Who?"

Sirens wailed, coming closer.

"Let's go up and get our story straight. We can't tell the locals we held a man in the laundry. Hurry. Can't leave this either." He scooped up the beans with a dirty towel, tossed it into the washer, and ushered us out of the room.

"Don't look, Jade. I don't want you puking again."

The third body was the man who'd led the charge from the table. A quiet kid from Oaxaca. Now perforated by automatic machine gun bullets. I turned my eyes away, but the sight had already burned into my memory.

"These are the men who lunched with us. Where's the last one?" I asked as we mounted the garden stairs, the sirens swirling up behind us.

Horacio's voice was low. "He chased them to the front. He was gunned down, too."

I felt numb. We sat down at the kitchen table. Mrs. P emerged with tequila and three glasses. Her face looked ashen. Mine probably did, too. I brushed a stray hair off my cheek and came away with a hand covered in cobwebs. I shuddered. What was taking the cops so long?

"Girl, I'll discuss how stupid you were later. Right now, we have to get rid of the weapons and agree on a story. How about mistaken identity. We've been targeted and hired the four guards to protect the house. We don't know who it is or what they're after. Pray the news about Aguirre hasn't gotten out. I called Bendicias. He's on his way with a team, but he doesn't have the senator's clout. We're going to need the Embassy. Horacio, you work for me, now. Bodyguard to my daughters."

The sirens faded into the distance. I got up and filled a plate with sugar cookies for the men and sat back down. No one helped himself.

"How did they get in? Was the gate open?" I asked.

"No, *señorita*, I locked up after the relief guards came in. I was to let the night shift out after lunch."

Mrs. P finished washing up the lunch dishes, clattering the plates together as she lifted them out of the water. She was shaking. I glanced at Quint and raised my eyebrows. He shrugged. If he didn't care whether she listened in, I guessed

I wouldn't worry about it.

"So you're telling me a gang of kidnappers climbed over the wall and killed the off-duty security then carried Anibal back over the wall and escaped? Oh, yeah, *and* took the day-shift with them." I shook my head. "Not happening. It was an inside job." I got up and grabbed the coffee and clean mugs.

"Yeah," he replied, voice raspy, the buzz of chainsaw.

I set a mug in front of him and poured then gestured the pot to Horacio. He nodded and I set a steaming mug at his place. I asked, "Who knew Anibal was here?"

Quint studied his hands. "U. S. Marshal's office, their L.A. branch... and Bendicias."

I thought for a moment, picturing the earnest young senator from the State of Mexico as I set the pot back into the coffeemaker. "I wouldn't have pegged him as corrupt."

"Money warps people," Horacio said. "It's how the cartels operate. *Plata o plomo.* Either you take the bribes or they kill you and your family."

A chill shot through me. "That's playing dirty."

Mrs. P grabbed a dish towel and approached, wiping her hands. "It's how these men operate. You see, there was no choice."

Quint took her hand. "Yes. We understand, *señora.* We're doing what we can to make your family safe."

"And the little girl?" she asked.

Lily! I hadn't thought about her. Was she okay? I missed Pepper, but he was busy protecting Lily.

"We've talked to her. She's safe with friends," Quint said.

Mrs. P lifted his hand and rested her cheek against it before turning back to her clean-up.

Horacio went on, "Everything about these *carteles es sucio*, dirty. But they have the money and the power. I am saddened for the state of my country, and it has escalated with President Calderon's war on drugs. He's paving the way for the Sinaloans to take hold. Mark me, the Beltran Levya Organization is systematically being wiped out. I give them two years. We put a wedge into their operations last night."

"You're saying Bendicias is one of them?" Quint asked.

"No, *jefe*. They got to him. But we got Farcía."

"You guys, I never heard. Tell me what happened. What did you do? Tonalli and the others? You didn't ki—.. choked on my words, the thought too horrifying.

"Absolutely not, Jade. Except for Cárdenas's man they found before I could move him out of the house, we left them hog-tied and gagged in the garage. Horacio caught Farcía and Lobo slipping out through the back with Anibal. They'll have mean headaches, but they'll both live," he said, sneering and tipping his mug toward Horacio. "Hopefully the police took 'em in. Unfortunately, I'm pretty sure it was they who called the police. Cárdenas certainly doesn't seek out law enforcement other than bribing it."

"What makes you think that? I thought you called. Or Bendicias."

"It's possible Farcía and Lobo planned what you *gringos* call a 'sting operation'. The *policía* came too late, *pues*, they were supposed to catch the Zetas."

"And if Cárdenas were arrested, the entire Mexico City human trafficking operation would default to the BLO. Think. But why was Lidia there?" Quint said, pinning me to my seat with his stare.

"I... uh, I—she hated Anibal?" I flashed back to what I'd overheard. "Out on the patio, Lidia was pissed at Farcía. She said he'd been well paid and Polo wasn't part of the deal. The deal was to give Anibal to Cárdenas, but I don't know what for." I looked between Quint and Horacio. "She didn't know where Polo was. She said it a couple of times. And I realized the Zetas didn't know anything about him, or us."

Horacio barked. "That *alecrán,* scorpion, Farcía got too

greedy. He's been smoothing the road for the BLO, and the senator was getting too close. He saw his chance. Lobo with his evil little sidekick Santos, set it up to get rid of the Aguirres and the Zetas. My guess is Lobo was going to be crowned kingpin of the operation. Young Aguirre was the bait."

"But, the Zetas had a different plan. We stepped into the fray. We kind of did the BLO's dirty work, didn't we? Quint, why didn't you detain Farcía and Lobo?"

Horacio answered. "Bendicias agreed to send a team to meet us at a staging area near the house. The team had the authority to make arrests; we didn't. When we picked up the tail on the mountain, I knew we'd been compromised."

"You called him again just now. Why?

The gate buzzer sounded. Mrs. P stepped out to answer the intercom, "*Dígame.*" I heard the static-y crackle and her response, "*Vengo.*"

The elevator door clanged and I heard the rumble of the box descending with Mrs. P inside. Quint and Horacio were shoving out from the table. "You know what to do, H," he said. Horacio nodded and bolted for the bag of guns and the stairs. Quint pushed past me as though I wasn't there. Something was happening and I wasn't invited.

Chapter 32

Lover's Lookout

I woke up with Pepper licking my face. He crooned to me, wagging happily. I threw my arms around him in a tight hug and buried my face in his ruff. A low chuckle wafted across the room. Pepper's ears shot up. He bounced off the bed to sit down beside a silhouette, tail thumping joyously. I sat up and turned on the bedside lamp.

"Dylan! How long have you been sitting there?" I asked, as I pulled the coverlet up to my chin.

"Moments. Your dog was not going to let you sleep. You okay?"

"Yeah, fine. Just tired," I said, running my fingers through my hair. Christ almighty—I'm a mess. This was hardly how I'd planned on next presenting myself to Dylan. He was going to hate me. "It was a long night. What are you doing here?"

"Gee, aren't you happy to see me? Quint asked me to bring Lily and the dogs home."

I was overjoyed to see him, but I wouldn't tell him that, at least not now. "Does that mean we're safe? Did he tell you what happened?"

"No, other than a quick call, I haven't had any communications with him. Señora Pérez let us in. He said we'd discuss the situation over dinner."

I yawned and glanced at the clock on the bedside table. 11:23. "Lily?"

"She's gone to bed. You girls sure have interesting rooms. This looks like a bordello."

"And you've seen a lot of bordellos?" I joked. "Hey, what happened to Sicario?"

"Senator Bendicio's team showed up and whisked them all away. Your Sicario was barely awake."

"Did you get him to talk?"

"Why don't you get ready to go to dinner. I know a great little tapas place that stays open late. Quint said you haven't eaten."

"He's coming? And Horacio?"

"Who?"

Ah, Quint wanted to grill Dylan, that's why the late tapas. "Never mind. I'll be down in ten."

Dylan stood up. "I'll wait downstairs then."

I jumped out of bed into a hot Navy shower. Dressing was harder. I wanted to look good for Dylan, but I was tired and couldn't decide what to wear. Jeans, a fitted scoop neck tee in coral with my patent leather sandals and what I'd started to call my "city" jacket—the bulletproof one. I slipped the Semmerling into my suede shoulder bag and daubed on some lipstick. I'd piled my hair on my head, letting tendrils frame my face. It was as good as it was going to get tonight. And why should I care? Quint was going to monopolize my potential boyfriend. Dylan wouldn't even look at me.

Dylan clambered out of his chair when I joined them in the kitchen and pulled a chair for me. The men were drinking what smelled like whisky. "Drink, Jade?" Quint asked.

I shook my head. "What's up? Are we going?" I looked at Dylan. Dylan looked at Quint.

He grinned. "I don't want to get in the way of young

love—you two go and enjoy yourselves."

I let out the breath caught in my chest. *Thanks, Dad*, I silently said. "We're safe to go out?"

"Dylan is, and I doubt we'll see any action tonight. They have what they want.

I frowned. "They who?"

"Well, ain't that the question?" he said. "Look, go have a relaxing meal and we'll talk about it tomorrow. H and I have spent the day digging. We have some information. And I've got vetted men on the house. That's Joe at the gate. He's expecting you. Go on, kids, git!"

Dylan, quite a gentleman, helped me up and shook Quint's hand. "Good night, sir."

Quint erupted in laughter. Dylan's cheeks colored. "Sir! Did you hear that, Jade? Your Dylan aims to pass muster with me." He laughed again. "Dylan, call me Quint. I didn't raise the girl. I have no right to say what she does. Anyway she's a woman with her own mind. She'll do what she wants whether I approve or not." He winked at me then motioned us out the door. "I'll take care of Pepper for you."

"Thanks, but I think we'll take him. It's okay, Dylan?"

"Sure. All the restaurants let dogs in. Come on."

We stepped into the elevator, pushed PB, and soon were being escorted to Seeger's car.

"Thanks. Joe?"

"Yep, miss. That's me. I'll be here when you get back," he drawled in what I guessed was a Carolina accent. Weird.

I gave the American a little wave and Dylan closed my door.

He looked handsome in black jeans, a grey knit shirt, and leather blazer. I was more interested in devouring him than the exquisite tapas that appeared in an endless stream of little plates. Another of his buddies from school owned the place and served up the royal treatment. Fred had studied at the Culinary Institute of America in the Napa Valley and gone on to apprentice under a famous Spanish chef in Barcelona. He'd come home in the last couple of years to open his own version of a Barcelona tapas bar. Fried *padrón* peppers, Spanish tortillas, something with clams, a cheesy croquette with smoky sauce, mussels in a garlic bath, chorizo, grilled asparagus, herbed olives, croquettes of ham and prawn, crisp fried potatoes in aioli, something with lettuce, and finally, dulce de leche crepes, called *panqueque* in Spain. I thought I was going to burst, but I still longed for the paella al la Valencia crossed off the menu board.

"Next time, Jade. We'll come back soon."

Pepper woofed and extended his paw to Fred in thanks. Fred had slipped him a stack of ham trimmings. "Not just ham," Dylan said, "but Iberico ham, the best in the world." Suddenly, I wanted this to be my life. I thanked Fred too, and promised to bring the gang soon.

We waddled out to the car. Back to reality. I kept my hand on the Semmerling, wishing I had a normal life. With Dylan and a family and—Dylan swept me into a warm embrace before opening the car door. He leaned down and kissed me gently, and broke away, smiling down at me. "I've wanted to do that all night. I know a cool place to go neck. Shall we?"

"Neck?" I grinned. "Sure! You have a lover's lane or an overlook where the teenagers go near here?"

"You bet sweetheart," he replied wiggling his eyebrows and putting the car in gear.

I fiddled with the radio until I found a station playing Mexican standards.

"That's Lucero," he said, about a song I vaguely recognized. "She got her start in pop and when she got too fat for TV and the pop stage, her producers took her off the pop scene and put her on variety shows doing old time music. It's all about image here."

"Same everywhere. The stars are pretty, sexy, stylish.

Didn't you watch MTV?"

"*Claro, moñeca.* You'd look good on TV."

"Doll? Give me a break, Dylan. Who says that anymore? Yeah, I could be a pop star, if I could sing!"

"*Moñeca* is a common term of endearment here," he said, defensively. "I'm an old-fashioned kind of guy."

"You old lug," I quipped and punched his arm.

He'd pulled onto a quiet street with lots of trees and few houses. We drove up a small hill, and at the end of the street he turned-out onto a vacant lot. Mexico City, or part of it, spread below us in a million glowing lights. I sighed as Dylan pulled me into his arms. Pepper plopped onto the back seat with a huff. He knew we would be here for a while.

American Joe greeted us at the gate when Dylan returned me to Amores. "Enjoyed your dinner, miss?" he asked with the hint of a sneer. I blushed. I must look a sight. My hair, no longer in a neat chignon, probably looked like a rat's nest. But who was he to comment on my business? Pepper growled and I gripped his collar.

Dylan winked at me. "Hey, man, great restaurant. You should try it before you go back to Alabama," he drawled.

I giggled.

"North Carolina, sir, ma'am." Joe responded as he pulled the gate closed and scouted the street for danger. Obnoxious but conscientious, I thought.

I asked, "Joe, what brings you to Mexico?"

"Orders, ma'am. My detail is here to collect the fugitive and provide security to you. Hard to do ma'am when you're out all night with someone we haven't vetted," he chastised.

That was enough. I was tired and not in the mood for some strange soldier to give me a ration. "You want to know who my date is? He's the surgeon who stopped a violent human trafficker from selling any more little girls and boys. That enough *vetting* for you? Now get out of my way." I let go of Pepper and pushed passed this self-righteous ass and marched to the door, dragging Dylan behind me. I threw my arms around him and pulled him in for a goodnight kiss, one eye on Joe. "DO YOU MIND?"

Joe melted into the shadows.

Dylan hooted. "You're a tough one, JadeAnne Stone. Remind me not to get in your way."

I kissed him and slipped into the house. Let Dylan work it out with the gatekeeper. I was going to bed.

Chapter 33

The Fat Lady Sang. Why Isn't It Over?

Sunday, September 2, 2007

In our couple of weeks at Amores, we'd developed a routine. First down would make coffee and warm up the *pan dulces* Mrs. P bought the day before. She thought we were nuts to eat them slathered in butter in the morning. "In Mexico—" she had the habit of saying to preface her disagreement with how we did things— "In Mexico, we eat the *panes* with hot chocolate in the afternoon when they come out of the ovens." Our little band was known to do *that,* too. But this morning, our housekeeper and her reprimand were not with us. Today we had strangers and no *pan dulces*.

Pepper and I arrived last. Cloudy skies dulled the morning light filtering into the kitchen and Quint stood in the gloom stirring scrambled eggs while Lily buttered toast as it popped out of the toaster. I flipped on the overhead light. A worn-looking Joe sat at the table, complaining about —everything. His coffee was cold, the cream tasted funny, he was hungry.... realized he was just a boy. Barely older than Lily. I pulled my sweater closer around me and poured a cuppa, dousing it with cream. God! If I didn't slow down with the cream, butter, tortillas, I was going to turn into a potbellied pig.

"Mornin', daughter. Sleep well?"

I warmed up Joe's coffee from the fresh pot. "Mmmm, yeah." I grinned, "Thanks."

"Lily dropped a stack of toast onto a plate in the middle of the table. "How was the restaurant? And Dylan?" She teased out his name.

Joe shut his mouth, straightening up. "She—" he stuck his thumb at me— "she's your *daughter*? I thought—"

"Hey Joe, *did* you think?" I asked. He looked at Lily and rolled his eyes. She giggled and grabbed plates from the cabinet and passed them around as another man tromped up the stairs and joined us. Not an American. Joe ignored him. I wondered how a snot nosed twit had been sent on what I'd consider a plum assignment.

Quint shook salt and pepper over the eggs. *"Buenos días, Rico. Siéntate aca."* He pointed to an empty seat next to a platter of steaming bacon.

I smiled and greeted the guard, nodding to the food. *"Sírvete. Hay más si quieres."*

He mumbled, *"Gracias, señora,"* without looking at me and started to heap his plate. Joe opened his mouth but clamped it shut when I said, "There's plenty to go around. Help yourself. Lily, come, sit. Have you met our security detail?"

She flounced into the chair next to Joe and giggled. Apparently she had. "Quint, don't let your eggs get cold," I admonished him. What was it about this kitchen that turned me into my mother? But *she* wouldn't be caught dead here.

"So, aren't there two more men guarding us?" I asked. Lily nodded, a question in her eyes. "You want to know why we have guards," I stated. She nodded again and we both turned toward my father. "Then tell her." My voice came out sharper than I intended.

"Why don't we eat first," he said. It was an order. "We

have a lot to sort and some decisions to make later."

He shoveled eggs into his mouth. The security guys did the same. Like locusts they cleared the platters of everything. I hoped Dad had gotten enough. If not, he could finish Lily's. She was just pushing it around.

Her fork clattered onto the plate. "I'm going to feed the dogs," she said and carried it to the pen. Maya's ears shot up and she grinned. The puppies woke up and started a rough and tumble play. The biggest clambered out and trotted under the table to play tug of war with Joe's pant cuff. Joe tried to kick him away, but Pepper lumbered to his feet and bared his teeth before nosing the pup back to the box. Lily fed him a pinch of egg and lifted him back in.

"Your dog growled at me," the kid whined.

"Son, did you get enough to eat?" Quint asked.

"Yes, sir. That dog was going to bite me."

"Maybe you shouldn't be so aggressive toward his pack. Now git. Your relief will be here shortly. Send the others."

Joe rattled down the stairs and slammed the door. Quint winked at Lily. "He's a real twit, ain't he?"

Rico's grin lit his face.

"Rico here doesn't like him either." I jeered. " You should have heard him when Dyl brought me home last night. He sure didn't approve. Puppy hater."

"What'd he do, Jade?" Several puppies madly licked at Lily's egg-y fingers while Maya washed the plate.

"Reproved me for going out late with," I mimed air quotes, "someone we haven't vetted. Rico, shall I make more eggs?"

"*No, gracias, señorita. Jefe, que amable, muy ricos huevos*."

"Sure thing, Rico," Quint said, and raised his hand in farewell as the security guard returned to his post.

"I'm going up to shower. Have fun making another breakfast. Lil, you staying here?"

"No! I want to go to my aunt." Lily's bright mood dimmed. She stood up, a wiggling puppy under each arm. "And I want to take my dogs."

"Lily, honey..." I began.

Quint interrupted me. "Please meet me upstairs at four p.m. to discuss our current situation. Now, go do whatever you girls do and let me feed the next shift." He gave me a stern look, probably in response to my expression. "Invite Dylan. I want him to know what we're up against."

Without Mrs. P, it looked like I'd be responsible for dinner. I'd washed, conditioned, and styled my hair, practiced my yoga routine, read the newspaper Quint left on the table open to a mention of Senator Aguirre and his mother, socialite Lidia Sotomayor, and watched part of an old *Cantiflas* film on TV with Lily. She'd descended into the dumps again and withdrawn into her little circle of dogs and television. Hadn't she had a good time with Dafne and Seeger? Or were all the security and secrets too much for her? If it weren't for Dylan, I'd be in the dumps, too.

I assessed the food situation with Pepper dogging my every step. I could make a salad, and I found a container of Mexican rice. Pepper looked hopeful when I headed toward the garden stairs. I dreaded going down; the yard was a place of terror for me after two invasions. But the freezer lived downstairs and our household was on lockdown. At least Joe would be gone.

"Come on Pepper, let's go outside." He did a little dance and wagged furiously. Maya galloped in with her train of mini-me-s and we descended to the yard. The dogs did their business and the puppies romped on the lawn. The garden looked much better since Tonalli had made a few trips to work in it. I hoped he was all right, although he'd be out of a job now that Lidia was dead. She'd been a scumbag bitch, but she was heroic at the end. And Polo? Quint must have gotten news.

Pepper had loped off around the house with Maya chasing him and I heard her barking her head off in the front. Six little pairs of ears pricked up and they charged toward their mother. I jogged after them, expecting to see someone walking by but found a security guard cowering in the foundation plantings.

"Maya!" She stopped barking and lowered her head, eyeing me guiltily.

A timid voice from behind a big gun. *"¿Muerde el perro?"*

Well, he didn't shoot her, but really, these guards were useless. "Come out. She's harmless. I'm JadeAnne, by the way. Quint's daughter," I said in Spanish.

He stood up, gripping the gun. *"Señorita,* you shouldn't be out here."

"I have to get food from the *bodega.*" At the word "food" Maya yipped and grinned. The guard looked terrified. "You can escort me," I suggested.

It was Sunday-quiet in the neighborhood. People were doing what people do on a fine day off. I heard bells from one of the churches nearby. Someone getting married. It was a good day for it. The young man guarded the door while the dogs and I checked the downstairs refrigerator and the freezer. Bless you, Señora Pérez! I found bags of her *albóndigas* and the sauce to go with. I also found a large bag of frozen cupcakes and plenty of lemons in the cupboard to make lemonade. I'd heat up several cans of beans and voilá —*comida.* "Shit, Pepper. No tortillas."

I'd send that twit Joe.

Dylan arrive promptly at four with a huge bouquet of sunflowers. I led him into the living room where Quint, Lily, and Señor Santiago from the Organized Crime Special Investigations Unit, SEIDO, waited.

Dad welcomed Dylan and introduced him to the bureaucrat while I poured him a beer from the bar I'd set up. He looked puzzled, but Quint told him to relax, we wanted an unbiased opinion, or something lame like that. I didn't hear it all as I carried my flowers to the kitchen to find a vase and check on my food. Everything was hot. All I had to do was cook the tortillas. We'd meet then eat.

"Señor Santiago," Quint was saying as I rejoined the men, "you've probably heard about the trouble in Tepoztlán Friday night?"

"No, Mr. Quint. What trouble?"

Aguirre and Lidia had been in the news, but nothing had been reported on their deaths. Yet, the Tsar of organized crime knew nothing? I said, "This stinks of cover up, Mr. Quint."

I poured myself a lemonade and sat next to Lily, across from Dylan. I wanted to gauge his reactions.

Quint began with, "You are familiar with the kidnapping of Senator Aguirre's half-brother after our meeting at the airport?"

"Yes. I understand the marshal and one of the assailants were killed. I believe one of the assailants is in custody, picked up by Aguirre's team at the clinic in Iztapalapa. The surgeon called it in?"

"Actually, sir, four men were arrested. One was a perpetrator in the shooting at the *taquería* in *el centro*. My daughter recognized both the man who was killed and the one now in custody. It was her friend, Doctor Porras here—" he gestured toward Dylan— "who was the surgeon removing the bullets. Knowing my daughter's history, he telephoned and sent me photographs of the man's tattoos, which JadeAnne was able to identify."

"What does this have to do with Tepoztlán?"

"Hold on, it will become clear soon. But let me digress to an earlier time this summer. Miss Flynn, Lily, and Lily's ten-year-old sister were kidnapped from their home in Los Angeles and illegally transported to Mexico, to the neighborhood of Lomas de Pedrigal—Calle San Augustín— a property owned by Lidia Sotomayor, Senator Aguirre's mother. The girls were held in a cell. A cave carved into the mountain really, with a dozen or more other children from Mexico, the Eastern bloc, and Asia, awaiting their sale."

Lily shook her hair over her face. I squeezed her hand. Dylan frowned, but Quint continued the history. "Young Aguirre had convinced my daughter to join his team under the guise of uncovering his cousin's murderer, which he claimed was something to do with the cartels. He harbored a strong resentment toward the Aguirre family and insisted Senator Aguirre headed a criminal organization based here in the capital. He created an undercover operation designed to lure JadeAnne into the safe-house where the trafficked children were held in order to include her in the shipment he had brokered to rival organization, Los Zetas. My daughter recognized the Flynn sisters as US citizens and insisted they remain with her. The rest of the children were loaded onto a helicopter and have not been recovered, although we know two locations where some of them were held. You closed one down and arrested the madam, Consuelo Garcia.

Santiago nodded. "Although you moved Miss Stone to Senator Aguirre's protection, she was kidnapped?"

Quint continued the story, detailing the events at ExpoCanina in Tlalnepantla. "One Fernando Torrens kidnapped, drugged and raped my daughter, leaving her in one of the dog kennels with that golden retriever," he pointed to Maya. Lily hugged her dog closer.

"I won't belabor the point, but the nursing dog led JadeAnne to her pups and the two American girls, caged and awaiting pick up by the Zetas. Before she was shot fleeing to safety with the girls, she recognized Cárdenas and two others: the tattooed man killed at the taquería Friday, and the patient arrested at the clinic Friday night."

Santiago steepled his hands and bent forward in thought. When he spoke, his tone held a tinge of disbelief. Lily cried softly into Maya's fur. I gave a quick shake of my head when Quint looked at me. Dylan's look was that of any normal, sane human being—horrified. The room went silent for too long. I took over the story.

"Mr. Santiago, you sat in the meeting Friday, you know Aguirre used his DEA position to broker deals between cartels and was in process of extradition back to the US with a U.S. Marshal, who is now dead. What you may not know is Anibal Aguirre was kidnapped and transported to a weekend home owned by Lidia Sotomayor in the town of Tepoztlán, Morelos. At the same time his half-brother, Senator Aguirre, disappeared, never arriving at a dinner meeting he had scheduled with Senator Bendicias. We learned of the house in Tepoztlán through our housekeeper, and her intelligence was confirmed by Bendicias. Both of these witnesses had been threatened by representatives of the Beltran Levy Organization, the originating organization of the Mexico City trafficking ring." I sucked in a breath and blew it out. No one stirred. "Is this getting too complicated? Maybe I can refresh someone's drink?"

Dylan held up his glass. I hopped up, shoving Pepper off the couch. Santiago frowned. Because he was lost? Didn't believe us? Or, because he didn't approve of dogs on the furniture? I poured Dyl's beer and slopped some whisky into Santiago's glass, shooting a spot of seltzer on top. I loved the seltzer dispenser. I'd get one for the Sarasvati.

Quint held his hand over his glass and picked up the story where I left off. Rays of late sun cut across the room, spotlighting the dust. I turned on a couple of lamps, tuning back into the story at the part where we were tailed. He described our rescue operation and called on me.

"The Tepoztlán house and patio had great acoustics like

an amphitheater; I could hear the conversation clearly. What my father has not mentioned is one of the key players in this was at the Senator's conference table with us Friday morning, Genero Farcía Luna."

I shut up, observing Santiago. He nodded, his expression one of vindication. His nose crinkled and he bared his teeth in something less like a grin than a terse fist bump "Yes!"

I opened my mouth to continue, but Santiago interrupted. "My office has had its suspicions. You heard him discussing his cartel involvement, Miss Stone?" He sat up, setting his drink aside. I'd gotten his attention.

Pepper, who had settled at my feet sat up, too, and turned toward the kitchen, ears straight up. He sniffed, cocked his head, and plopped back onto my feet with a groan. I paused, listening, but hearing nothing, I continued.

"I overheard Lidia Sotomayor inform her henchman, Eddy Santos, Farcía had been 'well paid and her son was not part of the deal.' Lidia was furious. She said the deal was for Anibal only. Guillermo Lobo was there, too. All talked as though they were fully aware Anibal was secured in the house and going to be turned over to someone expected to arrive. It turned out to be Cárdenas. But the Zetas planned their own double cross and went in shooting. Cárdenas escaped, but not before murdering Lidia and wounding the Senator—"

Horacio stepped into the room, stony faced. "He's dead."

I gasped.

"You can testify you observed Cárdenas kill Senator Aguirre and his mother?"

"Yes, I can," I said.

"What happened to Farcía, Lobo, and Santos?" Santiago grilled.

Horacio answered. "I took the *señorita* back to the car." He was protecting me. Had Quint done something to them?

"Wait. Eddy might have been killed on the driveway by

one of the Zetas. He went down and Lidia dropped on top of him. Didn't the police find them?"

"Mr. Quint, what happened to Farcía and Lobo?" Like a cop, this guy wasn't giving anything away, but I'm sure he knew exactly what happened to them.

"I left the two men unconscious and cuffed in the bushes in the back corner of the compound. Breathing," he stated.

"That is not the report I received."

"I can't help what you heard; I'm telling you what I did. Why don't we compare notes?"

Lily stretched and whined she was hungry. I agreed. I excused myself, and said, "Come on Lily, Dylan. Let's get dinner together. Mr. Santiago we have lovely *albóndigas*, best in the city. Won't you join us?"

I stood in front of him, Lily hanging off my neck and flanked by Pepper and the goldens. The man looked uneasy, but nodded. Dylan slid his arm around the other side of me and we trundled into the kitchen.

"What's going to happen, Jade?" Lily asked. "I want to go home. Those bad people are still out there."

Dylan embraced her and whispered something in her ear and she half-heartedly giggled, but I knew she was afraid. And I knew it was down to us to get the girl home.

"Dyl, don't you know someone who forges passports?"

"Are you out of your mind? Why would I know someone like that?" He flashed that adorable cock-eyed grin at us. "But I know who might."

Lily and I both yelled, "Who!" Then it hit me: Dafne. "You mean a certain lady we know?"

His grin took over his face. "Yep."

Sometimes he sounded more Californian than me. "Light the burner under that pot, will you?.. tipped my head toward the *cazuela* on the stove with the meatballs and sauce in it. Dylan saluted.

"Thanks. I think the dogs need to go out. Will you two

take them while I set the table and heat up the rice? Be vigilant, please. And tell the guards to send two guys up for the dinner trays in about fifteen minutes."

"Will do, boss. Come on, dogs, and my lovely guide. Let's go."

I microwave the rice, divided the salad into two bowls, and found a huge tray to fill with plates, utensils, glasses, and two pitchers of tamarind drink. Another tray I filled with everything to set the dining room table. I could smell the meatballs as I readied the dining room and gave them a stir as the pot bubbled.

I had the guards' food ready just as two stocky men stomped up the stairs and stood in the doorway shuffling their feet. I greeted them, smiled, and indicated their tray, and the shorter man nodded, mumbling something that might have been, "*Gracias, señora.*"

"*Por nada, Buen provecho.*" I handed over the trays.

The clatter on the stairs was getting on my nerves. I again thought about carpeting them. Which reminded me, with the landlady dead, what exactly would happen to us? My head ached. I longed for the Sarasvati's deck swept by clean bay breezes, even my boring office manager job, and my stuffy parents. But when I killed the Zeta, I ceased to live that life. I needed to get Lily to her family no matter what. And then? Where did Pepper and I belong?

I hustled the food to the table, yelled out the window for Dylan and Lily, and returned to the living room. Tension crackled in the air. Santiago definitely wasn't playing our game. I watched the men posture, bicker, and debate for a moment. They called this negotiating? I noticed the bottle had almost been emptied.

I interrupted. "So have you men figured out how we are going to get Lily home to her aunt yet?" They looked at me as though I were insane. "Oh, I guess not. Well, come on, wash your hands and have your *comida*. I'm sure you'll be able to think better with meatballs in your stomachs."

Horacio laughed and followed me into the dining room, Quint behind him. I went back for Santiago, whose natural expression must be confusion. "This way, sir." I directed him to the powder room under the stairs.

Santiago agreed, Mrs. P's *albóndigas* were the best he'd tasted, but he avoided the problem of Lily's return. If Quint and the Mexican government weren't going to help, Horacio, Dylan, and I would figure it out—if we had to smuggle her across the border ourselves. I sure hoped Dylan would agree to talk to Dafne, or let me. The sooner we took care of Lily, the sooner Pepper and I could go home. I pulled the plug to drain the sink. If only it were so easy to pull the plug on all my problems here.

Quint had asked us to meet with him over the dessert Señor Santiago had declined. He saw Mexico's organized crime tsar out to his car and collected the dinner dishes from the guards. Dylan was in the living room talking to his supervisor on the phone and Lily had gone upstairs with her favorite puppies. Maya looked worriedly toward the door and longingly toward the plate of cupcakes. Pepper snored in the puppy enclosure tangled with the remaining pups.

I sucked in a slow, sugar-laced breath and held it to a count of eight. The moment felt peaceful. Normal. I paced my exhale with another count of eight and relished the relaxation I felt. My shoulders slipped from my ears, my stomach unclenched, my jaw let go. I put the cupcakes and a stack of napkins onto the table as the room filled with the enticing aroma of cinnamon scented cafe de olla and sighed.

"Why the sigh, Jade?" Dylan whispered into my ear as his arms circled my waist and pulled me into his chest. I pivoted and slid my arms around him in a gentle hug, resting my head against his shoulder. "I convinced Diego to take my shift tonight so I can stay. But who is this relaxed JadeAnne

I'm hugging?"

"Shhh. I'm having a moment."

Dylan bent down and softly kissed my hair. I turned my face up to his and met his lips. He tasted like smoky caramel. A perfect dessert after thirty-nine days of nightmare and upheaval. I pushed my worries aside and let myself dissolve into him. After all, tomorrow would be another day.

The End

Coyote

Pursuit and Terror Across the Border

Chapter 1

Two Funerals, No Weddings

Saturday, September 8, 2007

I kept my hand on my gun and a sharp eye on the weekenders milling about the plaza as Dylan and I beelined into La Iglesia de San Juan Bautista for another funeral. This time, Senator Aguirre and his mother, Lidia Sotomayor Buendía, had been murdered—and the killer was after me, too.

I pulled my stylish bulletproof jacket tighter around my torso as we rushed through the carved doors. Dark-suited men with bulges under their jackets, wires curling into their collars, watched the mourners from positions around the church. Security detail to protect me and the fifteen-year-old girl I'd rescued from sex traffickers. I prayed they could keep us safe.

The senator's assistant Susana, met us as she scurried along the main aisle. "Hi JadeAnne. Dylan. I'm so glad you're here," she said, taping a spray of fresh flowers over the end of the front pew. She'd chosen black roses mixed with purple and white calla lilies. The black ribbon looked like real silk. She carried a flat-bottomed basket with half a dozen more sprays for the pews reserved for family and close friends. Thank God for Susana Arias de Barrera. Everything looked lovely, organized, and well protected. If ever there were a fairy godmother to wave a wand to get things done, she was it, I thought as I glanced around at the sunglass wearing be-suited men with bulges under their jackets stationed around the church.

"I'm ready to help. What shall I do?" I shouted over the organist's rehearsal.

"Help get the ushers pinned with the boutonnieres. No. Take the stack of programs and put them in the pews."

I nodded and picked up the half-fold stack with a picture of the senator and his mother on the front, along with their dates of birth and death inscribed in gold. Susana hadn't spared any expense. But why would she, I thought as I passed out programs, neatly placing ten per row then zigging around to the next row and zagging to the following. Still raw memories from the last funeral dogged me. I gulped a lung full of sanctified air and counted out another ten programs, the security detail comforting me only marginally.

As I zigged into the next pew, I was so deep into thought, I careened into a mourner.

"Whoa, there, girl! Let me help with that."

It was Dylan. Where had he been? I gladly handed over half the pile. He started down the left side of the church, winding between pews and kissing me in the aisle as our paths crossed.

Yep, a totally different experience than my last Coyoacán funeral. I was pretty sure the luncheon afterwards would be a lot more fun, too. I only had one concern—my would-be kidnapper and boyfriend mistake—Anibal. Hence the bullet-proof couture.

So far he had not turned up or been apprehended,

although half of Mexican law enforcement was looking for him. According to my dad, the cartels were paying the other half of Mexican law enforcement to protect him. Until he was safely extradited back to the U.S. I wouldn't let down my guard. Anibal Aguirre was not selling me to Los Zetas.

I stooped for a fallen blossom and surreptitiously scanned the mourners trickling into the church for suspicious bulges and ugly tattoos. If they were there, I didn't see them. Quint had hired a platoon of security, which he'd posted around the plaza and church; hopefully the bad guys would be kept out or nabbed by one of the men inside.

I'd learned exactly how the cartels worked this past week. With the aid and abet of politicians, bureaucrats, and law enforcement—they were getting wealthy off organized crime. It went all the way into the presidential palace, Los Pinos. At least that's what Polo's bodyguard, Horacio, said. I caught his eye and gave a little wave before sliding another ten programs along a gleaming pew.

Horacio predicted a major war over territory between the different crime groups, especially in the states along the border, the *plazas*. He advised me to watch which cartels were taken out. His prediction: Mexico's president would pave the road with Sinaloa's gold and welcome El Chapo in.

The idea fuddled my brain. I shook my head, dropped the last program and headed toward the front of the church. The organist had run through her repertoire and was talking with Susana. I recognized Loli Buendía hustling in with two giant urns of flowers and placed them at either side of the steps to the altar. The caskets, not open, thank God, shrank with all the stars, horseshoes, and crosses of flowers surrounding them. Urns and vases of more flowers crowded the floor in front the coffins, and sprays had been draped across Lidia's stark white lid and Polo's shiny black lacquer cover. The cloying scent of hothouse flowers was irritating my sinuses. I sneezed. Dylan handed me his handkerchief.

"You keep popping up from nowhere. Did you finish?" He held up his palms. Finished or ran out of programs. I went on, "Meet Loli, Lidia's great-niece. Loli!" I called and waggled fingers.

She beamed and came over. "It's so nice to see you again, Loli." I took her hand and held it for a beat. "I'm sorry for your loss, and to be meeting under such sad circumstances—again."

The twinkle in her eyes faded. "Oh, JadeAnne, it's hard to believe. Three of my family gone in a month. Aunt Lidia and I didn't see eye-to-eye on many things, but I'm sorry she's passed. It's Polo—" A little sob caught in her throat. "Polo and I were always friends. I don't know how I'll make it through his service. Do you know what happened?"

I knew. The last funeral flashed through my mind... my client's husband shooting her to protect his cartel money laundering. Now this poor family would lay to rest Aunt Lidia, shot protecting her son from the Zeta trafficker I'd been sold to. My stomach churned, a fan of blades whirling.

Loli didn't wait for my answer. "Have you seen Anibal?"

I grimaced, gut clenching, and raised my eyebrows at Dylan. "Loli, let me introduce you to my friend, Dr. Dylan Porras. Dylan, Loli Buendía."

He poured on the Dylan charm, taking her hand and looking in her eyes. "Please accept my deepest sympathy. If there's anything I can do to help you through this rough time, please call. JadeAnne knows how to reach me." Was Loli batting her eyelashes at him?

"Thank you so much, Doctor. I'll see you later at the meal?" She *was* batting her eyelashes at him.

From behind us I heard someone calling, "Loli, *ay*, Loli. *¡Hola!*" We turned to see the fat whore Consuelo García, madam of Lidia's "gentlemen's clubs," barreling up the aisle. Wasn't she in jail? As usual she looked like a brass fireplug teetering on stilettos.

Loli groaned, "Oh, no!" under her breath, gave us a shaky smile, and turned tail. Quint intercepted Consuelo as she tried to squeeze into the front pew with Senator Aguirre's brother and a handful of relatives. He steered her away from the flower marked rows, depositing her about a third of the way back with some suspicious looking men I didn't know.

The church was filling up. The ushers, Loli's boys, Polo's butler Chucho and a couple of young cousins I found out later, escorted mourners to the appropriate rows. Chucho smiled at me as he guided two of Lidia's little crows to the front left pew, like a falconer—one on each arm. I hoped I wouldn't be putting up with them again at the meal.

Oh, yeah, I hadn't eaten the meal at the last funeral. Anibal had dragged me out of the party to avoid one of the traffickers he'd swindled. If he showed up here, I might shoot him.

Quint seated me in the third row on the right. The family was bigger than I thought. Some of these folks must be Aguirres from Polo's dad's side. They weren't as well dressed as the rest of the bunch, but Lidia had to be *tía* to most of the people in the second row.

The organist glided in, black robes swirling, and began a hushed version of *O God Our Help In Ages Past.* I craned around again, looking for my men. Dylan thumped down next to me, our housekeeper Señora Pérez on his arm, decked out in a black dress, hat, and veil straight from 1950. She dragged a reluctant teen behind her. Poor Lily, trafficked from L.A. to Mexico City, unable to return home for bureaucratic idiocy, and now our housekeeper had dressed her in a dowdy, ill-fitting, black polyester sheath and patent flats. Insult after injury. I gave her a sympathetic smile.

Mrs. P nodded to me and I could see her red-rimmed, watery eyes. She actually cared for Lidia.

"Where's Quint?" I whispered to Dylan. He shrugged. I shifted forward and twisted toward the back again, scanning the crowd for my father. "Holy sh—" Dylan dug me in the ribs with his elbow. "Spirit," I finished, lowering my voice. "Turn around, Dyl. It's Lobo." I jerked my head backward.

"I've never seen him."

"I can't believe that scum showed up. He was the one

who actually drugged and transported Lily across the border. He knew we'd be here," I whispered.

Dylan shrugged. Mourners still streamed to seats. I stiffened as I recognized a couple of Lidia's associates. Cartel people. I bumped shoulders with Dylan and jerked my head toward the cluster of arrivals with a *why did the guards let them in?* look. *Ignore them*, he mouthed.

The music shifted to *It is Well with My Soul.* I was becoming an expert in funeral hymns. I looked at my watch. Right on time. The church hushed, the ushers came forward and took their places as a cellist and, it turned out, a singer, came out to accompany the organist. The singer's rich tenor filled the church. I'd always loved this hymn.

Finally Quint scooched in next to me from the arcade. I leaned against him and breathed, "Lobo." He nodded and put his finger to his lips. I burned to know how it could be.

The service went on and on, as I'd learned was the culture here, and the really good music was a pleasant surprise. Something outside of tradition I guessed. The cellist added depth to the hymns. I hoped she'd be at the meal. My stomach growled, but as I'd seen before—long lines of mourners, some I recognized, most I didn't, filed past the coffins to leave mementos and flowers with lots of crying. I wasn't going anywhere soon.

Everyone got up for communion, including Dylan. I spaced out with the music, keeping an eye on the faces passing. I nudged Quint and jerked my chin toward Senator Bendicias. Now why would he come to the funeral of a cartel woman he claimed he wanted to arrest—or the colleague he had betrayed?

Dad squeezed my hand. I realized he was as alert to the goings-on as I was. Perhaps more as he knew most of the players.

The stream of dirges and mourners finally ended; the family cried and hugged, cracked a joke or two, and invited everyone from the front rows back to Lidia's for lunch. I greeted Polo's brother and sister-in-law. Beto looked pretty broken up. This family's ties ran deep. And he'd buried his oldest daughter Lura, the woman I'd come to Mexico to find, thirty days earlier. I was glad wife Molly and daughter Alex fluttered around with kisses and kindness. Molly dealt with all the condolences; Alex held them both together with hugs. I started toward Dylan and Quint, waiting for me at the pew. That's when I saw Consuelo charging toward the immediate family.

I headed her off. "Well, well, look who's here. Consuelo, I heard you were in jail." Too bad they let you out, I wanted to say.

"It's you again. I should have known you'd push your way into this poor family's grief." She shot me one of her mincing looks.

I minced right back. "Funny, I was going to say the same of you. I think it's better if you don't bother the Aguirres right now, Consuelo. What are you up to now that your houses are closed?"

"That's for me to know," she said, twirled on her toes and teetered off in her too-tight skirt and too-high heels, her rear jiggling like an uncoupled caboose. I imagined her hiding behind a pillar to find out where we were all going.

The family started its procession up the aisle toward the door, and yep, sure enough, Consuelo popped out from behind a pillar. Luckily Alex's husband cut her off, and the Aguirre and Buendía clans escaped to their waiting cars. I watched Consuelo latch onto Guillermo Lobo's arm. I grabbed Lily and Mrs. P, and hustled our group out the door.

"Where'd you park, Dad? Follow us. Dyl got directions from Loli. The cemetery is kind of hard to find."

He pointed across the plaza in the direction of Xicoténcatl. I pronounced it for him. "Yep, that's the one. Where are you?"

I pointed towards Calle Felipe Carillo. "Over there on the left."

"I'll pull around. Wait for me."

Dylan nodded and clapped Quint on the back. My, weren't they getting chummy. I felt little warmth spread through me and surveyed the pretty park full of Sunday strollers and our security. I saw the balloon clown, and Archangel Gabriel was still doing his statue thing, and hopefully not blowing his horn. I didn't want any of the recently deceased climbing out of their graves.

Quint herded Lily into the park with Horacio following behind. Mrs. P dabbed at her eyes and scurried after them, reminding me of a squirrel darting out of the trees for popcorn.

"Dyl, let's cruise the plaza. Maybe the fortune teller is here. Last time she stopped the reading, packed up, and left when she flipped up the body stuck with ten swords in its back." I tugged on his sleeve.

"Sure why not. It's going to take Quint at least fifteen minutes to get around to us. "

"Probably twenty. Look at the traffic." I pointed across the plaza to a snarl of cars.

"Jade, you don't really believe that tarot mumbo-jumbo do you?"

I giggled up at him. "You obviously aren't from California."

We strolled arm-in-arm, trailed by two security guards. I noticed the white-clad ice cream man and headed over for two cups of coconut ice cream, the guards scurrying behind me. As I carried the paper cups to the bench Dylan sat on, I heard the throaty-voiced gypsy calling her trade. "*Vengan ustedes, tengo sus futuros.*"

"It's her. Come on, let's do it," I insisted, pulling him off the bench, and handing over the ice cream.

"*Buenas tardes, señora. Queremos nuestros futuras, por favor.*" I slapped a twenty note onto her table and we made ourselves comfortable in her folding chairs.

She barely looked up from the cards as she shuffled, pulled the King of Hearts, placed it onto the table, and nodded. With a smile, she laid the Queen of Hearts next to him. "*Ustedes, anamoratos*." She crossed the card with the Page of Swords and nodded again. "A young person, a girl, with a problem to solve. It will be delayed by..." she dealt the next card, the 5 of Wands. "Conflict. You will have to overcome this..." she said, and pulled the King of Pentacles. "He is a powerful and greedy man with many tentacles."

"Could it be a group rather than a person?" I asked in Spanish, flashing on the Zetas.

She pulled the Knight of Swords. "Possibly, and its leader is ruthless, impetuous. Gets what he wants. It will be a very destructive group that acts fast. Your success will depend on your planning. You must be ready. If not, this could be your outcome. " She pulled the ten of Swords again and looked up at me. "You!" she spat out, scooped up the cards and shuffled her deck, turning her back on us. But not before whisking the twenty *peso* bill into her pocket.

Dylan laughed. "What a load of crap." He took my hand as we walked off, but I felt chills run up and down my spine.

"Dyl, I'm not so sure. I got the King of Hearts and the Ten of Swords last time too. How do you explain that?" I said.

"You're proving your Californian citizenship—the land of fruits and nuts. Coincidence." He pulled me in close and gave my ribs a poke. I squealed. "My little nut job is ticklish!" He poked me again. I spun away from him laughing, and dropped my ice cream. I had come face-to-face with Anibal. And he didn't look happy.

"Run Dyl!" I shouted and took off, aiming for the traffic cop stopping cars for the pedestrians.

We dashed to the street, our security guards pounding after us, and jaywalked through the stopped cars to Dafne's yellow Beemer. Nothing noticeable about *this* car in a city of black cars. Horacio pulled the limo up behind us and beeped. We squealed out and headed toward the *panteon.*

Anibal shot me a middle finger salute as we rolled by.

About Ana Manwaring

Ana teaches creative writing and autobiographical writing in California's wine country. She is the founder of JAM Manuscript Consulting where she coaches writers, assists in developing projects and copyedits.

When Ana isn't helping other writers, she posts book reviews and tips on writing craft and the business of writing at www.anamanwaring.com/blogs/ Building a Better Story, and produces the North Bay Poetics, a monthly poetry event.

She's branded cattle in Hollister, lived on houseboats, consulted brujos, visited every California mission, worked for a PI, swum with dolphins, and out-run gun totin' maniacs on lonely Mexican highways—the inspiration for The JadeAnne Stone Mexico Adventures. Read about her transformative experiences living in Mexico at www.saintsandskeletons.com.

With a B.A. in English and Education and an M.A. in Linguistics, Ana is finally able to answer her mother's question, "What are you planning to do with that expensive education?" Be a paperback writer.

Learn more at www.anamanwaring.com. Please join her mailing list to keep up with news, events, giveaways and future releases.

If you had as much fun reading Nothing Comes After Z as I did writing it, please consider going to your favorite online bookseller and leaving a review. Reviews help authors continue to write their books for your enjoyment.

To find out about new books and upcoming events, please take a moment to sign up on my mailing list at www.anamanwaring.com.